Cherokee Rose

DRTᎰᎣᎥᏐᎠᏰᎩᎽᎠᎫᎬ᷂ᎻᎦᎯᎢᏕᎳᏍᎢᏳᎬᎷᎴᏯᏓᎤᎲᏛᏴᎾᏣᏬᎾᎵᎽᏃᎶᎤ

JAMES A. HUMPHREY

CONTENTS

DEDICATION

To the memory of my paternal grandmother Ella Waters,
great grandfather Andrew Waters (Dawes Roll Signees,)
and my ancestor Aney King who survived the Trail of Tears.

Grandmother Ella inspires my stories.

DRƚƠꞌiꞋꞋYAJEꞋꞋꞋꞋꞋꞋꞋꞋꞋꞋꞋꞋꞋꞋꞋꞋꞋꞋ

PREFACE

Public knowledge of Cherokee history, culture, and language is sparse. A partial reason for that limitation may be awareness.

The author, a citizen of the Cherokee Nation, inspired by his paternal grandmother, presents these story elements through fiction as an entertaining learning experience. He attempts to explore her world with dignity, appreciation, and respect. Cherokee is his "in progress" second language and while not having been raised in the culture, the author's intention is to present information and events from the Cherokee worldview.

Readers may determine their own opinions about his success.

Please be aware:
Cherokee Rose unfolds during violent years of Indigenous history. Those sensitive to turmoil may be offended by the events portrayed in this narrative.

ᏣᎳᎩ

ᏧᎴᎯᏌᏗ

ᎠᎡᏔᏯᎣᎢᏏᏯᏗᎩᏯᎠᏤᎦᏣᎠᎯᎦᎤᏪᏛᎠᏓᎬᎹᎠᏗᎤᎻᏚᏯᎦᏤᏊᎣᏂᏃᏈᎤ

JAMES A. HUMPHREY

CHAPTER ONE — Celebration

ᎠᎡᏔᏐᎣᎢᏐᏊᏴᎠᎫᎬᎵᏆᎯᎡᏫᏕᎳᏍᏈᎷᏓᎷᎵᎪᎷ᎕ᏋᏅᏝᏐᎽᏋᏍᏂᏃᎤ

In the year of 1838, the sweet smell of winter honeysuckle floats from creamy-white, two-lipped flowers over a freedman's farm in northwest Georgia. The luscious fragrance sweetens a family's observance of the dawn of a fresh season.

They dedicate their miniature, antebellum cotton plantation with a ritualistic crop harvest thanksgiving.

Ella Waters, an eighteen-year-old half-Tsalagi (ᏣᎳᎩ ja-la-gi, Cherokee) woman, performs the purifying Ribbon Dance and enjoys her folks' Green Corn Ceremony.

Her physical movements project purpose and self-control, unchallenged by significant deprivation or turmoil. Dance, to this family's oldest daughter, defines her bearing and demands a well-organized, fastidious presentation, more science than art.

Delighted that summer no longer imprisons, Ella's full-blooded mother, her younger sisters Bella and Lisa, and family friends dance individual appreciations of the new season around a circle featuring a crosswise framed fire pit.

Four logs, each aligned in a traditional cardinal-direction square, enclose a ceremonial bonfire.

Slave women mingle with the siblings and other Indian wives, unusual socialization but comfortable and reflective of the host's preferences.

Individuals wave sticks with colorful cloth strips attached to their tips. A floating visual riot of primary-color ribbons mix and float with the scent of flowers and an aura of equality.

From the corners of the fire's pit, long pine branches extend above the wives, the colors, and the sparks. A quad-pod, tied by rope at the top, anchors the limbs and dangles bright colored straps and ripe yellow fresh cobs. In the breeze, they swing in rhythm with the celebrants.

Sixteen-year-old Bella, shapely to a White man's eye, with tentative steps, mimics her older sister's dance moves.

She concentrates on her instructress but cannot suppress her indecisiveness and insecurity when she notices several men stare and follow her movements.

Lisa, fourteen, the youngest of three dancing Waters sisters, experiences the men's reactions. She glances at Ella, admires Bella, and laughs. The younger twirls toward a mature youth of her age who stares, enthralled. She rattles leg shells and enjoys flirting.

The boy steps forward, and the temptress, flush with experimentation but inexperienced and cautious, slips behind others and blends with dancing forms.

The exploratory teaser distances from her adolescent target.

Across the fire pit, Ella points with a censuring glare.

Young sibling winks, giggles, and waves ribbon sticks.

The mature daughter of the three slows pace as the youngest dances nearby. "You are fourteen years old, Lisa. Act that age. Don't pretend you're older."

The immature dancer flips ribbons in her sister's direction. "At least I'm not a biddy without a beau."

The multi-color strips women pop upon the soil imply more than a decorative and festive addition to the dance. Their serious pageantry prepares the ground for a renewal ritual.

***

Near the farm's main cabin in a gold-dyed, ceremonial buckskin shirt, the Mekko, Benjamin Waters, surveys the festivities.

From his neck, which exhibits old smallpox scars, a hand-carved stone water spider medallion hangs on a leather strap. The carving displays quality detailed craftsmanship exceeding normal native art.

This burly, ex-slave cotton farmer hosts his annual event from a hewn wood table. He watches his Cherokee wife dance and beams a smile toward his three daughters.

The youngest throws a kiss, and her parent claps.

The ceremony's host rubs bear oil on fire-broiled slices of venison, corn, beans, squash, and pumpkin.

One of Benjamin's slaves, Ezra, carries a pottery basin of the liquid grease at his landowner's elbow.

"You are the Mekko today, Benjamin." The slave whirls with the spirit of the dance and tips his bowl.

"Don't spill that. It's too hard to replace. Not many bears in Georgia these days." The older man steadies the younger's arm.

"I'll be more careful. It is an honor to help. I was showing off before the wife."

"Osda (ᎤᏍᏓ o-ss-da, good.) Celebrate the corn ceremony. This has been an excellent harvest, and the cotton crop looks promising."

"Promising…" the husband watches a youthful Cherokee woman support a swollen belly with one hand. She dances with the others, smiles, and waves ribbons at her husband. "… for a son." The slave beams.

"Daughters are good too." Benjamin interjects. "I wanted a boy but had three girls." The Mekko pauses. He grips the young man's shoulder. "I promise, your baby will not suffer a life of slavery."

Ezra focuses on his owner. "Your people don't live as slaves. You care for us as family."

"But my world doesn't treat slaves with grace. The girls, if I died, might sell the farm and property with no choice—which includes our workers. I cannot allow that to happen," Benjamin replies.

"You educated me with your children, encouraged my marriage, and provided a home. I owe you and stand thankful."

The two work in silence.

The younger man changes mindset. "But if you were to die, life might become difficult."

"I remember the day they gave you to me. I raised you from boyhood, but you owe me nothing. You earned a comfortable lifestyle." The Mekko's tone becomes serious. "My will is legal by the White man's code and filed with Judge Steel in Dahlonega. That document frees our slaves upon my death."

Ezra stands silent for a moment. "Why wait for when you pass, Benjamin? Release everyone today."

"I should and wish it were different. To buy seed each year, my property serves as loan collateral. The brokers include slaves in my assets as security. With free workers, I couldn't finance the cotton crop."

"More White man rules." The younger chuckles. "These laws you freedmen know."

"Someday, you learn their ways and what's legal. Be the Mekko of a clan. Wear the water spider."

"I'll be proud." The assistant smiles.

"Try on the medallion." Benjamin lifts the stone carving and drapes it over Ezra's head onto the younger's shoulders.

"The spirit of the talisman is not my heritage," the younger comments. "Thank you for the thought. Today, you stay the Mekko, even as I wear your symbol."

"I married a Cherokee girl when she was young. Before marriage, I realized our cultures must coexist. My new wife told me how the insignificant water spider brought fire to her people."

"The medallion's meaning?" The slave fingers the carved stone.

Benjamin expands the story. "Lightning struck a sycamore that stood in the water at the edge of a river. The tree burned. A brown crow flew in to capture the flame and scorched himself black, his color now. A barn owl saw this and struggled to catch the prize with its beak. The heat blackened its head feathers. Today, that bird is slick-headed. Other animals tried and failed."

Ezra preens and displays the medallion. His wife beams pride, and his peers see.

Benjamin elbows his helper, which focuses Ezra's attention. "This insignificant water insect saw failure by the others, wove a basket on her back, then seized the hot coals. Embers burned through the container. The lowly spider brought fire to the people, recognizable today because she carries a dark mark."

"Point of the story?" the younger man asks. "I believe you have one."

"You are the brown crow, turned black by the soot. Ella is the barn owl that tried and failed. I know she will always try. The girl detests failure. Wear the water spider medallion. Catch her fires on your back."

Ezra stares at his owner a moment, then takes the talisman from his neck.

He returns the engraved rock to Benjamin Waters. "An honor, sir. It is a higher call than I can do. I am a slave on an insignificant cotton farm in an enormous world."

"I don't need your promise. From a small boy, I raised you. I know you as well as my own daughters. When necessary, you will fulfill my charge."

The conversation stops as a voice intrudes, loud enough that heads turn in attention.

"No move to Indian Territory! Protest the forced removal!"

***

Under a tree, a representative of John Ross, the Cherokee politician, solicits petition signatures from a table.

A quill pen and an ink well wait atop the signing desk. "Fight the Treaty of New Echota! Support our most beloved leader!"

A volunteer steps forward. "I stand with Ross!" The signer flourishes the feather in the air. "I sign to stay in Georgia!"

Several others step into line.

Nearby, the only White attendee at the celebration, a sawn-off stump of a human, leans against a sycamore. In a heavy dark woolen suit with gray pants stuffed into boots, the man chews a wad of tobacco and watches the political action.

His hand rests on a "Brown Bess." The fine quality British Army muzzle-loading, smoothbore flintlock tucks in his belt.

The petition representative recognizes the observer but does not use his name.

"Support the cause, sir?" The solicitor extends a quill.

The bulky fellow spits nicotine slop onto the ground. "Name's Whitley. I'm White if you ain't noticed."

"I see you are not a tribesman. Many outsiders are against forced removal," the Ross supporter acknowledges.

"That so? Lot of 'Twenty-Niner' names on that paper?" The chewer bites off a fresh plug. Brown juice drips from the corner of his hairy mouth.

The prospector moniker reverberates.

Several Cherokee in the line suck in a breath and glance at the dark-clad man.

"No, sir. Afraid not. We have few miner signatures," the representative answers. "Most want deportation. They came to mine for riches in our soil."

"Most gold that's left is on Indian land." Whitley steps from under the tree's shade. Sunlight bathes his flat-brimmed hat. "So, we buy your property."

Polite hostility in the conversation escalates to tension.

Other Cherokees stop activities and watch the signature table.

"Your government wants to take it without compensation." The Ross organizer snarls. "That's theft."

"Your representatives signed the Treaty of New Echota and gave that property up." Whitley eyes the political representative. "Yes, I know your John Ross doesn't recognize the agreement and calls it stealing."

"So, you will not sign our petition?" The tribal delegate grasps the document and shakes it in the air.

The ex-miner places one hand on his Brown Bess. "No, but I'll make a fair offer for your land. If you don't sell, President Van Buren takes it and gives the property to another White man."

The conversation stimulates the audience, and grumbles rumble through the crowd—but the strain breaks.

"Begin the renewal ceremony!" the Mekko's voice penetrates the turbulent atmosphere. Tension surrounding the signature solicitation cools, and observers return to celebration.

***

Beyond the petition table and the ceremonial fire, many guests' tents and lean-tos host small smoking campfires.

Women break from the Ribbon Dance, scramble to these lodgings, and emerge with used clothes or worn furniture. They fling the items into the bonfire, a time-honored renewal act.

With shards of pottery, the wives scoop coals. They return to renew their individual fires from the sacred flames.

Ella, Bella, and Lisa walk together toward their log home. "I'm burning an ancient dress." Oldest presents an example for her younger sisters.

"You must think Paw will get you a fresh one." The second girl, Bella, empathizes.

"How fun! I want new!" The youngest, Lisa, chimes into the talk with self-interest top of mind.

"We burn old things to renew our spirit, not for pleasure." Mature sibling stresses the symbology of their actions.

"You're long past any hope of renewal!" Her immature sister snips and spins out of striking distance. "That's why no husband." She sticks out her tongue.

Ella grabs for her imprudent younger one, but she escapes.

***

From the celebration's hewn-log food table, Benjamin Waters watches his girls. He shakes his head as they enter the cabin.

The Mekko notices Dideyohvsgi (ᏬᏍᎯᏬᎣᏯ, di-de-yo-huh-ss-gi, Teacher) who sits on the family's front porch.

This venerable friend wears traditional garb with shaman accessories, a medical pouch and gourd rattle. Two eagle feathers poke downward out of his gray hair.

The fifty-eight-year-old "medicine man" reads an issue of *Cherokee Phoenix* dated June 21, 1838, printed in New Echota, Georgia. He chews tobacco and studies.

The newspaper's headline screams, "General Scott to Move Indians to the Territory." The older Indian throws the newspaper onto the ground. He spits slimy juice on the story.

Dideyohvsgi notices Benjamin Waters, laughs, and lifts a clay pot of Passv, a caffeine-laden yaupon holly drink. The dark-colored liquid froths white. The shaman shakes the vessel, and its contents bubble frothier. He swigs a mouthful of the purgative.

From Benjamin's side, Ezra places his bowl of bear grease on the rough-hewn log banquet table and walks to the news reader.

The slave scans the newspaper's headline on the ground. "I hear that General Scott always obeys commands."

"Especially presidential orders." The shaman nods to the young man.

"What do you think might happen?"

"I don't know. Unetlanvhi (ᎤᏁᏢᏴᎯ u-ne-tla-nv-hi, Creator God) hasn't seen fit to tell me."

With his soft-soled moccasin, Ezra foot-smears the splattered tobacco spittle and browns out the headline in personal protest.

Dideyohvsgi slaps Ezra's shoulder, laughs, and offers a swig of Passv. "The old ways return! Our youth take a stand. Drink in honor of President Van Buren. That man could use a drink of Tsalagi purgative!"

"Tradition won't change with wise medicine men still alive." Ezra sips and coughs with the strength of the Passv.

Embarrassed by the display of stomach weakness, the young slave checks to see if Benjamin Waters watches.

***

The Mekko presents his back as he hugs his wife and three daughters. He serves each venison and bear-oiled vegetables, symbolic atonement for sins. The family accepts the food with dignity and respect.

"I burned a dress in the renewal fire, Paw. Think I could get a new one?" Lisa glows up at her father.

"Yes. Your sisters, too. It has been a wonderful year. Come, stand with me and welcome our guests." Benjamin spreads his arms to embrace slaves and visitor friends. They file through his open arm's greeting. The Mekko embraces everyone and invites each to drink from the Passv pot.

The freedman encounters the miner-turned-land-purchaser. "Mr. Whitley. I am surprised you celebrate the Green Corn Ceremony."

"Am I not included?" the White man steels his body.

"This is our day of redemption. We accept every guest." Benjamin does not hug this visitor.

"Have you considered my offer?" The buyer extends his hand.

The Mekko pauses and ignores the handshake. "Yes. This farm is not available."

Whitley's face flushes red. He grasps the "Brown Bess" tucked into his waistline.

The man controls anger. "President Van Buren is moving you Cherokees to the territory, ain't you heard? This property will be much cheaper from the government, I suspect. It's wiser to reconsider. Take my fair offer, Mr. Waters."

"Have you noticed that I am not a Tsalagi, (ᏣᎳᎩ ja-la-gi, Cherokee?)" The landowner eyes the pistol in his guest's belt.

Whitley looks at Ben's wife and daughters and removes his hand from the weapon. "Your spouse and these girls are. Most say President Van Buren is not color blind, but I'm not one of those."

Ella, beside her father, fixates a fearful moment on the "Brown Bess" at the crude man's waist as he moves away.

"Paw," oldest daughter's lips move near her father's ear. "That's an awful weapon in his belt."

Benjamin smiles at his eldest. "People use guns in this world. Those weapons may not appear deadly. They may claim to carry pistols for protection from serpents. Problem is the shooter chooses his own target."

"You don't strap one of those things around your waist." Ella observes.

"No, I do not. Before I met your mother, I forget the number of snakes I killed. I hung my musket above the fireplace when we married, and there it stays. But it thrills my soul that you are aware of weapons." The father slips an arm around his girl. "Guns exist in a world beyond this corn ceremony's redemption."

"Why, Paw? It's not right."

"Because brown, yellow, red, and black snakes live out there." Benjamin Waters attempts an explanation. "Most are good. They eat rodents, rabbits, toads, worms and slugs. But a few are poisonous and need killing."

Ella watches Whitley mount his horse and turn the animal away from the celebration. "Who decides which snakes die?"

"Too often, those with guns."

"That man should never carry such power over anyone." The daughter hugs her father's waist.

"When it comes my time," he wipes the sun's heat and his anxiety sweat from his forehead with a forearm. He pats Ella's shoulder, "I hope someone as fair as you decides my fate."

CHAPTER TWO — Murder

DRᏆᎤᏅꞌꮖᏚᎤᎮᎩᎪᎫᎬᏇᏁᎯᎢᏕᏔᏍᎱᎬᎹᎠᏕᎤᎯᎲᏑᎩᎬᏖᎣᏁᏂᏃᏇᎤᵛ

The Green Corn Ceremony's fields of corn that promised renewal surrenders to a cash crop. New budding cotton's fluffy white balls pop open atop lush green plants. The healthy growth stretches in rows until they blend within distant haze that seeps from the earth.

Bolls march across the landscape, capped and plumed soldiers on parade. The ranks spread over the rich Georgia soil of the Waters' farm and promise prosperity.

Ella and Ezra walk through the chest-high crop. She picks a plant's fluff, and if perfect, the bloom receives a place in a neat row within her small basket.

Her father's young slave follows and steps with purpose and caution. The protector looks at the family's log cabin, a distance away.

Ella notices his glance. "You remind me of Headmaster Clay in Presbyterian school."

"Your Paw said times are changing. Farmers have reported trouble. I'm your bodyguard."

"What did my father say?"

"Said Old Man Ross's crop was torched 'bout a week ago."

"The Ross' daughter went to class with us. Remember Emily?"

"Yes. I liked the way she moved. Tried to get her attention but she was conceited and ignored my efforts. That southern belle was not the least bit interested in a slave."

"That wasn't fair. I could have talked to her. Mr. Ross wasn't that rich."

"Slight chance. That girl's walk didn't know this fellow was alive." Ezra continues. "Point is your father ordered me to stand guard throughout this day."

"While collecting mushrooms in the hills?" Ella giggles. "Today, a young, married man could do something more pleasurable than follow me around."

"Your Paw's my owner, remember? He said to watch out. My job's watching out for you, on or off the farm, even picking flowers."

"I'm capable and responsible. Most nineteen-year-old women have kids. Paw frets. He thinks his oldest girl is a child."

"Don't judge, Madam Critic."

"Spoken like you're married with experience."

"Remember last year? Your dad was fond of that fellow. You know, the guy with baskets of money?"

"He was rich but nasal. Had a breathing problem through Christmas. The fellow's most interesting quality was his sneeze. But I know my father loved his wallet. It was good for the farm. The fellow was a cotton broker."

Tilled and stone-removed surroundings display more rocks in the soil as the couple leaves furrowed farm rows.

Ella follows a stream uphill. It bubbles over fresh stones in descent from the Blue Ridge Mountains.

"I asked the fellow why the constant sneeze." Perfection in a suitor is a requirement as the oldest Waters daughter continues the man's description. "Poor man said he suffered from cotton allergies. Imagine a girl married to a merchant who can't tolerate his goods."

Ezra peers across the field at the well-maintained Waters farm as his ward talks.

In the distance, Benjamin dismounts a mule near his porch and waves.

The slave signals safety and "all's well" with both hands. When sure Mr. Waters has seen the signal, the young guard scrambles along the creek to catch up.

***

Ella's father pauses before entering the house and surveys the land.

The property lays peaceful in the afternoon's heat, but the owner's body language communicates caution.

The freedman listens.

A muffled stomp of a horse's hoof on dry ground from the distance focuses the farmer's attention.

The landowner steps to his porch's edge.

Across an expansive field in a bordering tree line, a limb rustles with no apparent wind.

Mr. Waters watches the brush.

More movement.

Ella's father backs to the front door's latch. It swings inward.

Through the open door with eyes on the distant foliage, Benjamin lifts his musket from wooden hooks above the fireplace.

***

Across the cotton rows, concealed by trees, Tesali (ᏘᎯᎵ, Te-sa-li,) a twenty-three-year-old Cherokee, wears a traditional loin cloth with leggings and watches on horseback. A saber slash's scar from chin up the face disappears under a calico turban.

The menacing figure stays silent.

His fingers tighten on a bear claw, one of many on his necklace.

In a beaded sheath, an enormous blade hangs at the man's waist. His belt also hosts two flint lock hand muskets. A lengthy musket rides in a sheaf suspended from his army-issue saddle.

The Indian observes the peaceful farm with two rough, sweating toughs—ex-miner "Twenty-Niners."

Both men's soiled blouses stick to skin with sweat.

One wears a battered black hat with a short brim.

The other protects his head with a faded bandanna.

"I say kill that girl and the Nigger we saw before we take the farm," Top Hat mutters. "Boss won't tolerate witnesses."

Tesali stares at the speaker but does not answer.

The man turns to observe the farm. "Whitley don't need to know. Pays the same."

The three men's horses drip lather from hard riding. The animals continue to sweat in shadow's speckled concealment. Tree branches at the edge of the Waters' crop offer temporary respite from the heat. The worn, lathered mounts wait. Riders burden their animals with muzzle-loading muskets and pistols. They snort in the heat.

"That old man on the porch looks like he's fired that musket before." Bandanna Head Niner lifts a branch to see better.

"What you say, Tesali? Take him first?"

The armed men and the warrior watch Benjamin Waters usher his and Ezra's wives into a low top-entry underground meat and grain storage bin. The freedman closes the lid over the women and hurries to the porch.

He settles into a rocking chair behind a water barrel. His at-ready musket points outward on top of the container.

****

Beyond the cabin and cotton rows of the fields, the brush line extends along Ella's brook. Upstream several hundred yards, the tributary turns in a depression between two ridges, and its banks nourish woods.

In those trees, Ella sits with shoulders against a trunk and watches Ezra sharpen a stick with a knife.

The slave notices the attention.

She returns to finger play with the bolls and mushrooms in her small basket. "Know why I never got married?" the oldest Waters sister muses.

"No, but I believe you intend to tell me."

"Lisa says I'm no fun. She's correct. The thought of marriage upsets my stomach."

"I've known you since childhood. If you think you are right, you take a position. Don't believe you consider fear, even of marriage."

"That's appearances." She glances at the married man. "Hidden terrors rack my mind. Matrimony, mistakes, and allergic cotton brokers are a few." Ella laughs. "That's a confession from an eighteen-year-old spinster. Truth is, I enjoy men, but run terrified from picking one. I am afraid of a bad choice."

Ezra wades into the creek with his sharpened lance poised.

Movement eddies the water.

The sharp stick punctures the surface, and the young fisherman jumps to retrieve a prize.

No catch.

"Picked too quick a fish."

His long-time companion laughs at the failure.

The slave offers the fishing gear.

Ella accepts, gathers a skirt hem at the knees, and wades upstream.

Color glints. She thrusts the spear. Nothing.

Her guardian explodes with laughter.

She bends in the wet stones and examines her target. The girl picks up a rock, a precious glittery object, a valuable bornite-quartz nugget. Delighted, she shares the glitz.

"That's gold." The young slave sputters.

The two scan the stream bed. Several more rocks sparkle.

Both gather nuggets and drop the prizes into the basket. "See any more? Look, is that another one?"

Ella's joyful pursuit of glitter ends as distant cracks of weapon fire echo over the hills.

The sound floats above the couple and shakes the trees. Echoes rebound from the mountains.

"Shhh. Listen." Ezra coils like a surprised water moccasin.

More rifle shots reverberate in the still afternoon's air.

The slave grasps his companion's arm and drags her at a break-neck run downhill along the stream.

The couple bursts from the foliage into a cotton field.

Across the expanse, smoke billows from the Waters' house. Its slave quarters crackle with flames.

Ezra tackles Ella and pins her, concealed in the plants, to the ground. The protector muffles her attempted scream with one hand. Both press against the earth.

Wide, panicked eyes peek above her protector's fingers and follow Tesali.

The Indian escapes on horseback along a cotton row followed by the two "Twenty-Niners."

The fugitives kick their horses' flanks.

The mounts spray lather from their necks as the perpetrators at a full gallop crash through the field.

The slave protector releases Benjamin's eldest daughter as the horsemen disappear. Both run toward burning buildings.

Thick, black smoke billows across white fields, and ash stains fluffy bolls gray.

Ella clumps her apron, along with its lumpy valuable contents at the waist. She runs with abandon, but the young man travels faster.

She slips in the soil, falls, and breaks her apron's strap. The garment dumps gold, cotton, and mushrooms on the ground.

Her brain ignores the loss, and her body stumbles the remaining yards.

Ezra captures Ella in strong arms. "Wait! You don't want to see!"

"Let go!" She fights away from her friend and stumbles ahead, then freezes.

With a musket ball's hole in his temple, Benjamin Waters lies near the log house's front door. The man clutches his single-shot muzzle loader and breech ramrod in dead hands. Spilled powder and flint lay at his waist.

Ella scrambles to the form. Sobbing, the daughter falls to knees and attempts to lift the man's hefty shoulders. Ezra helps and shifts the body for the daughter's embrace.

Terrified fingers tremble as she spreads her father's collar. The girl removes the water spider talisman from his neck. She kisses the object, slips it over her neck, and wails with grief.

Ezra stands and inspects the farm.

No one moves. All living quarters smoke.

The young man runs to the smaller, windowless, dwellings on fire. The searcher lunges into his family's cabin but jerks away from the heat.

The youthful husband surveys the farmstead.

The only shelter not burning, a food storage dugout, offers a hiding place.

He rushes to the sunken space. The wooden cover creaks as the man yanks. The slave stares for a moment, steps backward, and vomits.

Ella, crying, stumbles to the open doors.

Her protector attempts to prevent the daughter from looking.

She breaks loose.

Among baskets of corn, beans, and pumpkins, the ravaged bodies of Ezra's young pregnant wife and Ella's Cherokee mother drip blood over stored food. Their physical abuses match the skinned and hanging smoked meats.

Ella recoils and collapses. In a fetal curl upon the ground, the oldest child suffers with her parents' deaths.

Bella's voice calls from the cotton field. "Over here!"

The older sister gathers herself and twists to the voice.

Her younger siblings burst free from concealment. "Paw! Mom!"

The two girls run to the arms of their older protector. Ella prevents viewing the bodies.

"No!" Lisa screams. "That's mother."

Big sister grasps the youngest. "Not this. Remember her the way she was."

From her neck, oldest slips the water spider medallion over Lisa's. "Wear this. Paw's noble spirit protects and heals."

The three girls grieve tears of loss and hug to draw strength from each other.

"Do what she says, Lisa." Bella wraps the younger girl in caring arms. "Big sisters are always right. Never forget Ma. Try to become that woman, the way we both remember her."

Ella looks up at Ezra with wet eyes. "Your baby? Your wife? No!"

"Leave me alone, please. I don't want anybody to watch me cry." Ezra covers his face and stalks toward the fields.

Smoke billows and crowds the land. Its darkness conceals the young slave's grief.

***

As the Waters' farm smokes and the family consoles each other that night, miles from the murder, Tesali and the two Twenty-Niners wait near Dahlonega, Georgia. They camp in a brushy clump of trees.

Three men silhouette before the fire. Their saddled mounts stand tied to a spruce pine.

"Those squaws screamed loud as slaughter pigs!" Bandanna Head slurs his words. The White man sucks whiskey from a bottle.

"Shut up, Foul Mouth. There was no reason to scalp or skin those farmers." Top Hat frets and paces.

"Except fun. No extra charge," the offender snarls.

"Careful what you say." The second culprit jerks a thumb at their partner in a calico turban. "He's an Injun."

Tesali pulls a knife from a belt scabbard.

Cloth-wrapped adversary-head grabs a musket.

From the brush, an approaching horse snorts and interrupts the confrontation.

The three men snatch weapons.

Tesali positions his body in the shadows, a dim target behind the two whites.

Under the sights of their muskets, Whitley, an older Twenty-Niner in a heavy suit with gray pants stuffed in boots wearing a flat-brim black hat dismounts.

He leads his mare into the light of the campfire. "Did you get the job done?"

"Got the cash?" Top Hat replies.

The boss lifts his "Brown Bess" from a leather sleeve that hangs from a saddle horn. "You torch their cotton?"

"Wasn't enough time. Waters fought back. No telling who heard. Just killed the Nigger and his Injun wife."

"That so? I pay half now. When the crop burns—as we agreed—you get the rest."

The top hat Twenty-Niner points a weapon. "No. Pay us now!"

Whitley whips his pistol level. Both fire and die.

Bodies hit the ground engulfed in black powder smoke.

Vision clears. The man with the head bandanna turns to Tesali.

The "Injun" holds a long gun aimed at the man's chest.

"Wait! Partner! Top Hat's dead! More money! Makes an even split!"

The Cherokee stares with unemotional, intense eyes.

Bandanna Head drops to his knees with his empty musket. "Take the money. It's yours!"

With one hand holding his musket, Tesali fingers the bear claws on his neck.

"Yeah, I scalped those Injuns! Want to know why? Look!" The terrified human rips off his head wrap. A scarred skull displays scalping. "An Osage warrior took my topknot!"

The Twenty-Niner stumbles backward from a lead ball's impact. The mortally wounded man thumps to the ground.

Through the smoke, the warrior walks to Whitley's horse and searches the older man's pack. He removes his promised money and stuffs the cash into his turban.

Tesali returns to the body that squirms in pain. With both hands, the victim attempts to contain blood that squirts from a chest hole.

The Indian pulls a knife from its beaded sheath and drops to a knee by the trembling Twenty-Niner's head. With hard eyes, his hand clamps a palm over a doomed mouth. Void of expression, the Cherokee carves off his partner's pre-scalped skull scar.

The man writhes at his executioner's feet.

The murderer watches without compassion. He stares without a blink. To complete the killing, his musket butt smashes a skull.

Tesali drops to his knees beside the corpse and wipes the knife's blade plus the musket's shoulder rest on the dead's soiled shirt.

He stands and steps over the corpse to Whitley's body. The Cherokee picks up "Brown Bess," admires its craftsmanship, and stuffs the weapon into his waist belt.

Tesali cuts a bear claw from the collection on his neck strap. The warrior places the object in Whitley's mouth. Precisely positioned as a single fang, the Indian marks his prey. A foot's heel jams the identifier into place.

The warrior ties his neckwear together and peers at the dead "Twenty-Niner." With two fingers, he rubs the scar on his face.

Tesali smiles, mounts his horse, and nudges the animal with a bloody foot.

Without a glance at the carnage in the camp, the murderer rides into the darkness away from the killing ground and fades into the bramble.

CHAPTER THREE — Hickory Tree

ᎠᎡᏔᎶᏭᎢᏏᏍᎤᏝᎩᎩᎯᎫᏥᎬᏍᏘᏛᎠᎭᏗᎤᎳᏬᏍᎦᎷᎬᎷᏀᏇᎶ᎚ᏨᎯᎢᏵᏯᏴᎿᎠᏂᎯᏃᏇᎤᵛ

The following morning, on the remnants of her porch,
the Waters' eldest daughter watches the sun rise over her land
of cotton. The sky sparkles clear, and the horizon glows golden.
Smoke drifts in whiffs from cooling log embers that enclose
Ella's previous life, and she longs for better times.

Her mind's mists shift, and *she specifically remembers.*
"Paw, I love you."

*On her daddy's lap, six-year-old Ella rocks, warm from the
fire in their log cabin. Benjamin's wife, Walela (ᎦᏛᎳ wa-le-la,
Hummingbird,) knits in a chair. Ella gazes up at the dark-colored eyes she loves. Tiny spots of light reflect on his pupils from
the fireplace's burning coals.*

*Benjamin Waters looks at his oldest and kisses her on the
forehead. "Do you know what today is?"*

The little child nods. "No."

*"It's special." Her father continues. "White folks call
it danisdayohihv (ᏔᎯᏍᏛᏘᏀᎠᎳ da-ni-ss-da-yo-hi-huh,
Christmas.)"*

"Why? The snow outside?"

*"No, my dear. Years ago, I was a slave on a plantation. My
family took off work one day each year, in winter. The Whites
would feast, dance, gamble, and visit with each other. It meant*

a lot of extra labor for us, but not the normal. Mama and Paw worked because they were slaves, and I did also. My owner believed in Christianity. He celebrated the birth of his God's son, remembered on that day. Christians offer presents to each other on the child's birthday."

"Do you mean presents of something good like Bella and Baby Lisa, Daddy?"

"Your sisters are genuine blessings from your mother. The White owners would give little things, food, child's toys, objects that slaves made."

"Are you a slave now?"

"No."

"Why not?"

"My master gifted a sled to his only son one Christmas. His boy was my age. He took the toy to play outside. It was my job to pull him on the snow. He did not enjoy how fast I could run, so the child went down a hill onto a frozen pond by himself. The impact broke through its surface. I saved the fool from drowning. In gratitude, his parents signed my 'Free Paper.' After that, I met your Mom. We started our farm."

Walela sets her knitting aside and rises from her rocking chair. "Some parts of the White man's ways, I enjoy. One is Christmas." She leaves the room.

Benjamin looks at his oldest child. "Where is she going?"

"I didn't hear the girls cry. Don't know." The youngster shrugs.

Mrs. Waters returns with a small hand-knitted pouch. "Today, I have a gift. Wear this, Benjamin." She kisses Ben and her little daughter on their foreheads. "This is not about remembering a baby. It's in appreciation to my husband. He gave my three girls to our clan and your father raises you children in the Tsalagi manner."

Mr. Waters whispers his love and accepts a knitted sack.

He looks at his oldest. "What do you think it is?"

Ella claps her hands with pleasure. "Open it Paw! I'm so excited!"

Benjamin shakes the bag. Into his hand, a stone water spider medallion drops. "Look Ella, this is special. It is a fine gift, carved by an artist. This talisman holds deep meaning in your culture."

He turns his attention to his wife and his eyes moisten. "I will wear it with pride."

Walela smiles. "May it keep you safe and bring you home to your family."

***

The loving log cabin living room fades from memory, and Ella misses its humanity and warmth.

The cool morning's temperature chills, and the new Waters matriarch pulls a shawl around her shoulders as she looks across the front of her father's property.

Sisters sleep on the ground. Under ash-stained blankets, they rest in a primitive lean-to of two branches that support canvas from cotton bales as a temporary roof.

Impromptu shelters host slaves who survived by conceal-ment in the cotton with the Waters girls.

One, Ezra, coaxes a small fire and attempts to boil coffee. He glances at Ella with eyes that appear red in the morning light, swollen from a night of grief. He turns and checks the thick black liquid.

Ella looks from the fire over the cotton. She stands.

Toward the waist-high crop, the woman walks and droops her head. She searches and examines the tilled soil several yards ahead. Across rows, the young woman seeks her items abandoned in the fire's panic.

Near a broken plant, Ella's treasure lies. Nuggets of gold scatter reflective glints in the furrows.

The Waters' daughter glances behind at her father's burned farm. No one watches, and she inhales a deep breath of relief.

She drops to her knee, with her head concealed by the top of plants, and abandons the collected bolls and mushrooms. The young woman retrieves every nugget into her apron.

Completed, her fingers tie its cloth closed about the gold. In the privacy of waist-high concealment, she lifts her dress and attaches the garment around her stomach.

The oldest Waters sister stands. The treasure hangs between her legs, concealed by an ankle-length skirt. She shakes her hips to ensure the package stays. Assured, the new matriarch returns through the cotton to her carcass of a home.

Her sisters sift through the debris. "Where have you been? It worried me." Bella asks.

"Walking in the fields. We have an excellent crop to sell." Ella replies. "Just thinking and planning. Our father would do the same."

"The slaves wrapped him in canvas. They moved all of them to that old hickory tree. You know, the one Paw buried Grandma under." The middle Waters daughter watches her sister.

"Good," the older returns. "I asked them to move the bodies."

Lisa gasps. She spies something in the burned debris and lifts an almost unrecognizable toy doll from the ruins.

The younger bursts into crying. "Ma made her. I was six," the youngest blubbers.

"Be strong." Bella steps close and slips her arm around the girl's shoulders. "Someday you will sew a new Betsy and give it to your child."

"Never be another!" Lisa throws the destroyed toy into the charred memories of her life.

"Please, everything's changed." Bella urges cooperation. "We must stay together, protect each other, and love deeply. We want to get through this."

"Why don't you shut up?" the youngest retorts. "That doesn't fix anything! You just spout empty words."

"Bella's right. We must adapt." Ella insists. "We don't have a home anymore."

"Let's go live back East, Philadelphia or New York!" Lisa's voice relishes her suggestion.

"They freed slaves in Pennsylvania a hundred years ago." Bella rubs her eyes. "Without our slaves, we are poor folks. We can't afford to live up North."

"Fact is, we're without slaves now. They all receive free papers after probate." Ella looks at her two sisters. "Paw's will requires it."

"Looks like no New York." Lisa's voice drips disappointment.

Bella stiffens her chin. "That's fine with me. No human serves any man unless she wants to. If forced by another, she's a slave no matter the color of her skin."

"Bella! I'm delighted you have principles." The elder Waters woman claps her hands.

"I just hope life never places me in that position." Bella's eyes moisten. "You never know what you could be forced to do."

"Big sister will always be around to protect you." Ella postures with her new status. "That, I promise, and Paw's memory holds me to it."

***

The following day, near an old hickory tree several hundred yards across cotton fields from the Waters' charred farmhouse, Ella follows a wagon. Its flat carriage supports five canvas-wrapped bodies. The mule in front plods along a dirt road overgrown by weeds.

Under its shade, the only White man, a Presbyterian minister, wears a pressed clergy's collar. The symbol tucks under a black suit. He grips a Bible under one arm with its title in view, another symbol of his faith.

Cherokees, freedmen, a few slaves, and many of the guests that attended the Green Corn Ceremony trudge up the hill behind the makeshift hearse.

Dideyohvsgi, the medicine man and Benjamin Waters' friend, stands several feet from the clergyman and waits. The shaman watches Ella's ex-school master bow his head in prayer.

Ezra follows behind the family grievers as they move and notices the cleric at the hill's top. He touches his lifelong friend's shoulder. "Isn't that Headmaster Clay?"

"Yes. Now it's Pastor Clay."

The flatbed stops. The old medicine man leads a group of Indians and freedmen who unload the bodies. The men place canvas forms individually at five freshly dug holes. An older gravesite with a white-painted cross at its head begins the row.

"I'm glad they will rest with Grandma." Lisa leans near Bella.

"Yes, she was a Christian, a Presbyterian, but Grandma fought with mother. Your grandmother believed in the ancient Cherokee ways." Bella pulls her sibling closer. "Paw said she never accepted him, even after we were born."

Dideyohvsgi and the pallbearers, with rope, lower their canvas bundles into their respective sites.

Reverend Clay steps to Benjamin Waters' eldest, the new head of her clan. "Thank you. Your folks supported the church for many years."

"They did, Headmaster… excuse me, I should say Pastor." Ella stumbles on the man's title. The clergyman nods his affirmation.

"My parents believed everyone should learn to read and write. Your school provided education for their children." Ella clasps her hands.

"We did, but they were not faithful worship attendees. Not regular as most God-fearing Presbyterians, I'm afraid." Brother Clay looks about the gathering. "The freedmen I see here are pious. They are successful Christians. Your mother and father shared their success. Not in worship, but through the Lord's educational outreach."

"Paw paid to provide his girls and most of his workers an education. This is a farm, not a rich plantation."

The minister observes the slaves who stand beside the wagon.

"His laborers are a problem." Pastor Clay states.

"What do you mean?" The workers' owner focuses on the religious man's white starched collar. The clerical symbol supports an angry red face.

"Your father and mother were free souls. Some of these you wish to send into the Lord's Heaven are not."

The oldest sister, shocked into retreat by the statement, nods understanding as if she still attends the man's classes.

"John Calvin taught that Christians should relate all people as a community together. God is sovereign over all. But the church's General Assembly, a year ago, divided at the Mason Dixon line."

"Are you saying you won't officiate the burial of my Ma and Paw?" Ella stammers.

"I cannot, under the direction of my governing body. Your freedman father and his wife are fine. But ordinary slaves must find their path without me." The pastor firms his chin and crosses his arms. "My denomination does not allow me to pray over their kind."

Ella retreats one step from the man and his Bible.

Her cheeks flush red and her eyes flash anger. "Hypocrite! You hide behind your General Assembly. I demand you leave my property."

"As you require. Peace be with you." The bigot nods his head and stalks past the flatbed.

The empty body wagon, with its mule and driver, return down the hill. They do not match the Presbyterian's pace.

***

The Waters family and their slaves watch the departure.

"Do I still remind you of old Headmaster Clay?" Ezra whispers to his classmate.

Dideyohvsgi and the pallbearers lower the last canvas-wrapped body into the ground. The man spies the retreating pastor's back.

The shaman walks along the row of holes and joins the Waters' leader. "I see the Presbyterians do not include us. Or was it your slaves?"

"Slaves today, Cherokees tomorrow. Baptists next day, I suspect." The older sister takes the shaman's hand. "Will you speak? My Paw married my mother, so I'm sure Cherokee words fit him well."

The native shaman smiles. He steps to a hole. He lifts a shovel and dumps earth into the grave.

"Family, friends. To celebrate these lives, please take a turn. Return your parents, your families, your loved ones to the soil from where they came. I know some of you are Christians. I follow the spirits of our ancestors," Dideyohvsgi begins. "But together, we say to these who will join their makers, travel well, rest forever. We promise to cherish your memory."

The pallbearers shovel dirt into graves. They pass shovels to others under the shade of the Hickory tree.

Each person dumps a load. Earth heals the wounds in its body. Individuals pile each site high.

Dideyohvsgi lifts his arms. "Last spring, we enjoyed Benjamin Waters' hospitality at his annual Corn Ceremony. Today, I invite you all to a communal dinner. His family friends and neighbors prepared the meal. They have tables under the trees."

The funeral group walks together, many hand-in-hand, down the dirt road to the Waters' charred log cabin.

As they walk, the group's mood changes from dirge to community.

"Ella, it is so nice for everyone to do this dinner!" Lisa comments.

"It is." The oldest replies.

"Whom do we thank for the use of these mourning dresses? What would we have done without them? It worried me sick." Bella smooths her skirt.

"Worn what we had, I expect." The older Waters glances at her sisters.

"Had?" Lisa turns palms up. "Everything burned in the fire! Only clothes left are the old lady things in Ma's cedar chest."

The walkers approach the remains of the Waters' log cabin.

***

Under shade trees near the debris of the house, several tables support food. The attendees circle the refreshments. As they chat, people select their favorites.

Many guests express condolences to the Waters sisters. Others include Ezra.

"Ella, what are you going to do? You need a permanent place." One guest becomes practical.

"Paw would have wanted us to rebuild. We must carry on." She looks about her place. "He loved this farm. So do his girls. I will try to rebuild."

Dideyohvsgi, with a roasted turkey leg in hand, joins the conversation. "They respected your father in this community. The man was successful. His friends and family will miss him, and I am sure intend to help."

"Thank you." Ella dabs a tear from her cheek with a sooty handkerchief. "You were a lifelong friend to Paw."

For moments, the family and the old medicine man remember earlier days when Ben and the Shaman rode the paths of war together, battled the pox that scarred the freedman's neck, defeated the scourge of Mohi, and proved Son of Stone Cloud's creed.

"He was a good friend to me." Dideyohvsgi lowers his head and steals Ella's wipe for his own eyes.

CHAPTER FOUR — Probate

ᎠᎡᏘᏬᎤᎢᏚᏬᏈᏯ ᎠᏌᎡᏇᏈᎯᎢ Ꮙ ᏆᏚᎦᏣᎹᎩᎨ ᎤᎯᎲᏛᏯᏴ Ꮀ ᏅᎯ ᏃᏈᎤᵛ

Ella drinks from the farm's well and supervises construction of a new home. Many of the workers, neighbors, and family friends from the funeral and New Corn Ceremony lift and carry materials where her father's burned-out log cabin had been a few short weeks ago.

Several flatbed wagons sit loaded with hewn pine fresh from the sawmill. Hired tradesmen measure, cut, and hammer planks onto a stud-framed house.

Bella joins older sister at the farm's water well. "Ella, I'm so proud of you."

The oldest shares a tin ladle with its cool liquid. "And I of you. This raising is difficult. I need someone I can trust. You caught that short delivery this morning."

The middle sibling admires her sister. "But you marched into the bank in Dahlonega for the loan to rebuild."

"Easy. I pledged the cotton crop." Ella offers the ladle to Lisa, who joins the two.

The younger gushes. "I'm so excited. We've never lived in a proper house!"

Ella fakes surprise. "What? Our home was."

"I mean with flat walls, not logs, with windows, lots of them, and curtains. We have our own rooms!"

"Won't be real without Ma and Paw." Bella's voice cracks and bubbles as her eyes moisten.

"We still have to go through probate before it's legally ours." The eldest expresses her concern. "Court's next week in Dahlonega, and I'm not looking forward to it."

"You handled the bank well." Bella wipes a tear from the corner of one eye and grins.

"I went for planting seed financing before, with Paw." Ella drops the water ladle into her bucket. "They want new business. Court is different. I've never faced a state magistrate."

"It'll be fine." Bella grasps and squeezes her sister's hand.

"Judge Steel is White in a Georgia court. This is not Cherokee law or the tribal council. I go afraid of making a mistake that I can never correct. And what if he hates our kind?"

Bella leans closer to her sister. "Don't worry. Dideyohvsgi said he does not hate Cherokees. He says the judge married a Choctaw."

"You always make me feel better." Ella smiles.

***

The following week, Ezra, in Benjamin Waters' best, heavy woolen, go-to-meeting-suit, guides two mules. The animals pull a wooden-wheeled cart on the curved road before the Dahlonega Courthouse.

Beside the slave, Ella wears her mother's high-lace-neck Sunday dress. Her feet squash into a pair of store-bought leather shoes, black with low heels, and she squirms and slips them off at the heel.

The courthouse approaches. "Enormous building, Ezra."

"Probate's a big White man's justice plan. I remember that from school."

"Father preferred Cherokee councils."

"Your Paw sent me for an education with you. He knew which carried more weight."

"Maybe. It's been a few months since he was killed, and we have no justice from either."

Ella stares at the three story, massive courthouse. It sits upon an expanse of hornblende slate surrounded by the soil of a public square impregnated with small specks of nature's gold.

***

Lounge-abouts of White, Indian, and African descent drape the building's entrance yard and watch Ella's cart approach.

A Cherokee loafer stands and shades eyes against the sun's glare. "Whoo-eee, look at that Nigger in a fancy suit."

"Got him an Injun Master." A vagrant whistles derision. "Ain't he something?"

Ezra ties the mules, and Ella marches up stone steps to massive double entrance doors.

"Just the lady." Another lounge-about jeers. "You know you're not allowed in there."

The Waters daughter steps to the entrance. She looks at Ezra, who hesitates. "Come on with me. School together, court together."

***

Ezra steps behind his owner into the cool, dimmer courthouse.

She fusses with her uncomfortable shoes as a White male clerk watches their arrival.

Noticing his stare, she marches directly to the official. "I am Miss Waters."

"Yes, you are. But what is he?"

"He's..."

"I'm Benjamin Waters' slave, Ezra, the driver for his daughter, Ella."

"Judge Bennett Steel probates my father's estate." The black shoes hurt as she emphasizes her mission.

Unnoticed from behind, the magistrate, a thirty-eight-year-old Georgia attorney, enters and stands at the door.

The clerk holds his hands extended, palms forward. "Yes. But your companion must wait. Outside, not in here."

Ella's back stiffens. "Then I'll go with him."

"If you wish." The door guard wins.

The Waters heir's face flushes red. "No I don't. I insist Ezra attend this meeting."

"You do?" The man braces for additional confrontation. "Are you not half-Cherokee and part Negra? This courthouse does not allow Negras in these halls without shackles."

Ezra controls his indignant soul and steps between his owner and the bailiff. "My apologies, sir. I am a slave, but I am a beneficiary in the probate settlement. I believe the judge will see me."

The door guard sputters frustration. "This is most irregular..."

"But correct." The man's voice at the entrance intercedes.

The two visitors turn toward Judge Bennett Steel. In black robes, the man's body language communicates intensity and purpose.

"Usually when I come to work, my mind is on some docket case. Today, first thing, I make a ruling." He takes Ella's hand and escorts her toward his chambers while her slave follows.

Ezra looks back at the frustrated employee.

The clerk stands frozen with mouth ajar.

The young slave celebrates his minor victory imposed by a White judge without outward expression. Unusual for its time, the decision indicates the magistrate's independence and innovative vision.

***

In his office, the judge reviews papers on his desk as Ella watches from the opposite side.

Several feet behind, Ezra tugs up too-large pants.

"Miss Waters, my condolences. I met your father and mother and knew both to be upright citizens."

"Thank you, sir. Their murderers remain free."

"I suspect unscrupulous riff-raff land speculators, usually busted Twenty-Niners."

"Or perhaps limited interest in due process justice for a Cherokee woman and a freedman?" Ella's voice carries ice.

"I understand your frustration. My wife is Choctaw." The magistrate leans back in his chair. "But enough. We have business. Please, young man, sit." Ezra settles into a comfortable chair as the judge gathers probate items and studies legal language.

"Upon your parent's death, their entire estate transfers equally to you and two sisters."

The court pauses and looks at Ezra. "His will frees his slaves. It awards personal possessions along with a horse or a mule plus the sum of fifty dollars a person from the future sale of the farm or its cotton crop to each freedman."

Steel signs Ella's "Slave Papers" and pulls Ezra's from the group. "In the State of Georgia, I have few opportunities such as this. Sir, please stand."

Ezra jumps to his feet, and the magistrate presents freedom.

The lawyer concludes the life-altering present with a handshake—free man to emancipated ex-slave. "This act I believe is your race's right. Unfortunately, in this part of the country, that may not occur for many generations."

"I pray the wait is less. Thank you."

"There is another matter." The magistrate digs through the papers and hands one to Ella. "This is a financing note for your current cotton secured by land. The loan is due upon sale."

"I am aware of that. But the land's value was also ample security for a bank-funded replacement home."

Judge Steel grins. "That I am pleased to learn and concludes our business."

"Thank you, sir." The Waters family head rises from a chair.

"It does, and I express my thanks." The proud freedman nods his head in gratitude.

"You are both most welcome, but frankly, direct your appreciation to Benjamin Waters."

Ella and Ezra nod and step toward the door.

Bennett stops the exit. "You young people have been delightful. The manner with which you challenged the clerk out there was food for my starving soul. I don't remember a day in this courthouse I have more enjoyed."

"Pleased we graced your morning, sir. You blessed mine." The ex-slave grasps his free paper, tight.

"With your freedom status, there may be an occasion when employment becomes necessary. Come that time, please recall this conversation and apply with this jurisdiction." The judge shakes Ezra's hand an additional time. "And I wish you the best, Miss Waters. I hope that soon I will preside over the trial of your father's murderer."

"Nothing would please me more, your honor."

***

Instead of justice in Judge Steel's court, the pendulum of life swings, and weeks later, Ella and her sisters' bodies and minds refresh. Summer heat breaks, and the morning breeze stirs cooler over the Waters' farm.

Ella wakens with anticipation of a fresh season and new direction. She stretches from sleep and sits on her bed's edge. Dawn's light sifts into her room through embroidered curtains that shift gracefully in the breeze. She rubs the night from eager eyes and slips out of bed.

The woman pads to the bedroom window and peeks out.

Morning mists and floating fog tinge the farmland gray and still.

Ella considers time and circumstances and how Benjamin Waters' property reflects change. No slave quarters exist, and the limited charred evidence that they were ever in place barely influences Ella's view.

Acres of white fluffy bolls atop cotton no longer crest plants, now brown and crinkly from summer drought and little post-harvest care.

A muffled clank of metal and a stomp of a distant hoof disturbs the utter peace.

These sounds echo an unaccustomed alien presence.

Ella looks from the window in all directions for the disturbance, then jumps and rushes to her sisters' room. She gathers her siblings from bed. "Girls! Into the wood bin."

"What's the matter?" Lisa resists.

"Not sure." The oldest urges. "I heard something outside."

"I'll stay with you." Bella apprehensively climbs from her feather mattress.

"No! I think it was horses! Hide and care for her."

Bella lurches for a robe, but her younger ward struggles away to peek out the bedroom window. "Horses! Exciting! I must see."

Ella grabs the back of Lisa's cotton night gown and drags her sibling through a hall into the kitchen. She lifts the cover of an empty wood bin and stuffs the girl inside. "Not a sound until I say. You hear?"

Bella crouches into the space, and Ella pushes the wood bin's lid closed.

She searches the room. A small knife lies on a counter near the window where it dries in the ventilation. With the weapon extended blade first, she tiptoes to the door.

Ella peers through the opening into the hall. Nothing moves.

The inadequate blade in hand drops to the floor as she spies a real weapon. Desperation grips the girl as she hurries to the living room. She grabs a long rifle, her father's musket, from display pegs above the fireplace without knowing it hangs unprimed.

Ella carefully slips the house's entrance open and peeks.

* * *

In a regimented line, Georgia Militia Sergeant Hiram Colly and two privates sit saddles in the center of a line with three other White civilian volunteers, mounted and armed. Their militia uniforms fit the men uncomfortably and need upkeep and cleaning. The trio of volunteer soldiers lack signs of discipline and appear as prisoners fresh from a stockade.

The sergeant leader dismounts onto the porch.

He withdraws a paper from his coat and reads the document aloud. "By order of General Winfield Scott, Cherokee must be collected into gathering points."

The head of the Waters clan brandishes her father's rifle. "Not freemen landowners!"

The militiaman folds his order and slips the document into his coat's pocket. "You do not appear to be an ex-slave. Show me an owner that's not an Injun!"

"He's . . . dead!" the vulnerable woman sputters back.

Two of the Georgia militia, including a massive hulk in a calvary hat and black boots, jump from horses as Benjamin Waters' heir fumbles with her firearm.

"Don't resist." Sergeant Colly commands. "We have other Injuns to pick up today."

In his inappropriate US Army headgear, volunteer Frank Hale laughs. "That musket ain't even primed, fool." He clubs Ella with the butt of his weapon, and she drops unconscious.

CHAPTER FIVE — Internment

DRTᏠᎣᎢᎢᏚᎠᏐᏋᎩᎪᎫᎬᏋᏘᎪᏔᎷᏪᏔᏵᎷᎡᎨᎪᏋᏬᎣᎮᏮᏕᎩᎦᏖᎨᏁᎮᏃᎮᎣᎢ

The stench assails Ella's senses as she regains conscious-ness in a pile of filthy straw littered with horse and mule buns. Her awakened face drips sweat in the early summer humidity as Bella and Lisa wipe her perspiration with their dress hems. Both younger sisters sweat in rivulets, eroded on trail dust caked skin.

Others huddle under the wooden lean-to, a communal bed of filth. A few cough or mumble with fever. Most sit and stare.

Ella inspects her surroundings beyond the haystack. She lies in a corner near a two-level log cabin guard house. The intersection is one of four that encloses a hundred-by-eighty yard rectangle. The stockade's pine walls stand top sharpened and planted deep into hard earth. Several small trees dot the enclosure, but like the humans inside, they struggle for life on the barren terrain.

"How long was I out?" Ella struggles to stand.

"Three days." Bella replies. "Go easy, now. Not too much."

"Where are we?" The oldest Waters sister spits shreds of trash from her mouth.

"This filthy pile is the hospital." Lisa flicks dirty straw off her skirt.

"In the Fort Dahlonega internment camp, a gathering pen for Cherokee. I think we are south of town." Bella wipes her own face.

Ella gathers her wits. She cringes her bare foot away from a mule bun and struggles to her feet. "What kind of place?"

"That's what these militiamen call it," middle daughter continues. "I hear we are waiting until they gather a large enough group to start us overland to the territory."

"I've had plenty of this stinking horse feed." Oldest Waters woman takes a sister in each hand and steps away from the stench.

***

The assault upon nostrils improves as the sisters move a distance from the medical area, but a pervasive odor of sweaty, unbathed humans remains unavoidable.

Family clumps of men, women, children, and occasional slaves huddle. They claim small ground spaces. A few react with aggressive, protective gestures as the Waters clan nears.

The young women walk around these groupings in their search for space to settle.

Malnourished, pathetic people cluster together and stare back with swollen, tortured eyes, reflecting loss and disenfranchisement.

"What's the matter with them?"

Bella lowers her voice. "Starvation. They've been here a while."

"You've been unconscious." Lisa whispers. "You haven't seen this place."

***

Yards from the Waters clan, naked Cherokees sit and lie in the sun. With feet chained to a huge timber, several pitiful souls roll in the soil and babble gibberish. A father tries to bury himself under the massive log.

A brutish civilian in overalls, boots, and a calvary hat, the volunteer Georgia militiaman Frank Hale who rendered the Waters matriarch unconscious, stands over the pilloried prisoners.

Ella recognizes the escort. "That fellow was at our farm!"

Bella slaps Ella's pointing hand downward and covers her sister's mouth.

The overseer does not notice or care as he kicks a chained Cherokee woman near him. She does not utter a sound. The brute thumps her harder, enough to flop her head. The woman's dead sockets stare open, with pupils glazed.

Ella and her charges shuffle on to distance themselves.

Frank Hale's attention follows the women, especially the prettiest, Bella.

A few steps from the militiaman, Lisa whispers. "He's still watching."

"Shhh, girl. Don't give him a reason to come." Middle Waters hisses.

Ella does not look back as she pulls the others with her. Before them, inside the stockade near a corner guard house, a cart with iron rim wheels sits. Its tongue points skyward. Its heavier flatbed rear rests on the ground.

Little sister scrambles under the wagon's bed and into its shade.

Other Cherokee walkers in the area avoid the wagon.

Ella pushes Bella into the coolness under the bed with Lisa, and the three enjoy relative comfort. They crowd close, out of the grueling heat. Eldest gathers dirt to serve as a pillow for her youngest, and the most seductive Waters rests her head on big sister's leg.

"I'm so tired. It's cooler under here." Lisa's eyes droop.

"We've been too afraid. One of us has stayed awake day and night to nurse you. We're far beyond exhausted." Bella shifts her weight and finds comfort.

The oldest nods understanding. "Rest. I'll watch." In moments, the Waters' girls nod into slumber. Ella watches camp events through the spokes of the wagon.

Dozens of Cherokees walk about the compound. Most congregate around women in this matriarchal society. Children play near their family pods but stay quiet.

Armed Georgia militia guard under individual spots of shade but show little attention to the surrounding Indians. A few puff pipes in clouds of tobacco smoke. Others tighten facial tie-cloths against the stench. Several crouch with their backs against the pine walls and sleep.

The guards ignore Cherokee that nurse members who cough or babble with temperature. Many of these family units support sick infants and feeble members.

Through the wheel, the Waters eldest watches two men. Each drags a leg of the cadaver Frank Hale kicked. The men with the corpse do not notice the sisters underneath the cart. They drag the stiff form to the edge of the conveyance where its flat tail rests on the ground. Each guard grasps a hand and a foot. They swing and toss the carcass upon the wagon.

One limp arm and fingers slips through the spokes. It dangles near Ella's face. She recoils in silent fear and disgust. Bella wakens. Oldest clamps her palm over her middle sister's eyes and mouth until the militiamen retreat. She releases her sister, then shakes Lisa awake.

"We have to move. That poor dead woman may have a disease." Eldest herds her siblings from under the cart into the lot and joins other aimless walkers. As they wander, the Waters family searches for a space in the yard not claimed or protected by others. She trudges with a sibling in each hand but stops as she hears a muffled call.

"Ella. Bella. Lisa." Dideyohvsgi, the medicine man and her father's friend, sits against the stockade's wall and motions for the sisters to join him. Ella's tears dampen Dideyohvsgi's hair. She hugs the aged fellow.

The shaman wraps his arms around old friends. He embraces both of his former friend's daughters as if they were his own. "Cry, little ones, grieve often. Unetlanvhi (ꭴꮑꮵꮕꭿ u-ne-tla-nuh-hi, Creator God) cries with you."

"We're just so glad to find a friend." The oldest Waters gushes.

"Women weep for their families here. Mothers pass tears of strength." He pats her shoulder for comfort.

"I hate this place." Lisa sobs. "It's no fun."

"How long have you been here, Dideyohvsgi?" Older sister asks.

"Long enough to claim this spot. The militia brought me in two days ago." The old man shrugs. "They arrested me from a farm where a woman was having a hard birth. She died, and they took me. They must have thought it was my fault."

"We haven't seen you, but we weren't in the yard. Ella was in the camp's hospital." Bella points out.

"That explains your smell." The shaman wrinkles his nose.

"This place is abominable. How can we get out?" Ella stares at the healer.

"I am old and have little power. Mine faded years ago. You three are different. Before the missionaries brought religion to our tribe, the spirits promised me in a dream that good comes from evil. The owl spirit told me when a woman's tear fell, it was a seed to grow into a new blossom."

Lisa's teary eyes look up at the storyteller. "A flower?"

"A gold-centered, white Cherokee Rose." His hands hold an invisible bloom. "The center is for the valuable yellow metal stolen from our lands. The stem has seven green leaves that represent each of our tribal clans. These flowers and our people grow only on Indian soil."

Lisa looks at her biggest sister, and through the young girl's tears, a gentle, peaceful smile spreads with the story. "That is a beautiful story. My teardrops become roses."

Ella reaches to her youngest sister's cheek and removes moisture from her eye with a forefinger. She plants the tear into the land of Fort Dahlonega and forces a sample of its yard's dirt firm over the planting. Her big sister bows her head and blesses Lisa's personal tribal blossom.

***

In deference to the legend of the white rose and its yellow center, Ella, two weeks later, inspects a small, tender stem in the same spot that peeks from the soil. She pushes extra dirt around the tiny growth and presses it solid. "Grow, little Lisa," the older and responsible one whispers to the plant.

Sounds of enterprise from beyond the walls interrupt Ella's floriculture. She scoots on the ground a few feet away to the wall and peers through a break in the pine stockade. Dideyohvsgi sleeps in their family space with his back against the barrier, and Bella sits nearby. Lisa snores with her head in her sibling's lap. The alert sister looks at her older and shrugs a question to the noise. Ella tightens her shoulders in response, then presses closer to the peephole.

Several families arrive in two wagons loaded with belongings. Sergeant Hiram Colly rides and meets the newcomers. He lifts his right hand to stop.

The Cherokees disembark, and Georgia militia prod them with musket barrels to hurry. One of the Indians attempts to lift his belongings from the conveyance. A militiaman slaps his musket's butt across the defenseless man's face. Blood and teeth splatter the sand.

Ella cringes away from her view and grimaces with the victim's pain.

Items transported include baskets of beans, squash and corn, smoked sides of venison and pork, a packed bale of cotton, pieces of furniture, and individual apparel.

The guards herd the arrivals into the fort.

Sergeant Colly dismounts from his horse and inventories the cart as three Indian riders approach the caravan. They join and inspect the wagon.

Ella clenches her fists as she recognizes the lead warrior. He and the White man talk. The leader counts cash into Colly's hand, and he tucks the money into his uniform's coat. The militiaman turns his mare and rides into the fort.

Tesali, the warrior murderer of Benjamin Waters with a facial scar, passes his horse's reins to his partner. He takes control of the conveyance that he purchased and moves out of Ella's view.

Ella relaxes her clenched fists and rubs them together. Cuts from her fingernails, forced by tension, smear her palms red. She wipes the blood on her apron and settles next to Bella for sleep.

***

That night, Ella's bad dreams transition without her awareness into reality as forms slink in the yard among the detainees. The threat transfers from one household group to another. At each stop, a new woman either waits or joins the collection.

Two men, followed by several subjugated women, creep closer to Ella's camp.

The men become Frank Hale, who directs Sergeant Colly to a youthful, appealing victim asleep with her people. In stealth, the massive militiaman bends low, captures the shapeliest Waters female, and sweeps her from the ground.

Ella, comatose with her arms around Lisa, stirs but does not awaken.

Bella struggles and gasps for breath. Her captor's immense palm prevents breathing and sight. Sergeant Colly strikes the prettiest sister with the butt of his hand-weapon, and she collapses.

The men slip away into the darkness with the woman in Hale's enormous arms. A small group of Cherokee captives follow, without calling out or warning other families, resigned to their fates.

***

Next day, the rising sun colors Ella's eyelids orange before they flutter open. She focuses on the sleeping medicine man nearby. Ella kisses Lisa and rolls over to waken Bella, whose blanket lies empty.

A calamitous noise erupts.

In fear and panic, oldest sibling looks across the yard. Dideyohvsgi grabs the older Waters by the ankle before she screams.

Two Georgia militia beat metal tubs.

The sound reverberates around her group and all the sleeping prisoners. The area awakens, and occupants stumble in the noise's direction.

"Corn!" The medicine man struggles to move his aged body to his feet. "It's been days!"

A mass of Cherokees surge toward the militiamen, and both leap upon nearby tree stumps. They broadcast kernels of dried maize as if they feed chickens.

Ella and her family lunge into the crowd and press past bodies in a desperate struggle. Each hand full, she drops into her soiled apron and fights to trap more. Youngest sister and the shaman dive to get food.

A larger Cherokee woman knocks the younger Waters girl off her feet and steals the girl's life-sustaining morsels.

The old shaman pulls struggling Lisa to her feet. "Dance, little one! This is the White man's Corn Ceremony!"

The men on the stumps shake their metal containers bottoms up as the last bits fall, then throw the empties aside. Fronted by several armed militia patrols, a food broadcaster tugs a small barrel cart from the storehouse, uncorks spigots and allows liquid to pour into each tub.

The militia prevent the mob from getting too close before the vessels are half full. They cut off the flow and pull the vehicle back into the repository. Guards slam its doors.

Indian men, women and children, young or gray, struggle against each other to touch and sip a taste of wet.

An elderly fellow, from the press of the crowd, falls into one tub and tips the metal pail. Others leap to lick the moisture from the ground before it soaks into parched soil.

***

The Waters clan huddles together. The medicine man eyes Ella's smock as she drops to her knees between him and her family member. A pitiful few dried corn kernels lay in the garb, and the oldest sibling divides them into four piles. The shaman eats his pile, Lisa consumes hers not so fast, and the server takes one grain at a time. She savors each morsel and wraps her missing sister's portion.

A nearby commotion attracts Ella's attention.

Frank Hale with a musket in hand drags a stumbling Bella by her tangled hair to her family's patch. He throws the young woman at the head of the clan's feet.

"Be ready when I come tonight." The brute turns and strides away.

Bella's eyes stare blank and swollen, and her dress hangs ripped at the shoulder. Tears drip along the girl's cheeks as she collapses into loving arms. The sister trembles as she attempts to speak, but Ella covers her sibling's lips with her fingers and strokes her spasming eyelids.

The traumatized victim shakes her head and empties a piece of salt pork from her skirt.

Lisa's eyes focus on the protein.

Ella offers the exhausted and numb woman her minuscule collection of kernels wrapped in an apron. Her sister stares at the corn, motions no, and succumbs to sleep.

The Waters matron sits in the sun and strokes her beloved Bella's hair until she sleeps.

The youngest whispers to her wiser sibling as Dideyohvsgi listens. "I missed her the entire night."

The old man holds a tiny bowl. He squats, careful not to spill a drop of its precious liquid, "The Guards took her."

"Where? Why? That is so exciting. Wake her so we can hear the complete story!" the youngest babbles.

"Don't ask her, Lisa. She will not tell you."

"Oh! I can't wait to get older so I can go with the soldiers!"

Dideyohvsgi grabs Lisa's hand. "Bella did nothing with them."

"Then where was she?" The innocent child's eyes swell with curiosity.

The shaman takes the youngest's hands. "Unetlanvhi called her to ride a white horse through the clouds and around the moon. On the trail in the sky, she fell to earth and landed with her family. Such a fall hurt her soul."

"It did?" Lisa looks into the old man's eyes.

"Your sister will never want to speak of it."

"And never ask her." Ella adds as she glances at Dideyohvsgi's small bowl of liquid. "Is that the water you could draw today?"

"No. This is special and not to drink. They boil willow root—for cleansing of the dead—much more valuable than any White man's drinking ration."

"How did you get it?" the big sister questions.

"I got the wash from a father whose son I cured of the pox. He smuggled the medicine in through the stockade."

"Through the wall?" The oldest of the girls reacts.

"Goods come in through the soldiers' outhouse for money. Inside or outside, the smuggler pays Sergeant Colly."

"That's criminal. I think you should take the stuff back." Ella protests.

"Wait, there's more. The father told me someone paid to meet you on the night of the full moon."

Older Waters recoils, shocked, which jostles her sleeping patient, and she awakens. Middle daughter looks at her nurse and her eyes flood. She attempts to speak with trembling lips, but her sibling reaches out and calms the tremors with her fingers. Dideyohvsgi passes the small bowl of boiled willow curative to her therapist, who dips an edge of her apron into the cleanser and dabs Bella's cheeks.

The protective oldest Waters woman stuffs her emotions and hopes the liquid tree root cleanses the White man's squalid obscenities from her sister's soul.

CHAPTER SIX — Fiasco

DRTᏬᎤⁱᏕᎤᎥᎩAJEᏒᏝᏗᎻᎦᏜWᏕᎡGMᎯᏛᎤᎻᏗᎩᎾᏇᎾᏁhZᏇOᵛ

Sunday afternoons, an hour before sunset, Cherokee Christian believers within the Georgia internment stockade expect a wagon at the main gate. A Baptist preacher, accompanied by his wife, arrives every Lord's Day.

Militia guards within watch the clergyman in a black suit and hat and his spouse in a gray dress and bonnet arrive and climb out of their carriage. He ties his team to a post outside the wall's entrance.

The minister reads Bible passages until someone opens the gate and the two missionaries enter.

By arrangement with the Georgia troops, the proselytizers offer Protestant preaching and soul saving to the defined-by-White's unsaved heathens. A few converted and faithful parishioners also attend.

This Sabbath ritual draws attendees as the only allowed contact between the prisoners and the world outside the fort.

The unsecular worship occurs segregated to Cherokee only. White guards do not watch.

The preacher and his wife pass through the walls and join a group of Baptist Cherokees. The Indians patiently wait for their weekly religious service, and it appears to be more than worship.

To Ella's clan, the event provides a diversion from monotony.

***

The Waters family watches separate from the service in a cooler afternoon shadow cast from the palisades' wall. "The soldiers allow that Christian to hold his meeting." The shaman's brows furrow in complaint, "but I can't sing the Unetlanvhi chant."

"Why don't you turn Protestant?" Lisa elbows the older man.

"Smarty mouth." He smiles and enjoys the attention.

"Let these people worship." Ella rubs a hand through her hair and watches the White preacher open his black Bible.

"If that book grants freedom, I'll be a Baptist." Lisa, at her age, insists upon the last word. "But it won't get me out of this place."

The sisters return to their camp spot. Youngest trails, then stops. She turns to the Protestant service and observes for a moment. The spontaneous Waters girl smiles and mumbles to herself. "But being clergy might."

***

Later, after the moon shines high in the sky that night, her group settles for the evening. Ella relaxes with one eye on the yard and dreads the next arrival. Bella attempts to find comfort and sits cross-legged. She rocks and hums a child's sleeping song for calm and inner strength during the hours between sunset and Frank Hale's collection.

Lisa, unaware that her sisters fear an intruder from the dark, sleeps with her head upon her arms.

Dideyohvsgi does not rest in camp with the Waters girls. His absence and her middle sister's vigil keep the clan's matriarch alert and watchful. This night, Ella scans the fort for militiamen patrols. She observes little movement. The detainees sleep.

The oldest checks Bella who, as the time nears for her tormentor's arrival, withdraws from reality into an insulating physical and repetitive rock.

Ella assures herself that her sister has withdrawn before the oldest slips away. She crawls across the yard on her belly and creeps between dark sleeping human forms. Imitating a ground squirrel, the conspirator lifts her head and surveys her surroundings. A murmur of whispered voices attracts her attention. She worms closer to observe.

"We need guns." A young man points an imaginary rifle at the sky. "We cannot overpower these soldiers without them."

"Or knives and war clubs." Another shakes his fist as if it contains a weapon.

"You men are young." Dideyohvsgi spreads his hands palms downward for caution. "Most of us are ancient, or women and children. Weapons for the few able to fight will not break this imprisonment. We must find a better way."

"My wife can slit a militia's throat slicker than any of you." A Cherokee demonstrates the technique.

"No, the elderly shaman is right." A wiser young warrior points a forefinger at Dideyohvsgi and then, at himself. "I am Onocona, son of the brave Waya. You knew my parents. I do not fear the White men. My father was courageous, but he was also shrewd. With the militia, we must be sharp as he was."

"Quiet. Someone comes." Another dark form whispers and pretends that he sleeps.

Ella drops her head upon the ground and fakes rest. She watches an ominous shadow step around sleeping Indians nearby. The armed threat stops, checks his surroundings, and bends to grasp a nearby young woman's arm. He jerks her onto her feet. She does not protest but follows the militiaman on her nightly ritual.

As the escort and the woman walk through the night toward a corner log house, Onocona raises his head. "A warrior cuts that guard's neck. A sane man pretends sleep. Are we smart or cowardly?"

The others murmur with each other. Someone rises to his knees. "There are seven of us and only one of him."

"That is not true." Dideyohvsgi holds a hand high for attention. "We saw one guard. Slit his throat, and a replacement appears. Resist, and they become an army."

"We must use their weight against them." Onocona clenches his fist. "Their power is numbers. Armies need organization, communication, logistics, and command. We are few. A few can disrupt many. That is our strength."

Ella, unseen by guards or the rebellious plotters, crawls away from the conspiracy through the darkness.

Minutes later, the eldest daughter creeps into the space her family claims. Youngest lies sleeping. The oldest gazes at the ugly present.

Bella is gone.

She entered the lower world of evil with Frank Hale, and her older sibling was helpless.

Frustrated, Ella settles next to her Lisa and battles for sleep.

***

The following morning, the Waters' conspiracy leader and returned shaman wakens with the clan.

Lisa sleeps beyond the healer.

Nearby, the family matriarch rests and listens to bird cries from outside the stockade and within, the groans of stirring humanity.

"Dideyohvsgi, you are awake?" Ella props to one elbow. "Yes."

"Where were you last night?"

The conspirator remains still and considers the question.

He sits. "I have given my word. I cannot speak of this."

"Then I will tell you." Ella's tone rings accusatory. "I found you and the others after midnight. A few young warriors plot against the Georgia militia. You plan a Cherokee uprising. You walked the path of war with Dragging Canoe and John Watts. More than anyone, you know our people have done this many times. Another retry is useless."

"We do not rebel." The old medicine maker sputters. "We resist, disrupt, annoy."

"You exasperate the Whites, and they react. They slap a fly on a horse's ear." Ella slaps a mosquito on her arm. "The soldier's guns squash pests and all their relatives."

Dideyohvsgi looks to the rising sun. "But the insect may grow into an eagle."

"No. It will just die and fade from memory." The conscientious sister concludes.

That day, the prisoners in camp move nervously, and clumps of Cherokee men talk in small groups. Several impromptu meetings suffer interruption by militia, concerned by the activity.

***

Later in the afternoon, six guards with muskets follow Hiram Colly into the yard. Sergeant Colly commands the detachment. He draws and fires his pistol into the air. The weapon's blast reverberates, and the yard's occupants respond attentively. Colly holsters his firearm. "This morning, a civilian pilfered the store house. The intruder mixed cow pies in the flour bins. We will not tolerate harassment. The State of Georgia offers an award of twenty dollars to any deportee with information."

A mummer of conversation and a minor ripple of laughter sweeps the assembled Indians. A voice yells out. "Save that flour for the guards!"

Colly whips his attention to the callout. Nobody moves. "We suspend individual food rations until you report the Injun that soiled the supply . . . and until you turn over the person who just spoke for discipline." The sergeant pivots to his guard detachment. "About face! Forward march!"

***

No corn ration falls on the imprisoned chickens this day, and the prisoners grumble and complain. Another night of restlessness comes. After the hulk shadow of Frank Hale gathers Bella in his round up, Ella sits in the blackness with her youngest. "Dideyohvsgi has disappeared. I'm worried, Lisa."

"An old man like him won't get in too much trouble." The younger sister shrugs the concern away.

In the darkness, several shadows creep around the interior edge of the stockade. A militia patroller approaches the

64

creepers, and they drop to the ground. The conspirators' shapes blend with other sleepers. As the guard continues his pace along the wall past the forms, they advance and attract Ella's attention. Much too spry to be Dideyohvsgi, the matriarch suppresses any concern for others. Her tension focuses on her Bella.

Sleep comforts at intervals throughout the night. Before dawn, Frank Hale delivers his prey. "You earned your keep tonight, Squaw." The degenerate throws Bella onto the ground and stalks away.

Older sister gathers her shaking loved one into her arms and attempts comfort. Blank red eyes stare empty. The girl's lips smear with gloss and her cheeks blush pink from White woman, whore-style face paint.

Ella purges her personal guilt with tears as she hugs her sibling. "I am so sorry. Paw wants you safe. I fail him—and you. Please forgive me."

The second oldest Waters sits and stares, expressionless.

***

As the two sisters sit together inside a wood stockade in Georgia, the morning sun paints the sky's clouds golden, and Ella's surroundings waken. Someone in a family clump nearby coughs. With a snort, a militia guard with his back against the fort's wall wakens, grabs his musket from the ground beside him, and inspects his prisoners. A baby cries with hunger before its mother satisfies.

The matriarch of the Waters clan spies Dideyohvsgi bent low to blend in the yard's shadows, with another Cherokee as they scramble toward her plot. Both, out of breath, drop to their knees at Ella's side.

65

"This is Onocona." The medicine man looks back where he has come for anyone that may follow. "This is my friend Ella. We can trust her."

"With our lives?" The young warrior stares directly with cold eyes. "You have not seen me. You do not know me. Do you understand?"

Wide-eyed first sister nods understanding, and the Indian continues. "We resist. This old fellow tells me you support us."

"My friend knows me, but he does not speak for me. What do you want from me?"

"We organize to hurt the Georgia troopers, and if all goes well, to escape confinement. I cannot tell you how, but our plans need money. Can you help finance our efforts?"

The Waters eldest scrutinizes the older shaman at the warrior's side, and he smiles. She swings her attention to the fighter. "Will your actions improve things?" Ella attempts to read the warrior's eyes. "And not make this place worse for all of us?"

"Yes, and we all may become free." Onocona's voice carries the conviction and optimism of youth.

On her knees, the oldest Waters girl shifts her back to the two men and reaches under her blanket pillow. From a beaded purse, she removes part of its contents. She turns and hands a wad of cash to the young fellow.

"Thank you, Ella, and you, Dideyohvsgi." The warrior pauses. "Your money helps us hurt the White troops." The Indian, low to avoid notice by the guards, slips away.

The Waters matriarch watches the young man slip away and turns to her father's friend. "I gave him a third of our wealth." Ella shows her medicine man the remaining money.

"Good. That leaves the bank short and us committed to this prison struggle. I know their plan, and I swear by Unetlanvhi, if it works, we well spent our cash." The old one grasps Ella's hands.

Lisa wakens and rolls to face her sister. "Did I hear a voice? A young man?"

"Yes, but he's gone. He has much to do."

***

As the day wears on, the prisoners grow restless. Many walkers stumble through the yard and avoid the militia guards. Their nervous movement creates a breeze, a respite from the midafternoon sun. Several wanderers' ribs press against skin. They ignore their bodies' evidence of starvation's onset. Women cuddle infants under their dresses for protection in the shade, and children sit and stare instead of play.

Ella, Lisa, and Dideyohvsgi huddle under a lean-to with a blanket roof that hangs from their shoulders and extends over their heads to anchor under Bella's sleeping body. It shades the three but allows a view of the yard.

A Cherokee mother drops to her knees in front of the family. "My daughter is dry. Her baby starves. Do you have milk?"

Those in the shade nod no. The woman moves to the next group.

"These poor people cannot go much longer." Ella watches the distraught grandmother as she searches. "May Unetlanvhi watch over Onocona." The oldest sister's eyes implore Dideyohvsgi.

"Who's he?" Lisa perks her attention level.

"No one. Check on Bella."

"You do it. Why me? She's older than I am."

Afternoon shadows cool the stockade's grounds, and the Cherokee groups settle. A gentle wind stirs and offers additional relief.

Lisa allows the air to flutter her hair as Dideyohvsgi slips away. "Where's he going?" She follows the medicine man's form until he blends with others.

"Some of his old war buddies meet and brag about their conquests." Ella pats her younger sister's knee.

"I thought he only told those stories to me." Lisa giggles and settles into her blanket.

Not long after, the young girl sleeps while her older sisters sit in the darkness and wait.

Bella begins her trance-like rock, and soon after, Frank Hale collects his merchandise.

Responsibility for her youngest sibling presses the mind of the matriarch of the Waters clan, and doubt grips her skull. She weeps regret for her tragic failure to protect her Bella.

Musket fire breaks Ella's depression, and she panic checks her family.

Only Lisa rests beside her and stirs at the noise. "What's that boom-boom?"

Older grasps her little sister's hand and scans the compound for Bella and her medicine man. Neither appear as others in the encampment wake, jump to their feet, and question the weapon fire. More muskets boom, and screams of pain assault the wall barricades.

Locked from the outside, the stockade's wooden gates fling open, and horses stampede into the yard, several with young Cherokees on their backs. On their heels, dozens of Georgia militia pound into the enclosure in pursuit. They discharge long guns and pistols.

The enclosed prisoners fall to their stomachs, and parents protect their children.

A last warrior on horseback, with a hatchet in hand, charges the grouped militia. Several guards' weapons explode smoke, and the man on the horse falls dead.

Black powder mist floats above the detainees as a terrified silence descends over the prisoners. Guards collect runaway horses and pull bodies of youthful men out the gate.

"I'm here and unharmed." Ella jumps, startled at Dideyohvsgi's voice.

"And Onocona?" She looks behind the medicine man.

"I think they captured him, but I am not sure." The old shaman drops to his hands and knees.

"Who's Onocona?" Lisa inquires a second time.

CHAPTER SEVEN — Consequences

DRTᎶᎣ'iᏃᎣᏙᏯAJEᏇᎮᎯᏔᎾWᏚᏩGMᎯᏚᎣᎻᏚᎩᎾᏖᎾᏁᏂZᎯOᏉ

A rising sun warms the internment camp, and the Waters clan groups together the following morning, except for Bella, who has not returned. Others also cluster and expect reprisal for the activity of the evening prior.

At one corner of the stockade's yard, hewn pine storehouse doors fling open. Militiamen roll the death wagon into the compound. They turn the conveyance so that one of its wheels faces the crowd.

Two soldiers drag Onocona and tie the young warrior spread eagled across its wheel.

Cherokee detainees mill around the militia, unsettled from the night's rebellion, and observe an uneasy armistice. A foreboding atmosphere hangs from the sky like a premonition of disastrous defeat.

Sergeant Colly joins his detachment and steps atop a stump. "Last evening, we had an unfortunate incident." The soldier surveys the crowd. "Deportees bribed a civilian employee and got weapons. They stole horses from the corral and attempted mutiny. All perished, except for three."

A ripple of concern and curiosity sweeps through the sergeant's audience.

He waits for quiet. "With interrogation, two of those prisoners died. They identified their leader. A few of his followers, they informed us, disappeared and blended into your numbers. You know who they are." The militia sergeant turns to Onocona on the wheel. "This prisoner is the third. He will hang here until he—or one of you—name the others." The Georgia noncommissioned officer pivots and walks back into the shadows and coolness of the storehouse.

The day progresses as detainees stand around Onocona. Sun beats upon the yard, and silence pervades.

The state's military overseers spell each other in shifts and provide most of the stockade activity as the sun becomes hotter.

Late in the morning, a Cherokee woman steps from the crowd. "I knew Waya, father of Onocona. His son will never betray another warrior to the Whites." She carries a small pottery container of water and moves toward the wheel.

A militiaman leaps from his station and clubs the mother to the ground.

Her pot breaks and moistens the yard's soil around a blood stain from her forehead.

"He won't last long in this sun." Ella whispers to Dideyohvsgi.

"He'll name the rest of us, I'm sure." The medicine man restrains his voice. "But there's nothing I can do."

***

Midday passes and the vigil continues. No daily corn disbursement or water ration offers relief. The Cherokee in the yard grumble and whisper complaints to each other as they scorch in the afternoon sun.

"That militia monster has not returned Bella." Ella leans to her friend's ear. "Do you think it involved Bella some way?"

"I asked Unetlanvhi to protect her." The shaman covers his mouth as his lips move. "I don't see a way she could get swept up in the uprising."

"You're one of the rebels. That connects you to those who know. Can you find out if she's alive?" the Waters matriarch presses. "Someone in your group should know."

"Not today. We cannot communicate." Her old friend's eyelids flicker. "The guards are everywhere."

Conversation stops as the storehouse doors swing open and Sergeant Colly strides out of its darkness. The soldier inspects Onocona's condition.

His prisoner hangs from the wagon's wheel with chin on chest. When he realizes Colly's presence, the warrior left in him raises his jaw in defiance.

"You ready to name those who escaped?" The interrogator speaks only loud enough for his captive to hear.

The Indian on the wheel spits and splatters Colly.

The soldier freezes. "I think not. Too bad, Injun." The man wipes his face with his sleeve and turns to the throng who stands in surprise by the act of defiance. He waits for an under-tone buzz to squelch. "No one has reported any escapee from last night's rebellion," the Georgia official informs the crowd. The sergeant paces back and forth before the wagon. "You may have noticed there has been no food or water ration today. When the Militia captures the escapees, those rations will resume." The officer stalks into the warehouse.

Frank Hale leads two Cherokee, burdened with timber from the storehouse, into the yard. As the brute supervises, the

Indian slaves make a pit. They dump their loads on the ground and start a flame in the hole. Smoke soon rises from a fire.

Militiamen with a huge, raw beef roast on a board between them exit the depot. They place the meat on the wagon bed near Onocona.

One reenters the storeroom and returns with a pointed iron spit with a ring on its end. This cook places the spit in the flames as the Cherokee slaves pound "Y" stakes into the earth at opposite sides of the pit.

"Look at that beef," Lisa whispers to her older sister.

"I see it, but we eat corn kernels and salt pork." Ella grits her teeth. "That steer is rations meant for distribution. I wager my life on it."

"If you keep whispering." Dideyohvsgi warns, "you may lose that bet. Some guard will think you're conspiring."

***

Another hour of late afternoon sun creates weak knees and dizzy minds in most of those who maintain Onocona's vigil. A few families wander away and resume their imprisoned lives.

Ella stays. Her vision blurs in the heat without water, but she forces focus and watches Frank Hale step to the cooking pit. He rips a tattered buckskin vest off one of the Indian attendants. With the cloth protecting his hands, the brute grasps and extends the iron spit into the air. The pointed end of the spit glows red. The torturer steps to Onocona and brands a sizzling stripe across his thigh.

The warrior's head jerks backward, and his eyes pop open. He grits his teeth and chokes on his pain.

Hale snorts and slaps the hot poker against his prisoner's stomach, holding it in place.

The captive's lungs bulge and his body trembles in shock. A terrified and anguished primal scream reverberates across the yard.

Hatred burns into Ella's heart like the red rod that created the sound. Every spectator shares the pain.

"Where is our Bella?" Ella steps forward as she watches. Dideyohvsgi and Lisa clench her between them. The oldest sister struggles against their restraint. "That monster took her!"

As the Waters daughter fights for self-control, Hale yanks the poker with welded belly skin melded to its surface and steps to the wagon. He jams the iron through the roast, smiles at the hiss, and suspends the meat on the spit above the fire.

Smoke and the smell of roasting meat floats around the detainees in the yard. Several viewers eye the cooking food, and an undistracted few maintain their respectful vigil.

The unconscious collapsed and branded prisoner remains on the wheel.

The sun's heat, lack of water, and the sniff of roasted beef to those who consume kernels of corn daily overcomes. "Ahuli was one!" A Cherokee indicates a young fellow who stands with his family. "He rode last night!"

Militia captors surround the indicated.

Frank Hale strides to the accuser and points at the youngster. "This Injun?"

The traitor collapses to his knees. "Yes! I saw him!"

The brutish soldier whips his elbow under the chin of the informer and snaps his neck. "Then you were there!" The tremendous beast laughs as he curses and kicks the broken-necked body.

Militia club Ahuli's father, who steps in front of his son to protect him, and the husband falls unconscious. The soldiers drag the young boy's body into the storehouse.

Hale carves a piece of juice dripping protein off the spit roast and tosses it to a bystander. "See! I have a heart!" The man clutches the food and slinks away as his server dances an insane jig around the fire pit.

***

Afternoon evolves into twilight as the guards and their supervisor share the remaining meat. The White men eat while starving Cherokee watch the banquet.

With his belly full, Frank Hale extracts the spit and plays burning games upon the alive but unconscious Onocona strapped to the wheel. Each time iron burns flesh, the torturer dances and sings with the fevered insanity of an Inquisition executioner.

"Ella, I'm here." Bella touches her older sister's elbow.

The Waters girl embraces her sister with joy. "I was so worried. Are you hurt?"

"What went on last evening? Something must have. The militia didn't sell us. Nobody ever came." The woman's sunken eyes betray her smile.

"Shhh, not in front of Lisa. You need to rest." The elder sibling guides her sisters, followed by the old shaman, to their plot in the yard.

At the wagon wheel, few observers support the vigil for a dead Indian brother.

***

As darkness deepens, the Waters clan listens to crickets chirping. Sounds no longer float from the abandoned cart where Onocona hangs, but faint scents of roast beef sweeten the air.

"Dideyohvsgi, should we free Onocona and take the body to his family? I think we should." Ella's sense of right and wrong overwhelms her fear.

"No. The guards may have gone, but they still watch." Her older friend urges caution.

"Frank Hale will cut him loose. He needs that wagon to transport his women." Bella, under her breath, remains more aware of reality than the others.

"And it might incriminate our conspirator." Ella looks at Dideyohvsgi.

"If I get through this day, I'll thank Unetlanvhi." The medicine man glances about his surroundings. No one watches or listens.

The group sits in silence, each poised with varying degrees of dread. "Look up there." Lisa points to the sky.

Above, a full white orb illuminates the yard with a cool blue and peaceful glow.

"It's the midnight of the perfect moon, Ella." The shaman stares up into the night. "Did anyone contact you?"

"No. Why?" The Waters matron shrugs, then recalls. "I remember. Your friend said someone bribed Sergeant Colly to meet with me. I know nothing more about it."

Lisa and the medicine man settle onto their blankets for sleep.

After a moment, Bella whispers. "Is little one asleep?"

Her big sister nods affirmative, and a concerned sibling keeps her voice low. "Who wants you?"

"Dideyohvsgi did not know. A buddy told him, a co-conspirator."

"When Frank Hale comes for me, if he draws you, I will die." Bella rolls her back to her sister.

"I can't live with myself each time he picks you." The leader of the family trembles, and her throat bubbles. "But there's nothing I can do."

Bella's voice in the night sounds strong with a hint of resolve. "No matter what happens, remember always that it was not your fault, and I love you."

***

Ella sits with her sister in the light of the new moon and waits while most of the rest of the stockade sleeps.

Bella grasps her knees with both her hands and arms as she stares at the gray hulk of the storehouse. Several women sprinkled in the darkness sit with their sleeping families and stare as she does. The granary door creaks as it opens, and an apprehensive inhale sweeps through the waiters.

Ella glances at Dideyohvsgi as he groans and scoots his back closer to Lisa for warmth in the cooler night.

A shadow in the distance near the storehouse moves from one waiting woman to the next. Without a sound, each victim joins their militia procurer.

"I think it's best you pretend you're asleep," Bella whispers.

Older lies beside younger and watches a dark hulk become Frank Hale. The militiaman grabs shapely daughter and jerks her to her feet. This night, he shakes Ella from her feigned sleep. With no choice like the other young women, she goes silent and submissive.

Bella's big sister does not resist, but the animal procurer holds her mouth covered and drags her with him like a knapsack.

At the granary, the beast directs Bella to the Death Cart. She joins a small group of other girls. Ella attempts to join her sister, but Hale grabs the back collar of her dress and yanks her off the flatbed wagon. Under a two-man militia guard, four Cherokee men pull the haul of women into the darkness.

Hale, the prowling militia animal, pulls Ella behind him through its open door into the granary.

Inside, Sergeant Colly leans against a wall and holds a candle. The pimp inspects his new arrival as if she is merchandise. He assures himself that she is fit for delivery.

"I didn't touch the squaw," Hale mutters as he turns and moves out the storehouse to follow his debauched women.

Head militiaman stands in the depot in front of his prisoner.

She clenches her hands behind her back. Their fingers grip each other to prevent nervous tremors.

"You're Ella Waters, eldest daughter of a cotton farmer freedman named Benjamin?" Colly's voice vibrates low and menacing.

"Yes."

The Georgia soldier steps to a list and, by candlelight, reads from a sheet of paper. "You live with an elderly medicine man?"

"He was a friend of my father's."

"An informer identifies him as a leader in the mutiny." The official lays the note on a bench and waits for a retort.

Surprised that the woman shows no backlash, the sergeant continues. "How old is the shaman?"

The matriarch of the Waters clan clears her throat and replies, "I am not sure. I suspect late sixties."

"I should arrest and hang him, but I am not inclined to do so." The militiaman waits for a reply. He receives none. "You have influential friends. Do you know Judge Bennett Steel?"

She nods a lie. "No."

"You don't? Well, he knows you. One of his clerks paid a hefty sum of money to see you." The sergeant jerks his head to follow as he pulls his flintlock pistol from his belt and blows out the candle on the table.

His captive follows the man as he steps through the granary door into the night.

A strange moon shines on Ella's face outside the stockade's wall. Light dances on whiffs of clouds under a harvest orb. Beyond a cleared protective circle, pine tree woods block the view of whatever awaits.

Sergeant Colly escorts his prisoner a short way through the pines to a wood slat outhouse and opens its door. He shoves her into the shack and closes the entrance.

Alone, the apprehensive female backs into a corner.

The privy features a long flat plank with eight holes mounted to three of its walls. Slats in the roof allow stripes of moonlight to paint the interior space.

Door hinges creak, and she crowds back into her safety cocoon.

Light illuminates a store-bought White man's brocade shirt, belt, trousers, and boots as Ezra stands before her with a small basket. His eyes tear as he extends help and guides her to a seat on the long plank. From his pocket, he offers a piece of smoked venison.

Her hands tremble as she accepts the meat. She bites, chews, and her jaw trembles from the sensation.

"We have little time." Ezra cautions. "I paid that sergeant one of the smaller nuggets we found in the river."

"This venison's worth more than gold."

"Please, listen. You will find a small door behind the camp hospital, where they push out corpses. Be there tomorrow midnight, and I'll smuggle more food to you."

"No, you can't. They'll catch you."

"Not likely, and I'm leaving soon. Judge Steel hired me. He wants me to be his clerk and study for the bar. His family's leaving on the water route to the territory. He plans to take me."

The outhouse swings open, and Sergeant Colly stands by the exit.

Ezra looks at his old schoolmate, pats her hand, and leaves into the night.

The militiaman escorts Ella to the stockade. He pushes her into the granary.

"Search her for contraband." The man in charge orders.

The prisoner cringes away, but Frank Hale grabs her neck and violates her person as he searches. The pervert drools as he lingers at Ella's crotch.

The Waters woman steels her body and her stare.

The molester slaps his victim across her face and shoves her out of the granary into the yard's darkness, a place of misery and continued imprisonment.

The shocked and humiliated soul stumbles through sleeping families to her own and collapses. She cries herself to sleep.

CHAPTER EIGHT — Revenge

DRTᎣᎤᎤᎥᏚᎤᏒᏗᎩᎠᎫᎬᏍᏇᏗᏂᏌᎠᏔᎤᎠᎫᎨᎷᎫᏏᎤᎤᎶᎯᏛᎶᏂᎳᎤᏁᎤᏂᎰᏃᎯᎤᎤ

The following morning, Sergeant Colly stands on a stump outside the granary's door as Frank Hale beats a metal corn pail. Cherokee from the yard stir and gather around the militiamen.

Ella helps Dideyohvsgi struggle to his feet. She checks for Bella and finds her returned and asleep. Lisa watches over her sister as older sibling and the medicine man join the crowd.

"General Winfield Scott orders detainees to prepare for relocation from Fort Dahlonega to Fort Wool. Custody will transfer from the Militia of Georgia to the United States Army. Purpose, final deportation to Indian Territory." Sergeant Colly steps from the stump.

Conversation in English and Cherokee ripples through the gathering.

A family nearby celebrates. One member jumps to his feet. "John Ross and the National Party leads our people to paradise!"

A different group overhears. "The Treaty Party signed three years ago, not the Chief! That's why we go!"

Dideyohvsgi surges to the argument, but his friend pulls him back. "Please, Ella. They should hear from Unetlanvhi!"

"They don't want your politics or your religion." She drags the medicine man away from the controversial discussion.

***.

That evening as exhausted-by-rhetoric Indians snore across the compound, the two older sisters watch the granary and huddle together for warmth and security.

"I find it hard to believe that you just sit here and wait for that scum to fetch you."

Bella sits in silence for long moments. "What would you prefer, big sister?"

"Protest, yell, scream, cry, make a scene!" Ella sputters.

Again, second sibling rocks serenely. "You have not been where I go. That monster and Colly exploit our Cherokee women for profit because we are helpless." The victim whispers. "If we resist, we die. To them, we are subhuman. They see only profitable products that sell well."

"Colly's the leader?"

"Yes. But he only collects the money. The militia beast-master manages and controls the girls."

"If they took me, I just couldn't bear it." Ella collects her sibling's hands.

"Nor can I." Bella murmurs. "But I have no options."

The two women sit it silence until Frank Hale creeps from the darkness. He drags Bella to her feet and leads her away. She strains to look at her beloved sibling. "Remember me to Lisa the way I was."

"Shut up, whore!" Her captor twists his prisoner's arm and propels the woman forward.

Bella's words float through the air. "Not how I have become."

Night swallows the pair, but the older one holds her attention focused for a long moment. Darkness conceals her sister's plight. Helpless, in angry and frustrated silence, the head of the Waters family cries until the midnight moon shines high in the sky over the stockade.

A guard strolls on patrol along the pine wall. He looks in her direction, but she does not move or dare to breathe. After a moment, the man continues. Clear, Ella slips into the dark.

***

The oldest daughter crawls between sleeping family groups to the haystack infirmary. Several sick Cherokee patients suffer without nurses.

A woman focuses feverish eyes and whispers weakly, "Help me. Water, please."

The stealthy sibling freezes for the time that the person calls, and then illness fogs the woman's sight and voice. Ella moves on and creeps to the stockade fence. She looks both ways along the wall for the silhouette of a militia guard. She finds the small wooden corpse removal door.

She taps on the wood quietly and hears Ezra open the door's latch from the outside. "Take this chance for escape. Scoot through. I have a wagon."

"You know I can't leave Bella and Lisa!"

"What I expected. Take this." The voice shoves a blanket wrapped bundle through the gate.

"The Waters family thanks you, old friend." Ella collects the package.

"A guard's coming." Ezra warns.

The door shuts near Ella's chin and the latch clicks. She slips back to concealed safety in the hospital's hay, one body of many.

85

The wall guard paces to the haystack infirmary, covers his face with a cloth, and hurries through.

After moments, Ella feels safe and slithers through the dark yard to her resting place. She unwraps the blanket. Venison jerky, fresh corn, and other foods lay before her.

A deerskin bag with a leather tie, the only nonfood item, attracts her attention. Ella opens the sack and pours out its contents. In the moonlight, gold nuggets from the stream above her father's farm sparkle. Included are the ones Ezra collected.

The Waters matriarch looks around but sees no observers. She ties the pouch under her skirt.

***

The next morning, she and Dideyohvsgi eat pieces of venison jerky. They hide their food bounty from the yard's view. Lisa sleeps nearby.

"Quietly, or everyone will join us." The medicine man warns.

"I'm worried sick. Bella's not back."

"The others, I meant, not your sisters. May Unetlanvhi protect her."

Ella's voice cracks in concern. "That White beast hasn't returned. She talked with me last night before he took her."

"I hope Lisa's white horse lifted her for an extra trip around the moon." The old man raises his hands to the sky.

"I was impatient with Bella, I'm afraid." Ella visually searches the yard in emerging sunlight.

"Won't be long before another corn ceremony." Dideyohvsgi comments.

Other Cherokee groups watch the granary for disbursement. The doors swing open and the Cherokees surge for food.

Instead of corn throwers, several armed militiamen step out and form ranks on both sides of the door. Two other militia haul the death cart and turn it so that one of its large wooden wheels faces the crowd.

The guards reenter the storehouse. They escort Bella into the lot. She walks quietly and peacefully with a soft smile. Sergeant Colly supervises as they tie Bella's wrists outspread to the spokes of a wheel.

The prisoner does not struggle or resist in any manner. She sees older sibling but shows no recognition. Her satisfied expression does not change.

Ella leaps to help her sister, but Dideyohvsgi restrains her.

"Today, we execute the Cherokee Bella Waters for the murder of Georgia Militiaman Frank Hale." The officer stares at the assembled crowd.

No one protests or objects.

"Sentenced by militia court-martial and a tribunal of her peers, she dies by the lash." Sergeant Colly retreats through the granary doors.

Benjamin Waters' murderer, Tesali, with a long leather whip entwined at its end around metal studs, strides out of the darkness.

Colly nods authorization, and the warrior sweeps his hand backward, followed by the snaking leather that hisses as it coils. Slingshot recoil splits the air as its length flies and pops. Studs rip the cloth and skin of Bella's back. Her knees buckle but she does not scream.

Ella's tears spot the soil and plant Cherokee roses as the terrifying damage of the beating reverberates across the yard.

"Dideyohvsgi, it's my fault. My stupid false sense of right and wrong!" The oldest sister sobs into the medicine man's arms.

With a third vicious stroke, Bella screams in agony.

"I'm a self-consumed hypocrite." Ella faints.

***

During the following day, the execution weighs upon older sister's shoulders, and her mind repeats a conversation. "I find it hard to believe that you just sit here and wait for that scum to fetch you." Bella sits in silence for long moments. "What would you prefer, big sister?"

Ella walks as a convalescent. She mutters under her breath with each step. Her blood-shot eyes flick back and forth. Children in the stockade yard shrink away from the old crazy woman. Without purpose, the lost soul wanders. She searches for, but cannot recover, her humanity.

Lisa and Dideyohvsgi watch the oldest Waters. When either intervenes, their attempts to help and comfort meet hostility. The head of the clan stumbles forward with no life-spark, commitment, or recognition.

"Can you help, Shaman?" Lisa watches and grasps the old man's elbow.

"Your sister is in transformation. An Aniyvdaqualosgi (Thunderer) inhabits her mind. Her heart lives in the sky and commands thunder and lightning." He watches the oldest daughter of his best friend wander, lost in the shadows of self-accusation.

"Sometimes I believe you do know." Lisa crosses her arms. "Do you think she could hurt herself, or us?"

"Aniyvdaqualosgi are powerful and dangerous."

Dideyohvsgi's eyes widen with respect for old terrors. "But they are usually physically harmless."

Ella stumbles along the stockade's walls.

A militia guard, with his back against the posts, straightens and lets the crazy woman pass.

Near the storehouse corner, the oldest Waters sister leans her forehead against the stockade fence and cries silent tears. Outside action, viewed through a crack between two pine uprights, captivates the Thunderer's hazy view.

Crates with canvas covers as tablecloths work as display tables. Upon their cloth tops, the Georgia militia offers rations and supplies. Intended by the military for Cherokee consumption, items cost little. Farmers and their families circulate through the tables and buy goods for personal use. Hiram Colly supervises the enterprise, and his men serve as merchants.

Ella's eyes focus on the sergeant. He manages profitable misuse of government assets. The man overseas the entire illegal business. His clerks empty their tills regularly and transfer money to the overseer.

With accumulated cash in a leather satchel, he carries loot from the sales tables to the corner storage blockhouse. Ella drifts along the palisade to the corner storehouse and fumbles upon a crack between its uprights.

Inside, alone, the sergeant counts the take. He separates the currency into equal piles. He stuffs one batch in his blouse. The second stack the man places neatly in a lockbox. He records that sum in a logbook. After the transaction, Colly returns to his men and the market.

Ella stumbles from her view of the storehouse's interior and continues her aimless roaming around the stockade.

Near the warehouse, a young militia guard crosses his legs for relief and surveys his surroundings. Many Cherokee sit or lie in family pods. A few walkers drift nearby. The yard looks quiet and normal to the young fellow, overwhelmed by the need to urinate.

The militiaman scurries to the storehouse, leans his musket against the wall and disappears. He heads through the space for the outhouse beyond the stockade's walls.

Ella approaches in her haze of self-castigation. Unaware of surroundings, the eldest Waters sister kicks the musket's butt and stumbles. She feels the impact on her foot and focuses.

Fortuitously, Sergeant Colly enters the granary with his leather satchel stuffed with more money. The man fails to notice the cracked door, ajar and open to the yard.

Ella watches through the opening as he counts bills. She looks at the long gun near her feet. With trembling hands, Bella's sister picks up the weapon and cocks it. She freezes in fear at the sound. A quick glance assures her the militia manager did not hear the lever action. The long gun's butt settles with purpose against her shoulder as she slips her finger onto its trigger. Along the barrel, Colly's head centers at its end sight.

Ella's index tremors for brief seconds, and her focus on the sergeant's head shifts out of focus to sharp with the sight off the target. Bella's avenger breaths deep and steadies her aim, then relaxes. Bella's sibling steps aside from the door and leans with her back against the wall. She lowers the musket against the wall where she originally kicked it.

With a purposeful and rejuvenated step, the matriarch of the clan walks away from the weapon with renewed mental health and a fresh resolve to rejoin her family.

As Ella distances, the young recruit returns from the outhouse outside the walls and interrupts Sergeant Colly's count. "What are you doing, Private?" the senior noncom demands.

"Returning from the privy." The boy stammers.

"Get back to your post." His commander orders.

The soldier hurries through the storeroom and into the yard. He picks his musket from where he leaned it, does not notice a cocked hammer, and returns to his posted position.

Ella hears and watches the fellow return.

He inspects his surroundings. The butt of his weapon impacts the palisade wall and discharges.

The Waters eldest jumps in reaction.

A young boy child in a nearby Cherokee family falls dead from a musket ball in his chest. His kin erupt in hysteria.

Ella jolts herself into complete normality and leaps to give aid. "Get something to stop the bleeding!" she joins the family group.

The lad's mother sweeps her son into her arms. She extends the body to his father and drops to her knees in grief. The patriarch grasps the boy's lifeless carcass to his chest and sobs.

From the storeroom's door, the money counter within calls. "What's the commotion out there?" Colly steps out of the storehouse. "Who fired that shot?"

The young soldier guard stands meekly with his smoking musket and points at the dead child with its frantic family.

The dead boy's father's face boils red with rage. He lumps his son's corpse into Ella's arms and charges the commander.

Colly draws his pistol as the grieving Indian lunges forward. The White man blows a hole through his attacker's neck. With gun lowered, he steps to the father on the ground and with his boot rolls the Cherokee over to insure no further threat.

"Private, you're on report!" The irritated officer spits through clenched teeth.

"For what? It was an accident!"

"Disturbing my count, you Cockle Burr!" The sergeant slams the storehouse door.

Ella, with the son's lifeless form in her arms, stands slack-jawed and stares at the storeroom. She questions her return to sanity and her fresh insanity invitation.

She granted an authentic Aniyvdaqualosgi amnesty and escape—by sacrifice of an innocent Cherokee boy—for the death of her beloved Bella. May Unetlanvhi forgive and forget her.

CHAPTER NINE — Sacrifice

ᎠᎡᎠᏍᏳᎣᎢᏎᎣᎢᏴᎠᎫᎬᏫᏯᎲᎢᏥᏍᏫᏓᎳᎬᏓᏣᎹᎠᎴᎣᎲᎯᏴᏯᎾᏛᎾᏂᏃᏔᎣᏐ

Unaware that Ella passed on her revenge opportunity, Lisa sits alone in her prison yard family space. The bored teenager watches a young Cherokee man pitch and catch a small ball with a hickory mallet. With dexterity and natural showmanship, he controls it up and down within inches of basket stick.

The boy notices Lisa's attention but ignores her interest and continues. Pretending loss of handling, he bats a round deerskin ball near Lisa and jogs to retrieve it.

"Hello. I am Yona."

"You play with grace and strength, Yona. My name's Lisa Waters." The girl shows no timidity or reservation.

"That name invokes peaceful rivers and plentiful hunting grounds." The athlete smiles and focuses his attention on the girl.

"Yona translates as 'Bear.' Thank you for the compliment." Lisa hands him the ball.

"You're not Cherokee?" The boy accepts the toy and bounces it in his hand.

"I am half." She responds. "My father was a freedman in Georgia."

"Was? I see you walking with an older man."

"That's only an uncle." Lisa does not blink over her misrepresentation.

"Stroll with me?" The ballplayer flips her the ball. "My name sounds rough but I'm harmless."

Lisa catches the deerskin wrap and stands. "Yes, let's walk. I have been sitting too long."

The two young people wander around the yard, unlike most of the deportees, inspired by youthful connection and budding friendship.

"I hate this place. Wish I could leave." Lisa experiments with the new relationship.

"Did you know Onocona?" Yona's tone implies respect. "Escape is difficult. Look what happened when he listened to your uncle."

"But you are braver, and I am smarter." Lisa charms her compliments.

"The man was the best stickball player in Georgia. I am not as courageous, but I think you're more intelligent." The young fellow chuckles.

"I have an idea." Lisa leans close and presses the issue. "But my plan needs a partner."

***

Across the yard, other conspirators meet. Dideyohvsgi sits in a ring of five men. They gamble with peach pits. The old shaman throws three seeds marked on one face into a center of the circle pottery bowl. Two settle with marked sides facing up. The gambler repeats the pitch, and none comply. He passes the native dice to the player on the right.

"You are unlucky, my friend." The player accepts the seeds. "But this day it does not cost lives."

"Onocona planned the break. It succeeded and failed." Dideyohvsgi glances around the group. "We made a mistake. With another opportunity, we steal rifles before horses."

"No more chances. We transfer to army custody. These Georgia maggots vanish." Another gambler pokes his thumb into his palm. "Beloved leader John Ross instructs the clans to travel with the soldiers to the territory."

"Onocona died from a guard's torture. His sister's husband is my uncle. My family prefers to stay." A third's voice ripples hatred. "And kill militia."

"We might arrange another escape." Dideyohvsgi crosses his arms at the chest.

"With whom? Everyone I know follows Ross." The first player hands the dice. "You are a shaman. Read the days ahead. Those that wished to fight lie beaten. Here, take the seeds. Play. Let luck predict."

The old medicine man accepts. He rolls. They settle in the dish with marked sides down, and he frowns.

***

As evening descends, Lisa and Yona continue to walk together. "Tomorrow is Sunday. I see no reason to wait." Lisa pushes her personal desire.

"The militia guards are wary. It is too soon after Onocona's attack, but I am also impatient." The young man nods in agreement.

"Then we try?" Lisa hugs her new hero.

"No, Lisa. This is not a child's game. We do not try. We escape." The boy's eyes flash rebellion and determined defiance.

That night around their small campfire, Ella sleeps as Lisa and Dideyohvsgi talk. "Your sister returned from the spirit world. Bella released her grasp." The old one softens his voice not to disturb.

"No. She was always our strongest. She worked her way through the fog." Lisa glances at Ella.

"Oldest always feels responsibility." The shaman stares at the sleeping form. "She blames herself for Bella's death. That guilt she may always carry."

"I don't think so. Bella's free. Ella knows it and is jealous. This family searches for liberation, not liability." Lisa stares at the old fellow. "You know the urge for freedom. A boy I met today said you were one of the escape's leaders."

"Which led to many deaths." The medicine man's voice drips bitterness. "Freedom from the Whites always leads to death."

"Or emancipation," Lisa replies.

Dideyohvsgi peers across the small fire at the youngest Waters sibling for a moment. "You plan a run. I know the look."

Lisa stares back. "My sister and I do not fear rebellion."

"Listen. Escape is not one of your talents," the older man warns. "Soon, we leave with the United States Army. That is a true escape from these stinking militiamen."

"I don't want soldiers around at all. Bella went with them, and it led to tragedy. I prefer to travel with Cherokees. I wish to see unknown lands, have many babies, and start a new life."

The inexperienced and the old sit in silence for moments. Lisa speaks first. "Am I selfish? Do I ask too much?"

"No, child. I only admire your enthusiasm." The medicine man rubs his forehead.

***

The following afternoon, Sunday, a wagon stops at the stockade's main gate. Driven by the Baptist preacher and accompanied by his wife, the carriage arrives on its weekly schedule.

Sentries watch the husband, always dressed in a black suit and hat, and spouse in a gray dress and bonnet, climb out of his conveyance and tie his two-animal team to a post outside the entrance. The missionary does the same each Lord's afternoon. He carries a Bible and reads passages until guards open the gate.

This preaching day, as they always do, the minister and choral assistant walk to a group of Christian Cherokees who wait for their weekly religious service.

Lisa and Yona watch from a cooler afternoon shadow cast from the palisades' wall. Lisa wears a standard gray long dress, much like the one worn by the preacher's wife.

The Baptist begins. "Gather here, you wicked unbelieving Israelites, God's visible people who live under means of grace. Come, listen to his word."

"The guards open the gate and don't even look," Lisa whispers to her young co-conspirator.

A group of Cherokee stands around the preacher as he delivers a fire and brimstone sermon. "Notwithstanding the wonderful works that he wrought; you do not understand the cultivations of heaven. You brought forth the bitter and poisonous fruit of rebellion and mutiny."

Yona points. "When they leave, the couple must walk past that cart over there. We'll hide behind it."

"That action always exposes destruction, as one who stands or walks in peril falls." The pastor opens his Bible. "Expressed the same in Psalms Seventy-three, verse eighteen, 'Thou dist set them in slippery places; cast them out'."

"Then what?" Lisa leans close to Yona and slips a hand around his waist.

"I'll use his hat and coat. You wear her shawl." The young warrior clenches his jaw with conviction and commitment. "These people walk away. No one watches the preacher. The guards won't either. We stroll out the gate."

"As those that walk in perilous places are every moment apt to fail." The Baptist increases his volume. "They can't foresee whether they shall stand or sink. When they fall, as did your brother Onocona, there is no warning."

Lisa and the young man maneuver through the listening crowd toward the wagon.

"They are liable to slip of themselves, without being thrown by the hand of another," the preacher presses his point. "As the leader of the rebellion stood and walked on slippery ground, he needed nothing but his own weight to fail."

As two young people engrossed in each other, Lisa and Yona walk arm in arm and duck into the wagon's concealment.

"The reason he has not fallen before, and only falls now, is that God's appointed hour had not come!" The Baptist slams a fist into his palm for emphasis. "When due time arrives, his foot shall slide inclined by his own weight. God won't hold rebellion up in slippery places any longer!"

Concealed behind the cart, Yona pulls a Cherokee hatchet out from under a deerskin vest. Lisa spots the weapon, and her eyes grow wide. "What do you plan to do with that?"

"Take the Baptist's hat and suit." The young warrior grips his weapon.

"At that very instant, mutiny shall fall into destruction! He that stands in such slippery declining ground on the edge of a pit where he can't stand alone, the soul falls, lost!" The preacher pauses for his words to penetrate the collective Cherokee mind. "The word that I now insist upon is this. Nothing keeps wicked sinners at any one moment out of hell but the pleasure of God."

The preacher's wife joins her husband as the speaker spreads arms in invitation. "Come forward, sinful sheep. Repent and prepare your hearts."

Several Indians profess faith, and the satisfied minister, after wishing his flock a good evening, takes the wife's arm and strolls toward the cart.

The crowd breaks. People mill and drift into the imprisonment yard.

The Baptists walk near the wagon. Lisa's warrior grasps the preacher. He whacks the husband across the head with the flat of the hatchet. The younger Waters sibling grabs the wife and covers her mouth. She shakes with fear and attempts to scream through Lisa's hand. Yona clubs the woman into unconsciousness. He rips the bonnet from her head and hands it to Lisa. "Put this on before the guards catch on!"

Yona pulls the black jacket off the preacher and tugs at the unconscious man's pants. Out of sight behind the wagon, he dons the preacher's clothing; Lisa draws the hat low over eyes.

"Walk stiff. Imitate the wife." The rebelling boy directs.

"She's not going anywhere." Ella interrupts.

Lisa spins around to face her older sister. "What are you doing here?"

"Dideyohvsgi said something was up." The eldest Waters yanks the head cover off her sister. She drops it onto the unconscious minister's wife.

"I will not lose another sister."

"Are you coming?" Yona glares at Lisa.

"No. This is not fun anymore." Lisa draws away from the youth.

"You are a just a spoiled child!" Yona shakes with frustration and disgust.

The determined boy escapee tugs the preacher's hat low over his own eyes. He tucks the clergy's Bible under an arm and strolls toward the stockade's exit. As the disguise approaches, entrance guards swing wide the gate.

Ella drags Lisa from the unconscious Baptists concealed under the cart. "We have to get you out of that dress." The two sisters mix and blend with others as they move away from the religious service area.

Ahead of Yona, tied to a post, the preacher's carriage waits. The boy tugs his brim lower and strides outside the stockade.

A guard's voice interrupts, "Where's your wife, Pastor?"

Lisa's young accomplice throws his head disguise to the ground and dashes for the waiting conveyance. He yanks the team's reins from a hitch and leaps for the seat. With the pull, one horse squeals and attempts to rear while the other backs away.

Yona turns the animals for the road away from the stockade. Several musket balls splatter into the boy's back from many discharges. The young man struggles to stay in the wagon but fails. The defeated escapee lands dead in the free dust outside the encampment.

Inside the fort, Lisa slips on a skirt as Ella burns her gray dress in Dideyohvsgi's cooking fire. "You can be a scattered, undisciplined brat, as that boy said!" Her older sister fumes.

Lisa's eyes mist as she looks toward where the shots rang out a moment before. "He wasn't a boy. He was a Cherokee brave warrior."

CHAPTER TEN — Collection

ᎠᎡᏣᎰᎣᎢᏍᎠᎱᏴᎠᎫᎬᏊᏇᎮᎢᎦᎠᏌᎳᎦᎵᎬᎹᎿᏓᎤᎢᎲᏨᏴᎾᏓᎤᏁᎻᏃᏊᎤ

Several days after the death of Yona, all detainees leave the stockade under militia direction, out of their detested enclosure but not free. Ella's thoughts dwell on the recent past as she departs. Bella's execution and her sister's deposit in the wall's community body pit cloud her mind.

Ella realizes she may never return to her sibling's cold and lonely unmarked but final home. With Lisa and Dideyohvsgi and tears swelling her eyes, she trudges away from the stockade past a wagon.

Sergeant Colly sits in the conveyance with the Baptist pastor and his spouse, both with bandages on their heads. As the Indians parade before them, the Baptists cannot identify their assailants. "Anyone look familiar?" The militiaman waves a hand across the travelers.

"No. We saw them, but it happened so fast. Couple of big braves." The wife wrings her hands.

A long file of Cherokee move in mass from Fort Dahlonega southward along the Federal Road. Georgia militia on horseback escort on both sides of the column. The horsemen herd the people, keep them moving unconcerned with their condition, and often corral stragglers.

Civilians who travel the roadway for other reasons ride with the pedestrian Cherokee. Those travelers steal and bully walking individuals or families without militia objection. Satisfied, or with whatever possession the thieves want, these miscreants leave with impunity.

Ella, subdued by watching repeated injustice and barefoot, attempts to keep pace with the column. Blisters from the road's punishments bleed her tender feet and they protest with pain.

"Can't walk on those all day." Dideyohvsgi reaches for his footwear. "Take my moccasins."

"Then you won't make it." The oldest sister stops the shaman.

"Don't be a martyr. These have bottoms."

Ella welcomes the shoes. "We are so unprepared."

"Supplies, horses, travel clothing, weapons, money," the old man counts the deficiencies on his fingers. "The White man's dole may not be enough to reach the territory."

The Waters matriarch touches the lump under her skirt where her gold hangs. "We'll get there despite them. Our priority now is shoes."

"I would prefer a spit-roasted buffalo rump." Dideyohvsgi licks his lips. "I can't eat moccasins."

***

The following day, the column of unprepared, forced travelers approaches a United States Army encampment and collection point outside of Fort Wool.

Georgia militia mounted men, including Sergeant Colly, ride on both sides of the file.

The Cherokee detachment, driven from the primitive rations and conditions of internment on a march without preparation, suffers. Their lack of food, wagons or mounts, ravishing thirst, and—as Ella on the first day—worn or no footwear oppress the Indians as they walk the underdeveloped road.

The Georgia militia, in sloppy civilian clothes with few marks of rank or uniformity, contrast with a crisp, mounted US Army unit that approaches the Indian travelers from the north.

Outside the walls and across the river from Fort Wool, soldiers stand guard around a large space with tables in rows. Under the shade of overhanging trees, provided food, clothing and drinking water await. Civilian tents and lean-tos crowd the compound and sell tobacco, trail supplies, and whiskey.

Ella watches the official change of sentries and steals quick glances at the comforts.

The Georgia militiamen meet troops and transfer their Cherokee charges into federal custody. The militiamen dismount and wait with their horses.

"Look at those soldiers. They are my age." Lisa claps her hands with delight. "Clean and crisp, very exciting."

"They remind me of your Yona." Ella quashes her sister's lack of self-discipline. "Except they're White."

Captain Jessup, commander of the collection depot, guides his horse to speak before the Indians. "By order of Major General Winfield Scott and the United States Army, the troops assembled and assembling, have orders from the president, Martin Van Buren. Cherokees remaining in North Carolina, Georgia, Tennessee and Alabama, must travel to the west, according to the terms of the Treaty of 1835."

"What's old Fuss and Feathers think we been doing?" A militiaman's voice rises above the gathering.

Jessup's physical bearing, to Ella, displays military contempt and disdain for the undisciplined militia. He pauses and scans the men for the complainer. "I read General Scott's orders." Captain Jessup removes a document from his topcoat. "Troops must show every kindness, compatible with removal."

A vocal current of derision and "hoots" bubble from the militia.

"If, in the ranks, a despicable individual should inflict wanton injury or insult on any Cherokee man, woman, or child, the duty of the nearest good officer is to interpose, seize and consign the guilty wretch to the severest penalty of the law."

Before the Commander continues, most of the Georgia militiamen remount and ride in the direction they came from. A few, including Sergeant Colly, join the army's mounted soldiers.

"I think Fort Wool's going to be much better than Dahlonega," Ella whispers to her friend at her elbow.

"May the spirits make it so." Dideyohvsgi looks skyward.

Captain Jessup surveys the Cherokee before him. "Within the purpose and spirit of that general order, detainees will equip and prepare for removal."

The column moves past the troopers and a sign that reads "Fort Wool Federal Collection Camp." Its name marks the entrance to a large, unfenced compound encircled by US Army armed sentries positioned at ten-yard intervals. Guards stand alert.

Civilian barkers yell from non-government individual tents and lean-tos, "Hey yah there, get your South Carolina tobacco here!"

A barked order, "At ease!" relieves the soldiers at attention, and well-disciplined troops relax their postures in unison.

Deprived and hungry Indian families gawk at bountiful provisions. Comparison of conditions, militia to United States, stun the starving, oppressed observers. Astonishment succumbs to curiosity, and the collected Cherokee break into families and clans.

Peddlers join the din. "Whiskey! Cheapest prices in Fort Wool."

Ella, Lisa and Dideyohvsgi walk together as the crowd explores peddler's wares. "You ever had any liquor?" the younger sister giggles.

"Once. Paw let me taste some. Made me sick." Elder rubs her stomach.

"Makes me roam in spirit land." The medicine man smiles. "But we can't afford these things. Only visit the army ration tents."

The Waters matriarch pulls the shaman out of Lisa's hearing range. "I have a surprise."

He pays attention. "What?"

The oldest extends her hand. "Accept this. We are more comfortable than you think." She displays a gold nugget. "Can you sell this for money?"

The old gentleman leans back in surprise. "I know someone in another clan." He slips the rock into his vest and withdraws currency. "Spend what we have left. Lisa's going to need it, and I must have new moccasins." Her friend chuckles. "You took mine."

A Baptist preacher in a wool frock coat greets the party. "Come, take food and water. Our Lord cares for his sheep and his flock. Welcome to Fort Wool's Collection Center." A clergyman converges upon Ella from the opposite side with a Bible and his own message. "Children, may the peace of Christ be with you."

Dideyohvsgi shies away from the White Baptist and Presbyterian clergymen who serve as civilian hosts.

The pastors encourage individual Cherokees to eat, drink, and listen to the words of their God, read from thick black books. The Baptist bellows as he points at whiskey vendors. "Beware of false prophets, which come to you in sheep's clothing, but inwardly they are ravening wolves."

"Which am I?" the shaman mutters. "A false prophet or a hungry wolf?"

Lisa notices fashionable dresses on tables heaped with clothing under a massive army canvas. She rushes to the provisions. Ella enters the tent with caution, inspects the area and its goods and occupants, then turns to her father's friend. "Go, Dideyohvsgi. We need more money."

The oldest sister's hands tremble with anticipated normality as she helps her sibling choose a clean new wardrobe from a supply table. She glances at her own soiled garb with its apron stained by sweat and blood. Her tears spot the ground as she selects fresh clothing and two pair of moccasins.

Lisa holds a skirt in front of her. "Look! We must find one for Bella…" The young woman's eyes fill, and she drops her chin. She hugs the new dress.

Ella pulls her little sister close. They stand together and remember.

***

Moments later, the siblings shop and select items through civilian tents. Older reminds younger. "Not too much. What we buy, we carry."

Dideyohvsgi returns and interrupts, "I believe you need to see something." The old friend motions to follow. Ella gathers her selected pieces, pays with his cash, and follows him from the pavilion.

Several military and temporary structures stand further along the line. The medicine man points at one. The tent's sides strap to its top. Inside, an army sergeant supervises privates who sit at small tables. Two of the soldiers talk with Cherokee men across their desks. A sign reads, "Deportee Suggestions."

"I believe I have business here." Bella's sister pauses and instructs her friend, "While I take care of this, do you think someone might want to sell a wagon with a team?"

"I can ask. Sounds more interesting than dresses."

The older one unloads her new clothing into Dideyohvsgi's arms. She enters the tent and seats herself at a private's table.

"Your name?" The trooper fills out a form with a quill pen.

"Ella Waters."

"Race?"

"Cherokee."

The private stares. He does not write.

"My mother was Indian. My father was a freedman." Ella's voice trembles. "So I'm half."

The boy writes, then giggles at his own joke. "Which part of you gets removed to the territory?"

"And how about the other part?" The oldest sister's curiosity overrides her wisdom.

"I was joking, sorry. I'm from Pennsylvania. That is in the North. Your suggestion for us?"

"My recommendation is… is that you, the army, I mean, take action." Bella's sibling gathers her strength. Ella's emotions break through her personal dam of fear and resentment. "The militia raped my sister and murdered her by bull whipping!"

The young private sits quiet and motionless. His eyes swell with moisture, but he does not leave eye contact for a long moment. "Sergeant, I need help here."

"I heard." The supervisor steps to the table. The noncommissioned officer leans forward. "Your plight may be heart rendering, Miss…" he consults the paperwork on the desk "… Waters. This matter is above our pay grade. We are under orders to refer such items to our superior officers. Captain Jessup is hearing issues of this nature at sixteen hundred hours. I suggest you relate the incident to him."

***

Later, Bella's older sibling sits on a wooden bench outside the suggestion compound and waits with several other Cherokee men and women. The tent's sides hang to the ground on three faces. The front stands strapped open for circulating air.

Dideyohvsgi joins the waiting woman. "Are you all right?" Ella nods affirmative, and the medicine man shares his search. "Wagons are not for sale in these parts. Too much demand with army freight moving. Most of the teamsters prefer oxen. Stronger, they say, and forage well, less upkeep."

"Which means we walk to the territory." She shrugs. "We Waters women are not strong."

Medicine man elbows his friend's oldest daughter. "You may have been that way back home, but times have changed, I suspect."

The oldest sister stiffens her back. "I hope you're right. Check on Lisa, please. I am fine."

Ella sits and waits on the bench. The heat presses, and her head spins with the memory of the Georgia militiamen as they reenter the granary and escort Bella out into the yard, who has a soft expression on her face. They tie Bella's wrists outspread to the wheel toward its spokes.

The prisoner does not struggle or resist in any manner. She sees her sister but shows no recognition; only continues her delicate smile. Ella's musings return to the sound of mounts as they approach the tent.

Captain Jessup dismounts with several officers, returns the guard's salute, and enters with his entourage.

Older sibling listens, but the canvas muffles the conversation within the pavilion.

The mumbles become louder as her mind watches her own tears spot the soil. The crack of the bull whip reverberates across the yard.

"Dideyohvsgi, my fault. My stupid false sense of right and wrong!" She sobs into the medicine man's chest.

With the third lash, the victim screams in agony.

"I'm a nasty hypocrite." Ella faints into Dideyohvsgi's arms.

"You are next." A soldier stands at the bench outside the suggestion tent. Ella shakes her head for clarity, rises, and follows the escort.

Inside, Captain Jessup sits behind a table with his officers at ease but on their feet. Without looking up, the officer addresses Ella. "Miss Waters?" He looks up, and she nods yes.

"I have read your recommendation. I fear that you were not aware of the facts in the matter of your sister's death." The military commander stands. One administrator hands his leader a document. "They convicted your sister of murder. Georgia militia court-martial sentenced her, with a Cherokee tribunal of your peers, I might add. The sentence was an execution for her heinous act." The man offers the record. "The court's recording, if you wish to view those proceedings."

She nods no. "Bella did nothing evil in her entire life."

"This matter is closed. Next, please." The Captain hands the document back to his officer.

Ella's escort takes her elbow and walks her out of the tent. Outside, Ella looks at the face of her usher. He is the same Pennsylvanian private who registered her suggestion.

"I did not see the record, Miss Waters. But I do not believe it would read the same in my state."

Ella nods appreciation to the young soldier. "Thank you. When we get to the territory, let us hope it will be another Pennsylvania."

CHAPTER ELEVEN — Duty

ᎠᎡᎢᎣᎤᎥᎦᎧᎨᎩᎪᎫᎬᎭᎮᎯᎰᎱᎲᎳᎴᎵᎶᎷᎸᎹᎺᎻᎼᎽᎾᎿᏀᏁᏂᏃᏄᏅ

That night, Ella lies on the grass with Lisa and Dideyohvsgi around a small campfire, one of many within their encampment. Peaceful, well-fed, no walls conditions soften her mind, but her individual encounters with the Georgia militia affront her sensibilities. She watches other Cherokee families and remembers her missing sister. Some of the groups she eyes also miss members passed from sickness, malnutrition, or broken souls. Whisps of smoke, sparks, and small red embers rise from their fires, like Ella's, resembling funeral pyres.

A flutist plays in this distance, accompanied by a banjoist who sings, "Old man, old man, your hair is getting gray. I'd follow you ten thousand miles to hear your banjo play."

The elder Waters sister's head sways in rhythm to the tune as the flame's light dances on her eyes and reflects bitterness and anger. She stares across the fire at her little sister who also gazes in return. "You know I failed again. That army captain molded me easier than pottery clay."

"Old man, old man, you live to hear me say." The song drifts over the two women. "I'd follow you ten thousand more to walk another day."

"Stop blaming yourself. They were military," Lisa empathizes, "with all the power."

"Duty called for Bella's older sister to stand up for her pure life." The Waters matriarch lifts a chin in defiance. "The soldiers did not allow me to tell her story."

"You stood up." Lisa scoots around the fire and rubs her sister's shoulder.

"White people don't listen to Cherokee stories. Ask any medicine man," Dideyohvsgi's experience strengthens his words.

"They convicted your sister of murder." Lisa mimics Captain Jessup.

"A Georgia militia court-martial." Ella frowns and joins younger sister's mockery. "They passed judgment. That means guilty!"

"The part most absurd was 'a Cherokee tribunal of peers.' Those people were paid in salt pork and corn kernels!" Dideyohvsgi's disgust matches Ella's, but his parody does not.

Lisa completes the rant. "That officer said, 'the sentence was an execution for a heinous act.' The only abhorrent action was that sanctimonious court-martial."

"Bella's death never had a chance for justice. Same for Ma's and Paw's." Ella's voice trembles with bitterness and resentment. "Legal is not for Cherokee."

Family frustrations float skyward with campfire smoke, and the group settles into individual thoughts.

The fire, where Ella's family lounges, glows in the darkness, one of hundreds within the Fort Wool collection center. The bustle and din of daytime life disappears. Serenity prevails, and a thousand fireflies flicker. Night's natural light show announces early evening.

Lisa abandons the circle of light warmth to catch a firefly in cupped hands. Returning, she sits and peeks into her captured lantern at the campsite. Inside the darkness of her palms, the green-white glow of the insect's tail dims but blinks to illuminate anew.

"Small one, if I let you go, will you highlight the night as a star?" the younger sibling coos.

The medicine man and her older sister enjoy watching the happy young girl.

"You are that firefly." The shaman opens his hand and clenches it shut, then repeats the move. "Shine, then fade, only to blink again. That lamp in your hands may lead you forever."

"Such a little thing to light the darkness." The youngest peeks at her captive.

"But you are brighter." Ella hugs the spontaneous youth. "With glitter that makes our days better!"

Lisa allows the insect to escape, and they watch the star soar. The firefly hovers in the sky above the congregate of a once proud Nation reduced to homeless clans clustered in the care of a larger land- and resource-consuming cross-continental expansion.

***

Exploited and confused men stagger around ground fires with feet that stumble for balance from too much liquor, but most camps glow warm, and displaced families rest from the toil of the trail.

A new person steps within the Waters fire's warmth. "I found you." A non-Cherokee, dapper-dressed civilian joins the group.

Ella claps in delight, an instant transformation from the gloom and introspection moments before. "Ezra! We thought you left for the territory!"

"In three more days." The freedman drops to his knees and shakes hands with Dideyohvsgi. He tweaks Lisa's nose. "Where's Bella?"

At the mention of the sister's name, the campers dampen the joy of Ezra's arrival, and the flight of the firefly into their throats and their mood returns to somber.

Ella chokes back tears and looks at Ezra for comfort. "They murdered her."

"They? Who? What are you saying?" The freedman guest sputters his words.

"The White militia. A Cherokee tribunal. The removal." The older sister hides her sorrow from her childhood friend. "They called it an execution for killing an animal named Frank Hale. They bull whipped her to death, Ezra. Tesali, one of our own tribe, snapped the whip."

Her father's lifelong younger friend and ex-slave gathers the woman into his arms and rocks. "I am so sorry."

"The spirits weep." Dideyohvsgi looks skyward, palms upward.

"They will not stop mourning until her murderer dies." Ella lowers the shaman's hands and hugs her freedman friend.

The group sits around the fire and gazes at its hypnotizing flames. Red-hot coals pop, and sparkles of rising and white burning dust sweep upward with the heat.

The young visitor breaks the silence. "I don't think even Judge Steel could take action."

"What do you mean, son?" The medicine man turns to the statement.

"Bella's death is one of many—not only murders but a host of other cases." The younger freedman refers to his job.

"We have rights in a White man's court?" The shaman's voice rings, incredulous.

"Yes, but Steel's jurisdiction is overrun and by nature, such a case is an appeal. Since the argument first appeared in a military setting, as a retrial, it requires the same. To start in a civilian tribunal, your appeal stands in line behind many others."

"Cherokee are always at the back of the line." Ella mutters, but her freedman friend hears.

"I understand the implication, but the entire group of litigants are Indian," the young attorney in training clarifies.

Ella pounds a fist on her knee in frustration. "Why? This world is not fair. I lost my Bella! I want the murderer whipped until he dies!"

"Vengeance is mine, saith the Lord," Judge Steel's protégé quotes.

"When did you become a Bible spouting Christian?" the oldest Waters daughter mocks.

"The White man's God, the Cherokee's Creator God, and the law books in the law library say the same thing. That black book provides the example." The fledgling attorney evades the question.

"Please. I apologize. I am bitter but don't want to lose a partner. You are one of the few that I have remaining." The childhood classmate remembers their history. "Did I offend?"

Ezra addresses the oldest Waters sister with concern in his heart. "Do you know what you're facing?"

"I have no power to correct her execution." Ella lowers her chin.

"Not with Bella's death, with the months ahead?"

"Yes."

"I don't think so. The army plans a land route to the territory. The trip will take an eternity. There are many rivers to cross, wider than you can ever imagine." Ezra's concern tinges every word.

"I'm the one that was good in Geography." The older sister points out, "Headmaster Clay gave me an 'A.' You got a 'B' because you couldn't name all the original thirteen colonies."

"That wasn't real. This is." The young freedman sweeps a hand to the sky. "There will be mountains so high the only way up is to crawl."

"I've crawled before, with you, in the cotton."

"On your father's land. Where you go are wild lands. Most have little law or justice."

"The United States Army protects." Dideyohvsgi's voice drips sarcasm.

"Bella's trial shows that security." Ella nods agreement.

Lisa crosses her arms across her chest. "We don't have to travel. Let's slip away. Ezra shall lead."

The head of the clan steels her shoulders. "The government promises a different home. We have nothing now. We can't just leave with nowhere to go."

"No place will replace the one the United States stole from you." Ezra's comment tinges bitterness. "And winter comes soon."

"Nothing is worse than losing a sister." The Waters matriarch stands firm.

"True, Ella." Ezra agrees. "Since your father's probate, the White men and their soldiers have taught me valuable lessons. They frequent Judge Steel's court and seek counsel."

"We know this for sure," Dideyohvsgi pipes in, "our people go to Indian Territory by order of their Nation's chief. With no choice. This detachment is first. They round us up like a herd of buffalo. Cows describe us better. If we don't move, they will shoot."

"This is only one collection point." Ezra surveys the many campfires that surround. "Others also travel. Look at these campers. You are not prepared. None of these people are."

"You say we have no choice but to go." Lisa looks at her friend.

"With no coats, few blankets, and until today, barefoot?" Dideyohvsgi stands and surveys the camp sites that cluster in the night.

"Army talk says to journey north because of more water, through Tennessee, Indiana, and Illinois." Ezra drops to his knees and draws a crude map in the dirt. "Two major rivers block the route, both so wide the opposite shore waits in mist. Missouri and Arkansas become mountain barriers before the territory."

"That is where a home must rise and where we go, but I hear you." Ella pays attention to Ezra's words. "I believe that the journey will be difficult."

"That's an understatement." Ezra smears his map with one hand. "But an alternative exists."

"A Cherokee rebellion?" Dideyohvsgi's voice crackles with excitement.

"No. The soldier's guns and cannons would end resistance. Do as Judge Steel plans." The freedman draws a second map in the sand. "Take the water route up the Tennessee River, onto the Mississippi to the Arkansas, and into the territory—six weeks at most."

"We could." Ella considers the idea. "But the cost? We must settle there. We might not have the funds. I cannot make a mistake."

Ezra looks at the Waters matriarch for an extended moment. "Your parents cared for me, educated me, and gave me free papers."

"Father loved you and all his people."

"My point is I am in debt to you. I will travel to the territory with you as a payback."

"No!" Ella's face reddens.

"Why not?" Lisa claps her hands.

"That's not right, and I refuse to allow it! Go with the judge. Become a lawyer. What a lifetime opportunity! Offer justice in that unknown land," the oldest insists.

"You rode with Benjamin Waters before these girls were born." Dideyohvsgi stares at the freedman. "You owe him. Protect his family."

"Paw pampered us girls. We never faced life choices." Ella's voice and posture calms. "Ezra, the person who owes now leads this clan, not an ex-slave. I failed his memory when Bella died, which increases my debt."

"Your father was a brother to me." The shaman remembers. "The man knew all the important families who take the water route. If forced, he planned to sell the farm and book a river passage."

"Paw thought no one could seize his land." Ella clarifies. "But reality is that security is gone. There's not enough money to afford steamboat tickets, to establish a farm and plant new cotton."

Lisa nods agreement. "You never know. A long hike across Ezra's north may be fun. Won't be boring, sounds like."

"Long is a certainty. And the trip is extremely dangerous." Ezra pulls a burlap-wrapped package from his jacket.

"That sounds exciting!" Youngest sister giggles.

"You must face reality. Take this." The young man unwraps a new percussion-fire Paterson revolver. "This is a revolving pistol invented last year by a gunsmith named Samuel Colt. It fires five thirty-six caliber rounds without reloading."

Ella recoils from the weapon. "Father was a slave who became a farmer, and he worked hard and endured his difficulties without weapons."

"In the peace after the Treaty of Tellico Blockhouse. I knew him before. His legacy requires this," Ezra demands.

"He protected his folk," Dideyohvsgi agrees. "Before he married Walela, your father knew violence."

"No! Benjamin Waters wanted nothing other than peace, love and equality. We undertake a new life, and the only time I saw him with a gun, he was dead in our front yard! I won't accept that tool of death and domination."

"You are a determined woman, Ella." Her earnest friend surrenders and wraps the weapon.

"My father is gone. Now, I am responsible for the clan. My duty is to lead the family as he did."

CHAPTER TWELVE — Departure

DRTꭳꮎꭲꮪⱺꭲꭹYAJEꝏꝑꭴꮝⱮꮃWꝺꮁGMꭱꝏꭴꭳꮒꮀꮰꭹꮎꭶꮀhZꝗꮳ

A breeze swirls dirt around Ella, Dideyohvsgi, Lisa, and the assembled detachment of Cherokee families who wait on departure day. Dust peppers hundreds of bare feet. Most of the assembly stands without boots or moccasins.

"Unetlanvhi wind blows change." The old medicine man studies the thick and dark gray passing clouds.

"Feels good. It greets us." The oldest Waters sister smiles into the breeze.

Large, loaded US Army supply wagons and an enormous barrel of water mounted above a two-wheel axle sit ready with teams and drivers. Several smaller Cherokee owned conveyances carry children, the ill, and old people unable to walk. A few wealthy Indians not from the internment camp join the group from the surrounding areas with mule- or oxen-drawn Conestogas. A few beef cattle and milk cows, tied, follow supply carts. US Army soldiers and civilian guards, plus a spattering of Cherokee, hold on horseback.

The mounted military detachment stands in formation and awaits commanders.

Most Indians clump together in clans and await instructions. These groups differ in size from two to seven or eight. Adults support shoulder strap packs, primitive collections of supplies and worldly possessions, on their backs. Homemade canvas bundles or blanket wraps vary in volume with the strength of the carrier, including children.

The women and girls dress in wrap-around skirts of woven fiber, deer skin, or mild summer homespun dresses in the White man's style.

Men and boys wear breechcloths and leggings in the tribal manner. Older men's faces and bodies host massive tattoos of ceremonial designs, but that adornment the younger generation resists.

Most stand barefoot. A sprinkling wear moccasins. These foot protections show significant use and abuse. An occasional man wears military-issued boots. Few family groups display any signs of preparation for lengthy travel in less inviting climates.

Soldiers shuffle in the ranks as a bugle call splits the morning air. With flourish and ceremony, US Army Captain Jessup and several officers ride to the head of the line. This detachment pulls a flatbed on wheels. They stop and move the cart forward. It functions as a stage.

The commander climbs and stands atop the wheeled platform alongside a Cherokee translator. He addresses the group in English. "By order of General Winfield Scott, the detained Cherokees now encamped at Fort Wool will leave for Indian Territory!" He mounts his horse and points northward along the road. "Ho!" The officer moves along the Federal Pike's dirt roadway. Several junior officers follow.

The translator repeats the order, and deportees move into line. The Captain and the people flow forward. Occasional mounted soldiers drop back on both sides of the column to keep the Cherokee together like uniformed outrider cowboys with their longhorns on the Chisholm Trail.

Ella, Lisa, and Dideyohvsgi hoist their packs upon their backs and step into the file. They adapt their pace to the group, and the column's momentum moves like an extended worm on a ribbon of dirt. The soil path before them stretches into the unknown.

"You all right?" Ella checks on her younger sister.

"This is too much. My pack is so heavy. I don't think I can carry it." Lisa drops her load to the trail.

"Let me take a few of your things." The more mature woman pulls several items from the youngster's stuff and transfers them to her own backpack. Ella's attention diverts to two horsemen who gallop past on one side of the file. She grits her teeth together as she watches Tesali and Sergeant Colly clatter by and move forward to trail Captain Jessup and his officers.

"What are they doing here?" older Waters asks herself.

The medicine man overhears. "Scouts. They forage ahead to find water and campsites. Without them, the army is blind."

"With them, the army is blind and misguided." The matriarch of the clan mutters under her breath.

The human detachment emits a traveling sound. Their mass moves with grunts, sighs, and occasional weeping. Vehicles creek and groan. Animals snort, and their hooves plop the soil road. Those audibles mix and shift like music into an ambient anthem of melancholy and despondency.

Military outriders watch and prod slow movers. Higher than the walkers, guards on horseback survey the masses and solve problems. They seldom offer encouragement, or any form of help, and their solutions involve force.

The detachment marches at a walker's pace, and those further back endure more grime and discomfort than those on point. Lead hikers follow the army and its conveyances, which generate their own debris.

"I can't breathe in this dirt!" Lisa spits.

"Dust means its dry and warm." Dideyohvsgi licks his lips. "Better than ice or rain."

Ella pulls cloth from her pack and wraps a mask around her nose and mouth. She offers protection to her traveling companions. "Wrap this over your face," she directs her sister. "Makes it easier to walk."

Ahead, Cherokee deportees cough and spit trail filth.

The blow increases in the afternoon, and a windstorm sweeps against the file as if the north warns, "Stay in Georgia."

***

That evening, they pitch a dusty camp in connected wide spaces along the dirt road. Abundant trees offer firewood. Most families feed wood to their fires and cook whatever provisions they have brought for the trail.

Ella and her small group roast strips of venison on sticks over their fire. Their faces cake travel dust, and without water, with their facemasks removed, they resemble unmasked bandits. Road grime clogs their eyebrows and eyelashes and cakes above their noses.

"This is all of the deer." Ella turns one stick to cook both sides. "So after tonight, it's the pemmican we carry."

"We saw a lot of squirrels and rabbits today," Dideyohvsgi observes. "How about I catch a tasty opossum tonight?"

"I refuse to eat those filthy looking things!" Lisa recoils and wrinkles her nose.

"The army will issue rations soon, I think." Ella looks at the shaman and spreads her hands apart. "Those wagons are full."

"Hello." A visitor intrudes from beyond their fire circle.

Big sister stands. "Step into the light where we see you."

An older Cherokee female steps forward as Dideyohvsgi and the younger sibling rise to meet their guest. The woman's voice trembles. "I knew your father. Benjamin Waters was a good man."

"I remember you. He was, thank you." Ella's voice softens. "You and your family were at our new corn ceremony."

"Then the militia took our farm. A White militiaman struck my man with a club because he refused to leave." The woman's eyes tear in the firelight.

"I am so sorry." The Waters matriarch extends a hand. "When was that?"

"Three weeks ago," the woman sobs. "And then they took my mother and me. We had no time to gather supplies before they herded us into this march."

"Is your husband all right?" Ella's voice carries genuine concern.

"They crushed his skull. He died that day." The woman pauses and clears her throat. "Miss Waters, you know we do not beg, but we have no food."

Ella removes the roasting venison sticks and gives them to the visitor. "Take these to your family."

"You are most generous. Thank you. Tonight, we have a meal."

"Good. Tomorrow on the trail you need your strength." Ella slips an arm around the hungry.

"But you give me your dinner?" The woman hesitates.

"No person should sleep with an empty stomach on the first night of this journey." Older sibling smiles, and the visitor nods her gratitude and backs out of the warm circle into the darkness.

"And what are we going to eat?" Lisa watches supper disappear.

"Too early to get an opossum." Dideyohvsgi points at the youngest sister.

"But not for pemmican." Ella digs into her pack.

The group sits and stares into their crackling flames. They munch bluish hunks of a mixture of tallow, dried meat, and berries. "I wonder how many of these people have no food?" Ella looks at the campfires that surround as she chews.

"What do you mean?" Lisa shows an interest.

"I mean unprepared, burdened by a family, with no actual idea of this trip we face."

"Count us in that group." Dideyohvsgi jokes and looks around the fire for a response. Nobody laughs; they stare in return.

After a moment, the mood breaks. Ella confesses, "If you had not been at Fort Dahlonega, I would not be here. We lost Bella and I'm responsible for that. But without you, Shaman, Lisa and I could not have come this far."

"Nor could I have survived." The ex-rebel conspirator coughs and clears emotion from his throat.

Oldest daughter nods and turns her head. She observes the army's encampment.

Many military-issue tents surround a central pit. Horses munch buckets of grain, each animal standing tethered in a remuda near a smaller tent containing saddles and gear.

Soldiers in camp warm themselves while army cooks boil beans and bake bread in heavy black cooking pots and pans. A shot deer roasts, and the aroma drifts. The smell of venison and cornbread floats through the entire encampment.

"Let's have dinner with them." Lisa smells an enticing invitation.

"See any Cherokee around that fire?" Dideyohvsgi cups a hand above his eyes and looks.

"Only Georgia militia types dressed fancy." Ella slaps his arm away from his face.

As they view the army campfire, a group of Indians march to confront their captors. They confer with a soldier who trots to a command tent and sticks his head through its flaps. In blue pants tucked into riding boots and suspenders over a gray undershirt, Captain Jessup steps out of the canvas and talks with the delegation.

From their distance, Ella watches the discussion animate. Several soldiers near the meeting edge toward their rifles propped as tripods nearby. The conference calms. The commander enters his lodging, and the delegates return to their campfires.

Soon, individuals from family groups pass rumors to the next group. A boy delivers the news to Ella's circle. "Army says there will be a food disbursement. Starts at dawn."

Dideyohvsgi settles into a comfortable position on the ground with his back to the fire. "Get some sleep, ladies. We're rising early."

***

The following day, as the murk of middle night cycles to gray, Ella wakens at the sound of a wagon. In the center of the

129

Cherokee encampment, an army supply cart stops. With several armed guards disbursed around the conveyance, three soldiers unload and stack crates. Before dawn, early risers wait.

As light breaks the horizon, the troops pass out packages from the cartons. Each recipient carries two packs away.

Ella rises and walks toward the food distribution. An Indian with bundles approaches.

"Good morning. You've been to the wagon. What do you have, there?" The oldest sister looks at the man's packages.

He spits on the ground in disgust. "Salt pork and flour. White man food. They said this is for a week. I even had to sign a receipt for this trash."

Older sibling joins the waiting Indians around the supplies. A soldier hands her a couple of burlap-wrapped packages. "Name?" the soldier demands.

"Ella and Lisa Waters."

"Signature or mark here," the army concludes its transaction.

The eldest sister returns to her camp. The others waken and sit up upon her arrival.

"They gave me a week's food for two. It's not much. Get yours, Dideyohvsgi. We're going to need all of it."

The shaman inspects the burlap packages and rolls his eyes. "Salt pork and flour."

"More to carry on our backs." Ella lifts the bags for weight.

Noise from the wagon attracts their attention. A loud argument erupts between a woman and a soldier. The army supply man strikes the complainer. She collapses.

The protester's husband leaps to his wife's aid, and the private grabs his rifle. The soldier and the spouse struggle for the weapon. One of the guards shoots the woman's partner in the side and he falls beside his wife. The soldiers brandish rifles, and the supply disbursement halts.

"You men fetch the surgeon!" The sergeant in charge of the detachment controls the tension.

Ella watches the surrounding troops prevent any approach to the wagon as the husband squirms and screams. His cries echo through the oldest Waters woman's brain, and her mind's eye recalls her sibling tied to a wheel. "Please, help the man!" Bella's older sister covers her ears and sits to hide from the pain.

The suffering husband's howls diminish to low moans as the guards of the supplies wait.

Ella lies on her back, blocks the cries from her ears, and watches light in the sky brush the clouds, yellow, golden, then white.

The army's surgeon arrives on a horse. The doctor dismounts and steps to the patient. He feels the husband's throat for a pulse as the wife stares.

"This fellow's dead. Next time, Sergeant, don't bother me. Just pack the body to the infirmary," the physician orders the supply wagon's commander.

The deceased's partner falls onto her spouse's chest and wails with grief.

Ella turns from the scene to Dideyohvsgi. "Pity. That poor man died for two days' ration of salt pork and flour."

CHAPTER THIRTEEN — Struggle

ᎠᎡᏓᏬᎢᏍᏙᏝᏴᎠᎫᎫᎦᏆᏗᎤᎶᏛᎬᎦᏪᏝᎤᎾᎲᏣᏯᎨᏖᎠᏂᎭᏃᎬ

Several days later, Georgia's Oostanaula River blocks the detachment's progress. The river's waters push against brushy banks one hundred yards apart as it flows south from Tennessee. A rope tied to a tree on each bank extends across at the intersection of the Federal Pike. Tervin's ferry, a flat-bottom raft large enough to support two wagons, creeps along the cable.

Slaves onboard pull by hand. W.J. Tervin, the ferry's owner, supervises. Cherokee families and four soldiers watch from the craft as it progresses over the narrow but fast-flowing torrent. Army mounted troopers, a dozen Indian groups, and three conveyances transported earlier wait on the north side. Far more bake in the heat on the South Pike and wait their turn.

A soldier rides near the Waters clan, who stand by with the others, and shouts information. "Fare for the ferry, one dollar. Pay and get your ticket here."

Ella and Lisa sit with Dideyohvsgi and lean their backs against the wheel of the next wagon in line to load. They hold army issue buttons, small round tickets purchased for a ferry-boat ride, featuring an eagle with spread wings. The wagon's bed above their shoulders provides shade.

"That's three dollars for us." The medicine man calculates.

"Ridiculous!" Ella protests. "I saw a sign. It read twenty-five cents per person."

"Right! Two bits before the army got involved." The shaman claps his hands in ridicule.

The transport unloads across the river without incident and, empty, begins a return. Slaves on the ropes work less, and the boat slides over the water faster on this trip.

"Looks dangerous to me." Ella follows the ferry with her eyes. "See how much easier it goes since they unloaded?"

"Your first ferry ride?" Dideyohvsgi leans closer.

"Yes, and I hope one of my last. I swim like a stone. What if you fall off?" The older sister's voice ripples with concern.

"I won't be able to help you. I wade only where it's waist deep," the shaman vows.

The Waters matriarch considers her traveling companion. "How many rivers between us and the territory?"

"I don't know." His eyes look west. "But this is not my first ride. Chief John Ross has a fine farm downriver. Big two-story wooden house with a stone chimney at one end. South of him, Major Ridge lives. He owns the ferryboat I took."

"Peculiar they are neighbors, rich ones at that." Lisa comments.

"Think so?" Ella considers the thought. "They hate each other. You're right."

"A lot!" Lisa presses the thought. "One signed the New Echota Treaty, and the other leads the opposition! That's two enemies living next to each other."

"Surprise! Didn't know you were political." Dideyohvsgi laughs.

"I'm not. I only heard Ezra talk." The youngest pouts.

"And both aren't walking to the territory." Ella stands as guards approach with a group of Cherokees. "They went with Judge Steel and Ezra."

A mounted private leans from his saddle. "Tickets?" The three hand the ticket-taker their buttons and join the boarding.

***

The Tervin Ferry bumps the shore near the waiting party. "Load that wagon!" A soldier with black, bushy facial hair, on his horse, pushes one Cherokee man's back with his boot.

The Indian spins in anger and grabs the soldier's horse's reins.

An army issued spur rakes the protester's cheek, and he recoils in pain. The injured victim spits blood and staggers. He, with the others, shoves the wagon onto the ferry. W.J. Tervin attempts safety. "You fellows! Pull it forward."

Dideyohvsgi, Ella, and Lisa crowd on board, and the shaman pulls them closer to the wagon's side.

Troopers herd more passengers aboard the craft.

The oldest sister grasps younger close for protection as guards shout orders and press to load a second wagon. Cherokee men and women push the Conestoga onto the flatbed ferry deck. The soldiers crowd families around it.

"Balance the boat! Not too many!" The owner pilot calls from the ferry's bow.

The soldier with the immense bushy beard and blood on his spur waves his hat and shouts back. "More Injuns means fewer trips!"

"We've got capacity! I don't take responsibility for this!" The ferry master shakes his fist at the soldiers.

"You're just padding your pocketbook," the same hairy man yells. "At three-bits each, pack them together!" The bushy one pushes a family of Cherokee onto the rear of the barge.

Dideyohvsgi mouths to Ella, "Seventy-five cents? We paid a dollar."

The load lurches as the sisters grab the spokes of their wagon's wheel. It quivers as they clear the suction of riverbank mud.

The eldest Waters acknowledges the medicine man's math. "The guards pocket the extra twenty-five."

"That's robbery!" Lisa shakes her head negatively.

"Somebody's getting rich off this." Ella looks to the shaman.

"Same story. White men make money, slaves power the boat, and Indians pay the fare." The old Indian spits in disgust.

"Sergeant Colly's got his hand in this for sure." Eldest agrees.

"So does President Van Buren!" The medicine man laughs. "And General Scott."

Muscles conquer the ferry's cable, and their deep voices chant together, "I'm a 'going, I'm a' going. Bend your back to this rope that's a' holdin." Tervin stands at the prow and supervises his slave's efforts as they propel two loaded wagons with passengers against the river's current.

As the craft gains momentum, the slaves pull harder, and the pace quickens. The cadence of their song increases. "I'm a' going, I'm a' going. Walk this boat with what we done a' loadin', I'm a' going, I'm a' going."

Ten vessel lengths into the river, the press of humanity on the bow pushes a child overboard. The child's mother screams and people, unaware of the calamity, shift away in reaction and fear. As bodies move, balance changes and the ferry lists. Items on deck slide toward the rear and force more Cherokee to crowd closer and weigh the boat's stern. The current catches its deeper keel, sunken from the extra transferred weight, and pulls the craft to one side. As the barge shifts, more people panic and scream.

"Move forward!" Tervin's voice vibrates over a spontaneous grumble of dread and concern. "Balance the boat!"

The passengers vibrate with fear as the vessel shakes. Parents grasp and clutch children close and crowd away from the ferry's edges.

Several of the boatmen, experienced at propelling the craft, sense eminent danger. For their own safety, the river men dive into the rushing torrent. "Stand firm!" the captain screams orders to his slaves. "Pull!"

Two pullers slip and fall into the water as it swings into the current. One submerges, but the other clings to prevent drowning.

The wagon in the rear leans and knocks a Cherokee family off the vessel. They thrash and scream, but the river flushes them away.

Both wagons on the deck share a rope lashing them together for stabilization, and the second wagon's corner wheel slides into the muddy water. The wheel's axle catches the boat's edge and sticks. It holds the conveyance on the listing craft.

Ella and Lisa struggle with their footing and slide into danger.

Dideyohvsgi fights to hold on to both women with one arm and the Conestoga with his other.

As the front wagon slips, its weight increases the ferry's tilt, and more individuals and goods slip backward and invite disaster.

The rope between the two wagons whips taut with a snap as the second drops its last wheel overboard. The current tugs at the wagon, and its cargo capacity floats. People scream in panic and scramble for safety as the weight of the Conestoga tilts the entire transport and pulls the craft's stern deeper.

***

On horseback in the river, Tesali rides on a swimming horse. He urges the animal closer. The scout leaps from his mount and bounds to the rope that ties the two Conestogas. With his calico turban damp, his vicious large-blade knife flashes in the sunlight. The strand that holds wagons together falls loose.

The hazardous second wagon with its occupants slips free and tips sideways into the river. The current catches the conveyance's sides and yanks it off the barge. It sinks and pulls several Indians under the water with its weight. Individuals scream and fight to swim as the flood sweeps the floating wooden box away.

Ella's wagon recoils to its original position at the front of the raft, and the craft levels.

W.J. Tervin twists around the remaining cargo to view the sinking second. "Save those people! Throw them ropes!"

"They're drowning!" Ella screams as she covers her ears and eyes. She hides from the wails of her tribe.

As the eldest Waters uncovers, Tesali pulls a child from the water. He deposits the kid across the pommel pockets of his saddle. The scout turns his swimming horse and grasps another girl by the back of her wet dress. He hoists the juvenile to safety.

The murderer of her sister stares at Ella and Lisa for a moment as they huddle at the wheel of the righted supply wagon.

The two siblings watch as the bald army soldier with the bushy beard that forced loading issues bobs out of the water next to the Indian's horse. The non-swimmer trooper blocks his mouth and nose. He gasps for air and slaps with both arms.

Tesali's boot crushes the soldier under the edge of the sinking wagon. Bubbles burst the surface as the man drowns. The murderer looks back at the Waters sisters. They turn their heads away.

With the two Cherokee youngsters, the army scout goads his swimming horse toward shore.

Ella shivers and grabs Lisa closer. "You all right?" Older sibling inspects her little sister, then turns and watches women and children splash. Those too sick scream and drown. She twists toward Dideyohvsgi. "Do something! They're drowning."

The old man looks back at her and shrugs. "I can't swim."

Ella jumps into the water and grabs a bobbing woman by her bonnet. The shaman flops to his stomach on the ferry and extends a hand to her thrashing arm. He pulls his friend's daughter and the floundering lady she holds to the safety of the raft. The saved bodies cough river bubbles as they struggle to breathe.

Lisa slaps her big sister's back. "What are you doing? You don't swim either!"

Dideyohvsgi pounds the rescued woman's back and her lungs expel more liquid. She sputters, "I'm alive! You saved me!" The old medicine man points to Ella who hangs onto her little sister. "I didn't. She did."

The thankful woman hugs Ella with gratitude. "You are wonderful. My husband and my children thank you."

Lisa, on her knees, beams pride. "You knew you couldn't swim. What are you doing jumping in that water?"

"Learning so I can teach you, sister!"

CHAPTER FOURTEEN — Fear

DRTᏛᎣᎥᏚᎣᏝᏐᎩᎪᎫᎬᏇᏙᎱᏝᎲᏜᏔᏛᎱᏩᎷᎠᏍᏬᎣᎢᎯᏛᎩᎾᏛᎾᏁᏍᏃᏇᎤᵛ

Near Red Clay, Tennessee, Blue Hole Spring bubbles in a pool beneath a limestone ledge. Air pockets in fresh, pure water pop at the surface and give the locale a pleasant, welcoming ambiance. The water flows into Mill Creek, an unimportant tributary of the Conasauga and Coosa Rivers.

An open-sided wood building with a roof, the Cherokee Council House is the dominant feature of this traditional gathering ground. Its weather protects dozens of families.

In a meadow between the spring and the meeting room, Ella and Lisa prepare blueberry cornbread on their campfire. The oldest sibling mixes powdered maize with water and pork fat in a pottery bowl while younger sister nestles a pan on a hot flat rock tucked into their small fire.

"Where did you get this civilian food?" the youngest girl chatters.

"I bought this stuff at that farm a few miles back. I thought we might celebrate," Ella replies. "The farmer charged me fair prices."

"He must have Cherokee blood." Lisa laughs with her own joke. "This smells fantastic."

"Think I'll add salt. We're running low, but it sure perks up the flavor." The cook digs a small bag from her pack and sprinkles her mix. "We use pounds of this stuff. Makes every-thing better."

"Does it appear that each time we draw rations, there's less?" Lisa looks at the supply.

"Our allotment has nothing fresh like these blueberries you picked." Ella adds the fruit to the blend. With her fingers, she pours and pushes the mealy mixture into the hot pan in small lumps. The concoction sizzles and pops on contact, and its aroma drifts around the fire.

Dideyohvsgi returns with a bag of flour that displays a US Army stamp.

He shows the stuff to Ella. "They give us White man's corn, but it will never smell as good as your 'hoecake'."

Lisa perks her ears. "What kind of cake?"

"Hoecake!" the medicine man repeats. "You never heard it called that?"

"I think only you do!" The youngest elbows the older man.

"No, not only me. That's what Georgia women named it."

"Hoecake?" the little sister blushes and stuffs her giggle with both hands.

"Not what you assume, girl. Ella, you need to talk to this sister of yours." Dideyohvsgi points an identifying finger. "Whites named it that because you can bake it on a garden hoe." The old shaman points to the cooked delicacy. "They use the hoe to tuck the food in the fire as you did in that pan."

"Hush, you two. This cornbread's a luxury compared to our normal rations." Head cook takes the flour bag from the medicine man. She puffs her cheeks and blows air. Dust powders her face as her younger sibling points and laughs.

"Don't laugh. At least they feed us. It is edible, and we're out of corn." Ella cleans her lips.

Lisa licks a forefinger and pokes it into the powder. The finger comes out with its tip white. She tastes the flower and grimaces. "The army calls that food?" She shakes her head and hands the bag back to Dideyohvsgi, who sits and reaches for his pipe.

The shaman stuffs his smoker with flour, picks two sticks from the ground, and pinches a red-hot coal from the fire. He attempts to ignite the powder, but it extinguishes the light. In disgust, he pops the pipe against a rock and dislodges the un-smokeable stuff, then stands and looks to see if anyone noticed his drama. Disappointed, the shaman smears the flour from his pipe into the soil with one foot.

Armed soldiers patrol the camp and guard its perimeter but pay no attention to the shaman's antics. An army command tent sits at one end of the encampment. The Cherokee deportees from Fort Wool surround, but hundreds from other collection areas, with their campfires, wagons and guards, extend past the medicine man's sight.

The older fellow gets comfortable and relaxes back at the fire.

Ella serves him, along with her sister, a piece of hoecake.

Dideyohvsgi juggles his hot item from palm to hand to cool before he takes a bite. "Hmmm, love the blueberries."

Head cook stiffens. "It's the salt. That's why those berries taste so good."

"Salt's the invisible savior for lots of people." The shaman swallows his mouthful. "Which makes me think, did you see the scout in the calico turban back at Tervin's Ferry?"

"You mean last week, the fellow that cut the rope?" Ella pretends ignorance.

Lisa claps her hands. "My, yes! Wasn't he exciting?"

"No! Not in the least." Older sister's voice firms and her glance toward younger sibling steels.

"I thought he was!" Lisa expresses her admiration.

"Ezra and I saw him before, in Paw's cotton. He was one of those who did it." Ella's voice hardens with hatred.

"He murdered Ma and Pa?" Lisa's tone switches to serious.

"You have to be sure, Ella." Dideyohvsgi stares. "Accusations like that can be very dangerous."

"I did not see him butcher them," the Waters matriarch clarifies. "But one of them did."

"His name's Tesali." The older man raises hands to the sky. "They call him 'the Great.' He's the new Army Chief Scout."

"I swear by our ancestors and by the spirits, I know he did it." Ella viciously stabs a hoecake with her knife. "He and two others fled through the cotton near Ezra and I."

"Justice—in its own time—always comes. But not now. Be patient like the deer hunter. Wait your day." Dideyohvsgi lowers his hands and touches fingertips to his chin.

"I listen, my friend." The matriarch of the Waters clan bows her head. "But I am too weak and might die of old age before I see due process."

"Come, you two. Let's enjoy our cake." The youngest extends a hand for another piece.

Ella widens her eyes. "I am afraid. That fiend did not see me. If he knew, I believe he would murder me. And Ezra."

"Never speak of it again, Ella," the old man warns. "Or you either, Lisa."

"Why not? For a change, I agree with Ella. We should scream it to the world." The younger sibling crosses her arms at her chest.

"If Tesali was aware that you witnessed your father's murder, Unetlanvhi could not protect you." The shaman's voice tinges with his own fear.

***

After dinner, as the campfires' embers no longer spark but only glow with the stars, the oldest Waters daughter watches the sky's lights twinkle. She fades into sleep and dreams.

Ella sits up, focuses on the leaves of the surrounding trees and prays. "Oh Unetlanvhi, whose voice I hear in the wind." A leaf drifts and brushes the woman's nose. "Your breath gives life to the world."

The dreaming woman stands and extends her hands to her night's sky. "Listen to me. I need your strength and wisdom." The white orb in the night flares into colors and falls as tiny blinking droplets of hues. "Let me walk in peace, and make my eyes behold the red and purple moon fall."

Ella turns and drops to her knees by her younger sleeping sister. "Make my hands respect the objects you have made and my ears sharp to hear your voice." Lisa's image transcends to their mother's and father's sleeping forms, cuddled in bed together. "Make me wise so I may understand the words you have taught my people."

The sound of a galloping horse, like hooves on a harpsichord, beckon Ella's attention. A warrior dressed in black leggings, breechcloth, and calico turban approaches. "Aid me to stay calm and strong in the face of what comes for me." She trembles.

The dreaming Waters daughter searches the ground. "Let me learn the lessons you have hidden in every leaf and rock." She picks up a stone and prepares to defend against the charging Tesali.

Ella drops her weapon to the earth. "Support my pure thoughts, actions, and intent to help others."

The attacking Tesali's facial scar glows red, and his eyes flash white. Ella's terrified soul prays. "Use me to find compassion without hate overwhelming me." She throws her arms up to protect her skull. "I search for strength, not to be greater than my brother, but to fight my greatest enemy."

The helpless human peeks through her protective hands.

The horse rears with its front hooves flailing inches from harm. The rider transforms to a wild-haired, wild-eyed buckskin-clad woman wielding a Cherokee hatchet. Ella's own reflected image flashes fire from her lips as she screams. "My greatest opponent is myself!"

The apparition vanishes and the eldest Waters daughter lies trembling in her own sweat, "Make me always ready to turn to you with clean hands . . ." She stares at the peaceful stars that shimmer in the night sky above her " . . . and straight eyes." Her view inaugurates the slow transmission of the sun's yellow glow. "So when life and the night's darkness fade, my spirit may come to you without shame."

Ella squeezes her eyelids shut, fearful of the light and terrified by the advent of a new day.

***

Days later as they continue travel, Ella, Lisa, and Dideyohvsgi walk exhausted near the front of the column from Red Clay as they top a ridge and move into the valley of the

Fort Cass, US Army Garrison. They gaze past the military establishment upon the Hiwassee River and view an immense United States-operated internment camp.

Indians wait at this gateway to the main trail west to the territory. Thousands of campsites along the stream fill the basin. Summer drought parches the land, its vegetation, its wildlife, and reduces the tributary to an unnavigable trickle.

"Look! There's more of our people than I have ever seen." Lisa babbles in awe. "Not only Cherokee, Chickasaw, and Muscogee, but the Seminole and Choctaw Nations, and their slaves. I'm so glad Paw freed ours." Youngest looks to her older sister.

"If he hadn't, it was our responsibility, and we would have." The Waters matriarch nods. "Look how low the river is. This drought cooks the land. Think those river travelers got to the territory?"

"They made it. Rich folks get the simple trip with a head start." Dideyohvsgi crosses his arms over his chest.

"I just hope Ezra and the judge made it."

Several army officers on horseback approach the column. The contingent's commanding officer meets the file's escorts, and the group confers for a moment. The meeting concludes, and one of the mounted guard trots past Ella's party with orders. "Turn the detachment west to Blythe Ferry. No supplies or water here."

Eldest Waters daughter glances at Dideyohvsgi and turns. "These people are suffering."

The march continues, and Ella watches their drinking wagons roll into the valley to Fort Cass. Her attention shifts to several approaching mounted civilians.

Men without uniforms ride their horses into the marchers. "Natachtie! Natachtie!"

A soldier stops their progress. "State your business."

"The Injun Natachtie owes me money!" A White bully scans the Indians.

The guard points to an old Cherokee man near Ella. He stands with his deaf, mute son. The boy proudly wears a red bandanna.

"He stole that!" the civilian rides to the youth and jerks the scarf from around his neck.

Dideyohvsgi jumps to help, but the civilian's horse thumps the shaman backward. He falls and skins his forehead on the rocky road.

With his musket's butt, the accuser smashes into the youngster's face. Blood spurts from the adolescent's nose, and the confused child spins to his knees.

The boy's aged father leaps to defend his son.

Attacker on horseback clubs the parent to the ground. His panicked horse tromps the fallen.

"That's an Injun that'll never steal from me again!"

The deaf, mute son crawls on hands and knees. He cries over his father's body as the insensitive mounted lout laughs and rides, unimpeded by soldiers, out of the column.

Cherokee, including Ella, scream and shake their fists at the occurrence in protest. One Indian drags the puffing and protesting White man off his horse.

With several others, Ella leaps and pummels the offender as he attempts to protect himself from the onslaught. In her mind, the oldest Waters' own image flashes fire from her lips as they scream. "My greatest enemy is myself!" Fear of her own passion grips Ella's heart, and she jumps away from the offending civilian. The trembling sister backs against Lisa.

"Come. This is the White man's way, not ours." Lisa calms her sister's tremors, and both young women join the old medicine man.

They move onward with the column.

CHAPTER FIFTEEN — Betsy

ᎠᏣᏓᎣᎢᏍᎣᏫᎩᎠᏧᎬᏉᏢᎯᎦᏌᏫᏓᎡᏀᎫᏓᎣᎯᎲᏛᏯᎾᏪᏯᏂᏃᎠᏳ

The next day on the Tennessee River at Blythe Ferry, a woman shades her eyes from the sun and looks across a quarter-mile wide narrow of Chickamauga Lake. In the distance, her husband William captains his flatboat. Paid freedmen row the eight-wagon loaded craft through the water. Its spacious size and stability contrasts with the smaller same purpose boat at Tervin's two weeks prior.

Nancy stands on her porch and watches an immense collection of people, organized chaos, move. Cherokees gather on her side of the lake, but near the deck, the deportee Waters sisters walk back and forth with Ella's apron dipped in water. They nurse an enormous bruise and skin scrape on Dideyohvsgi's forehead. He lies under a tree in shade.

The wife of the owner steps from the deck and approaches. "My name's Nancy Field. I'm Cherokee. My husband's William Blythe, who owns this ferry. What happened to your friend?"

"Hello, Ella Waters. A White thug on a horse roughed him up outside Fort Cass."

"Ella Waters? Are you Benjamin Waters' daughter?"

"Yes. You knew my father?"

"Years ago, he shipped cotton out of here. Stayed with us for three days. Fine fellow."

"Thank you."

"Come on in. The old man's head needs nursing."

Nancy Field helps the sisters move Dideyohvsgi to a floor mat in the principal room of her frame house. With Ella's wet apron across his forehead and in the cool and comfortable dwelling, the medicine man nods into sleep.

The women sit on wooden benches and watch the crowd.

"You're full blood Cherokee?" Ella studies her hostess.

"Yes. Born in Alabama. Married Mr. Blythe and moved out here. He had this tract on the river. We didn't know what to do with it."

"Wish I could find a man with property." Lisa blushes.

"It wasn't his idea to start a ferry. The growth out here forced him into it. Too many people asking him to row them across." Their hostess remembers earlier days.

"I'm half-Cherokee. Why do you think they deport me to the territory while you get to stay here and enjoy life?" Ella's question carries no malice, just curiosity.

Nancy Field senses the intended spirit of the pointed inquiry and thinks for a moment. "They don't count me because I have a White husband. If he were Cherokee, we would be traveling."

"You never see Indian men with White wives." Lisa blushes a second time. "Why is that?"

"They are all being herded to the territory. Women are too smart for that and want to stay home." Ella winks at Nancy, and the three laugh with understanding and empathy.

The oldest Waters sister enjoys the laughter, a pleasure lacking on the trail. She turns and looks through the window. Her eyes focus on a coiled bull whip strapped to a saddle. Tesali rides up to the porch and cat-fast dismounts to its plank deck. He pounds on the door.

Ella steps back into the shadows of the room as Nancy Field answers.

"William Blythe?"

"He's out on the water."

The scout turns and stares out across the lake at the distant boat. "On that large but very slow ferry? The army contracted for two days. How many more days to transport the detachment?"

"Lake's low. Longer, but talk to my husband. He might tell you if you ask him nicely."

Tesali raises his hand to strike the impudent Nancy Field, but spies Ella in the shadows. He controls his temper. "You! Step into the light."

Oldest clenches her hands in front of her and steps forward.

The Indian sneers, "I know you. I saved you from drowning at Tervin's Ferry."

"But many others died." Ella grips her fingers.

Tesali's expressionless dark eyes stare at Bella's sister. The scout studies Benjamin Waters' eldest daughter as if he senses a past connection.

Nancy Field intervenes. "Take your issues to my husband. I said he's out on the lake. He'll come in after the last trip."

The visitor clears his throat and spits on the woman's clean floor. The Waters women grimace at the brown spittle stains on a well-kept floor.

Without apology or the slightest sign of remorse, the scout turns and bounds out the door onto his mount. He gallops away.

Ella stares at the brownish splat. "Makes my stomach sick."

"That's one Cherokee brother with little upbringing. Some men I dislike." Nancy Field mutters.

"If you only knew his soul. Thank Unetlanvhi he's gone." Ella peeks out the door.

"Wild men I find exciting." Lisa glances at the other two women's expressions. "But you watch them from a distance."

The three women move to the house's front porch. In the overhang's shade, Nancy drops woven straw mats. She reenters the house and returns with blankets. "Only one bedroom inside, but you will all be comfy out here. In fact, the night air off the river is cool. You'll enjoy it."

The group settles on the deck to people watch the afternoon's crowds. The ferry loads several trips as they watch. People move without press or panic. No passenger purchases tickets with money needed for food as transpired at the earlier ferryboat.

"Last crossing cost us a dollar a person, but the troopers took some of that." Ella's scorn translates to Nancy Field.

"Tervin's Ferry cost that much?" Nancy Field's eyes widen with amazement.

"Yes, the normal fare was twenty-five cents. At least that was what their sign said." The Waters matriarch looks at her hostess.

"That's robbery!" The wife of the barge owner shakes a fist.

"That's not the only hustle. The soldiers sell our decent rations to White civilians on the trail." Lisa responds. "We get salt pork and flour. They market the jerky, corn, and beans."

"Profitable." The Cherokee sympathizer understands. "I will tell my husband. He contracted with the military at twenty-five cents a head and a dollar per wagon."

"Ask him to increase his prices next time. We are the first detachment. Others follow," Ella advises.

"I'll make sure the army pays, not the passengers." Nancy Field guarantees as she rises and enters her house.

The ferry owner's wife returns with a whiskey bottle and four glasses. "You folks have endured hard travel. This might ease the pain."

The woman pours and serves her guests.

"I've never tasted liquor." Lisa looks up with anticipation. "Is this fine with you, Ella?"

The older sister accepts her glass as Dideyohvsgi joins the women. "Neither have I. What do you think, medicine man?"

"I think I will, and I have sipped whiskey before." The old shaman nods thank you to Nancy Field. "My head feels much better thinking of it."

***

That night, the matriarch of the clan sleeps relaxed from her whiskey. She wakens on her sleeping mat. Ella sits up and loosens the blanket wrapped around her.

From the deck of Nancy Field's home, she peers across hundreds of campsites.

A White man's whiskey wagon conducts business nearby. A bonfire in front of the saloon welcomes men who barter their possessions for drink. Many of the wagon's customers stagger drunk, howl, and carouse.

William approaches the porch. Nancy Field opens the door and steps onto the deck to greet him. "Saved your supper, Bill."

Blythe notices the guests and removes his hat. He nods hello and looks to his wife.

"This is Ella Waters. You remember Benjamin Waters? She's his daughter."

The host shakes his head in a hearty welcome. "Good man." Blythe's smile becomes serious. "Sorry to hear he passed, but I'm afraid they'll never find who did it."

Her father's eldest gestures. "Thank you. I think you're right."

"Stay with us." The owner turns to his wife and hands her his hat. "I closed the ferry for the night, Nancy, but I guess I should've run off the whiskey peddlers first."

"Little late, William." She opens the door. "Come inside. It's been a long day. We had a visitor that I need to tell you about."

The oldest settles onto her sleeping pallet and checks on Lisa. Her spot is empty. Ella jumps from the Blythe house porch and searches.

She spies a blanket-wrapped form asleep under a tree and yanks its covering. A boy stares, awakened.

A drunken Indian stumbles and jostles the Waters matriarch as he passes.

The searcher moves toward the whiskey wagon.

Several other drunk Cherokee men notice the woman and try to put their hands around her. She struggles away and around the makeshift saloon. Near the rear, Lisa sits cross-legged before a bearded White vendor. She giggles and claps, enthralled by the dance of a straw doll that performs before her.

Older sibling rushes to her sister and sweeps her into protective arms. Together, with younger struggling in protest, they run through the darkness to the light of the Blythe's house and settle on its porch. "What do you think you're doing? That man could have taken you away!" Ella's voice trembles, and her hands shake.

"You mean like Bella?" Lisa looks at her sister with round, open, innocent eyes.

Ella's guilt and concern for her youngest sibling overwhelms her heart, and she bursts into tears. "I could not bear losing another sister."

"I'm sorry. I swear I'll never do anything like that again." Lisa hugs her older sibling.

***

The next morning on the water, the two sisters wrap a clean bandage around Dideyohvsgi's head. They work at the feet of William Blythe as he pilots his ferry onto the shore of Chickamauga Lake.

The craft bumps against the bank. The ferry master steps near Dideyohvsgi and hands him a red bandanna-wrapped package. "For your travels. It'll make that lump better."

They wave thank you after a walk across sand to join the mass of Cherokee who have crossed previously. Others, from morning arrival, swell the crowd. The entire group waits around the edges of the Great Road to Nashville.

Dideyohvsgi opens his red bandanna and unwraps a big, rectangular chunk of pressed tobacco. He bites a corner, chews, and smiles over his nicotine rush.

Along the route's edges, White men run several tents that sell whiskey, blankets, clothing, food, and water. As the older sister naps, one tent features straw dolls and catches Lisa's eye.

She forgets her promise from the night before and wanders to the display, stands, and stares at the toy babies.

Ella jolts awake and spies Lisa. She jumps to join her little sibling, but Dideyohvsgi stops her. "Rest," the man reasons, "Let me handle this."

The shaman walks to his youngest friend's side and looks at her soft smile. "See something pretty?"

The girl points at a figure with large, painted eyes.

Surrogate father barters with a White woman salesperson. "The price?"

"How much you got?"

"Enough."

The tent's keeper bends toward the child customer. "She your granddaughter?"

"No, she's not." Dideyohvsgi spits on the ground.

"You are paying, or is she?"

Frustrated, the medicine man walks little sibling to Ella. "Wait with your sister. I'll reason with that clerk." The shopper then moseys to the canvas store. This trip, keeper's husband meets him. The Indian points at the toy. "What's your best price?"

"What you chewing there?"

The shaman displays his block of tobacco. "Good South Carolina stuff."

"You got a doll, Injun."

The medicine man flips the seller his chunk of tobacco, takes the straw figure, and marches back to his young friend.

Lisa hugs the doll and beams. "I love her, Dideyohvsgi! I'll call her Betsy like my doll when I was little."

CHAPTER SIXTEEN — Insobriety

ᎠᎴᏘᎯᎣᎢᏍᏚᏆᏯᎠᏨᎤᏉᎯᏂᎤᏪᏛᎶᎹᎠᏨᎤᎢᎲᏛᏯᎾᏖᎾᏂᏃᏆᎤ

The detachment treads along a tree line in the hills of Tennessee. Thousands of steps, barefoot or soft-sole moccasin clad, press foliage flat and wear a trail across the land. Ella, her sister, and her medicine man pack loads heavy for a mule, much less a woman. Their backs bend, and ascending becomes tedious. They force one foot before the other.

Their plight multiplied by hundreds, a mass of human sufferers align in a column resembling a mile-long centipede. The people struggle to transport their lives and livelihoods. Farmers carry seed. Blacksmiths lug tools. Leather makers tote needles and sinew. Ella hauls two bottles of whiskey tucked in her pack, purchased from peddlers before departure at the last stop.

The oldest Waters lags several paces behind Lisa and Dideyohvsgi. As she treads along the trail, she sneaks slugs from her hidden stash.

Lisa turns and walks backward. "You're lagging."

Ella skips forward a few steps and catches the group.

"You all right this morning?" Her concerned sibling's face sags with worry. "You're not with us."

"Whew! I smell liquor." The medicine man rubs his nose.

Ella removes a bottle from her pack, takes a drink, and passes the booze to her older friend. The shaman grins and drinks. "Good stuff. Where did you get it?"

"White whiskey peddler back at the ferry." Ella's words slur.

"You can't even talk right!" Lisa responds with disgust in her voice.

The three souls, in line with many others, tote their loads through Tennessee with little further conversation.

The older sister swigs her booze. She offers the enticement to her medicine man friend. After two acceptances, Dideyohvsgi declines more.

Midday, Lisa pulls pemmican from her backpack to share for lunch as the group marches. Ella ignores food, but the younger woman and the shaman enjoy the nourishment.

As the afternoon's journey continues, the liquor loosens the older sister's tongue.

"You make lousy companions," she swaggers. "Let's sing."

"Ever heard me sing?" Her male companion laughs.

"Cherokee wise men are songbirds." Eldest points at her friend.

"We chant. That is a different skill." The old man looks to the sky. "I speak inspired by the spirits. My voice in song sounds like a coyote on peyote."

"Nobody wants a tune. Then I do!" Ella staggers a step. "Will you come my Phillis dearie to the wild mountain free, where the river runs so pretty, and ride along with me, and you shall be so happy with your Jacob by your side, so wait for the wagon, and we'll all take a ride."

The drunk hangs an arm over her sister's shoulder and belts the chorus. "So wait for the wagon, Oh! Wait for the wagon, Oh! Wait for the wagon and we'll all take a ride. Oh! wait for the wagon and we'll all take a ride."

Lisa pushes her sister away.

The woman stumbles as she steps to the trail's side and slings her empty bottle into the trees. She loves the song as she rejoins her companions. "I thank you, Mister Jacob, but I'm not inclined to go, your wagon is so clumsy, and your team so very slow."

Young sibling glances at the other walkers that surround her group and pulls her sister close. "Enough. You're embarrassing me."

"Whose talking? I remember your handsome, dashing Yona. That boy died catching a wagon for you."

"Shush." Lisa attempts to control her older sister. "This is not you."

"You played with your Jacob! You were not inclined to go. He was so clumsy, and you were so slow!" Ella chuckles at her own cleverness.

A mounted guard notices the disruption in the column's progress and trots his horse near the Waters party. "Keep moving! What's the problem? Is that woman drunk?"

The Waters matriarch turns to the trooper. "Is the US Army blind?"

The soldier guides his mount through the travelers to the oldest sister's side. "You are. We'll fix that." The sentry throws a lariat around his target and ties the rope on his saddle horn. The horse drags the stumbling drunk to the edge of the column.

"Please, don't hurt her!" Lisa screams.

The guard jerks the rope. "This way she stays with me."

Ella, unsteady on her feet, lugs a full pack on her shoulders and stumbles along, tied to the animal ahead. Running with both hands gripping the cable, the oldest Waters woman leaves her clan.

"We can't let her go." The younger sister grasps her companion's arm.

"Not much choice," the medicine man reasons. "With these packs, try to catch her."

***

Far forward at the column's side, the trooper leads Ella at a walk. She stumbles but keeps her footing. Cherokee families in the detachment watch the guard and his prisoner pass. A few look with compassion. Most stare with blank eyes devoid of any emotion. They watch another detainee marched by force to the territory.

Ella's vision spins as she struggles. The sky hangs under the trail, and the surrounding trees point downward. Her throat gurgles, and her stomach empties alcoholic slime in three violent heaves. At once better, the woman's steps become less shaky.

The soldier who drags Ella stops at a small wagon with four walls and a roof with no windows. The guard dismounts and pulls the eldest Waters girl to a door in the back of the cart, which he opens. "Get in there!" The trooper removes the rope around his prisoner's waist and prods her, with her backpack, into the darkness of the conveyance.

A woman cackles from the interior.

Another voice screams, "Shut that! The light hurts."

Ella hears the guard ram a peg into the door's lock hoop and return to his horse.

In the darkened space, other murky and unidentifiable forms sit and stand.

One pitiful shape in a corner babbles, "He did, she did, it did. Who did? I did. Did I? Why? High fly, do I, in the sky. I lie. Cry."

As the oldest Waters sister's eyes adjust to the darkness, details of her surroundings focus. Across from her, against the wall, a wild-eyed woman sits naked and drools. The poor soul rearranges her clothing on her lap from one on top to another item in its place.

Ella shifts her pack from her shoulders to her side and removes her second bottle of whiskey. None of the crazies within the wagon notice. The Waters daughter uncaps the jug and swigs.

"Share that, lady?" A male voice penetrates the darkness. An old man crawls near, close enough to be visible. He cups one hand before him. Liquor fills his palm, and the crawler's tongue laps the alcohol in the manner of a feeding feline. With the liquid gone, he settles his back on the wall next to his bartender.

"Splendid stuff. Thank you. Might want another in a minute?"

"What is this place?" Ella whispers.

"No need to whisper." The fellow scoots closer. "This is the crazy wagon. Army troops pull it with the cattle and horses. You and I are prisoners. The rest of these folks are touched. What did you do?"

"These people are mad?" The new prisoner uses a low voice.

"Yes. That's Lucy there, the naked one. She can't decide what she wants to wear. The hairy man beside her never talks. The woman next to him is Emily Brooks. Heard them call her name when the soldiers threw her in here. She hasn't said a word."

"When was that?" Ella leans closer.

"Last winter sometime. It was freezing. They parked the wagon outside the Fort Dahlonega stockade."

"You've been in here for months!" Ella's voice vibrates amazement.

"I could sure use another hand of that whiskey." The man leans forward.

Ella pours a handful and slugs a belt herself. "They picked me up for drinking on the trail. Why are you in here?"

"The same as you, a rule violation." The prisoner empathizes and pats Ella's shoulder. "I gutted my wife and ate her gizzard."

The oldest Waters woman recoils and distances herself from her new friend.

"Mind if I have one more sip?" The old man's missing teeth attempt a smile.

Ella imagines human remnants in his gums. "You keep your distance. Twice a day, I'll bring you a drink. Rest of the time, stay on the other side of this wagon," the liquor vendor stresses.

***

Later, Ella sits in the semi-darkness of the crazy cart as it lurches along the trail and slugs from her bottle. A woman with stringy hair and unkempt nails crawls to her side. "Are they coming?"

"Who?" Ella shies away.

"Peter, Paul, Matthew, the Disciples." Wild eyes expand as if she divulges a secret. "And Mark, Luke, and John."

"Soon." The oldest Waters sister pats the woman's hand.

"They were here yesterday. I talked to Luke, the physician. He told me I was with child." The disturbed pats her belly. "Can you believe? At my age."

"If he said so." The younger woman attempts to pacify her elder.

The old lady cackles, "If you don't have faith in a disciple, you're crazier than I am."

The vehicle lurches to a stop and the crazy panics. "They're coming. My time is here. Tonight, I'm going to talk to Paul."

Ella discovers a tiny crack in the wood slat wagon wall. She presses her eye to the split and views a slim slice of activity. Soldiers walk by, and an occasional horse moves through the woman's sight. The army pitches night camp with no Cherokee visible.

The newcomer makes herself as comfortable as possible with her mind on crack view. She notices Emily Brooks staring. "Come. Sit by me. I think we both need a friend." Ella pats a spot next to her.

The woman, without changing her expression or stare, moves close.

Secure with a newfound companion beside her, the wagon's newest prisoner returns to her minimal view. For hours, little changes. Nothing moves around the wagon, and the eldest Waters sister's eyelids flutter near sleep.

That relaxation perks awake and aware of the pungent smell of burning pipe tobacco. She looks through her portal, but it offers only blackness.

The prison wagon shifts as a smoker relaxes his back against its wood sides.

Ella gestures for silence to Emily Brooks, who sits at elbow length and fixates on the new captive.

"Psst! You out there. Can you hear me?" Ella whispers.

"What?" A male voice responds.

"Do you need to make some money?" The prisoner attempts to see outside.

"I'm listening."

"You're hearing a deportee," Ella begins. "Take me to my family. They'll give you a gold nugget for your help."

Silence meets the proposal.

"You hear me?"

"Hearing's one thing. Believing's another." The voice rings suspicious. "This is the crazy wagon. Why are you in there?"

"Too much whiskey. But I've dried out now," the drinker lies.

"Where did you get your valuables?" the exterior voice doubts the claim.

"We brought it from Georgia. You can have it."

After an eternity, the weight against the cart shifts. "Maybe. I'm sure this wagon's locked. I'll look." The man's talk returns to the crack. "It's not, just a wood peg holds it shut."

Ella views her benefactor's stubble facial hair, a male slave's countenance.

"Be patient. I will return in an hour. You and I can't walk out of here together. I have to bring something to hide you with."

"What's your name?" the prisoner sputters.

"Matthew, you?" The slave smiles.

"Ella. Take care."

"You have no worries. This slave has a plan. I'll get you to your family and your gold buys me a freedom trip to Ohio." The face disappears from the crack.

The captive slugs a shot of whiskey from her bottle and notices the wife killer staring. "Listen to me. I'm leaving the wagon soon. Don't make a sound, understand? I promise to leave this for you. Look, it's half full." Ella waves the liquor in plain view.

The old woman also watches. "You going to the promised land?"

"Yes, I am." The Waters eldest responds.

"Paul's coming to visit me. I'll meet you there." The lady shudders. "Matthew will baptize me. See you when we get there."

***

A while later, Ella hears someone. The peg slips from its latch and the door swings open. "Climb in here." The old slave lifts a large bundle of hay from an expansive wooden barrow with a metal-rimmed front wheel.

Emily Brooks hovers behind Ella and smooths her hair with both hands. She grabs the escapee's elbow. "Take me with you. I'll die in here."

The Waters woman sets the whiskey bottle on the cart bed available to the wife killer and slides out.

As Emily Brooks attempts to follow, the slave blocks the exit and closes the door. He drops the wooden peg lock in place.

Brooks' muffled voice from within tears. "No! Don't leave me. Take me with you. Ugggh, thump."

The free Waters woman listens to Emily Brooks' silence, created by violence.

Ella escapes with no time to investigate.

The escapee curls in the barrow, and her accomplice conceals his ward with hay.

The barrow creaks away for a distance, then a soldier interrupts. "Where are you going, Matthew?"

"Taking fodder to the horses, private. Nice night, hey?"

"Yeah. Wish I was back home."

"Soon will be. Heard you have only six more months on your enlistment," the slave responds.

"A long time. You drinking, boy? I think I smell whiskey."

"Yes, sir. Had a cup to help me sleep. After I feed the animals, I'm going to bed."

"Afraid I have guard duty until midnight."

The barrow wheels pass the night sentry and bumps over a hill to a remuda and a makeshift pen of cattle.

As Ella rides along, she extracts the small pouch of gold nuggets under her dress and retrieves one.

The motion stops, and Matthew lifts the hay and throws food to the horses. "There are many families beyond that tree line." The old slave points at the foliage. "How can you find yours?"

"How will you get to Ohio?" The oldest Waters woman hands her savior a gold nugget, and the man's eyes widen with amazement.

"One step at a time. First, I'm going to steal a horse. They won't miss it for days."

"Same here, Matthew. I slip through that tree line. The soldiers won't know I'm gone. They don't care. It's the crazy wagon."

CHAPTER SEVENTEEN — Fall

ᎠᎡᎢᎣᎤᎥᎦᎧᎨᎩᎪᎫᎬᎭᎮᎯᎰᎱᎲᎳᎴᎵᎶᎷᎸᎹᎺᎻᎼᎽᎾᎿᏀᏁᏂᏃᏄᏅᏆᏇ

A month later, rolling hills show late color. Oak, maple, dogwood, and yellow poplar leaves dance around Ella's worn moccasins. She treads along the Great Road to Port Royal, Tennessee. The traveler removes a bottle of whiskey from her pack and sips.

"Please stop drinking that stuff, Ella." Lisa touches her sister as she walks alongside.

"Leave me alone." The older's hands shake as she caps the jug and returns it to her backpack. "I'm exhausted. I didn't sleep last night."

"You're sweating too much," the younger sister observes. "Maybe walk slower. Should we drop back?"

"I am sick to my stomach." Ella stops and vomits.

The walking deportees in the column veer around the Waters clan and space away from any sign of sickness or disease.

In migration, imitating ants on the landscape, farmers, blacksmiths, traders, and merchants with their mothers and children amble. This cross-section of life forms the first detachment led by the United States Army to march what they later call the Northern Route to Indian Territory.

The freshness and cleanliness of departure fade over weeks on filthy travel and the millions of steps that Cherokee travelers force. Their excited anticipation and acceptance of a new home from their government, with each worn, destroyed moccasin, repudiates their traditional pride and independence. Suspicious evaluation and resignation bred from lack of hope creeps into their collective psyche.

The water-deprived and calorie-depleted mass of pitiful humanity moves with a helpless, unchanging momentum toward daily goals defined by herdsmen.

One official army wagon creeps along, pulled by two military mules. Weeping women walk in its rear. Children's bodies, devastated by measles and dysentery, pile as cargo. Several slaves, tasked by owners, escort the cart as substitutes for family.

Ella speaks to a slave. "Don't you fear walking so close? Those children died of many kinds of disease."

The man shrugs. "I can't choose when it's my time to die, my master does."

"But you flirt with death right now." Older sister walks closer. "You may be his property, but your value is much more alive."

The servant shakes his head negatively. "He values his family's lives more than mine, so I escort his son."

"That he does." The Waters matriarch claps her chilled hands for warmth. "We and he go along this road, a slave to someone. We have a taskmaster, or we would choose otherwise."

"But your owner doesn't use a whip." The poor fellow shrugs his shoulders.

"One did. On my sister's back until she died. She might be alive today if I had stood up for her."

"Why didn't you?" The walker turns to his new companion.

"Because I was afraid." Bella's big sibling digs in her pack for whiskey.

"I walk with death and live my fear." The victim whispers, then his voice strengthens. "As do you, I see."

Ella's hands tremble as she uncaps the alcohol.

"I may be a slave, but I control my dread." The man grasps and caps her bottle. He turns and throws the liquor high in the air. It sails beyond the column and crashes with a sprinkle of glass against a tree. "Face yours." Her reflection's eyes penetrate Ella Waters' hazy booze-soaked brain.

***

The column moves on. Walkers pull blankets tighter as a cool fall wind blows out of the north. Most wear summer clothing, the women in light cotton homespun and the men in breechcloths and leggings. They walk with moccasins, most soft without soles, or with no footwear. Slaves tread barefoot in old and worn-out work clothes, often with straw hats.

An occasional White man, intent upon profit or pure vicious harassment, rides with the Indians long enough to sell whiskey before they spot pestilence. They abandon their profits as too high risk, and the march continues.

The front of the detachment slows as it approaches a toll house tucked in the trees beside the Great Road. The column stumbles and lurches to a stop.

Hiram Colly and an army officer converse with the operator, unheard by Ella as she watches.

The agent shakes his head, refuses the army's offer, and points across the rolling hills. Column leaders turn the marchers into the much rougher transverse of Tennessee fields.

Its hypnotic cadence reclaims the detachment. The children's body wagon lurches over a rock. A young boy's torso, speckled by measles whelps, falls off the cart.

Ella reacts and moves toward the carcass. Dideyohvsgi and the youngest restrain her and pull her away from the pestilence and into line. She trudges onward but stares to the rear. The walkers and wagons split around the fallen child as they continue forward.

Breaking from her place, the matriarch of the clan runs back. She pulls the boy's corpse to the trail's side.

Lisa and Dideyohvsgi follow, and they pick up stones to cover the individual. They attempt burial.

The detachment plods forward, and few notice their efforts.

The same slave who spoke to the oldest sister about facing fear carries a sizable chunk of stone to the grave. He drops the load on the pile and looks at Ella. "Cherokee woman, I want you to know that I am no longer afraid." He lifts another slab.

She picks up a rock nearby. "They still have whips."

The man totes his load to the heap. "We are in Tennessee. North is Kentucky, and after that Illinois or Indiana. That's where I'm going."

"Both above the Mason Dixon line. Go, and may Unetlanvhi watch over you." Ella smiles.

"After I help you bury this boy." Her new friend lifts another piece of granite.

"Don't delay. Your master will look for you soon." Ella waves her hand and indicates the man should leave.

"I expect not." The laborer hauls more rocks. "He has much on his mind. His master's taking him to the territory."

***

A few days later, at the mouth of Big Springs in Kentucky, groundwater flows from under an outcrop and creates a small river. Moisture along its bank glistens and forms fresh ice on the stone. Soft snow drifts from a dark sky.

Ella, Dideyohvsgi, and Lisa crowd together under one blanket at a fire beside the river.

Along the freshwater spring, others camp and huddle around their own fires for comfort in an unseasonal temperature drop.

"This is exquisite." Youngest sister catches a snowflake on her finger, examines its delicacy and puts it in her mouth. "We had so little snow in Georgia."

"We don't want this so early," Dideyohvsgi warns. "Our trail is north."

"But tonight, I love it!" Youngest lifts both hands skyward and cups her palms.

"What are those two doing?" Ella watches Hiram Colly and a soldier press through individual camp sites. They carry army issue rations of corn and blankets, "Blankets!" the men call.

A family patriarch struggles to his feet with arms extended. The father stumbles barefoot. "We need blankets!"

"Got money, Injun?" the distributors demand.

"Those are ration supplies!" The Cherokee points at the "US" on a cloth corner.

"Means they're warm and will last through the winter! Good blankets! Ain't enough for everyone! Just those with cash!"

The protester slips on the snow and falls to his knees. They shove him aside and move to the next potential customer, a more prosperous family group.

The Waters matriarch turns, lifts her dress and apron, and opens the pouch that dangles under her skirt from a tie at her waist. Ella hands a gold stone to Dideyohvsgi. "Buy blankets and corn."

Lisa jumps in front of the medicine man and looks cross-eyed at snow on her nose. "Lots of covers!"

"Not with this. They'll steal it." The older friend rubs the gold with his thumb.

"Trade with our people for federal money." Ella pats Dideyohvsgi on the shoulder.

Hiram Colly reaches a mother with a girl child. The Indian hugs her infant close and trembles from the temperature. "Help, please! Her father died from dysentery. She'll freeze!" The woman lunges for one blanket carried by the soldier assistant, and his boss boots her away.

The man turns to the Waters sisters, who concentrate on their fire, and he moves on to the next potential customer.

Ella motions for the parent with a child to join them at their small campsite. The guest crowds beside the younger woman and holds her offspring to the warmth. The mother sees Lisa's doll. "You love your baby. That is good, but she is straw. Please take mine."

"What?" Lisa withdraws and her face wrinkles with repulsion.

"Raise her as your own. My time is ending." The birth mother extends the child with both hands.

"What do you mean, ending?" the potential surrogate parent inquires.

"I spit blood."

The youngest Waters stares at the older mother for a moment and softens. "May I, Ella? She will be my sister, my Bella."

"You can never replace Bella."

"Please, she's so cute." Lisa reaches for the little girl.

"No, you spoiled planter's kid! No baby. It must eat, can't walk, needs an education." Oldest attempts reason but resonates pouty resentment and impatience. "You're a child yourself."

"I wish you died instead of Bella! I hate you!" Lisa retorts.

"Come, you women. Neither one of you has the patience of your father." Dideyohvsgi returns with federal cash.

"Find Colly. Buy blankets and extra corn." Ella looks at the trembling child in her mother's lap before the fire. "Include enough for them."

The woman with the infant wrings her happiness into her hands. "Miss Waters, thank you. My baby dies without you."

"I think Lisa might get buried first if she had a real baby." Ella tightens her shoulders within the mother's hug.

***

Days later, the column moves through Caldwell County, Kentucky, on a thin trace crowded by woods on both sides. Snow continues to fall, and many of the walkers' massive packs loom even larger as flakes collect atop them.

Ella and Dideyohvsgi struggle through the snowstorm loaded with supplies but warmed with purchased heavy coats and army issue blankets. "Where do you think we are?" she turns to the older man.

"Heard someone say we're in Kentucky." The shaman shifts his pack for more comfort. "But it feels as if we've walked to Massachusetts."

"Wonder if he made it." Ella stares northward.

"Who?" Her older friend wrinkles his eyebrows.

"That slave." She firms the muscles in her chin. "The one who helped us bury the boy and ran away north."

Lisa carries the blanket-wrapped infant girl, and the child's mother trudges along beside her. The woman coughs often, and blood splatters red on the whiteness under her feet.

The head of the clan shivers in the cold. Ella walks backward into the wind and glances back at the red-spotted trail that follows their exhausted group.

Wind whips through the trees on both sides of the trace, and gusts of white obscure the view ahead.

From out of a gust of snow, on his army issue horse, Tesali approaches along the column's side. "Keep moving. Two miles to camp and water!"

Ella eyes Tesali's heavy leather winter-ready military coat and his warm boots lined with deer pelt. The scout wears his calico turban, but a raccoon skin hat provides additional protection.

As the Indian rides, he notices blood spots on the snow, turns, and tracks the red drop marks to the infant's mother.

The rider swoops upon the parent, grabs her by the collar, and drags her along as he gallops toward the rear of the column.

Ella watches the coughing woman prisoner bounce, trip, and fall to bump again alongside Tesali's mount until they disappear around a curve in the trace.

"Spirits of the snow, help that sister find warm summer pastures," Dideyohvsgi prays.

"This is not fair! Why do I have to carry her kid two more miles?" Lisa kicks the snow.

Ella turns to her younger relative. "You want to just leave her?"

"Yes!"

Oldest slaps her sibling for the first time. "Shut up! You said she was going to replace Bella!"

Lisa backhands her sister in return. "This baby's not mine!"

Ella Waters hold the red slap mark on her cheek. "Then be a White man. Abandon the youngster in a blizzard!"

Youngest puts the baby on the ground and walks forward with the column many yards, then relents and runs to save the infant.

From her backpack, Lisa withdraws the straw doll that Dideyohvsgi traded his tobacco to buy and leaves the figurine in the baby's spot on the trail. She returns to Ella.

"I think you're growing up." Her oldest sister smiles.

Younger snuggles the kid to her body and wraps her child in the blanket. "Ma sewed my first Betsy. An old medicine man gave me my second. This one, I'll also name Betsy."

The detachment trudges in a curve on the trace. A clearing in the trees opens to a view for the moving mass of people.

The family matriarch does not respond to her sister. She steps ahead and stares into the foliage beside the trace. Ella trembles before she firms her shoulders and faces her fears.

From a leafless tree in the middle of the expanse, with a noose around his neck, the dead body of the slave who helped bury the boy on the roadside swings in the late day's north wind. The slave faced his fear and ran north but never made Massachusetts.

CHAPTER EIGHTEEN — Birthright

ᎠᏓᏛᎠᏟᏍᏗᏴᏯᎫᏤᎧᎮᎠᎮᎦᎬᏯᏛᎵᏅᎹᎦᏋᏒᎣᎯᎲᏛᏯᎾᏟᎾᏂᏌᎪᎤ

The image of the slave suspended by the neck from a tree haunts Ella as she struggles through thigh-deep snow. The woman and her family follow a trail crushed by those ahead. White wind continues to sweep against their progress.

Each leafless forest skeleton, in her troubled thoughts, suspends another human by necktie. Several she envisions as slaves, but most dangle Cherokee brethren.

One step she advances after the last. Each surge forward hauls extra weight and strains energy and muscle. Her right ear tingles, frozen and exposed to the wind. She rubs the appendage.

"That's turning red." Dideyohvsgi notices the color as he pushes ahead. "Here's another blanket."

Her old friend removes a bundle from his pack and wraps its warmth around his travel mate's neck.

Lisa waits for her companions. "I'm freezing. Betsy's icy. When do you think we'll stop and camp?"

"Couple of hours, I expect. Lot more daylight today." The medicine man surveys the sky.

The three crowd together and forge ahead. They face the wind and snow behind others who suffer less and many who endure more.

Betsy cries and escalates intensity to a wail. "She can't take this." Lisa snuggles her closer.

Ella removes her extra blanket from around her shoulders and tucks its warmth around the child.

The family fights forward through the blizzard. Forms that precede become white shapes, indistinguishable from each other and almost invisible in the wind-driven snow.

***

Afternoon passes in a haze of effort as they toil through ice. "Your ear," Lisa reaches and touches her older sister, "is pale."

"I don't feel your fingers. It's numb." The eldest explores her skin.

"Not good." The medicine man removes his own wrap and pads his companion's neck and ears.

Frosted forms in front of Ella's family slow and stop. A guard's voice from forward floats with the whip of fluffy ice pellets. "Hold! We dry camp here."

The Waters group collapses where they stand. Ella shivers as her sister and the shaman forage for anything combustible to serve as firewood.

Dideyohvsgi returns with an armload of small winter die-off tree limbs and sticks. With two of the longer and sturdier branches, he constructs a lean-to to block the wind. A canvas suffices as the roof and provides protection. He stomps a flat spot, protected from the blast by the wind breaker. With rocks, he builds up a small platform.

From his pack, tinder straw and dry mushrooms offer material that his flintstone on pyrite sparks ignite. As the source smokes, the fire starter blows and adds sticks tepee-style.

To Ella's joy, the heat warms the calmer air under the family's shelter. But she shivers in blankets and her speech slurs, "I am so tired, can't walk. I want to sleep."

The sick woman battles frostbite and hypothermia as her exhausted eyes shut and her body demands time to heal.

*****

Sleep drifts in Ella's mind, and the snow around her melts in the warmth of Georgia's sun. Benjamin Waters greets his oldest child atop a hill. "Come, Daughter. Walk with me." The cotton farmer takes his girl's hand, and they stroll together among flowering Bottle Brush Buckeye bushes that clump close in the warm southern air.

"Paw, do you know I let Bella die?"

"Yes, your mother and I see her often." The man's soothing voice comforts. "You're troubled? Over when you join the family? I have passed. Faithful ones will follow in your own time."

Ella looks into her father's eyes. "No, Paw. We are different. You were owned by your maker and your beliefs are enslaved. You bowed to his morality, unable to express the desires of your humanity, and lived in servitude."

"Yes, I was a servant to a human owner." Ella's father puts a burly arm around his offspring as the two walk and pulls her closer. "The apostle Paul said in Ephesians, 'Slaves, obey your masters with fear and trembling, in singleness of spirit, as you embrace Christ; not only when watched, and to please them, but as servants of Him, doing the will of God'."

"Your owners were men. But not now?" The Waters eldest looks to her parent for a response.

Benjamin shakes his head positively. "I had only one master, but man enslaved."

"If a choice exists and I have the will to choose," his daughter's voice steels as she pounds a fist into her palm, "I'll be free from both."

"I hear, beloved child. You have that option. Do choose for yourself." He hugs her close. "But you need care, protection, hope, and love from a higher power."

"I am a woman. Christian history degrades us from creation to revelation." Ella's voice rings resentful.

"There is no record where Jesus disgraces, belittles, reproaches, or even stereotypes your sex." Benjamin steps back from his offspring. "He treated your gender with dignity and respect."

"But he is not mine. His church believes in a male God, prophets, disciples, apostles, and its teachings are man-centered." Daughter turns from her father's ideas. "In my world, women serve his congregation, not him."

"Living has been difficult since you left Georgia." Benjamin views his wayward offspring.

"Peace, compassion, and forgiveness are important in your Christian faith, Paw." Oldest sibling reaches out with her hands. "But in life you fought heretics and sinners. Everyone was an enemy. You sent me to school. I learned about the Inquisitions, the Crusades, and wars against Jews. Everywhere, violence. 'Spare the rod and spoil the child,' my friends' parents said. Your religion endorses slavery and brutality toward women."

"Yes, too many people differed with each other." Benjamin clasps the hands. "Because they defined their morality based

on personally endorsed religious beliefs. But Jesus taught new lessons in his Sermon on the Mount. I admit that few listened."

The Waters parent becomes the "Mekko" as he stops between two Bottle Brush Buckeye bushes.

"I love you, Ella. You were the light that I worked to shine. Now you are dim, and I can no longer lead you to enlightenment. Your mother may be better skilled."

The man leans over and kisses his child on the forehead. He sweeps a hand forward. "I cannot go further. Walk through this gateway to your other birthright."

As the Ella steps through, she glances behind, and her father no longer accompanies. Before the feverish woman, her other parent waits. Young, as in an old Christmas dream, in fresh buckskins with beaded moccasins, her Cherokee mother, Walela, spreads arms in welcome. The fringes from her sleeves flutter in the calm breeze, and a neck piece highlights the love that shines from her face.

"Mother!" Ella embraces family thoughts.

"Daughter, you walk troubled in my lands."

"I am sick. My mind fails. Check my forehead."

The woman in buckskins covers her daughter's skin with a palm. "You have a fever. We must prepare a potion. You suffer frostbite."

"How is that possible, Ma? It is so warm in your land."

"You visit from the winter." Maternal instinct embraces its own. "But we cure your flesh and mind."

"The heat in my head boils from my soul." The daughter relaxes and cuddles in the woman's arms. "I journey with Lisa over hard trails and . . . I lost our Bella."

"To the wrath of the White man." The matron's countenance darkens. "You suffer because you take responsibility."

"I carry guilt, Mother."

"I cannot absolve that shame, Ella. Only your actions do that. Helping ears that feel numb and feverish is much easier." The Cherokee leads her daughter to medicinal plants.

Mother and elder sibling move across the hill to cattails on its far slope. The Indian harvests the plant. "Pick only every third stalk. Then there will be medicine for others." She presents its cob, resembling a modern-day corn dog, to her patient. "Eat. Sooth the heat in your soul."

Both women munch the brown fruit and walk together. "I have been with Paw, who tried to help me with his religion." Ella relishes the food treat.

"Benjamin lived his faith. That was a reason that I loved him. But those beliefs were not mine."

"Nor for me." The daughter pauses. "But trouble always awaits, and I need something to guide me."

"Talk with Unetlanvhi." The older woman offers another cattail. "Let him expose a spiritual view, and become healthy. You must have a sense of direction and follow the righteous, harmonious, and balanced."

"My pathway has no purpose. I struggle each day. There's nothing good." The daughter droops in confession.

"You have not prayed. Pray for help to walk across these lands."

"No, Mother. Your Cherokee ways are not mine. My blood is only half. My father was a slave, and you wear moccasins. I am both. Who marks my trail?"

The wind increases from the north, and Ella's mother's hair blows as she turns to face an incoming storm. Lightning flashes on the horizon, and rain streaks distant clouds.

"Our time here is ending, Daughter. I wish that were not so, but you must return to winter while I walk in summer. Know that I love you. Take care of Lisa. Remember me well."

***

The sky darkens and thunder rolls in Ella's brain. The rumbling becomes her sister's voice. "Can you hear? Wake up!"

The eldest daughter's vision brightens from dark to light, and she smiles up at Lisa's face. Behind, Dideyohvsgi leans over the young girl's shoulder and watches.

"Welcome back. You're going to make it." The medicine man offers his diagnosis.

"You've been out for days." Little sibling extends three fingers.

Bundled in clothing and blankets with her head in Lisa's lap, both women sit in a melted clearing carved around a fire in deep snow. The blanket lean-to stands, now larger and reinforced by more canvas and tree limbs.

"That long?" Ella mumbles.

"Yes." The shaman shivers. "It's been too icy to travel, but the blizzard stopped this morning. The column's camped and not going anywhere soon."

The oldest Waters feels her ear with one hand.

"You had frostbite. The other day, we pitched camp just in time." Lisa tucks blankets around her patient. "Our learned medicine man made a smelly poultice and smeared it on the burn. Your ear healed, but my nose rotted."

187

"Thank you, Dideyohvsgi." The ill woman smiles.

"You talked in your fever." The traditional Indian medicine man takes his friend's hand.

"I dreamed wild dreams. I ate cattails and almost became a Christian."

"Too many brown cobs." Dideyohvsgi chuckles.

Ella nods in response, but her heavy eyelids weigh into slumber, and fresh thoughts fill her mind.

In Georgia, Ella sits in the rear of a canoe behind her father. They row in a river and view a violent place where water circles. Benjamin steers to the river's bank and waits for the torrent to smooth.

The whirlpool approaches wider and wider until it draws them into a vortex. Daughter and parent battle the current. The craft tips and both flop into the cascade. They swim, but suction pulls them under the surface.

A giant fish attacks Benjamin, and as it swallows, Ella's father screams. "We're saved by the sign of my faith." His words echo in his daughter's mind as she realizes Dad cannot help.

The non-Christian woman spins round and round to the very lowest center of the whirlpool. Upon reaching the narrowest part of the maelstrom, the water opens. A company of people wave. They beckon to join.

Ella recognizes Bella as she extends her hands to help.

Another circle current catches Ella and sweeps her from reach and rescue. The torrent bores her soul outward and upward. As she distances, Bella continues to struggle and grasp below her.

CHAPTER NINETEEN — Ohio River

ᎠᎡᏔ ᎤᎣ ᎢᏍᏙ Ꮙ Ꮿ Ꭰ ᎫᎬ ᏛᎦ ᎵᎪ ᎹᎯ Ꮥ ᎣᏨ Ꭵ Ꭴ Ꮻ ᏂᎻᎯ

Weeks later and deeper into winter, heavy snow
continues to fall and accumulate on large numbers of US Army
flatboats. The rafts, constructed of uncured Kentucky Catalpa
trees from John Berry's property along the Ohio River, wait on
shore to transport detachment wagons and deportees.

Three of the ferries' transports, heavily loaded with
carts and Cherokees, transit the wide expanse. Hundreds of
Cherokee watch the flatboats' movement from the river's icy
and snowbound eastern bank.

The first vessel, partially obscured by snow whipping in the
wind, nears the western embankment through floating, current-
driven chunks of ice. The crowd that waits to board whoops
and cheers the boat's advance from the East.

Dideyohvsgi points at the conveyance, and Ella shades her
eyes against the glare. Lisa watches with her adopted baby girl
tightly wrapped and warmly snuggled to her chest.

A large berg drives with the current against the distant boat
and slips under its side. It lifts that edge above the freezing
water's surface. Two Conestogas slip to one end of the far
transport, and it flips. Cherokee screams of fear penetrate and
dance with the air-driven snow across the Ohio.

Ella claps her hands over her own mouth and stuffs her empathy scream.

The wagons slide and crush deportees. They dump passengers into the water as several non-swimmers splash and drown.

The second flatboat rises over another berg and empties its human cargo to follow the first raft's doomed souls.

The third craft stops before half point, and its prow turns eastward and returns its load. A low moan of relief for those saved swells from the crowd on shore.

"The river spirits deny us," Dideyohvsgi comments. "They drink our people and dunk our wagons."

"Nobody's crossing that for a while." Ella stares across the river. "And I believe it's the ice, not your ancient ones."

"My great advisors weaken the further we travel from Georgia. They tire of this trek across their lands. By spring, I fear they will find other followers to protect, and this waterway will never let us pass." Dideyohvsgi shakes his head in fear.

"I know my spirit weakens as we go," Ella sits on the snow. "So I don't blame yours. By thaw, I may be too old and weak to challenge this crossing."

"But at least no more walking for a while." Lisa flashes a giddy smile.

***

That night, the snow thickens into a blizzard as Cherokee families huddle and shiver around open-air campsites on the east side of the river. Most cringe under canvas lean-tos and richer ones enjoy wagons with tops, including sturdy and trail-tested Conestogas. Most of the travelers, including Ella's group, make do with coats and blankets and a protecting hearty fire.

"Dideyohvsgi, I believe we settle here for a while." The oldest sister rubs her hips for warmth.

"Weeks, maybe?" The medicine man inspects their surroundings.

"We should buy a wagon. We can use our Georgia gold." The Waters matriarch searches for options.

"We should. Winter signs are brutal." The shaman rubs his hands together for friction's warmth. "I have asked several owners. There are none for sale."

"This baby will freeze out in the open air." Lisa's voice cracks with concern and worry. "Ella, we mustn't lose another one I love."

"In the morning, we will build a better shelter." Big sister touches Lisa's infant. "Just get Betsy through tonight."

"I saw a dead chestnut in the woods. Lightning struck it." Dideyohvsgi looks in the direction the column arrived.

"So?" The Waters matriarch shrugs.

"You're too young to remember, but in the old days, the Cherokee built warm and comfortable wattle and daub homes." The shaman drops to his knees and draws in the snow. "They used tree branches as a frame, then covered the limbs with mud and grass to fill in the walls. We made the roofs of chestnut bark."

"Three of us can make that?" Ella studies the drawing.

"We're not building a Waters homestead here, just a shelter for a few weeks." The medicine man points at his blueprint in the snow.

"Doesn't sound easy, but life's not very fun anymore. Nothing's simple." Lisa kicks fresh snow onto the illustration.

"We don't have a choice. We'll start building something in the morning." Ella rises from her knees.

The three sit together in silence and stare into the flames as frozen moisture accumulates ankle deep outside their fire circle.

"Why did somebody hang that slave who helped us with the rocks?" Lisa breaks the mood.

"This world's cruel, a place where humans die because of the color of their skin." Older speaks with empathy and sorrow.

"Who did it?" Younger's voice cracks with apprehension.

"It wasn't hunters. There was too little time, and I don't believe his Cherokee owner had the money to pay." Ella's thoughts drift to the young slave, and she remembers his work at the grave site.

"It was somebody. Maybe your army scout that murdered Ma and Pa?" Lisa's speech tremors fear.

"No. The judge in Georgia told me they wanted Pa's land." Eldest Waters rubs her forehead. "But I think that I know better now. If Steel was right, a White man must have hired Tesali."

"I've been a medicine man my entire life. The color of a man's skin means little." Dideyohvsgi philosophizes. "What counts is the color of their hearts."

***

A month of snow and an eternity of boredom and deprivation later, the three deportees and their baby huddle together on the bank of the Ohio. They crowd around a small fire inside a tiny lean-to hut made from branches and covered by the bark of a dead chestnut tree. The hut's interior glows dim from flame as sunlight cannot penetrate the roof's snow and ice cover.

"Army rations are even running low." Ella watches the shaman chew on a frozen turnip. She attempts to eat a small piece of salt pork from their tiny ration. "If we make it through this winter, this food makes me wonder what provisions they will have for us in the territory."

"Our people talk and say nothing grows there," Dideyohvsgi observes, "so this may be as good as it gets."

Lisa sings quietly to her adopted baby as she kicks and thrusts her little arms uncomfortably. "When the fast-fading day leaves a gray sky, twilight comes, and I hum lullaby." The surrogate parent places her palm on her baby's forehead. "She feels warm."

Ella feels for temperature. "She may have a fever, or you've got the poor thing bundled up too much."

Younger sister loosens the blanket around the child, and the baby girl's eyelids sink as Lisa sings, "Dream on, mother is holding you, ah yah, ah yah, dream on, night is enfolding you, ah yah, ah yah."

Ella warms cow's milk in a small clay pot on the fire. "I can't believe you found the genuine stuff for Betsy, Dideyohvsgi."

"She needs her food," medicine man responds.

"Yes, but she hasn't been eating well the last couple of days." Younger sister kisses the child.

"Yesterday I walked back along the trail to that farm for milk, the one we saw on the way." The shaman adds a small stick to the fire.

Lisa hugs the old man. "Thank you. You found what my baby needs."

"I met the farmer and bragged I had the prettiest infant in the entire world at my camp on the Ohio."

"A White landowner cared?" The youngest daughter looks at the medicine man.

"He asked me why I was camping when I should walk across the river to the territory over its surface. I informed him no, not me."

"You did! What did he say?" Lisa becomes more interested.

"I told him if I walked, several thousand others would, and the ice is too thin," Dideyohvsgi pauses for complete attention.

"And?" Youngest sister leans forward with anticipation.

"His cow didn't love Cherokees, which made her sour, so the spirits guided me behind his farm to a better one not so greedy."

The youngest sibling claps with delight. "You stole the milk?"

"No, the cow liked Cherokee children, and her owner wasn't watching."

"Dideyohvsgi's joking you. He paid our week's stipend for that milk." Big sister clarifies the story.

"You should have stolen the stuff, Dideyohvsgi." Lisa hugs her baby close.

"I think we should thin it with water and make it last longer." Ella grabs a clay vessel and dons a heavy winter coat. "We need fresh water." With the container, she moves aside a makeshift lean-to door. Sheet ice hangs in its place. "Look at this." The older sister breaks the barrier with a metal cook pan and digs her way out through its several-foot snow topping.

The Waters matriarch shields her eyes from the glare as she stands and wraps an extra blanket over her coat tight against the temperatures. Nothing stirs as she surveys the snowbound landscape.

Hundreds of glistening mounds surround her, each a covered family encampment. Many, like her roof, feature small holes on top that smoke from interior fires. A few sit silent as frozen tombs.

Ella gazes at the Ohio River and sees no texture change from the bank to the far shore. She struggles, one step after another, through thigh-deep snow with slow progress toward the ice-covered water.

Ella stops to breathe heavily and view Berry's farm. No soldiers stand guard over the Cherokee encampment, but heavy smoke billows from its brick chimney. A corral near the farmhouse encloses dozens of unsaddled horses and cattle that huddle together and snort condensation, which ices into frost. The animals stomp their hooves for warmth.

Ella's mind drifts to Dideyohvsgi's farmer story as the army cows appear to lack care and milking. Their meat and milk sustain the troops, which elevate the animals' status above the Cherokee and are off-limits to the detachment.

Army voices argue over poker from within Berry's home, but those words drift intelligibly at a distance. The contrast between the army's warm land-of-plenty and the silent lumps where Cherokee gnaw salt pork and whisper hope to each other assaults Ella's eyes and hardens her heart.

Her inspection shifts offshore several hundred yards. The sun reflects from the actual flow in a narrow channel at river's center where a few bergs float downriver.

Ella reaches the river and stomps a heel through the watery shore ice. She attempts to fill her pot.

The opening shows muddy, shallow water under the crust. She moves upriver for a better, cleaner spot.

Snow with each of her steps stops mid-calf as the searcher makes progress around a bend to a deeper part. The woman drops to her knees with her container. She watches clean, fresh liquid flow into her pot but jerks in distraction at a sound behind her.

Darkness smothers Ella's vision as a hand presses a blanket over her mouth and prevents her scream. A captor drags his target from the shoreline as she struggles against the force.

Another's hands grab and lift her ankles, while the first, with the help of a partner, carries their prize away. She feels brush scrape her back and legs as they move into surrounding trees.

"You shout and I'll kill you, woman." A slaver twists his captive's arm behind her back.

"She a Nigra or an Injun?" his accomplice questions.

"We got lucky. The Garrison Pen in Louisville pays good for slaves."

"Shut up! Somebody's coming." First kidnapper warns.

Ella's blanket hood shifts and allows her to see with one eye, even though she cannot speak through the grip across her mouth.

In a break of the surrounding trees, Tesali's mount puffs condensation from its nostrils. The warrior carries a musket pointed directly at Ella and her captor. The horse slips through the snow toward the slavers.

"Keep your rifle on him," the woman's abductor instructs his helper.

"You know him?"

"Yep. He's the scout. Shoot him if he moves. The Injun's a bad'un."

"No worry. The commission we pay Hiram Colly protects . . ." the partner begins.

Before the sentence finishes, a Cherokee knife thumps to its hilt in the slaver's chest. The surprised scum releases his grasp around Ella and collapses to his butt. In the snow, he fumbles for his dropped weapon.

Tesali dismounts and walks to the dying victim. He pulls his blade from the torso without taking his eyes off the other slaver.

The accomplice jerks his rifle off his mount, cocks and whips the gun toward the scout. He squeezes the trigger. A lump of ice clogs its jaws' flint and frizzen.

"Don't! We're partners, you hear! Hiram Colly gets paid for every slave we steal from the Injuns!"

Without speaking or even blinking, the Cherokee warrior steps to the fearful, trembling man.

"No! Please! I'll double what Colly pays you."

The scout slits the man's throat, which gurgles dead air and mucus before his back stains the snow red.

Tesali turns, whips the blanket off Ella, and stares at her face for a moment. "You're the woman from Blythe Ferry."

"The same one who walked with the lady who coughed blood. You took her and left her child with me." Ella stiffens her body against a likely response.

"Do you cough the same?"

The Waters daughter shakes her head negatively.

Tesali continues his steely stare. "Did I know you? In Georgia?"

She nods no, more emphatically.

The scout stands for another moment, then drops to his haunches and brandishes his knife. "You see this?"

Her voice chokes in fear. "Tesali's weapon?"

"No, the White man's blood."

Ella gathers her nerve. "Better than Cherokee's shed. The sick woman's spittle, remember, you took her from the trail."

The man's expression does not change. "The woman was near death. She passed her sickness to others, not the guards. The great Tesali saved lives that day, more than at Blythe Ferry." The warrior turns his blade from under the prisoner's chin and smears the slaver's blood on the blanket covering her shoulder. He stands and looks at the expanse of the Ohio River. "Get back to your camp. The clumps on the river melt. Soon, we take to the boats."

Ella wipes sweat from her face, and her hurried breathing condenses in the frigid air.

Steely eyes watch the oldest Waters scramble from the clearing and hurry along the river's bank toward the Cherokee encampment.

The scout slips neckwear from his neck and removes one claw.

His boots crunch the snow as he steps to the dead slaver and places the bear's symbol under the carcass's lip where it extends as a fang.

He kicks the man's chin and drives the object into the cadaver's gums.

The warrior scout rubs his facial scar as he unemotionally stares at his prize. The body's distorted death mask hangs an

Indian extension from its upper jaw, like a lifeless and bloated walrus.

In a fluid motion, Tesali bounds back to his horse, mounts in a continuous graceful action flow, and rides alone into the woods.

CHAPTER TWENTY — The Gristmill

ᎠᏣᏍᏎᎤᎢᏍᎭᏫᏯᎠᏎᎬᎯᏣᎦᏦᏓᎳᏫᏍᎦᎺᎭᏍᎤᎲᏃᏯᎾᎦᎾᏍᎭᏃᎪ

Between two springs and near a Presbyterian church in Illinois, Ella, Dideyohvsgi, and Lisa huddle in the snow around their campfire. They loom bulky with winter coats and blankets for protection. Large flakes drift in the afternoon's gray winter gloom. Ice crystals settle and hiss when they melt in the fire's flames.

Youngest rests her head as she weeps.

Ella sits beside her sister and attempts comfort. "The Bear Healer will bring peace to you."

"No, he won't. Those spirit things died in Georgia." Lisa stares into the fire.

"I pray not." The medicine man opens his arms to support loss without spiritual offense. "But perhaps we need to pretend they did."

"Then suppose no pox." Youngest stares at the shaman.

"Many of our children have sickened with the chicken disease. Now it visits us, and we lose Betsy." Dideyohvsgi moves closer and slips his arm around the young girl's shoulder. "I understand your heart pains with loneliness."

"My soul is numb from the pain of this journey. I am sick of it." Lisa looks into the old man's eyes. "But thank your spirits for sharing you with us."

A short distance from the camp, a gristmill's wheel turns in a stream and grinds army corn for Cherokee rations. With each turn, it groans at its apex from a slight imbalance before momentum and cupped water weight propel wide blades downward.

Beyond the gristmill, cemetery marker stones stand atop a hill, sentinels on watch, and their gray shapes dot white against the background as the guard.

"We are fortunate. There's a graveyard past the mill. We can bury baby Betsy today, as is our practice." Dideyohvsgi nods his head.

"Cherokee custom? Betsy's actual mother never had a grave," Lisa mutters. She raises her head and voice in protest. "Her spirit coughs on the trail with us, or maybe Tesali just left her in the woods for the wolves."

"We bury the child because we loved her," Ella speaks. "Not because her parent couldn't care for her."

"In a White man's cemetery?" young sibling questions. "My Betsy died of a White's curse; they even named their pox after their chickens."

"Yes, a White's grave on non-Indian lands but by Cherokee hands." Ella rises. "I am sure burial takes a White's permission as required by his law."

"And how do you pull that off, Big Sister?" Lisa snaps with immature insensitivity.

"I'm not sure, but I believe it's my duty to try." The head of the Waters clan steps away from the warmth of the fire and marches through clumps of other family campfires toward the gristmill.

A Cherokee woman rises from one campfire. "We are so sorry that Lisa's baby passed. What can we do?"

"Thank you. There is nothing," The matriarch pauses.

"What did she die of?" The concerned mother inquires.

"The White man's chicken pox."

"Terrible. I know many others. Ahtsila's son yesterday. Maylee's daughter the day before. Those are only the children." The Indian shakes her head with empathy.

"I knew of old Wahali and his wife. Are there more?" Ella stops.

"Several. The hope is we travel to an army station soon or we may have to bury our dead beside the trail." The lady reaches out and touches Ella's arm. "You are brave and courageous, leading your family out of Georgia as you have. Many of our women have noticed. Please lead us to a place for our families to lie in peace."

The Waters matriarch squeezes the woman's hands. "We have buried enough of our people under stones along the road. I will ask the Presbyterians for a spot to bury our Betsy. I hope they listen. If they do, I will ask for you."

The mother kisses the elder sibling on her forehead. "Thank you."

Ella walks on through the encampment as the concerned matron watches. "There goes a true Cherokee, the daughter of Walela and a freedman, who earns her birthright. She always wants to help our people."

***

As Ella moves closer to the gristmill, a US Army soldier guard stops progress. "The gristmill's off-limits."

"My family lost a baby. I need to talk to the landowner. I want to bury our child in that Presbyterian cemetery."

The guard raises the butt of his musket. "Did you hear me?"

Expecting a blow, the eldest Waters cringes.

Beyond the trooper, a White man steps out of the gristmill and halts the confrontation. "Stop!"

"She's just an Injun." The surprised youngster spins to confront the command.

"And I'm George Hileman, an elder in the Presbyterian denomination and owner of this place. If your commanding officer wants his corn milled, do as I say!"

"Yes, sir!"

"You were going to strike that girl, were you not?" Anger seethes in the elder's voice.

"She ain't a girl! She's an Injun!"

The mill's proprietor calms. "I do not tolerate violence against any female on my land, soldier. Or any frump, witch, streetwalker, Negra, or any other label your decayed vocabulary can spew."

The guard snaps to attention.

"Report to your commanding officer and tell him to send me another gristmill guard at once!"

The trooper salutes and relaxes with a foolish expression. Aware the Presbyterian is not a ranked superior, the young man reacts with resistance.

"Now, Mister, or you will regret meeting me." Hileman sweeps his hand toward the army's tents.

The soldier follows Hileman's order and stalks a few steps away.

Hileman switches his attention to Ella. "And your issue, ma'am?"

"My family lost a child this morning to the pox. It is our custom to bury the dead the same day or if impossible, the next." The Waters eldest stands her ground.

"Look at this frozen soil." The departing guard stops and points at the ground. "She can wait for an army site."

"I own this land, private." Hileman looks at the enlisted man. "And I relieved you."

"Yes, sir!"

The Presbyterian elder turns back to the woman. "Psalm 46 tells us that God is our strength and ever-present help. Therefore, we will not fear."

"I am fearful of that one and his buddies." Ella watches the guard walk toward his quarters.

"Do you believe in Christ?" The landowner peers at his intruder.

"Your deity that allows men like that trooper to club and rape Cherokee women? No, I do not."

"Then, I am afraid I cannot help you." Hileman turns and takes several steps toward his mill's door.

The man stops and twists his attention to Ella as he wrings his hands. "Last Christmas, I lost my son to whooping cough. I cannot refuse you."

Ella's softens her voice and her attitude. "Matthew Five, Verse Four, says blessed are those who mourn, for they will be comforted. And I know how you grieve. I suffered my sister's death."

"You sound as if you are religious." The man's tone shifts to cooperative.

"I am not sure." She nods, uncommitted.

"But you quote the Bible." The devout religious landowner lifts his hands, palms up.

"Thanks to a good Presbyterian school." The Waters woman smiles.

"I see. I own the land under this church and its cemetery, the one on the hill over there. Our Presbyterians will disagree, but I tell you to gather the dead of your camp, including the children, and we will bury them." The landowner drops to his knees and grabs a handful of his soil. The dirt trickles through his fingers. "Go before I feel the need for a congregational meeting."

"Only our Christians?" The family matriarch bends to the earth.

"No, everyone. Your group's departed may rest in my ground this day at my expense. Now, sister. Make that known."

The Waters elder grasps a chunk of frozen dirt and rubs it between her hands. "Dust and pebbles return to the earth without labels."

***

As the day ends, George Hileman stands in the Illinois ice atop his Presbyterian cemetery hill with his palms clasped together under his chin. He prays as light snow falls below him on a small cortege of Cherokee deportees who follow a death cart up the incline.

Ella supports Lisa as they and Dideyohvsgi walk with the people carrier along the path up the hill into the White man's graveyard. The group moves at the pace that pallbearers pull the wooden makeshift hearse. Many of those who parade behind the cart weep.

Gravediggers, four freedmen and two Whites, lean on shovels and picks. They wait at fourteen fresh holes in a line that extend from one grave that stands atop the hill with a new marble marker.

The cart stops at the dug graves with dirt piles which support fresh fallen snow.

George Hileman unclasps his hands and steps a few paces toward Ella and her mourners. "I must tell you that the new marker is my son's," the father whispers.

"He lies loved, as will our Cherokee and slaves." Ella responds. "They are Christians, and I believe a couple are your denomination, so he will not be alone."

The landowner spreads his arms. "All are welcome in my cemetery." He chuckles under his breath. "Even my own Presbyterians."

Grieving families carry their dead children and relatives to their rest atop the hill in the snow.

With the cart emptied, Dideyohvsgi steps to the first fresh grave and offers a traditional prayer of lament, "Wi na de ya ho, wi na de ya ho, wi na de ya, wi na de ya, ho, he ya ho, he ya ho, ya." As he finishes, the shaman glances toward the father and church elder.

He repeats in English, "We ask the spirits of the earth and sky to weave for us a garment of brightness that we may walk in beauty where the birds sing."

The medicine man ends and peers again at the grieving parent whose silent form collects snow on his shoulders as he toes his son's soil. The older shaman takes the White man's elbow and leads him near his son's cross. Dideyohvsgi lowers his chin and closes his eyes.

George Hileman glances at the Cherokee families who stare back at him.

One by one, they bow their heads.

The grieving father swallows. "Our Father, who art in Heaven, hallowed be thy name, thy kingdom come, thy will be done, on earth as it is in Heaven."

In Cherokee, the Indians joins the Presbyterian elder and speak the last phrases of the ancient Christian invocation their natural way. "Daily our food give to us this day. Forgive us our debts the same as we forgive our debtors. And do not temptation being lead us into it. Deliver us from evil existing. For thine the kingdom is, and the power is, and the glory is, forever. Amen."

The White boy's father whispers, "Amenuh (ᎡᎣᎯᎣ a-me-nuh, Amen.")

As the prayer ends and its meaning hangs over the peoples' burial, a commotion from the bottom of the hill attracts attention. Ella and her group, including George Hileman, turn and look.

At the base, an army officer leads a column of four on their horses, in dress uniforms and shiny boots. The soldiers gallop up the path toward the graves, and their metal-shod hooves clatter on the path's stones.

A flag bearer's red, white, and blue banner flaps in the wind next to a bugler followed by two riflemen. The horsemen halt before the property's owner.

"Captain Jessup sends his compliments, sir!" The officer nods. "He suggests an honor guard to eulogize your son."

The Presbyterian elder glances at Ella, who smiles.

"Lieutenant, pass my gratitude to your commander, but tell him I fear he is late. My boy died last Christmas when we buried him here."

The trooper stammers, "He ordered me . . ."

The mill's proprietor interrupts, ". . . to make sure I still grind army corn?"

"No. That's not what he said." The young trooper contradicts as he notices the line of fresh graves. "He wished to honor those you bury today."

"Then you may have your bugler blow taps over our departed Cherokees and slaves interned here," George Hileman finishes.

The mounted officer backs his horse several steps. "Cherokees and slaves . . . there has been a misunderstanding. I must check for amended orders, sir. Good day."

Troops clatter back on the hill's path.

The landowner extends one arm over Ella's shoulder and they, with the other mourners, smile and watch the honor guard depart.

Snow collects and swirls at the group's feet for a moment before the leaders step away from the graves and lead their civilian burial column from the hill's most unusual memorial, a recognized by man but un-eulogized by military burial site.

CHAPTER TWENTY-ONE — The Mississippi

ᎠᏍᎦᏲᎢᏍᏓᏖᎥᏯᎠᏡᎦᏯᎲᎠᎢᎦᎳᎾᏗᎦᎹᎭᏓᎤᎯᎲᏙᏯᏀᎬᏴᏃᏁᏃᎥ

Two weeks later, near Willborn's Ferry on the Mississippi River at the Cape Girardeau Trace, the Cherokee detachment works to set up a winter encampment.

Ella, Dideyohvsgi, and Lisa toil and erect their lean-to in the snow before the night's temperatures envelop the river's east bank. The medicine man stops work and gazes across the water. The older sister looks. Most of the deportees pitching camp stare with their hands by their sides.

Stretching before them, frozen at its banks with ice to its center, the majestic national waterway symbolizes the gateway to the West. A wide channel flows in the middle.

A huge White man's boat belches heavy smoke from two smokestacks. Columns, doors, and windows punctuate each level. Music floats across the Mississippi's waters, and golden light glows from the boat's decks. A large American flag flies from the bow of the craft. In the back of the flatboat, a massive wheel with horizontal paddles strikes the icy water. It lifts ice blocks until they slip and splash into the torrent.

Ella and Dideyohvsgi watch the boat churn past and around a bend. They look at each other, shake their heads with awe tinged by jealousy, and focus on their night's camp.

More noise draws their attention. Flatbed boats move in the river's channel. Three mules walk on stern treadmills and power paddle wheels that propel each craft.

US Army troopers, led by Hiram Colly, meet crewmen who throw ties and lash the crafts to stakes driven in the ice. The cargo beds of each small vessel appear large enough for two wagons.

Ella and Dideyohvsgi turn from the river and help Lisa into their lean-to's night accommodations.

***

Next morning with no snow, the winter sun rises above the Mississippi warmer than normal for the season, and the Cherokee camp stirs early.

The shaman skins a squirrel while the eldest prepares a breakfast fire.

Youngest sibling rigs a spit from sticks to cook the animal.

"Lisa, a wagon with fresh water arrived. I think it sits by the ferry landing. Fetch a pail for drinking." Ella hands the girl a pail.

"We'll wash this carcass with what's left from yesterday." The medicine man shakes his butchered meat. "If you know there's fresh."

"The teamster woke me before dawn with his foul language." Ella looks to her sister.

Youngest, without enthusiasm, lifts the pail and steps away from the campfire.

"Sometimes, I wonder if that girl will ever grow up, Dideyohvsgi."

"I have seen much more maturity since Fort Dahlonega."

The reluctant younger sibling watches other Cherokee groups as she trudges through the snow. Most prepare meals and celebrate the unusual and welcome warmth of the sun.

Lisa spots the water wagon and heads in that direction. It sits on a flat section of foot-stamped ice.

Several Indians fill pots from its spigot as three young soldiers watch. Ensign Henry Bullock, privates Elkanah Millard and James C. Arnett stamp the ground to keep their feet warm at the end of the cart.

Teamster Jake Conally feeds a bucket of grain to his four mules that stand unhitched but tied to the wagon's wheels. His size, with a barrel torso increased by a huge and thick buffalo skin coat, presents an imposing and intimidating presence. His belt supports a big blade knife and a quirt with metal studs knotted in its leather lashes.

Elkanah Millard, the boy of the three, notices the girl approach and elbows his taller friend. "Whoop! Look at what's coming." The young fellows turn toward Lisa.

She spots the young men.

Private James C. Arnett she notices first, a tall rail of a figure with several days' growth of stubbled beard. His youthful face features a friendly grin, and his blond hair falls free from under his nonregulation slouch hat. He commands the other two boys with his maturity and demeanor.

"I say we mess with this little Cherokee princess." Private Millard rubs his hands together.

"Shut up, Elkanah! You do, and I'll have you for breakfast, I swear." James C. elbows his friend.

"What's the matter with James?" The boy solicits support from the ensign as Lisa approaches.

"Injuns raised him, you idiot." Bullock points at his friend's waist. "You see the Cherokee hatchet in his belt?"

The tall soldier removes his hat. "Miss, please allow me to introduce myself. James C. Arnett, Private, United States Army. May I be of service?"

She blushes and surveys the young man. Her gaze lingers on the Indian weapon at his waist.

"I am Lisa Waters, from Georgia."

"It is my pleasure." Tallest trooper returns his slouch hat to its perch. "Let me introduce my friends."

The budding woman flirts. "Love to meet them."

The blond-headed man offers his elbow. "My arm, and I'll take your water pot. I'll have one of them fill it for you."

"That's most gracious, please do." Lisa beams up at the tall fellow.

The couple steps to the other two young soldiers. "These are my friends, Ensign Bullock and Private Millard."

She curtseys. "Gentlemen."

"Henry's from Indiana, and Elkanah is from Alabama."

"I have met no one from either state. And where did you grow up?" Lisa edges closer to her new acquaintance.

"Georgia."

"We have something in common."

"More than you know. May I call you Lisa?"

She nods affirmative, so the boy steps closer. "My parents died when I was twelve. A Cherokee family supported me until I was old enough to join the army."

"And they raised you well, James." The Waters sibling turns to a commotion at the water wagon.

"Over there, that spigot. That's where you draw!" Teamster Conally pushes an elderly Indian away from the grain bucket that he uses to feed the wagon's mules. The confused fellow stumbles backward, grabs the teamster's grain pail and feels his way along the wagon's side.

"He can't see well." Lisa steps to help.

"Jake don't take to slow folks." Henry Bullock pulls a forefinger across his own throat.

"And Injuns not as quick as he likes, for sure." Elkanah Millard stretches his neck to see.

Half blind, the gentleman makes progress along the water wagon with one hand and lugs the container with his other.

"You! Where are you going? That's my grain!" the teamster demands.

Stopping the grope and disoriented, the Indian lifts the bucket closer to his eyes. The grain at its bottom spills onto the snow. He hugs the canister and reacts away from the teamster's loud and demanding voice.

The reaction infuriates Jake Conally, and the brutish bulk leaps at the poor defenseless man like a bear on salmon. He yanks his quirt from a belt and lashes. The metal studs in the quirt's leather rip through the back of the elder's head and neck.

"No!" Lisa screams.

Bleeding, the panicked gentleman twists in pain. He grips the container tighter. "My pail," the senior stammers, and the supervisor's eyes widen in fury.

Conally whips a knife from his waist.

"He just wants water!" the youngest Waters yells a plea.

Before the attacker can thrust his blade into the blind man's stomach, a Cherokee hatchet thumps several inches into the teamster's forehead.

The brute freezes in surprise as his blood spurts upon the snow. He collapses to his knees and falls backward. Teamster Conally lies on his back with his legs bent under him. Blood gushes from the weapon embedded in his skull and puddles around his ears, rich red against white sparkling ice crystals.

Lisa looks at Arnett. Both his buddies stand in awe and fear next to the private.

"Can't bear that brute knifing a feeble old man." James C. spits on the ice.

"You killed him." Ensign Henry Bullock whispers. "What are we going to do?"

"We have no choice but to report it." Elkanah Millard's hand tremors as he rubs his forehead.

Lisa collapses and drops to her knees. She sobs into her fingers.

"I'm not sorry, Miss Lisa." The tall boy bends and by her elbows helps the girl back to her feet. "I meant to do it."

Lisa looks at her hero and wipes her tension tears. "I know you did. I only wish I killed him, but I could not have been so on target."

***

That night around Ella's campfire, the youngest sibling stares into the flames as the oldest sister and Dideyohvsgi sit and watch.

The Waters matriarch speaks. "That will be the end of it. You were just there. You did nothing."

Lisa's tears focus on her older mother substitute. "James is a good man with a clean soul. I could see it in his eyes." She shakes her head. "I didn't do a thing, but I was there, and I wish I had thrown the hatchet. I swear I do!"

"No matter what happens, you were not to blame." Elder reasons with her little sister.

"Do you think they will hang him?" Lisa's eyes widen with apprehension.

"They might. The soldiers have their own ways." Ella replies.

"And their own laws that we can never understand." Dideyohvsgi shrugs.

"I can't let that happen." Lisa's voice firms. "I believe I love Private Arnett . . . I mean James."

Ella looks at the medicine man, rolls her eyes with exasperation, and leans back on her elbows further away from the fire.

***

The following morning, the night's campfire glows and smokes in the meager dawn light. The clan from Georgia sleeps under layers of blankets, their top covers dusted by snow.

Two horses stomp into camp. An Army Sergeant and an armed private disturb the matriarch. As she rubs her eyes, the soldier dismounts and prods Dideyohvsgi and Lisa's forms with the barrel of his musket.

"Which of you is Lisa Waters?" the noncommissioned officer on horseback demands.

"I am." Ella responds. "Why do you want to know."

The rider shifts his weight, and his saddle leather creaks. "By order of Captain Jessup, you will come with us to a

217

military hearing concerning the death of Jacob Connolly, a civilian teamster employed by the United States Army.”

Lisa and the medicine man strain awake and remove their blankets.

“And why do you need me, Sergeant?” Ella stands and resolutely faces the horseman.

“As a witness. Gather your things.”

“I am Lisa Waters. She is my sister.” The sibling stands.

“And I am her father.” The shaman rises. “May I go with my daughter?”

Frustrated and annoyed, the summoning official includes the group. “Everyone, fall in line.”

They trail the two horses in the tracks made by the animals through the snow.

***

Hours later, Ella and her clan sits on a wooden bench in the Willborn’s Ferry operational house. The downstairs space features benches where civilian teamsters and military officers wait. One chair remains empty at a table by a fireplace and nearby, Lisa, Private James Arnett, Ensign Henry Bullock, and Elkanah Millard squirm in four stiff chairs.

An officer descends the stairs. “Atten-hut!” Personnel on the ground floor stand and snap to attention as Captain Jessup follows the officer.

The civilians, unsure of protocol, rise or wait until others move, then settle upon their feet.

The commander glances around the room. He steps behind the table at the fireplace. “At ease.” The presiding official begins. “This hearing is not a court-martial but an informal inquiry into the death of an employee." Jessup sits in the chair behind the table. "Is the civilian's supervisor present?"

"I am." Civilian scout Hiram Colly rises from a bench in the center of the room.

"You supervise the teamsters in the army's use that service this detachment, do you not?" The captain appears bored with the proceedings.

"Yes, sir. The teamster who lost his life was Jacob Conally, and he was an employee under my supervision. He signed on at Fort Wool and served the army with loyalty and distinction."

"At his death, what were the employee's duties?"

"He loaded, carted, and disbursed fresh water by wagon from the river to our encampment here at the ferry."

"And was he executing his duty to the best of your knowledge, Mr. Colly?" Jessup continues.

Dideyohvsgi squirms on the bench and whispers to Ella. "I don't have as much fat on these old bones as I had twenty years ago."

"He was, sir," the scout responds. "My eyewitness interviews tell me he died preventing a theft of army property."

The captain pauses for a moment. "My records say that interview was with an Elkanah Mallard. Private, stand and discuss this inquiry."

In a chair next to Henry Bullock, the boy jumps to his feet at attention. "Sir!"

"You saw this incident?" The commander looks at the boy. "Tell me what happened."

"One of the Injuns stole an army grain pail. To carry water, I believe. He could barely see. Doesn't figure he knew anyone saw him take it. The teamster went to retrieve the item and met resistance, so he pulled his knife. He did not secure the government property. A thrown Cherokee hatchet implanted its blade in Conally's forehead."

The captain sits silent for a moment. "The records before me read an Indian did not throw the weapon. One of our own, a James C. Arnett, did. Was that what you saw?"

"Yes! But he's an Injun in a White man's body."

The officiating officer stares at the tall blond youth on the bench. "And you are he?"

The lanky trooper next to Lisa leaps to his feet at attention.

"Did you throw the hatchet?"

"I did." The boy glances at the girl beside him.

"Are you confessing to a murder?" The captain leans back in his chair and waits for an answer.

"No, Sir. The teamster intended to knife an old and confused blind fellow because he thought he could use a bucket to carry water to his family." Private Arnett's voice rings clear without remorse.

Lisa smiles up at her young fellow.

"Wasn't the teamster preventing the theft of army property?" Jessup leans back in his chair.

"No Sir, he was quirting a defenseless, vision-impaired Indian. Studded lashes ripped the old man. And he was going to stick his blade in the blind man."

"He protected government property." The captain implies a decision. Jessup sits and reads the transcripts before him on the desk for a moment before he speaks. "There were two more witnesses. Ensign Ballock, you will stand."

The young soldier leaps to his feet at attention.

"You saw this?"

"Yes, sir! Most skillful and exact hatchet throw I have ever seen!" Most of the people in the room laugh or chuckle, which the boy notices. The reaction inspires him. "Plus that old muleskinner was a stinking bully and deserved it."

"That's enough." Jessup regains order. "And Miss Waters, I understand you saw the murder?"

Lisa hesitates and then stands. "I did, sir. James killed that teamster, but he was only defending a senior who could not defend himself. I thank him for it." She lowers her head.

"What do you mean? Who was the old man to you?" Jessup presses.

"Just a gray-haired Cherokee, half blind and confused over a pail, searching for what has been most scarce on this forced journey, water and safe passage." Lisa's truth floats above the room as she sits.

Dideyohvsgi leans to Ella and whispers, "What were we saying about her becoming an adult?"

"Hush! That captain's going to skin her alive."

Captain Jessup stands. "This matter is closed. Private James Arnett will at once transfer to Fort Wool for official court-martial. The charge is murder. That ends this inquiry."

CHAPTER TWENTY-TWO — Missouri

ᎠᎡᏔᏓᎣᎢᏚᏌᎸᏯᎠᏧᎬᎤᏜᎠᎲᏟᏫᏛᎡᏇᎷᎷᎠᏛᎣᎯᎻᏛᏴᎾᏛᎤᏂᎻᏃᏌᎣᵛ

Burdened with heavy travel packs, Ella, Dideyohvsgi, and Lisa walk with the detachment column along the Old Wire Road. The older sister's eyes inspect the trail that moves beneath her feet as she plods. One step leads to another on the frozen path—forever forward. A few drops of blood stain the ground and she follows the spots.

Several yards before the family, a second clan trudges in the ice. The group's mother flaps her moccasins with each stride. The top and sides of the footwear hang loose from her ankles. Without soles or even a hide bottom, her foot bleeds.

The people ahead stop, and the Waters sibling passes. As she walks, Ella watches the bleeding matron.

The woman's husband removes his own moccasins, road worn and ragged but held together with soles. The man drops to his knees beside his wife and takes her moccasin ankle bracelets. He slips his shoes onto the mother's feet. Without comment or complaint, they follow the family.

Ella shivers. "I miss the warmth of Georgia, Lisa."

"Your memory ages, sister," youngest laughs. "It wasn't all that warm in the winter."

They continue walking on the trail. Woods devoid of leaves crowd the route. Their skeletal forms sparkle in the light from thin coats of ice and stand as ominous sentinels. These frozen pickets mark the way.

"You're not talking." Little Waters looks at her sister. "But that's better than drinking."

"This day does not welcome us." Older sibling looks at the leafless trees as they pass. "This gloom fills me with dread."

"What do you mean?"

"Look at this country. There is no happiness, hope, or future." Ella's voice tinges with bitterness and resignation.

"What are you saying?"

"We travel to a home we have never seen. There's not much reason to go on."

Lisa looks at her substitute mother as they shuffle and considers her concern. "Try love?"

"What? Something on your mind?" Ella looks at her sister.

"You know, I didn't care for that private."

"His name was James."

"At Fort Dahlonega, I hoped I loved Yona. He only used me for escape. The soldier was the first man who showed me any nice attention."

"He was a pleasant lad, I felt." Ella smiles. "And his soul was Cherokee. That won't help the poor fellow when he's tried in a White man's court."

"What do you expect will happen to him?" The youngest sniffs as her eyes moisten. She wipes her nose on her heavy coat.

"Nothing good. The army takes him to Fort Wool for a trial, but I don't believe he has much of a chance." Oldest pulls her wrap closer.

"Think they might hang him?" Lisa's voice quivers.

"Yes. I do."

Lisa breaks and sobs.

Ella pulls her sibling closer with one arm around the girl's shoulder. Both lean forward against the wind on the icy trail.

"We are the same as your young soldier." Dideyohvsgi speaks after a moment of silence. "We walk with the army to our graves."

The oldest sister watches a Conestoga ahead. Its prosperous Cherokee owner coughs often as he walks to the left of his lead Red Durham.

"Listen to that cough. There may be a nice wagon for sale soon." The medicine man points.

"Stop it!" Ella retorts. "Careful with your words. You have influence with Unetlanvhi."

"Hope so. That's a fine team." The shaman admires the oxen.

"You're right. Those animals look as if they could pull that load to the Pacific Ocean." The Waters matriarch stares.

***

In the column ahead, several children slide on the trail's frozen surface and play a mobile stick ball game as they move with their families. Most of the kids wield a hickory cane in each hand that curves upon itself with sinew webbing. Handmade, with the wood curved in the heat of a fire, the children's mallets chase and control a puck. With a rock in its center, animal and human hair wraps around its core, secured in a pelt stitched with more leather.

"The kids enjoy Anejodi, even in this terrible weather." Dideyohvsgi pretends he catches and throws.

"Like a child, old men always find fun." Youngest watches the shaman's moves.

"The game makes us warmer." The oldest sister imitates her friend.

Laughing and running in pursuit of the ball, childish joy and exuberance around the wagon ahead contrasts with the somber mood of the column.

One boy, eight years old, plays with more rambunctious energy than his siblings. Laughing, he runs beside the Conestoga and catches his mallet between spokes. The child laughs as the spoke snaps the hard hickory. Torque from the break flings the youth to the wagon's wheel. He slips on the slick icy ground and falls.

As the Waters matriarch watches, the youngster slides under a rear rim, and the massive conveyance lurches over his neck and shoulder blades. Ella screams and rushes to help.

Dideyohvsgi follows as the Cherokee wagon master hears the scream and looks back. He sees Ella bend to aid the injured and directs his oxen out of the file to the edge of the road.

The commotion attracts an outrider army guard, who spurs his horse to the accident.

"Bring the detachment surgeon!" Ella yells.

The trooper prods walkers that have become gawkers and gestures to keep the column moving. He bumps several watchers into movement with his mount and clubs another into motion. "Move that wagon off the road! Rest of you, get going!" the outrider guard directs.

The boy's family in various stages of panic and concern crowds around the injured child. His mother drops to her knees beside Ella and wails into her hands. The youngster's father rushes to aid his son, surveys the injury, and trembles with panic and shock.

Dideyohvsgi joins the emotional group. "I'm a medicine man. I can help."

The father attempts to focus his fear. "We're Baptists. Your ways died in Georgia," he responds. "But get the detachment physician!"

The shaman sits back on his haunches, rejected, and turns to Ella. She motions go.

"We have to move him. He'll freeze out here in the open." The oldest Waters urges the boy's family.

The man nods agreement. Ella's and the child's mother lift the small broken body and carry it into the shelter of the wagon.

Ella sits beside the unconscious child on the warmer, wind-blocked side of the conveyance. The youngster's relatives hover over him. The wagon's owner paces in nervous circles behind them and coughs. "I'm so sorry. I didn't mean to run over him. You saw it lady. Tell them."

"Yes, I did. My name's Ella Waters. It was an accident."

"Don't leave him on this icy ground. Please put him inside." The wagon master opens his home.

The helpers and the family ease the lad to a mat in the wagon out of the ice and snow. His mother covers the child with a nearby blanket and makes his broken, unconscious form as warm as possible. The child's father checks the rear entrance in hope the detachment doctor arrives.

Ella, unable to help the injured boy further, sits and looks around the interior. She observes its sparse contents, and the owner notices her look. "I live simply."

"I see you do."

"My name's George Sears. My wife and son died from dysentery at Berry's Ferry, so I need little anymore."

"I'm sorry, Mister," Ella replies. "We lost too many on that crossing."

"That we did." The man looks at the clan matriarch. "I may know you. In Georgia, I was a cotton broker. Was your father Benjamin Waters?"

"He died before they deported us, but yes."

"I understood someone murdered him . . . and your mother. Sorry for your loss. Heard land grabbers burned your farm."

"Or paid someone to burn it." Ella turns to sounds approaching.

Dideyohvsgi jogs beside the detachment doctor's horse.

The doctor leans into the wagon's rear. The boy lies on a mat several feet away. From horseback, the surgeon inspects the youngster. "What happened. Is he conscious?"

Inside, the family nods no.

"An accident. My wagon ran over the child." George Sears lowers his head.

"He won't make it." The doctor's diagnosis prompts hysterical crying from the boy's mother. The father's jaw hangs open with incredulity.

Dideyohvsgi watches the doctor ride back the way he came and mutters under his breath, "The White man's medical care doesn't include our people, even Baptists."

The amazed, distraught Indian stammers, "He didn't examine my boy!" He droops his head in grief and notices the shaman. "Can you save him with the old ways?" The parent pleads with his voice and his eyes. "Even after what I said?"

The medicine man climbs into the Conestoga. "I do nothing alone. If Unetlanvhi wishes, I believe she/he and I can comfort Baptists."

As the medicine man settles, Tesali rides upon the wagon and looks into its rear. "Get this thing moving!"

"We had an accident," Sears replies.

The scout gazes at the injured child for a moment. "Your party slows us. Back on the trail. Move!"

"We're leaving. I'll take the boy, his folks, and the Benjamin Waters family in my Conestoga." The owner climbs out past the Indian.

Tesali freezes at the mention of the patriarch's name. He turns and fixates on Ella.

The scout remembers.

Their horses drip lather from hard riding and continue to sweat from the heat in their speckled shadow concealment. Overhanging branches at the edge of the Waters' cotton offer respite from the warmth.

Worn and lathered mounts stand, burdened by men and heavy, muzzle-loading muskets and pistols.

Both White gold miners' soiled blouses stick to their sides. One wears a battered black top hat, and the other protects his skull with a faded bandanna. "Do we kill the girl and the Nigra?" a Twenty-Niner asks.

Tesali clears his brain as he stares at the oldest sister for a moment before his mind revisits Georgia.

In the distance, a young slave peers across the cotton field at the small, prosperous and well-maintained Waters farm.

Benjamin dismounts his mule near the porch of his home and waves at his daughter and her escort. Ezra responds with both hands, then scrambles after Ella as she moves upstream along the creek.

Tesali's image of scrambling by the water focuses into Ella's terrified face as she cowers away from the Indian at the opposite end of the wagon.

The army scout slides off his mount into the Conestoga with his tomahawk. His eyes glare at the sisters. He reaches for Whitley's "Brown Bess" tucked in his belt.

The Waters daughters suck deep breaths and huddle for safety.

The father of the injured boy addresses the intruder. "Those two were here when the wheel ran over my son. They helped me move him."

The focused Indian turns to the family of the maimed child. He realizes witnesses are present.

The scout looks at the group, shadows in a gloomy interior, a mood like the day when he, carrying a bullwhip, strode out of the dark Dahlonega store house.

A Cherokee woman hangs from a wheel before him. When ordered, his whip curls across the yard and rips into the woman's back. The crack reverberates, followed by another. With the third strike, the victim screams in agony.

A girl in the crowd, the same that Tesali now threatens, cries to an old shaman. "Dideyohvsgi, this is my fault. My stupid false sense of right and wrong!"

The scout's menacing expression remains etched around his facial scar as he pats Ella on the cheek. "You are favored among the Cherokee. You escaped from the White brutes in Georgia."

Tesali's hand trembles as he caresses the disfigurement on his face.

The murderer grasps and rips Lisa's father's water spider medallion from her neck.

Tears from fear swell the girl's eyes.

The scout examines the talisman and rubs a finger over the carving. He drops it around his own neck to join his bear claw necklace.

The Indian scrambles and leaps to the back to his horse and commands George Sears. "Get this wagon moving."

The owner pulls one of his oxen's ears and leads the massive animal, with its injured cargo, as it lumbers onto the trail.

Ella creeps to the rear of the Conestoga and peeks out.

Tesali stands his mount in the center of the road and watches. As he stares in thought, the scout fingers the bear claws at his neck.

The oldest sister sees the Indian lift and kiss a bear spirit's appendage death symbol.

The Waters woman ducks and sucks air to catch her breath. Her eyes tear as she peeks above the wagon's tailgate.

With blurred vision through watery sight, *Ella's mind follows the murderer and his two armed "Twenty-Niner" accomplices as they kick their horses' flanks and charge through cotton rows yards away.*

In horror, the woman drops low and concealed in the wagon. Ella confronts her fear and peeks out a second time.

No human, animal or spirit appears in her view.

CHAPTER TWENTY-THREE — Sear's Wagon

DRTⱭꝰiꙅⱭꞮⱯYAJEꝗꝒꟼHꝼꙆWⱮᏒGMꟼꝺⱰIHꙅꙋꞵᏫꝉꞵⱰhZꝯꝍⱱ

Inside George Sears's wagon, Dideyohvsgi sits cross-legged on the bed with a medicinal fire smoking in a ceremonial bowl. The injured boy, crushed under a wheel two weeks earlier, lies in a coma near the medicine man.

The boy's parents sit and watch. Their exhausted eyes droop and nod between short respite naps. A lurch shakes the couple to attention as a rim bounces over a stone.

"I recognize you brothers and sisters do not believe as I do." Dideyohvsgi peers through herb smoke. "But we have much in common."

Father of the boy nods agreement. "You have kept our child alive, and we thank you. The army doctor was not interested."

Medicine man spreads his hands with positivity. "More, we both have a responsibility for the land and those who live in it."

Herbs burn in the miniature bowl that rests in the middle of a sacred hoop. Musky scents float through the wagon. The hoop's spokes, each a primary color, align to cardinal directions.

"We both worship and revere a supreme being." The medical man inhales smoke and blows it toward the father.

He sniffs the herbal vapors and looks again to the shaman.

"We both admit repercussions from good and evil." The old fellow rocks as he speaks.

The boy's parent listens and shifts his weight. "We Baptists have faith in the teachings of Jesus Christ, his virgin birth, crucifixion, and resurrection." The father stares at Dideyohvsgi and determines that the reaction is not negative or aggressive. "He offers salvation for even you. Believers have everlasting life in heaven as a reward. Hell punishes the others."

The shaman nods understanding. "Before you knew of this Christ, our people lived in a culture of love, oneness, and connection with nature in body, mind and soul."

The boy's father stares at his comatose son for a moment. He whispers to himself, "I began with Unetlanvhi, who rules over evil and is the one power." He shakes to empty his head of herbal smoke and sits straighter.

"We believe in systematic worship services defined by the seasons." The medicine man coughs from the heavy mist. "We celebrate the spirits who control nature in each season."

"We have much in common." The parent smiles with empathy but not complete agreement.

Dideyohvsgi clasps his hands with his forefingers together. "Sad. Christians are arrogant. They claim we misunderstand what they do, how they do it, and that salvation is the only way. Because we do not agree, we are wrong."

The child's father nods approval.

"Then they tell us their God will destroy or punish nonbelievers, either now or in our next life."

The boy's parent agrees a second time.

Dideyohvsgi sits and stares back at his Cherokee brother. "Does that make sense to you?"

Ella's and Lisa's eyes blink from the floating herbal vapor. "I can't breathe in here." Lisa clears her throat.

"Think I'll get fresh air." Ella moves to the front and pokes her head through the entrance. Younger sister joins her.

"When the shaman in him gets going, he becomes tedious." Lisa glances back into the wagon to ensure no one overheard her comment.

"Dideyohvsgi cannot abandon the old ways. I love him as a father." Ella looks at her sister. "And many of our people cannot accept the traditional today. I cherish them as brothers and sisters for their independence."

"I know you." Lisa chuckles. "You intend to remake both."

The two watch George Sears, who walks before them with his oxen through knee-deep snow. Each animal labors. Pull foot from snow, plant next step forward, and repeat for miles. The man coughs as his team continues to plod. The animals, trained to heel to the wagon master but keep a space between them, show their quality.

"George needs a break." Ella pats her sister's shoulder.

"Better you than me. Even with Dideyohvsgi in shaman paint, I prefer the warmth."

Ella gathers her blanket around her shoulders and climbs out of the front. She jumps to the ground, slips on ice, and lands on her rear.

As Lisa chuckles, Ella deploys dignity and struggles to stand.

***

The detachment ambles along the road, and its parade plods into the falling and drifting snowstorm. Many pull purchased army issue blankets around their bodies against the chill. A few, with extra feet wrapping up to their knees, step warmer than those with only summer moccasins.

Ella joins Sears. "Freezing out here, George. I'll lead the oxen for a while. You go get warm."

"Miss Ella. I hear the locals say it's the coldest winter they can remember."

"Not good for your cough. Get in the wagon."

"Yes, Martha." The man coughs as he grumbles.

"Who?" Ella palms up her question.

"My dear wife, bless her soul." His teeth chatter. "Wise woman, she was. Even chose these Red Durhams for me. Their names are Hetty and Lulu. I was going to buy two mules." George Sears allows Ella to replace him at oxen lead and suppresses a coughing fit as he climbs into the Conestoga.

Ella rests her hand upon the oxen's yoke, a fifty-pound cottonwood beam carved with gentle slopes that seat over each of the animal team. Hickory u-locks encase each animal's neck with the free ends through holes secured by wooden pegs. She scratches the lead ox behind the ear as they trod through the snow.

Guards, equipped with military winter gear for themselves and their animals, herd the travelers from horseback, trail hands with cattle. They lead the first few. Followers track with determination. The detachment moves as a unit, unaware of its destination toward a goal. If that search plunges the group over a cliff, most will perish in line.

Many Indians succumb to the temperature and drop out of the column. With their family, or sometimes without, a Cherokee walker collapses in the snow, and the herd shuffles away from the straggler. Once immobile, in this winter's temperatures, the poor soul becomes an ice sculpture. Remaining walkers cough, sneeze, and wipe sick noses as virus and disease weaken struggling humanity. Measles, mumps, dysentery, tuberculosis, fever, and other sufferings plague their march. One army hospital wagon offers no respite and serves as a morgue.

Before the team, a family walks, and Ella's oxen catch up to the exhausted clan. "You folks take a rest." Ella stops them. "Ride up in my Conestoga for a spell."

Ella stops her animals to help the people climb into the warmth.

"We've walked every inch from Georgia, but today the colder miles are longer. How can we thank you?" the mother in the group gushes.

"It's warm in the wagon. Gather your strength. Rest, then let somebody else ride." Ella replies. "That's how to say thanks."

"Bless your soul, Miss…"

"Ella, Ella Waters."

"We'll call you Miss Ella and think of you as our Cherokee mother."

Ella laughs. "A parent, I'm not. Never married. Let's think of me as the Cherokee old maid." She pulls the canvas of the wagon's entrance closed tighter and returns to her oxen.

Inside the wagon, the new passengers cuddle together for warmth next to George Sears but eye the boy that Dideyohvsgi treats.

"He's not sick, only injured. You won't catch a disease." The shaman notices their concern.

"Pray for my son. It has been two weeks now, and he still sleeps." Lisa holds the boy's mother in her arms as the woman looks at the newcomers.

"And for me because he's there." George Sears mutters.

The new arrivals stare with curiosity but do not question.

A parent gazes at her child. The boy does not move and does not appear alive, except his chest expands with each breath. Lisa rejoins the wife and wraps her shoulders in an added blanket.

"Are you good folks Baptists?" the medicine man inquires of the arrivals that cluster in their own group.

"No, Presbyterians," the clan's matriarch replies.

"We practice healing by the old ways in this wagon." Dideyohvsgi extends his hands over the boy. "If it offends your Presbytery, then you should vote. I suspect the majority will not want to walk in the snow."

"Not until after they have debated it in committee," the woman jokes. She chuckles to herself. Her family catches the secular humor and enjoys the levity.

"You Protestants enjoy the weirdest things, communion for example," the shaman concludes. He shakes his head in resignation and returns to his patient.

Dideyohvsgi sweeps both hands clockwise over the sacred hoop.

"Do you think you help him?" Lisa watches the old man.

"Yes. I align nature and the earth with morning sunlight," the old shaman replies.

"Maybe you did in Georgia. But now we're west of the Mississippi." Younger Waters looks at her father's friend as if he lacks sanity.

"Sun and earth past the big river act the same." The healer closes his eyes. He sits back on his haunches and sings a traditional chant. With the words, Dideyohvsgi pauses over each spoke of the sacred hoop, birth, youth, elder, and death. "Looking behind, I fill you with gratitude. Looking ahead, I fill you with vision." He holds over the second sacred symbol. "Looking upward, I fill you with strength from the spoke of youth."

Smoke from the herb pot floats and gathers under his cupped palms.

The shaman opens his enclosed cures and blows the accumulated mist over the head of the comatose child.

"Looking within, I fill you with peace." The old medicine man slips toward the boy's mother. He cups her cheeks in his smoky fingers.

The woman tears and nods her appreciation as eyelids flicker and the boy awakens.

A proud shaman beams at Lisa. "The detachment's Baptist doctor couldn't do that."

"But you did." The young Waters smiles in amazement.

The fresh arrivals look on in awe. The family's mother spreads arms over her son. "We ride in a holy medicine wagon with a great man of healing. He calls the old ones to cure our children."

Dideyohvsgi beams his pleasure and winks at Lisa. "I didn't help the patient, the ghosts from Georgia did."

The boy's father scoots to his son's side and assures himself the youngster is alive and returned from his coma. "It's a miracle! Dorcas and Lazarus!" The man cups the youth's head in his hands and kisses his forehead. "Praise be to God!"

George Sears rises to his knees, extends his palms to heaven with guilt release and calls to his wife. "Martha, look! The child lives. I didn't kill him. Our Conestoga is a miracle wagon!"

CHAPTER TWENTY-FOUR — Massey Iron

ᎠᏕᏦᎣᎢᏍᎣᏞᏯᎠᏤᏇᏇᏗᏝᎦᏭᎦᏟᏋᎹᎿᏍᎣᎲᏛᏲᏋᏁᏋᏍᏂᏃᎠᎤ

Along Maramec Spring in Missouri, the detachment rests
near a stone iron works wall and large pit of red ore. Inside, a
blazing fire looms in the evening light. Beyond them on both
sides of the water flow, many single-room log cabins, with
fireplaces for winter heat at one end, house the factory's slave
laborers.

Operational seven days a week, twenty-four hours a day,
blasts from the bottom of the furnace increase the temperature
to melt ore. The oxygen burst from the heater blower blasts
past two cylinders that stroke at sixteen strokes per minute.
Powered by a huge water wheel, they drive an octagonal axle
thirty-five feet long.

Forty tons of wood burn in manufacturing and creates a
dark gray landscape. An ear-deafening clamor vibrates at a
high decibel roar.

Cherokee camps with small night fires fill the drab grounds
that extend from the iron works over ice-hard ground. Water
bubbles beside many of the encampments. The creek flows
unfrozen, a harbinger of a warmer season.

Late winter's breath blusters from the north, and Ella pulls
a blanket under her chin. She cuddles her wrap and leans her

back against the wagon's rear wheel. She watches campfires flicker in the night.

Snow dots the sky as the Waters eldest lifts a hand to catch a few flakes.

Gentle flurries waft with the wind. Thin but fresh white fluff collects in spots on the dirty gray grounds.

Dideyohvsgi steps to the wagon. "Isn't this something? I can't hear myself think. Somebody's making a fortune."

"His name's Massy. Riches on the backs of slaves." Ella covers her ears against the racket. "Fifty work that factory day and night."

"Yes. I understand many run away." The shaman sits beside his friend.

"Saw three slave catchers with dogs on the trail coming in." Ella shakes her head negatively. "Makes me sick."

"Look. Our Cherokee fires twinkle in this grayness."

"Too many to fit in the territory where we're going." The oldest sister scans the sky.

"I only hope that land has no iron works." Dideyohvsgi jerks his face to the heavens. "You see that shooting star?"

"Yes." Ella looks at the sky. "Was that one of your spirits talking?"

"No." The shaman listens. "Around here, they whisper."

"I think it was George Sears leading the way like he always did with Hetty and Lulu."

"You might be right. Are you ready? He is."

The Waters matriarch steps with her father's friend to the wagon's rear. On the ground, a blanket-wrapped body lies. "He was good. Without his wagon, we could not have survived these last weeks." Ella stares at the blanket wrap. "At least he doesn't hack and hurt anymore."

"Too many people who rode in his Conestoga cough no more." Dideyohvsgi drops to his haunches and lifts the body by its shoulders. The elder sibling slips her arms under its wrapped knees. Together, they carry their benefactor through spots of snow to a small cemetery beyond the iron works.

Four shallow unmarked graves lie close on the side of a gently sloped hill.

The Waters sister and the medicine man strain to lower their friend into one hole.

"He's with his Martha now, I expect." Eldest sibling stands and peers into the grave.

"But we must care for the living." Dideyohvsgi takes Ella's arm, and both walk away. In their view ahead, the Conestoga's canvas cover glows golden from a candle that flickers.

Lisa's shadow and several others silhouette on the cloth from the light.

"And our dead." Ella sighs.

Within the Conestoga, another smaller blanket-wrapped child waits. Lisa sits by the remains and comforts the boy's mother. Father and family sit near, and their sad, grieving eyes yield their youngster.

"The spirits took him despite my sacred hoop." Dideyohvsgi looks at the group and acknowledges failure.

"It was Unetlanvhi (ᎤᏁᏡᏅᎯ u-ne-tla-nv-hi, Creator God.) My son walks with our ancestors." The father nods to the medicine man.

The mother lifts the lad and extends him to the shaman. "But you gave me days with the boy. That time I cherish."

The old man nods and accepts the body into his arms.

The Waters sisters follow the blanket-wrapped child and his family to the burial. They lower him into the hole next to George Sears.

Another family fills the other two holes with their kin. Ella's people and the relatives pick up shovels and drop soil onto their loved ones. As they work, snowfall's flakes become larger.

Ella dumps a shovel load into George's grave and watches the earth separate into small pellets as it falls. The dirt spots the frozen clean white base accumulating in the site's bottom.

She looks up into the sky, and her head swims.

Above, snowflakes drift around each other and cascade downward. The intricate ice drops descend, tiny white doilies from black bleakness.

"Something wrong?" The shaman notices his friend not working.

"I'm fine." Ella breaks her reverie and kicks her shovel into the earth. "We better finish this. The snow's falling harder."

***

Later, the Waters party tracks through ankle-deep snow toward the camp. The boy's family ahead stops, and the father turns to Ella. "Time to return to our own campfire," the man begins. "We are in your debt for what you have done. We leave to make room for others in your medicine wagon."

The child's mother hugs Ella. "May God and Unetlanvhi (ᎤᏁᏟᏅᎯ u-ne-tla-nv-hi, Creator God) bless you."

"And you." She hefts her spade upon a shoulder.

The woman clasps her hands. "On this trail, people say a mother's tear falls and plants a flower in the soil to bloom in the spring. You are that blossom for us and all the people; you are our Cherokee Rose."

Ella turns and looks back at the lonely graves on the hill. "I hurt with you. I feel like our peoples' grave digger. There is no good in this."

The boy's family moves on into the darkness, and the Waters group watches them go.

"There is value here. Custom says bury the dead as soon as possible." The shaman grasps his friend's shoulders and peers into her eyes.

"Not what I was saying. Do you believe I was right?" Ella clasps his hands.

"What?" Dideyohvsgi peers into her eyes, confused.

"Taking the boy in Sears's wagon?"

"Yes. Unetlanvhi helped wake him—but allowed the child to die again, just the opposite of the new religion's Christ."

"George exposed many to the coughing death. Many are sick but have not died."

"Further we get from home, the less this old man's beliefs protect. Illness is only one of our wolves."

"What are we to do, Dideyohvsgi?"

"The White man gives no choice."

"And that is wrong. This injustice is one of many. But they have guns and soldiers. And powerful Cherokee support this march. Our people accept their ways and religion." Ella shakes her head in resignation.

"We bury the children and travel on—without Unetlanvhi's attention." Dideyohvsgi lowers his head. "They pay us less mind the further we get from Georgia."

"It breaks this woman's heart." Ella places a hand on her chest.

"Mine has broken too many times and hardens with age."

The driving, late winter snow paints four cross-cultural, conflicted, unmarked graves white.

***

Next morning, Ella braves the cold and stands silent in remembrance of her benefactor, George Sears. She unties Hetty and Lulu from his Conestoga wagon's wheel and leads the animals to the creek for water. An early spring's south wind blows through her hair, and she loosens the blanket tie at her chin.

The rising sun sparkles in the sky as she opens her blanket wrap. Her body welcomes the signs of spring.

The beasts drink from the flow as Ella watches other deportees at the US Army ration tent. Each accepts corn, salt pork, flour, and cornmeal. In addition to rations and water, they receive a government dole of sixteen cents per day.

Lisa and Dideyohvsgi wave from the line as they creep closer to the entrance. She returns their acknowledgment, then leads the oxen back to the Conestoga. As Ella guides the animals, a Cherokee woman stops her. "You are the owner of the Unetlanvhi medicine wagon?"

"Are you asking about the injured boy who died? Or where the others caught the blood cough?"

"Your shaman gave that boy's mother many days with her son. That is powerful," the Indian replies.

"It was owned by a person who did not survive the deep cough. He spit blood in the snow since we left the Mississippi.

I lead the wagon, but his illness taints our route." Ella's tone reflects her fear of the disease.

The Cherokee ignores the worry in her words. "My daughter can't walk. Unless you help her, she has no more days." The mother pleads, "Please, take her into your wagon."

"No, my family is not ill. If we took her, it is much too dangerous for them. I'm sorry, but I cannot accept any more diseased and injured." Ella walks away from the distraught clan member.

The head of the Waters group moves on toward the Conestoga a few yards, then stops. She shifts her attention to the concerned relative. "Take her to the detachment's doctor. I've seen too many die. I don't want to watch more."

"You know the White doctor doesn't care." The woman's voice trembles.

Ella walks her oxen to the wagon and ties them to a wheel. She moves to the opposite side and adds a stick to the campfire. A movement distracts.

Hiram Colly stands before her, and Ella steps backward to the protection of the Conestoga.

"I need to see George Sears. He owes his conveyance fee."

"He's not here."

"Not here, huh?" The scout stares at the oldest sibling for a long moment and then his eyes light with suspicious recognition. "You're the sister of the one who testified for Private Arnett?"

"I am. What happened to the boy?"

"He was a murderer. Tried to escape on the way to court-martial and killed a guard named Elkanah Mallard from Alabama."

"Mallard was the boy's friend. Too bad. I thought Arnett was a nice young man." Lisa's older sibling remembers.

"If dead murderers qualify. I'll be back at departure for the money." Colly stalks away.

***

As the morning sun pushes higher in the sky and the detachment organizes, the oldest sister tightens her oxen's yoke straps and watches the column form. The wagons fall in line, and the walkers gather with their packs on the ground. She rubs one animal's rump and turns.

The Cherokee who requested that her daughter ride in the Conestoga holds her sick child in her arms. Beyond and around her, two other parents with pleading eyes hold ill children.

Dideyohvsgi returns with a pot of fresh water from the creek and sees the people. He looks at Ella and shrugs. "Maybe you're Unetlanvhi?"

"Not me. Maybe you. medicine man. More likely Lisa is."

The shaman points a forefinger. "But they're calling you Cherokee Rose."

Ella drops her hands in resignation. She motions for the women with ill children to follow as she walks to the back and opens an entrance flap. With the last new patient loaded, the older Waters helps each parent make their child comfortable on mats that Lisa arranges.

When departure ready, Ella climbs over the wakis chest in front and jumps to the ground.

Hiram Colly rides to the wagon. "I need to see George Sears."

"He's still not here."

"You tell me that one more time and you'll feel my quirt." The money collector spurs his mount to the rear of the Conestoga and looks. Pitiful, feverish children cough and stare at him.

The scout jerks his horse away from pestilence and then peeks again. He stares at the youngsters for a moment, then turns back toward the front of the wagon. Colly looks at Ella, starts to speak, and changes his mind. He rides past the Waters matriarch onto the day's trail.

CHAPTER TWENTY-FIVE — The Danite

ᎠᏰᏘᏍᎣᎢᏍᎤᎭᏴᎠᏎᎬᏉᎠᏟᏫᎾᏛᎦᎹᎯᎣᎢᎲᏴᎬᏈᎣᏁᎯᏃᏆᎣ

A blue norther's winds flap a canvas corner of Ella's Conestoga. Dideyohvsgi blows on his hands for warmth as he ties the top. He pulls his coat around his shoulders and jumps from the wagon to the ground.

The medicine man jogs to join his friend, who walks with and leads the oxen. Snow mixes with the wind, and tiny ice pellets sting Ella's face as she walks the animals on the trail.

"This freeze never ends." Dideyohvsgi shivers.

"Nor does this march." The Waters matriarch blows in her palms.

"We were three months between the Ohio and Mississippi."

"In the coldest winter that part of the country ever felt." She slaps her hands together for warmth.

"Do you ever want to quit?" the medicine man looks at Ella's expression as she grimaces.

"Every day. Know what keeps me going?" Elder sibling nudges the old shaman. "Anger."

"At the Whites and their army?"

"No. But, yes. Not that." Ella stutters as she composes her thoughts.

"I am angry with our people, our leaders, our Chief John Ross—they maneuver for political favor. That's the nature of it,

I guess, but no one rises above their petty interests to work for everyone."

"Hmmm, I hear, but are you too perfectionistic?"

Ella digests the old man's words.

"The Cherokee and our leaders are human. They try. These times are not easy. And one time we were many, but now we are fewer." Dideyohvsgi eyes his companion.

"I think they believe in what they do." She pats Hetty. "But they stumble forward, as we do now, along a road to nowhere, led by no one with nothing except these animals."

"My life's direction comes from super-pull cows." Dideyohvsgi rubs an ox and laughs at himself.

"In Georgia, it came from the ones you milk!" Ella imitates milking.

"Quit complaining and go check on Lisa and the children." The medicine man points to the warmth. "Get warm in the wagon."

"Good. I will. It is warmer in there." The Waters matriarch allows him to replace her next to the oxen, and she scrambles for wind protection. The woman climbs into the interior of the Conestoga as her friend and the team plod through the snow.

***

The travelers navigate the rolling hills of Missouri's Salem Plateau with little effort and less attention. The shaman and the animals move half asleep and scrunched together for warmth in freezing temperatures.

"You the medicine wagon?" A Cherokee rider reins his horse next to the oxen.

Dideyohvsgi sways his head awake and focuses on the voice. "No, the detachment's wagon's up ahead."

The horseman peers forward and shrugs his shoulders. "I know. They have my son."

"Then why did you ask?"

"My boy has the pox. I want to bring him here."

"We have no doctor, no medication, and little else but the old ways." Dideyohvsgi attempts to rid himself of this distraction. "Go away. This is a death cart."

The father dismounts and leads his horse as he walks beside the oxen's leader. "The army doctors do nothing. Food is scarce. They treat us as if we are not alive. Your wagon may be for dying. Here, at least, he crosses as a Cherokee."

"We can always take one more." Dideyohvsgi pats the fellow on his shoulder, then smacks his lips. "Got any tobacco?"

As the medicine man solicits his addiction, Lisa and Ella care for sick passengers but stop, distracted by outside noise.

An enormous human in a heavy, long, knee-length woolen coat climbs into the back of the Conestoga. He wears a flat-brimmed hat and flourishes a modern revolver. "Don't you women scream or you're dead," he commands.

Except for Ella and Lisa, the other occupants lie prone, too ill to care.

"Get out, Mister. These people have diseases. You want the pox or dysentery?" older sister confronts the intruder.

"No, but I must hide. With the sick is good. My name is Hyram, and I'm a Danite."

"You're a what?" Lisa's voice trembles in fear.

"The militia's on my tail. If they catch me, they die." The gunman waves his pistol.

"Why you?" Ella pushes the handgun's barrel in another direction.

"You folks are Cherokee. That must be why you know nothing. I am a member of the Church of the Latter-Day Saints. We won the battle at Crooked River, but they captured me. I broke out three days ago."

"Broke out?" Ella edges away from the dangerous gunman.

"In the Missouri Mormon War. They take our land." The man twists to the sound of horses.

Outside the wagon, several mounted state volunteer militia pound up to Dideyohvsgi and his walking partner with the oxen. "Whose horse is that?" a militiaman demands.

"Mine." The sick boy's father responds.

"That mount ain't been rode hard." Another militia rides closer to Dideyohvsgi. "You people seen a Danite?"

The two on foot look at each other, perplexed . "We've seen nothing the last five miles except frozen Missouri hills." Dideyohvsgi shrugs. "I don't know about Danites. You tell me how to find one and what one looks like, then maybe I can help you."

"Ignorant Injuns. Come on, men!" The militiamen move away.

Inside the Conestoga, the armed intruder relaxes with the sound of departing hooves.

"You Whites fight each other in Missouri?" Ella eyes the Danite's firearm.

"No fighting now. Many of us escaped and flee."

"Ride with us for a while. It's warmer than running from your enemies out there in the ice." Ella smiles at the fugitive. "We also run away from people that took our lands."

"Lady, thank you. Seems we have much in common." The intruder tips his hat over his eyes and goes to sleep with his pistol clutched on his chest.

***

An hour later, Ella wakes the sleeper. "Hiding here is too risky. You must leave."

The escapee observes the sick. "I agree. It is too dangerous for both of us."

As she watches, the big fellow climbs out the rear of the wagon and drops to the ground. He looks both ways and scurries on foot off the trail into the underbrush.

Lisa touches her sister. "He's gone. I'm so glad. I was afraid."

"We want no involvement in any White man's war." Oldest shakes her head and checks her patients.

Dideyohvsgi's walking partner from earlier rides to the rear of the Conestoga. "Miss Ella. You in there?"

She opens the canvas flap. The horseman carries his sick boy. "Dideyohvsgi said you could accept him. He has the pox." The father extends the boy's form.

"Ride closer. I will." The nurse reaches out her arms.

***

The next day, Ella leads Hetty and Lulu, and the medicine man rests. The oxen's breath frosts with each exhale in the colder air. The Missouri terrain proves more laboring as they move southwest, but the wagon matches the pace of the column.

The Waters matriarch watches an army outrider guard clatter past at a gallop, toward the front of the detachment.

Dideyohvsgi sticks his face through a canvas opening.

"Heard that horse. What's going on out there?"

She shrugs and leads the animals forward. After a while, Ella spies a group of riders approach opposite her directional flow. Two guards and four Missouri militiamen move past Ella's position. The militia wear black boots to the knee, woolen pants, fringed sleeve jackets, and carry arms.

Dideyohvsgi sticks his head out a second time. "Heard more horses. Something is going on!" The man gathers his heavy coat upon his shoulders and jumps to the ground. He joins his friend at the lead oxen.

"Think it's got to do with that ruffian yesterday?" Ella asks.

"Could be." The shaman looks concerned. "What did you say he was?"

"He called himself a Danite." She clucks the animals forward.

"Hmm, never know with the White men. That could be one of their prophets, or maybe an apostle."

"He stated he was Church of Late Saints, so it might be." The Waters eldest favors one foot. "Lead the oxen, will you? I think I'm getting a blister."

"Sure. Out here, I won't miss any excitement." The curious shaman peers at the column in the direction that the mounted men rode. Dideyohvsgi hops as one foot impacts a hard object.

The medicine man leans over and picks the unusual rock from the ground. The rock's shape mimics a small red rose, and he tucks it into a leather pouch at his belt.

As the bitter day dims and the time for encampment approaches, Dideyohvsgi's droopy eyelids rhythmically bounce. Each step forward brings the sound of a man's painful moan.

The old medicine man shakes the stupor from his brain and stares at the sound. Mounted riders plod through his line of sight.

Several of the same group from earlier in the day lie stomach down over their saddles and drip blood. One dead is an army detachment guard.

Three ride upright, including the second trooper, but another militiaman clutches a bullet wound in his side and struggles to maintain his mount. None of the defeated speak to each other as they plod toward the front of the column.

Dideyohvsgi watches the battle-scarred group and shakes his head. "A Danite's no prophet, too deadly."

***

That night after encampment, the old man sits behind the wakis chest and views the wagonload of sick children as they moan and turn. One little girl stares with feverish cheeks and mumps' puffed jaws.

Dideyohvsgi withdraws the Barite Crystal rock he found from a small pouch at his waist. Red crystals form flat concentric circles - reminiscent of petals - a desert rose. The Indian holds the object into the light. It glitters.

The child's expression does not change.

Lisa looks at her father's friend, who notices her attention, and he points to his audience.

The medicine man scoots across the wagon's bed and touches the blanket hood around the ill girl. Her serious eyes blink from a sickly face. One eye is blue and the other brown.

With two fingers, he turns the rock so she can view its sides and colors.

Her lower lip trembles.

The old fellow lays the object on the floor of the wagon, inches from the girl's mat. He returns to his place next to Lisa.

The sick girl stares at the red display for a moment and then pulls it under her blanket. Her expression remains somber and sad.

The shaman nods into sleep.

The oldest Waters wakens him. "Dideyohvsgi, waken."

The old medicine man moves. "I'm awake."

"You don't look it."

"I am. What's the matter?"

"Nothing."

"Then why did you disturb me?" he sputters.

"Shhh! Just listen."

They freeze motionless and silent as the night's sounds penetrate the canvas top and whisper in the wagon. The wind flaps a loose corner of canvas, and outside, nearby tree leaves rustle.

A horse's measured breath stirs wisps of frigid air.

Ella slips to the wagon's rear. She looks back at Dideyohvsgi and he nods yes. She dislodges the entrance ties and lifts a flap. The woman peeks outside the wagon.

Inches from Ella's nose, the pale and colorless countenance of the Danite hangs. His corpse's eyes stare open and its mouth twists, distorted by a bear claw jammed into its upper gum. The head resembles a swollen single tusk boar. He lies over the rear of a saddle.

Frozen in fear, the older sister's lips tremble as she looks up at the rider.

"Ella Waters, daughter of Benjamin, you cannot hide my enemies." The steely eyes of the scout do not blink. "Even in your medicine wagon, Tesali knows and can find them." The warrior heels his horse and clatters away.

Oldest sibling sits in her wagon and trembles. She looks to Dideyohvsgi, who cowers in the wagon's opposite corner.

****

As daybreak drifts through the rear canvas and falls on closed eyes the next morning, elder sister jerks herself awake and peeks out of the wagon.

The encampment stirs. A few Cherokees enliven exhausted fires with sparks of preparation. Breath frosts in the air, but nowhere lies any evidence of the night's visitor.

Ella sighs and attempts to shake her night's dream from her mind. She focuses on the frozen ground at the rear of the wagon. A pool of blood stains the soil.

Ella's movements waken Dideyohvsgi, and he looks through the wagon and stretches. Nearby, the sick little girl from the day before sleeps. The medicine man moves to the youth and uncovers the child's head.

Her small, lifeless face stares back; lips frozen in a smile.

One delicate hand death grips her red rock rose.

CHAPTER TWENTY-SIX — Bell Tavern

DRTⱷO'ᎥⵕOᏐⵢAJEⵥꝯᎪⵎℂⱷWⱷℾGMᎡⱷOIH5ⵢⱰᏏⱺℶhZⱰOⵡ

Near Bell Tavern on the White River road, Ella and Dideyohvsgi pick and dig a child's grave in the frozen ground of Illinois' Wilson's Cemetery. The sun sets behind them, and the clink of their picks and shovels on the hard soil punch ice.

Mrs. Dye, the tavern's proprietor, watches and pulls her coat tighter. She supervises diggers at work nearby.

The medicine man removes cash from the pouch around his waist and hands the money to the landowner. "Two dollars, Mrs. Dye."

She accepts the burial fee. "Whose hole is that over there, where they're digging?" the lady points.

"One of the army outriders," Ella replies.

"Few soldiers buried here." The White owner nods her surprise.

Elder Waters rubs palms together. "It's good business. Government pays."

"They paid twelve dollars for that spot." The entrepreneur turns back to the smaller hole. "Yours is a child's grave?"

"Yes, a seven-year-old girl with mumps. She died in my Conestoga."

"You the medicine wagon's nurse?"

Ella stops digging, straightens, and faces the White questioner's eye. "They call me that, but a better title is Hetty's and Lulu's babysitter."

The proprietor stands in silence for a moment, then hands the two federal dollars to Dideyohvsgi.

Ella steps closer. "No, keep that. It's your land, and we pay our way."

Mrs. Dye gazes at her tavern where soldiers drink and laugh in its oil-lamp illuminated bar. "You have, far more than your share. That scum in my place travels for free."

She places the cash on the ground near Ella. "You can owe me. We will settle next time you come around Springfield."

Mrs. Dye turns and walks away toward her tavern and the loud soldiers. She meets Lisa, who walks from the encampment to join her sister. The tavern owner nods as they pass, then turns. "Hello. Are you the Cherokee Rose's sister?"

Youngest extends a friendly hand. "Yes, I'm Lisa Waters."

"I thought so. I saw you when your Conestoga rolled onto my land."

"Do I know you?" The younger sibling smiles.

"No, young lady. The Cherokee in your detachment talk of you and your relatives."

Younger beams. "They do?"

"You're becoming famous." The landowner nods approval.

"Thank you. You are most kind." Lisa turns.

"Wait." Mrs. Dye touches her elbow. "You've been in that sick Conestoga for weeks. Come with me. I'll pour you a warm bath, and I have a fresh dress that might fit you."

"How exciting! But I don't know you. Why would you do that?" Lisa steps away from the older woman.

"Because you and your sister have done so much for so many pitiful human beings. I can give you back at least one night of comfort. Go, ask your sister, and tell her she is also welcome."

"I am so excited! I will beg her." The girl turns and runs up the hill to where Ella and Dideyohvsgi dig.

Mrs. Dye watches the conversation at the gravesite. Youngest circles the grave and explains the landowner's offer. Ella's body language expresses doubt and distrust. Lisa talks with excited gestures. Two distinct personalities clash, and the impulsive one wins. Young Waters dances upon the return slope.

"Mrs. Dye. My sister says that I can, but she cannot. Her responsibility for that burial prevents her. But she said to tell you thank you."

"That's good, Child." The landowner slips her arm around Lisa, and they walk toward the tavern. "You deserve a night of fun."

***

Later, in an upstairs room, younger sister luxuriates in steaming bath water. She leans her head against the support of a wooden tub and suds her face with homemade soap. As she washes, the bather sings. "I have traveled this wide world over, and now to another I'll go. I know that good quarters are waiting. To welcome, I'll rosin the bow."

She dips under her bath's surface to rinse but breaks water singing, "I've always been cheerful and easy, and scarce have I needed a foe. While some after money run crazy, I merrily rosin the bow."

"Yes! Love it!" The proprietor bursts into the room with a fresh pail of boiling warmth and pours it into Lisa's tub. "I'll fetch that gown." Mrs. Dye closes the room's door as Lisa sings, "Some youngsters were panting for fashions, some new kick seemed now all the go, but having no turbulent passions, my motto is rosin the bow."

The benefactor reenters with a dress.

"That's so fancy!" Lisa's eyes light up like twinkling stars.

"When you finish your bath, I insist that you try it." The tavern's proprietor closes the door behind her. "I'll be back to brush your hair."

A few minutes later, Lisa stands in front of a full-length mirror and admires her reflected image. She twirls, and her hem sweeps across the floor.

Mrs. Dye pokes her head in the door. "How feminine you look! That fits. You must keep it. Someone staying at the tavern left it."

"No, I mustn't. Ella says nothing is free, and we don't have much money."

"You paid for it, my dear, nursing those sick children in your wagon." The proprietor strokes the gown's wrinkles.

"I can't. I will never wear it. Give it to a girl who needs finery."

"You! Come with me, you can help. We're busy downstairs, and there's even a fiddle player. I heard your song, come downstairs with me and rosin your bow!"

"Ella would say no. But she's a fuddy-duddy," the youngest gushes. "It's been forever since I enjoyed music!"

Moments later, Mrs. Dye and Lisa descend a stairway into the main Bell Tavern hospitality area. A fire in an immense fireplace dominates one end of the room. Large hickory skewers roast chunks of buffalo meat, and black metal pots of beans and squash bubble over coals.

Servers and cooks, including indentured servants, bustle activity. Many wooden tables fill the room's reception space, and White soldiers, a few locals, and Illinois volunteer militiamen occupy their chairs.

A servant stands by the chimney and fiddles "Buffalo Gals," a quadrille in six-eight time, and two tipsy troopers dance with each other before him.

Most of the men who watch from the tables drink homemade wine, whiskey, brandy, or bitters. They exchange boisterous conversation one decibel above the room's fiddler. Many of those turn their eyes to follow Mrs. Dye and Lisa, the only women in the room, as they descend the staircase.

"We attract attention." Young Waters leans forward to her host.

"If these boys get feisty, let me know." The proprietor scans the crowd.

Upon Lisa's arrival at the stair's base, one youthful dancing soldier deserts his male partner and bows low before Lisa in an invitation.

She looks at her older hostess, laughs, and nods yes. The two spin away into the quadrille.

Lisa picks the steps and whirls as she smiles. Another trooper taps her partner's shoulder, and they exchange. The new dress spins in the arms of more men, as others form a mixer line.

Mrs. Dye hovers and supervises the festivity; her presence keeps her patrons gentlemanly.

After three quadrilles, Lisa collapses into a chair out of breath but flushed and blushed with fun and frivolity.

Her first dance partner drops into a near seat. "I'm from Pennsylvania and you're a Cherokee beauty. I intend to marry you."

"Aren't you too tipsy to become a husband?" Lisa laughs and smiles at the boy.

"No! Back home, we get hitched at fourteen! I got a horse, six dollars saved, and this jug of whiskey we can drink!" The boy leans forward to kiss.

"Don't forget you're a gentleman." Mrs. Dye, at Lisa's side, holds a muzzle-loading single-shot Derringer at the tipsy soldier's temple. "And you've had enough. I say you sound retreat for the night."

The soldier boy looks at his proposed for a moment, then considers Mrs. Dye's ornate pistol. He smiles, stands, and winks at his genuine love. The boy tips his forefinger to his eyebrow and retreats out the tavern's door.

"I'm thinking it's sleep time. How long's it been since you slept in a real feather bed?" Mrs. Dye offers her elbow to Lisa. "I'll escort you upstairs and show you to your room."

"But I'm not ready." Young sister protests.

"I think you are, Dear. I work two more hours, and this Derringer is only a single shot." The proprietor laughs as she overrides Lisa's protest.

***

Later that night, from the wakis chest in her wagon, Ella listens to the music from the Bell Tavern and watches soldiers cut meat from a bison carcass that hangs on a wood tripod near its back door.

Both troopers stagger from drink. "Tastes better than beef." The shorter soldier smacks his lips.

"But it ain't tastier than rum!" The taller man belches.

"Enjoy your booze, do you, Corporal?"

"Mrs. Dye's got good stuff, but this meat is scarce. Rode half day to find this buff. Take a hunk in." The private hands a roast to his partner. He stops to wipe his knife on his pants before entering the tavern and looks at two Cherokee boys who watch nearby. "Git! That buff's military rations!"

The children stare at the soldier.

The short trooper lunges. He is too tipsy, and they are too quick. The boys evade and scramble away.

Ella climbs from her wagon and reaches for her knife. She tucks it under her coat. The oldest sister stops the pair as they run nearby. She gestures silence, and the three sneak through the darkness to the tavern. She peeks through a window.

Soldiers and civilian guards crowd the room, and Mrs. Dye scurries tankards of beer and shots of rum and whiskey to her patrons. An enormous fireplace dominates Ella's view with hot embers where cuts of bison roast on stakes.

The Waters matriarch guides the youths to the outside hanging meat. She carves two large chunks from the buffalo and gives one to each boy, "Take those to your Ma and Pa."

They scramble toward their campsites, and elder sister returns to the tavern's glass.

Inside, Hiram Colly sits at a table with another civilian and loud soldiers. The four relish drinks. "How come you signed on as a guard?" the Corporal stares over his glass.

"Wasn't doing that good in Georgia watching cotton planters get rich. Decided I could do the same," Colly replies.

"Takes land." The tall fellow points at the scout.

"That's why I took the job. When we make it to the territory, I plan to buy Injun property."

Mrs. Dye serves the four at the table more drinks.

"And if they don't want to sell?" the private gestures.

"Ha! You ever seen drunk Injuns! They'll need the money."

The proprietor turns and notices Ella's face in the window's corner. Older sister flashes a thumbs up. Her buffalo bloody hands stain red, evidence of what she had just done.

Inside, the server nods acknowledgment and smiles back. She mouths Lisa's name and cups her palms together to show sleep. The oldest sister nods understanding and slips away into the darkness.

***

The next morning, music, buffalo roasts, dancing, and drunken soldiers transition to morning-after reality. The column of travelers and Ella's wagon lumber forward. Ella leads the oxen, and Lisa, no longer in her party dress but clothed for travel, walks beside her. "And I slept in the most wonderful feather bed with duck pillows. I so wish you were there. It was delightful . . . and the music!" Younger bubbles her excitement.

"Did she give you breakfast?" The Waters matriarch guides the oxen by the tavern.

"No. She let me sleep until the sun rose. Can you believe that? How decadent I am!"

"Mrs. Dye is a decent woman." Eldest turns Hetty around the curve of the road by the tavern's back door.

Nothing hangs from the buffalo tripod, and the windows of the bar show dark in the early morning's winter light. The establishment's corral sits empty, and only a trail of smoke drifts from its chimney.

"Big party last night. They were loud. They were having fun, and I so loved the quadrille." Lisa beams to her sister.

Ella points. "But those folks weren't there."

A group of Cherokees fight each other for charred, black buffalo bits in the tavern's garbage pile.

CHAPTER TWENTY-SEVEN — Apparition

ᎠᏔᏍᎣᎢᏍᏆᏞᏯᎠᏤᏠᏇᏰᏘᎦᎷᎩᏫᏛᎥᏓᎷᏴᏋᏅᎯᎡᎩᏐᎫᏖᏫᏫᏍᎲᏃᎩᎣᵛ

Ten days later, as the sun rises, snow blankets the Cherokee encampment. In a large clearing surrounded by brush, the detachment readies for another day on the road.

Ella lugs a heavy yoke beam and two bows to her oxen and stands beside the team.

"Move your head." Oldest sister pats the ox nearest her. Lulu responds by swinging and holding her head far to her right. Collected snow on the animal slips with the abrupt movement, and powdery crystals drift to the ground.

With the near big skull out of the way, Ella steps in front and places the beam over the neck of Hetty, who stands furthest away. She lifts the other end of the yoke over Lulu. "Move, Lulu." Lulu returns, and the heavy wood rests on the team's necks.

The Waters matriarch hears a sound. She freezes and peers into the morning dimness, "Who's out there?" She listens for a moment. The brush looms as dark shadows, but nothing moves.

She continues yoking the oxen, fits the first bow under the neck of Lulu and fixes it with a wooden pin.

The woman pauses and resurveys where she thought she heard a sound.

Ella reaches under Hetty with the second and secures it with another peg. She watches her surroundings.

Glancing over her shoulder, the wagon master leads her team to the Conestoga for hitching. Centered on the oxens' yoke, two iron rings hang from its underside.

The first to connect is the round "tongue ring." She lifts the Conestoga's tongue.

"Back up."

Lulu and Hetty move as she guides its end through so that the wheels will turn when the oxen change direction.

Ten inches from the front, on the bottom, a metal projection, the "goose," blocks the rail from sliding any farther. On a downhill slope, the goose catches and prevents the cargo bed from rolling forward into the oxen's hindquarters.

"Need help?"

Ella jumps with the voice. "Oh my, you startled me, Dideyohvsgi!"

"What's the matter?" The medicine man looks at his friend.

"I think I'm just jumpy. Thought someone was in the brush a minute ago."

"Don't blame you. Missouri is hating and killing. Illinois was more civilized." The shaman wipes his forehead.

He lifts a long-link chain attached to a solid wooden beam beneath the front side of the carriage box. The shaman threads the free end of the cable through the second yoke ring, the keyhole-shaped "calabash." The man drops one metal oval sideways into the narrow part and secures it for pulling.

"I've been uncomfortable since that Danite hid with us." Ella checks the connection.

"That man knew his purpose. I wish that I were so sure of mine." Dideyohvsgi smiles.

***

Later that morning, the shaman leads Hetty and Lulu along the trail in Southwestern Missouri. Snow continues to fall as the frigid winter of eighteen thirty-eight and thirty-nine drags with the detachment's slow progress. Its weight and hardships test their resolve and purpose.

The detachment's levity on departure many months ago, before this season through the ice, feels frozen into a resigned and hopeless realization that the journey to a new home is not a promise but a curse.

Dideyohvsgi pulls his blanket over his shoulders against the temperatures and follows those in front, as if hitched to an endless team of animals that pull only forward.

As he plods along, his mind wanders to memories of long ago and a story told to him by a great Cherokee shaman.

In the beginning, the opossums and rabbits met with the buffalo and other wildlife in council as the birds perched in the trees above. Together, they complained of how man was moving into their world and how humans treat them and violate the wonderful place where they live.

The bison suggests trampling men in stampedes and breaking their bones. The rattlesnake suggests it share venom with people one by one. Other birds and animals list ailments and maladies that might afflict this menace. If any of their plans succeed, Indians die.

But nearby, listening, are the plants and herbs. Not being as troubled by man, they agree to supply a remedy for every disease the wildlife wants to thrust upon humankind. They select one Cherokee who they called "Didanawisgi" in human's language. The vegetation could not distinguish sex, but their choice became the first medicine woman—or man.

Dideyohvsgi's memories turn to when he was a young "tsila" (assistant) to the great Stone Cloud's son and his years of youthful study to learn about hundreds of remedies for medicinal and ceremonial use. The "personality" of each plant was the shaman teacher's greatest ability. Under him, Ella's friend remembers his practical training in hiskoliya (massage) using persimmon wood stampers and moxibustion. He relives countless instances of minor surgery and midwifery.

Dideyohvsgi focuses on Stone Cloud's son as he stands before a sacred fire and extends his arms and hands to the night sky. The son speaks to the teenage Dideyohvsgi seated cross-legged at his feet. "Interpret dreams, my Tsila, use them for personal growth, healing, and to gain knowledge. Know our stories, our myths, and our laws, for they give meaning to the world and help you find your place in life." The great man delivers the Cherokee language with its subtlety and power as he teaches medical lore.

As the young Dideyohvsgi listens, Stone Cloud's son reinforces the seven major tribal ceremonies. "Observe the first new moon of spring, the green and the mature corn harvest, and the falling leaves as festivals. Celebrate the winter ceremony. Use personal, family, tribal, and national traditions to support balance. This is your life work."

The teenage Dideyohvsgi stands and sweeps the smoke from the flames into the sky with both hands. "I swear to pay attention to the world around me, to how the sun and moon dance in the heavens, to the way men and women interact to water, fire, and the earth!"

Greatest medicine man steps closer and grips Dideyohvsgi's head. "I, Stone Cloud's son, give you elemental power to transform, to heal or doctor, to adjust one's mind, to bring luck, and always to protect the sick and the weak." Powerful shaman releases the youth, and he falls to his knees. The boy trembles at the feet of his teacher.

"You sick, old fellow?" A voice stops Dideyohvsgi's memory flight through his past life.

Ella's friend focuses, and the face of a Cherokee walks beside him and shows genuine concern in his eyes.

"I am fine," the older gentleman replies. "I have been reliving glorious days when I was young."

"But your daughter was trying to get your attention." The other points to Ella at the front opening of the wagon's cover, then moves on.

"Stop Lula, Hetty." Dideyohvsgi walks back to the Conestoga.

"Are you all right," Ella's voice ripples concern. "I called twice."

"The temperature dampens my hearing."

"Then you didn't hear it?" Her tone adds apprehension. "I was asleep, and horsemen scared me."

"No. No riders. They, I would notice."

"Are you sure? I woke in a sweat." Ella glances around the vicinity.

"Yes, I am sure. Go back to sleep. There were no mounted men." Dideyohvsgi closes the canvas and steps to the oxen. "Get up, Lulu!"

They rejoin the pace of the detachment column. Snow falls, and the dark day's clouds press the horizon against the trail.

***

An hour later, elder Waters joins the medicine man as he leads the animals.

"I'm fine. It's too frozen for you to be out here with me today." Her old friend blows into his palms. "Stay warm and spell me when I need it."

"Something's bothering me," the matriarch confides. "I think I need you as a shaman."

Dideyohvsgi's voice vibrates concern. "With all those sick people in the wagon, I am not surprised."

"Sickly, yes. But not that kind."

"Then what?"

Ella stares at her friend. "Most nights, I have dreams. Terrible, long nightmare experiences."

Dideyohvsgi pats Lulu's neck and walks for a moment. "The man who taught me mental talk was a great holy interpreter. Tell me your memory. I can help."

Ella's voice trembles from dread and not the cold. "They always begin the same way. I float in the sky, a butterfly in a lacy golden dress with expansive white sleeves that flow as wings from my arms. From cloud to cloud, I fly and join them together to make one fluffy one that is larger and stronger. Gliding through the heavens, I discover the exact cloud that fits with another, and when I cannot find the perfect fit, I become impatient and resentful. Then I flap my hands faster and harder so I may detect more to choose from."

Ella pauses and takes a deep breath, as if the story exhausts her.

"A busy night, but I hear nothing in your dream talk that concerns me," Dideyohvsgi comments.

"There's more. As I search for perfect fits, I become more and more critical of the clouds, and they sense my frustration. In response, they get angry and flush darker. They lash and throw lightening in crashing flashes at my lacy wings. Each hit burns a part of my wing black and useless—and I struggle to fly." Ella's voice cracks with the telling.

"People dream, Ella. Their dreams are windows into who they are." The medicine man touches and rubs his skull like a headache.

"But then a darkness moves within the mists far away. As I watch and hide, the black thing always follows me and becomes a blackbird larger than I am. It darts at me with evil yellow eyes and pecks my wings until I can't fly. When it knows that I am too weak and when I fall, it swoops and catches me in its beak. The last I see are its black pupils shaped like a bear's claw. Then I wake up." Ella's voice trembles in fear.

She looks up at the taller Dideyohvsgi for comfort and healing.

The medicine man coughs and clears his throat. "Your dream is most revealing. It flows from the deepest well in your spirit, and I do not wish to disturb it or its message. Lead the oxen for a while, and I will talk to the dream's blackbird over fire-talk smoke."

The shaman leaves the Waters matriarch with the animals and climbs into their Conestoga.

From the front, Ella watches Lulu and Hetty become one lumbering form, dark against the snow. Flakes fly in gusts across the road and drift against trees and bushes on their upwind side. Her eyes close.

She floats in the night sky, a butterfly in a lacy golden dress with expansive white sleeves that flow as wings from her arms. In flight, she joins small clouds with smaller to make them larger and stronger.

Her eyelids snap open. Before her, Cherokee plod forward on foot and clutch coats and blankets. Several wagons lead her, and each looms large and trails rivulets like comets in a winter sky of dry snow from their canvas tops.

A few Cherokees on horseback move, and their animals' snouts frost-breathe moisture white against their skin.

Dogs pad along the trail beside their masters.

Ella's eyes grow heavy, and the clouds above the wagons before her become angry and flush darker.

They throw lightening in crashing flashes at her lacy wings. Each bolt hits and burns a spot of her wing useless. She struggles to fly.

A dog barking startles the woman alert, and she grabs one of Lulu's horns for security.

Before her in the column, the noisy animal darts from its master under a wagon and runs forward between its oxen, nipping at their hooves.

The wagon's team panics, lays back their ears, snorts, and one ox hooks his horn into his Indian walker. The man grasps his side in pain and the two beasts stampede.

Cherokee leap from the careening cart's path as it plunges through the column.

Dogs, people, and other animals howl, scream, and lurch away from the chaos. The wagon tilts on its wheels as its pulling draft cattle gyrate from the trail and off the road into light brush.

The Conestoga impacts a small tree and bounces onto its side, but the oxen continue to run and drag the conveyance until its weight forces them to a stop.

Cherokee rush to help injured passengers. One man's leg twists under him as they lower him to the ground, and several children witnesses cry.

An army-mounted guard canters upon the wreckage at once and shouts orders. "The rest of you move onto the road. We'll take care here!"

Ella pushes to give help, but the trooper intervenes. "You! Back to your wagon!"

She returns to Lulu and Hetty. "Get up!" she commands, and the animals plod in response.

The Waters matriarch stares at the carnage behind her and flinches as the soldier shoots the dog that began the melee.

Dideyohvsgi rejoins his friend and the oxen. "You all right? Was anyone killed?"

"Two. The wagon master and someone else," she replies. "The escort didn't let me help."

"The army always helps us Cherokee." The shaman chuckles.

"I was daydreaming when it happened, the clouds and the blackbird." Oldest sister gapes at the medicine man.

"In the wagon, I spoke to the crow through a night fire-talk. He did not want to speak to me, but your dream's spirit made him talk. He is a blackbird with little soul but told me you invite him to peck you. Your standards on cloud fitting are too high, and when they fail, the heavens become angry. You are critical and demand perfection, which they cannot do, so they strike back with lightning. Only then do clouds call the raven, who has never had a golden dress or white lacy wings. In jealousy, he pecks away your ability to fly."

"How can I make his peace?" Ella inquires.

"You cannot until you pacify its anger. After that, you talk and set up a new relationship," Dideyohvsgi replies.

"You do help me, old friend."

"And may you have no more dreams." The medicine man sighs. "The talk with the raven drained my strength. If you control Lulu and Hetty, I will take a nap in the wagon."

"Do. I can handle the team."

As the Waters matriarch and her Conestoga continue on the trail, the mists gather denser and darker over the Cherokee detachment.

She shivers and pulls her shoulder blanket up around her ears as she plods forward with her people.

Rare winter lightning dances in the clouds before the detachment, and moisture condenses as thunder snow.

Ella watches the flakes grow larger and fall faster.

Elder sister looks behind her to see if the wagon wreck is still visible through the white frozen moisture.

She turns back to the column.

Ahead, alongside the detachment, Tesali approaches.

"Dideyohvsgi!"

As she observes the scout move closer, the medicine man joins her. "It's him!"

"Who?"

She peers into the snow. Nobody.

At that moment, the oppressive clouds break.

A ray of sunlight pierces the dark and illuminates a section of the column.

"The Spring Spirit, that's who." Ella sighs.

"The spirit says we near journey's end." Dideyohvsgi's voice cracks with exhaustion.

CHAPTER TWENTY-EIGHT — Timber Nigger

ᎠᎡᎢᎣᎤᎥᎦᎧᎨᎩᎪᎫᎬᎭᎮᎯᎰᎱᎲᎳᎴᎵᎶᎷᎸᎹᎺᎻᎼᎽᎾᏀᏁᏂᏃᏄᏅ

Smoke billows from the stone stack of an inn that dominates a curve on Telegraph Road. William Ruddick and his son-in-law, Samuel, stand on the expansive front porch of their two-story wood inn. They lean against the porch's support columns and watch Cherokee pass.

The building sits in a clearing in the woods surrounding the trail. An endless march of horses, wagons, and countless walking individuals moves a few miles from the border between Missouri and Arkansas. The Indians emerge from a long canyon in the trees, trudge past, and creep southward.

Ella leads her oxen and the wagon into the inn's front grassy space.

On the wakis chest with canvas open, Lisa brightens with new scenery.

Fresh spring grass interests the animals as the Conestoga groans to a stop.

The Waters animal-master walks to the porch. As she and William talk, Samuel chews tobacco and eyes the younger sister.

"Sell fodder?" Ella brushes trail dust from her skirt.

"Ten federal dollars a bushel." Ruddick states a price.

"Pay one," she replies.

"Got more customers than I need. Take it or leave it."

The chewer on the porch spits slop and steps to the grass. "Give you four bushels for that sexy little squaw."

Ella slaps Samuel's face, and William backhands her to the ground.

With a lip bleeding, she struggles to her feet.

An outrider mounted soldier guard rides up. "Get this wagon moving!"

"Timber niggers are begging for ox fodder. Ain't even paid for the grass their oxen ate," Ruddick sputters anger.

The trooper nudges his horse near the oldest. "You receive sixteen cents a day. Pay the man."

"That'll be three dollars." Ruddick extends his hand palm up.

Ella looks at the guard, pays the price, and returns to the team.

The mounted soldier turns and gallops away.

The Waters matriarch spits at her tormentor and walks her animals into the column.

Dideyohvsgi climbs from the wagon and joins his friend. "Got to watch what the oxen eat. No tough guy's grass." The medicine shaman teases.

"Not funny." Older sibling waves a hand. "The soldiers are no help. Afraid it'll be the same in the territory. Did you hear that scum? He called us Timber Niggers."

"To him, we are the same as the slaves, only we come from the forests where the white-headed eagle spirit watches. Which is worse, an Arkansas pig who believes we're Timber Niggers or a Cherokee slave master?" Dideyohvsgi waits for an answer.

"Your eagle symbol stands for our oppressive government, here and in the territory. Your watcher does nothing to help slaves. Both are false, the Indian's is dumber," Ella comments.

"The eagle is of nature and unaware." The medicine man lifts his hands skyward.

"Your holy one is unaware of slaves suffering?" Ella stares at her friend.

"No, just more interested in Cherokee." Dideyohvsgi concludes, "But White soldiers drive it west."

"There's nothing here that I can correct." Elder sibling finishes the conversation and the two walk in silence.

Dideyohvsgi breaks the mood. "In the ancient times, an entire clan asked the father of my teacher to stop encroachment by the people from the East. What he did slowed the flow onto our lands." The shaman stares into his friend's eyes with determination. "You will be fine without me. I'll take pemmican, but do not worry. I plan to return with Stone Cloud's medicine for slaves and our people."

The Waters matriarch watches Dideyohvsgi climb into the wagon and jump out of its rear with a small pouch of food. The old man looks both ways along the column for soldiers and disappears into the brush.

Lisa thrusts a head out of the front of the Conestoga. "Where's he going?"

Ella shrugs both shoulders. "To fight the White army and free all slaves, I think."

Younger sibling cups a hand over her mouth with surprise. "Hope he does nothing to hurt himself!"

***

Away from the detachment, Dideyohvsgi jogs through the trees and brush. Every few moments he stops and listens but only hears the rustle of the breeze through the spring growth on pine, oak, and hickory. As the old man travels, his eyes scan the sky.

Along the side of one hill, a creek of snow melt from higher elevations bounces over and across the country of northwest Arkansas, and the shaman stops to drink. He follows the waterway uphill, which climbs into the forest.

A weak-sounding whinny floats in the air, and the watcher snaps eyes to the sky. Pine and oak foliage obscure the view. The sharp-pitched bird call repeats, and he twists to spy the source. He throws both hands skyward. "I hear Noble Spirit, but I do not see! I follow!"

Scrambling through the brush, the old fellow stumbles and rolls into a gully out of control. His head impacts a tree stump, and he lapses into unconsciousness.

***

The medicine man wakens to darkness. A full moon and bright Milky Way illuminate the night. A black bear stands before him. "What are you doing in the woods alone, old brother of the Paint Clan?"

"I am lost, Great Elder," Dideyohvsgi stammers, "and search for support to survive the White invasion."

The animal shakes its head. "Your help flies in the sky. It calls to you by day."

"The pine trees stand tall, and the spirit is fast and flies above their tops." The medicine practitioner relaxes. "This old one drifts with age. I'll lie in this gully and wait for guidance."

"No, I reward you." The bear drops from an erect stance to less threatening fours. "I give you courage and strength to find help. But you must lead the people to bring the spirit's aid to a rightful end. The White men have powerful spirits, but with my help, I believe you can win."

"Yes. Show the way." The shaman bows his head.

"Prove you are worthy." The animal stands on his back legs and towers over the Indian. "Shamans change with the four seasons. The son of Stone Cloud trained you, or I would never speak to you in person, only pass you in the forests."

"He considered me special, but I understand your doubt. What do you need now?"

"Your help nests high in a majestic pine tree. There are seven eggs, one for each of the Cherokee clans. Bring the egg of your Paint Clan, and I will allow you to keep what you find." The black bulk drops to all fours and pads away.

***

The morning sun streams through the woods and shines in Dideyohvsgi's hungry face, so he eats half his pemmican. The old man climbs from the gully. On the bank, he examines bear tracks and smiles.

A high pitched, weak-sounding whinny of a bird call from above the surrounding trees beckons Dideyohvsgi. A huge, winged shadow darkens his face. He calls out into the forest. "Wait! I am here. The Cherokee comes."

The medicine man scrambles through the woods in pursuit of the shadow. A fallen timber and a dead branch snares his legging. The shaman falls, and his chin digs into the soft soil debris.

Before Dideyohvsgi's eyes in a den dug under the log, a small animal pair stares back. Long, bushy tails, orange color with black lower legs and white tips on their tails shows them as Red Foxes. The mother wiggles her ears. "Why do rush so, Shaman? Your elderly chin does not dig ground well."

"I follow a bird spirit to a nest where powerful medicine waits." Dideyohvsgi offers the last of the pemmican to the fox couple.

The high pitched, weak-sounding whinny from above the surrounding trees distracts and the patriarch fox peeks out of the den into the sky. "That is your bird spirit?"

"Yes, I am too slow."

"The white-headed eagle flies too fast to follow." The animal checks the clouds. "But you seek its nest, and I can take you there."

Dideyohvsgi sits up. "Why do that, Red Fox? I have eaten your brothers and sisters."

"Because my wife loves pemmican. That is her favorite meal. And you could not find the nest without guidance," the little one states. "I am sorry for you."

"Someday you will be old and need help." Dideyohvsgi rises as his guide climbs out of the den.

"This day is good for exploration. Feel the warmth of spring? We hunt during daytime in the winter. It feels right to try something different." The leader pads away into the woods and the shaman follows.

The elderly Indian trails his spirit through the pines and hickory trees. They stop for water at snow melt creeks. Late in the afternoon, the animal drinks from a creek and turns to his guest. "I will leave you now. We are here."

"We are?"

"Look above you to the top of that tallest tree." The guide points upward with its nose.

In the tree, an eagle's nest sways on its supporting pine limbs.

"How am I going to climb up there?" The tired Indian shakes his head negatively.

"I could never make it," the animal responds. "But you are the shaman, and I am just a fox. I thought you were crazy, but you wise men have your tricks and spells. I saw a rabbit at the creek we crossed, which I want to take to my wife for dinner. Good luck."

The fox pads away and leaves his guest standing in the woods with his head leaned backward and his eyes high.

Darkness descends and Dideyohvsgi leans his back against the eagle's tree and watches the stars until his eyelids become heavy and he falls asleep.

***

That night, resting in the mountains, Dideyohvsgi hears a noise, a rushing wind. The shaman looks above him where a white-headed bird sits on a limb and feasts on a small rabbit.

"Where did you hunt, Great Eagle?" The Indian eyes the bird and its prey.

"By a creek. I fought a ground-bound red fox and took it." The hunter replies but drops the hare as he speaks.

The old man grabs the carcass from the pine needles. "Hi-ya! I take your meal!"

The bald bird whooshes and lands nearby.

"I will give you back your food if you give me one of your eggs!"

"We have seven in the nest. Only three are of my clutch." The eagle paces around the shaman. "Four others are there but have other parents."

"I want a Paint Clan egg." The medicine man stands.

"They are similar. I cannot see many differences."

"Then get me what you think is correct." Dideyohvsgi steps closer. "If you can't tell them apart. neither will Black Bear."

With a burst of air. the white-headed predator leaps airborne but returns with one oval shell in its beak.

The spirit lays the object at Dideyohvsgi's feet. It snatches the rabbit from the man's hands and flaps back to its limb.

From its perch. the bird watches the old fellow tuck the offspring into a leather pouch and slip away.

***

As Dideyohvsgi nears the first creek at midnight, he spies a slight form curled on its bank. The medicine man drops to his knees beside the small animal and examines its broken leg.

"I caught the rabbit for my wife's supper, but your spirit attacked me and stole it," Red Fox rolls toward the shaman.

"I have seen the great white-headed eagle. But now you need care. A small splint will set your break," the medicine man comforts.

"A what?" the little animal moves.

"Shaman's magic. It will help you walk to your wife." Dideyohvsgi withdraws the egg from his leather pouch and lays it onto the pine needle blanket of the forest's floor. He extracts deer sinew.

With three sticks and the strip, the old man sets the fox's broken leg.

Just as the animal says thank you, his eyes grow wide, and a whoosh of air descends behind Dideyohvsgi. A dark shadow falls over the injured and its healer.

A much larger shape leaps out of the overgrowth and slaps the threat above the medicine man out of the air.

With a massive growl, claws rake the eagle and pound it into the earth.

Feathers fly as the beast rips the bird apart.

On two legs, the bear waves his immense paws, "I will not tolerate spirits that cheat and steal!"

The shaman and Red Fox cower before the great black hulk.

"The spirit traded you a white egg instead of your Paint Clan's and then tried to take it back. Gather the spirit's eagle's feathers. They fly in the sky and are powerful medicine. Use them against your White men. Brown Bear blesses your journey but leave my woods to the red fox and my animals."

CHAPTER TWENTY-NINE — Debarkation

ᎠᏣᎦᏴᎢᏍᏙᏆᏴᎠᏙᎬᏇᏯᏘᎢᎦᎳᏫᎦᎦᎬᎹᏘᏍᎣᎲᎭᏠᏯᎾᏖᎣᏂᎭᏃᏘᎧᎤ

Near the Fitzgerald Farmstead in the northwest corner of Arkansas, Ella walks the oxen along the Butterfield Mail stagecoach portion of State Road and enjoys the warmth of the spring sun. Her draft animals struggle as weight pushes their neck yokes against horns on a steep hill.

Lulu and Hetty brace their claws in the trail's dirt, but the wagon presses. The team strains backward, holds, but slips with movement forward.

The oldest Waters gives the animals their heads. Just off the trail, she spots a large, fallen log.

"Lisa!" Sister yells.

The youngest sibling sticks a head out of the Conestoga. "What's wrong?"

"Come here. Steady Lulu, Hetty!"

Younger replaces the lead. Ella runs and extracts a heavy chain from a storage box attached to the bed. She links the cable over an iron peg embedded in the rear reach.

As the oxen slide downhill with each step, Ella loops the metal strap around the fallen log and secures the timber. She leaps out of the way as the slack tightens, and the wagon pulls heavy wood onto the road.

The pressure against Lulu and Hetty relaxes as the weight mimics a sea anchor. Drag slows momentum.

Ella looks at Lisa and the oxen.

Younger smiles and claps hands above head in applause. The animals step forward without downhill chaffing. Oldest Waters rejoins the group.

"How did you know what to do?" Little sister expresses amazement with her older.

"I've been seeing that chain this whole trip and wondering what it was for," she replies. "Wagon master training was short, remember?"

"You solved it. Lulu and Hetty are glad. Now, where's Dideyohvsgi? Think something happened to the old man?" Lisa's eyes crease with worry.

"I am concerned. Nothing I can do. Frustrating. It reminds me of when I couldn't help Bella." Ella's voice quivers.

"I used to believe that was your fault. Today I'm older and know better."

The oldest kisses little sister on the forehead. "Get in the wagon and take care of those sick kids. I love you."

Lisa waves and trots to duties.

The Waters matriarch turns her attention to the steep decline. She steps forward at oxens' pace and moves to avoid ruts.

Off the trail and a distance up the next incline, a runaway Conestoga lies on a side with its team dead with twisted, broken necks. An Army outrider guard polices the wreckage and doesn't allow gawkers.

Older sister looks at her sibling. Lisa waves.

The younger sister plays a pickup-rocks-with-sticks game on the bed of the Conestoga with two Cherokee children patients.

As the oxen lug the weight of the added log up the next hill, they do not strain with the extra drag and plod forward.

The animals' leader looks at a fresh incline. Thick brush and trees crowd the road, broken only by an occasional rock formation. At the crest, atop a flat slab, a small red fox observes the column move toward his territory.

Ella notices the animal sits as a scout or sentinel. After surveillance, it scurries into the underbrush. She leads the oxen forward over the hill's ridge.

Now moving downhill, pressure from the wagon's momentum slips the animals' yoke tight against horns. Lulu and Hetty bear the increased weight.

Ahead, Dideyohvsgi steps from the woods onto the side of the trail and waves at his friends. The old medicine man carries a load of eagle feathers tied in a bundle with deer sinew.

"We worried." Ella greets the shaman. "It's been too long. Are you all right?"

"I am the best since we left Georgia." He looks to the heavens. "I have been living as a Cherokee." Her old friend falls in step with the oxen.

"You're skinny as a rattlesnake." She clasps the shaman's shoulders. "Lisa has salt pork and pemmican."

"Army dole? For free men? Not fit for the cattle that the soldiers herd. I bring Stone Cloud's medicine from the Great Eagle Spirit so that the Cherokee can fly above the White soldier to new lands!" Dideyohvsgi shakes his bundle of feathers.

Ella misunderstands. "Our people can't eat those things."

Dideyohvsgi's voice tightens with determination. "The Spirit's weapons are not for eating!"

The oldest Waters holds her hands in the air for surrender.

"They're for display, courage, and leadership!" Resolve shifts to a pout. "Stone Cloud used this symbol and led a rebellion."

"These are different days, my friend." Ella puts her arm around the man. "Today we lead by example, not with bird wings."

"That's why Brown Bear chose me." The shaman slips an eagle feather from the bundle and inserts it into Ella's hair. "You are my first warrior."

The contented practitioner takes two more from the collection and slides them under each oxen's yoke. "Lulu and Hetty, pull on, warriors. Carry our people past the White man."

Ella considers her friend for a moment. "If anyone can be an example, I choose you."

Dideyohvsgi beams with pride and slips another eagle feather into his own hair.

***

Two days later, without any sign of a massive Cherokee eagle feather-induced renaissance, Ella walks with the oxen and watches a parting.

Hiram Colly, with several soldiers, meet on horseback with Tesali. They talk, and the scout points up the trail toward the territory. The White boss pulls a money belt from his waist and pays the Indian a large sum of federal dollars, which he places in his tunic. Tesali nods, spins his horse for the trail, and notices Ella watching.

He studies the woman and rubs his facial scar, then he fingers the bear's claws suspended from his neck. Digging heels into his mount, the warrior bounds forward. At a full gallop, the man swoops at the oldest sister and reins the pony. The animal slides as the Indian lifts Ella's eagle feather from her hair.

Tesali sticks the symbol in his calico turban as he gallops away.

Ella plods past Hiram Colly and the soldiers. The White scout's eyes follow as her wagon passes.

The White man turns to the mounted troopers in his group. "We debark at Woodhall's Farm near Westville. Meet you there, men."

"Be glad to get rid of these stinking Injuns." A soldier slaps dust from his hat.

"These Injuns? Don't worry about them. If you value your life, watch for the one that rode off." Hiram looks ahead along the trail.

***

The following day, the detachment creeps into the Army designated debarkation point, a few miles from the Arkansas line inside the territory. Several log cabins constructed by the military, a corral for livestock, tents in the encampment, and many supply wagons surround the farm. Woodhall homestead with wood picket fences sits on a hill nearby.

The official processing center and depot dwarfs the early settler's farmhouse.

From beside oxen as they plod past the headquarters' tent, Ella and Lisa watch Hiram Colly. On a canvas-covered tent porch, he bends to a tabletop. Behind the table sits Captain

Jessup. The scout signs military release papers. "Our duty's done, Captain. What's your plan?" The now ex-scout lays a quill pen aside.

Jessup stands. "Army transferred me to Fort Smith."

"Think there's work there, sir?"

"I hear the courts are hiring deputy marshals. You should have no trouble getting hired with your removal service."

"Thank you. Might head that way."

As Ella's wagon moves by, Colly and the officer recede from view, and the Waters matriarch puts an arm around Dideyohvsgi. "We made it."

"Maybe. I'm not comfortable. Too many White men."

Lisa yells from the Conestoga. "It's glorious."

The shaman eyes the younger woman, drops back, and slips an eagle feather into her hair.

"Whoa!" older sister commands, and Lulu and Hetty stop.

The detachment column, a giant worm stretched into the army depot, lurches to a final halt, and a collective intake of territory air refreshes the exhausted wayfarers.

Lisa climbs from the wagon as her sibling collects two sick children.

Indian mothers gather. The oldest Waters passes their offspring into loving arms.

"Bless you, Cherokee Rose." A mother hugs the older Waters.

"Let's hope she continues to get better," Ella responds.

"Here's an eagle feather. Please wear it to protect your youngsters from the White man's doctors." Dideyohvsgi follows his friend.

Several other mothers pass youths to family and return to hug and thank the Waters group for the care and love.

The last patient unloads, and Ella joins Lisa and the shaman. They approach a short line that leads to a small table. A civilian official waits with a quill pen and an inkwell.

"Name?"

"Dideyohvsgi."

"Dideyos- what?" The bureaucrat struggles impatiently with the pronunciation.

"Just Dideyohvsgi."

"Didheyoyoisgy no last name?" He attempts to relate out of his culture.

"Dideyohvsgi Waters." The oldest sister interrupts. "And I'm Ella Waters. This is my sister, Lisa. You spell that D-i-d-e-y-o-h-v-s-g-i."

The fellow looks up, relieved, and enters three names on the paper before him.

Past the registration table, longer tables on wooden kegs hold blankets, food supplies, animal feed, and other rations from the United States government.

The sisters admire the bounty. "Look. A fresh dress," youngest sputters.

"You can tell the territory's different. I have a last name." The shaman rubs his chin.

An Indian in small round-lensed spectacles with a portable writing desk under his arm interrupts. "You're the medicine man. I met you once back in Georgia." The reporter introduces himself. "My name's Gabriel Wood." The two shake hands. "I write for Elija Hicks, the editor of *The Cherokee Phoenix* and *Indian's Advocate* newspapers."

"I know him and his brother-in-law, Chief John Ross." The shaman swells his chest. "Be pleased to grant an interview. Here, wear an eagle feather as a true warrior."

"Thank you, sir." The reporter sticks the symbol in his hair. "Isn't that Ella Waters, the woman known as the Cherokee Rose?"

On the porch of a blacksmith's log cabin, a better dressed man stands in a flat brim black hat. A colorful slash adorns his neck, and the man's pants tuck into high boots. He watches the crowd.

"Mr. Dideyohvsgi, can you introduce me? I intend to interview her." Gabriel Wood holds the medicine man's arm but stares at Ella.

The head of the Waters clan looks at the fellow in the black hat on the porch. She looks a second time, smiles, and runs to hug her old schoolmate, then she cries.

"It's good to cry, Ella. You've been through hardship, but you are strong and made it. Things will get better." Ezra picks up the bag by his feet and guides her to the shade of a nearby tree.

Dideyohvsgi pats the newspaperman on the arm and walks to a seat on the porch where the ex-slave stood. "Afraid she's busy right now. Sit. I'll tell you everything. Or did you already hear the story of the shaman and the Great Eagle Spirit?"

"That's the old. I want Cherokee Rose's account of our people's just completed migration." Gabriel Wood looks around the medicine man to Ella and Ezra in the shade.

Ella hangs on to Ezra's arm as they settle on the ground. Her young friend leans closer, "Judge Steel took the water route, only twenty-one days. I can't imagine what you endured."

"It was a grim winter, a terrible freeze that took so many." She wipes her tears. "Ice that I wish to forget."

"I'm so sorry. I should have gone with you. I've been in Tahlequah studying law at Judge Steel's court. My life has been comfortable."

"You have come far, my friend. I remember you, a young slave boy next to me in school, and now you have advanced so much. I am so proud."

"Chief John Ross wants the judge to set up a justice system with Cherokee courts." Ezra nods. "But I don't think he's going to do it. The president offered a federal appointment in Fort Smith."

Gabriel Wood steps closer. "Excuse me, Miss Waters. I'm a writer for *The Phoenix*, and I want to write of you and the trail, all about what you endured."

Ella looks up at the spectacled young fellow. "I have no tale. If you want something important, talk to this gentleman. His name is Ezra Waters. His journey from a slave in Georgia to a territorial attorney-at-law is worth a story."

"Please, Mr. Wood. She just arrived from an arduous trip with trials that you can only imagine. Another time?" Ezra's tone impacts the writer, who nods understanding and leaves the pair in private.

"How did you find us?" Ella looks back to her friend.

"Easy, been here only two days. The arrivals speak of the Cherokee Rose. Your father would be proud of you and what you did for those others."

"I'm just glad we've made it."

"You're not there yet. When I arrived, I registered you for a treaty's farm site. They have gone fast and there wasn't much left, but I got the best one. It's on a creek like in Georgia."

"We'll leave in the morning." Ella beams pleasure. "I'm excited."

CHAPTER THIRTY — Blind Eye

ᎠᏡᎦᎣᎢᏍᎣᏏᏯᎠᏤᏁᏆᎱᎦᏛᏬᏏᎶᎬᎷᎠᏲᎤᎲᎫᏯᏪᏈᎬᏂᏃᏋᎤ

Three days out of the debarkation station at Woodhall's Farm, Ella sits next to Ezra on the wagon's wakis chest.

Dideyohvsgi walks the oxen and approaches an established Cherokee homestead. They watch the fields approach at animal pull speed.

Around a mud block and tree log home, farmland supports cotton two foot high.

Six slaves hoe weeds, but they stop and stare as Ella's wagon passes. Four men work shirtless, and obvious whipping scars crisscross their backs. The women wear old dresses and pull long bags between the rows.

The workers look at the unusual clothes, transportation, and comparative prosperity of the passersby.

In contrast to the slaves, newer and better conditioned attire gleams from the wagon.

Ella wears a ribbon in her clean hair and a bonnet for sun protection.

Ezra sits beside her in his knee-high black leather boots and stiff brim hat, with a modern Colt 45 revolver strapped to his hip. Both wear Dideyohvsgi's eagle feathers.

One slave with a blind eye calls out. "There rides a free man!"

Ezra waves in acknowledgment. "Look at those poor people, Ella. They never had a master kind like your father. They're going to die of work and old age in that cotton field."

Their wagon passes and moves closer to the house. The oldest Waters shakes her head. "It's not right for any human to own another."

The attorney responds. "Slavery splits this country, North against South."

"And it divides my people." Ella lowers her eyes.

On the porch of the farmhouse, a prosperous Cherokee slave owner watches Ella's wagon approach. His wife joins her husband.

"Whoa, Lulu, Hetty." Dideyohvsgi halts the oxen near the portico.

"Welcome! We don't have many visitors." The Indian steps off his deck and observes the medicine man with his pouch of eagle feathers. "Stay awhile. I'll have a boy bring fresh water."

"A boy? No, please. We're eager to see our land." The eldest sister declines the offer.

"And where's that?" The farmer shades his eyes.

"By a creek in a valley, Allotment Parcel 318." The mature sibling expects a response. "Do you know it?"

The slave owner fixates on Ezra. "You got papers?"

"My free papers are in a safe at my law office in Tahlequah." The lawyer's voice hardens as his right hand rests on his Colt 45.

"You claim to be a lawyer?"

"No, I don't claim anything." The young man watches the Indian landowner. "I am one."

"Then I figure you understand what trespassing is. Get off my property."

"We'll move. Thank you for your offer of water." Ella waves Dideyohvsgi to continue. Instead, he steps toward the bigoted Cherokee with an eagle feather extended, but Ella's glare halts him mid-reach.

The Conestoga lurches into movement. As the wagon pulls away from the farmhouse, the family matriarch addresses her friend. "That pistol on your hip only solves issues army style."

"That scum wanted me in his cotton field." The attorney retorts angry.

"Your papers say you're free. Your education and wisdom keep you independent. The only thing that cannon can do is make you dead!" Benjamin's girl glares in return.

Both sit in silence. The young man speaks. "You are your father's. He was a young fighter. Older, he became a conscientious and ethical advocate for nonviolent change. I am sorry for the way I handled that. I learned plenty from your Paw, but I see I have more to learn from you."

The daughter leans forward and bumps Ezra's hat backward as she kisses her childhood friend on his forehead.

"Why don't I spell Dideyohvsgi with the oxen?" She smiles. "He's been walking in this heat for hours. That's why he tried to give that Cherokee bigot an eagle feather."

***

The midday sun beats the Conestoga's canvas, and medicine man sleeps against the side of the wagon's interior. His head bobs with each rut in the road, and he dreams that he rides his horse bareback on a buffalo hunt long ago.

Lisa plays marbles with stream polished rocks on the floor. Each marble carries meaning. The individual stones symbolize love and relationships found in her daydreams.

When the objects interact, the younger Waters reacts with a frown, or she squeals with joy.

A noise from the rear of the wagon attracts Lisa's attention. She peers into the dimness.

The youngest sister crawls toward the tailgate and bumps a large lump wrapped in a blanket. She notices movement and screams.

"What's the matter?" The shaman leaps to her side.

"That moved," the terrified sibling warns.

Dideyohvsgi pulls the cover. The blind eye slave from the farm that called out to Ezra stares with his good eye.

The medicine man flips the cloth concealment away as Ezra joins the inspection.

One eye, shirtless and shoeless, escaped from the cotton rows in a pair of dirty blue britches, the slave sweats.

"What are you doing in here?" Lisa's chin firms with anger.

"Watching Missy play marbles." His eyes project fear.

"How did you get in?" Ezra leans over the hideaway.

"I snuck in the tailgate. I heard you and the master. You are my vision of free."

"Got yourself a servant, Mr. Attorney." Dideyohvsgi points at Ezra.

The Conestoga lurches to a stop, and the four grasp what they can for stability.

"That's right, sir. Listen to the old guy." The stowaway struggles to sit as Ezra draws his Colt. "Don't shoot me, Brother!" The stowaway slave's one eye enlarges.

"Shooting's better than the whipping your master's going to give you." The lawyer waves his pistol.

"You don't want to take me back to that farm, freed man like you are. I'm a runner. He'll kill me as an example." The laborer clasps his hands together.

Big sister intercedes. "Put your pistol away."

"You should have thought of that before you ran, my friend." The attorney holsters his Colt.

"Please! Help me." The slave rubs his palms together like a prayer in motion. "In the name of Jesus."

"Wrong champion in this wagon." Dideyohvsgi grins.

"They won't miss me for days." The slave touches the medicine man's hand.

"We are not stopping to return anywhere. This wagon's been traveling for months, and we are awfully close." Ella looks out the rear of the wagon.

"Thank you!" One Eye blubbers and bows from his seat and touches the wagon's bed with his forehead.

"I didn't say we were taking you with us." Ella shakes her head negatively. "But I don't see options."

"I do. Leave him here." Dideyohvsgi points out the rear canvas opening.

"I will not abandon any human being to what's waiting for him. And he's not had supper." The oldest Waters relaxes. "Stay and eat. We shot a deer yesterday, so it's venison and corn pone."

***

Further along the road, as daylight ends, the wagon stops for the night, and the migrant group settles into camp. Older sibling unpacks cooking gear and watches One Eye gathers firewood. Ezra fills a black pot with water for coffee from the wagon's storage barrel.

"Ella, you realize that we are harboring a fugitive." The attorney warns his client.

"Maybe we protect a refugee." She glances at her friend.

"If your Cherokee council knew you hide a slave, an angry mob would attack this campsite." Ezra looks away. "And if White folks knew, this ground bleeds."

"Ezra. My father did not raise me to be over-influenced by ignorant opinions."

"That's true. Reminds me of something. Everybody at the courthouse in Tahlequah talks of this young lawyer and politician from Springfield, Illinois. His name's Lincoln, Abraham Lincoln. I understand he's just a few years older than I am." Ezra waits for a response.

"So?" Ella glances at his serious expression.

"Lincoln gave a speech in Springfield that made the newspapers. He spoke of the dangers of slavery, that the institution would corrupt the federal government. Lincoln warned that mobs of people who disrespect US laws and courts could destroy the Union of States."

"This Lincoln a White man?" Older sister peers at Ezra.

"Yes."

"I respect the rules and the law, but Illinois is far from us. Out here, you're the only lawyer within miles, and you don't make speeches, thank you." Ella peers into her childhood friend's face. "You think we should leave One Eye out here for a bounty catcher?"

Ezra watches the big laborer gather wood. "In the territory, under law, a Cherokee may own a slave. That's not only White rule, but Indian, reinforced by your tribe with the 1839 Act. You must return that man, as much as I disagree, to his rightful owner."

"Those same laws you speak of do not allow me to vote in tribal council or be a citizen of the Nation." Oldest sister pounds a fist into her palm. "My father was a freedman! His blood runs in my veins, same color as yours. I am not bound by White or Red man's law!"

"Afraid you are." The young attorney smiles. "Tell the soldiers you are not a member of the tribe and try to leave this territory. Then you'll become a target."

"All right, Mr. Attorney. What do I do with One Eye?" Ella slumps her shoulders.

"Take him with you. He works hard."

"What!"

"You heard me. There is legal and there's what works. Out here in the territory, what functions best? Judge Steel's not here." Ezra grins. "And you never asked me."

"If I ever need a lawyer, I hope he's you." Ella smiles back.

"And if I require one, my choice is that Abraham Lincoln fellow from Springfield."

"Someday, the best will be a woman." Ella nods.

The same night, the campfire beside their Conestoga wagon casts a flickering light orb around the campers. A partially eaten deer's hindquarter roasts on a spit above the fire. Tethered by a long rope, Lulu and Hetty graze outside the warmth.

One Eye finishes a piece of corn pone with a radiant smile across his face. "Miss Ella, you sure feed your slaves good."

"You may be a slave, but I do not own you. If I did, Ezra writes your free papers before we leave this camp."

"You going to turn me over to a slave catcher?" The big man's voice trembles.

"No. If they come, I'll hide you and do my best to protect you," the matriarch replies.

"Then in my mind, I am yours."

"Don't even consider it." Ezra interrupts.

"A victim accepts a condition because of no other choice." The oldest Waters lays her hand on One Eye's massive shoulder. His incredulous facial expression greets her touch.

The young lawyer looks at Ella. "Her father taught me that." He turns his attention back to the big man. "And don't call me mister. You are older than I. Ezra is fine."

"There is an additional thing." Dideyohvsgi holds an index finger beside his ear.

One Eye peers across the fire at the shaman as he rises and pads to the wagon. From his bundle, he extracts an eagle feather and returns. He steps to his fresh recruit and slips the symbol into the slave's hair.

"Wear that, even after a slave catcher finds you. It may be your only chance for true freedom." The experienced Indian pats the slave's hair.

Around the campfire, they stare into its flames in silence, with each person absorbed in his or her own thoughts until a nearby oxen grunts and shuffles away from movement and sound in the surrounding brush.

One Eye leaps to his feet and dives under the wagon. Ezra draws his Colt and faces the noise. Ella grabs Lisa, and together they crouch at Dideyohvsgi's side.

"Who's out there?" the young lawyer calls into the night. The foliage lies still and quiet. He cocks his weapon and steps forward. "Show yourself. I'm armed. If you value your life, speak now!"

"Be careful. I think it's a slave catcher." Ella peers at the brush.

The attorney ventures closer to the thicket, intent on any movement.

With a crash and flurry of sound, a doe breaks from hiding and clatters away.

Ezra expels air, and Dideyohvsgi explodes into laughter. "Bounty hunter? You're a deer slayer!"

"Wasn't funny, Shaman." The young lawyer sputters. "I could have shot myself!"

CHAPTER THIRTY-ONE — The Allotment

ᎠᏣᎦᎣᎢᏍᎪᎸᏯᎠᏤᏇᏓᎯᎦᏌᏴᏍᎦᎷᏕᎷ ᎠᏥᎦᎭᏳᎮᏃᎯᎡᏤᎾᎯᏂᏃᎤᏍ

The Boston Mountains in the territory display light-brown elevations as the sun scorches the Ozark highlands. Silty soils and reddish clay subsoils fade to hazy blue. Lulu and Hetty drag their wagon over mounds eroded through the eons from prehistoric and majestic palisades.

Ezra and Ella, with the oxen in front of the Conestoga, gaze across the hill into a valley. Dust blows with the south wind. Swirls dance amid rocky limestone outcrops that shelter stingy parcels of dry, infertile looking soil.

"This is it." The young man gazes over the landscape.

"Is it?" Ella holds the animals and surveys the location.

He points at a shallow creek that runs through a corner of the property. "Most allotments don't have fresh water."

"Not as green as the farm in Georgia." Ella rubs Hetty's ear.

"This is the territory. It'll be fine. I'll help get you settled," her friend replies.

Dideyohvsgi studies the land. "No Unetlanvhi lives here, too many rocks."

"This is no fun. Do we have to stay?" Lisa pokes her head out of the canvas top.

"These rocks won't grow cotton but maybe corn." One Eye bends and grasps a handful of gravel.

Ella turns to her sister and jabs hands on hips. "We didn't travel here for nothing, Lisa. It may be rocky, but they're our rocks!"

Younger sibling climbs from the Conestoga. "She's decided, Dideyohvsgi."

"Then we'll each need two eagle feathers."

The family leader clinches her jaw. "Let's get to work."

***

Three weeks later, the sun rises and warms a primitive house of fresh, earthen bricks stacked against hewn tree trunk beams.

The structure extends from a limestone outcrop. A sod chimney smokes from an internal fire. The residence rests near freshwater and a clump of hackberry trees.

The trickle of water drops from the top of an abutment through yards of small, bubbling mini-rapids past the timbers and over acres of land before disappearing as the valley curves.

Ella's two oxen graze in the shade of the hackberries, tethered on long lengths of rope, and chomp contentedly on three- to five-foot tall upright clumps of slender grass with blue-green shoots.

Dideyohvsgi steps out of the front opening of the sod home. He stretches both arms in the morning sun, then walks to water the animals.

Ezra's saddled horse munches growth near the oxen. It stands tied to a tree with a shorter rope.

The medicine man unties and leads the mount back to the dwelling. Ella and Ezra join him.

The young attorney straps a blanket wrap of supplies behind his saddle and turns to his friend. "I remember you did not want guns in the territory. That was then. You need this now." He extends his Colt 45 in a holster with an ammunition belt.

Benjamin's daughter frowns, her lips mouth no.

"These hills have bears and mountain lions." Dideyohvsgi waves at their surroundings as he looks at Ella.

She looks at One Eye. "And man hunters." The woman accepts the weapon. "Paw never visited the territory."

Ezra hugs Ella and waves to Lisa, who peeks out from the sod home's door. He shakes Dideyohvsgi's hand and takes his horse's reins. The attorney turns to the big laborer and extends a parting palm. "Remember you are never a slave. They are victims. Think as a free brother." The young lawyer nods.

"Yes, sir." An enormous, calloused, planting tool palm on the end of an arm engulfs the lawyer's grip.

"Not sir, just Ezra."

The massive human smiles, and the younger man mounts. He clicks the animal and trots away.

The oldest Waters daughter shades eyes from the morning sun and watches.

As Ezra tops the small incline out of the valley, he pauses and looks into the basin.

Ella waves, and the rider raises an arm, then disappears over the ridge.

***

Several weeks later, the older sister, on hands and knees, inspects a two-inch corn stalk in a neat row of hundreds of plants.

She pours water around the growth, then moves to the next spot of green.

The more agricultural craftsman, One Eye, works the rise beside her. Lisa stands nearby and watches.

"I'm so pleased you knew to soak the kernels overnight before planting. Look at these. They are wonderful," the Waters matriarch gushes.

"Shriveled seeds make poor eating corn." The big fellow pampers each plant.

"Without you, this farm could not be doing well." Oldest sister grasps the slave's shoulder. "I am thankful you chose our wagon to run away."

"Wasn't much other opportunity. A few visitors came. But you were the first with a free man that toted a pistol." One Eye laughs. "Figured you was an excellent choice."

"Our luck." Ella releases her grip.

"Time for lunch?" Lisa watches the other two.

"Get to work." Elder points at sister. "This corn's your food come winter."

"No! I can't live in this desert. I want to go back to Georgia."

"Grow up!"

"I am!"

"Then act that way."

"A happy life is a right!"

"Not if you're Cherokee!"

"Nothing to do with that! And I hate this dump." Lisa runs, cries, and slams a newly hewn hackberry front door.

One Eye watches the young woman flee. "Don't be so hard, Miss Ella. It's tough out here, and she's got no friends."

"She will be fine. The girl's tougher than she appears . . . and acts. You weren't with us on the trail from Georgia."

"No, but wish I had been, ma'am."

"I'm sure you feel that way." Older sibling looks at the fellow. "She and I are only half-Cherokee. That means little clan support. We're not completely welcome by Indians or Whites."

"Your daddy was a slave, right?" The big man peers at Ella.

"He was." Ella stands and adjusts her bonnet. "But a freedman, and there's not enough of them to champion anyone." She waters the next tiny corn stalk and glances at a far hill.

On its crest, two figures sit atop mules. In black clothes and wide-brimmed hats, both riders silhouette against the glare of the sun. The owner of the land watches as they ride on the incline into Ella's valley.

One Eye also watches the approach. "Spoke too soon."

Ella peers intently at the incoming horsemen. "Think they're slave catchers?"

"Could be," the massive laborer replies.

"Better hide in the house." Oldest sibling drops the water pot and runs with her friend.

Dideyohvsgi meets the two at the door.

"Get Ezra's pistol!" She waits and watches the threat approach.

The shaman returns with the modern Colt 45. Older Waters tucks the weapon into her apron and steps to meet the riders.

On mules, a man with a bushy beard that color-matches his dark clothing and a woman matching color but with a gray neck dust bandanna instead of facial hair carry no visible arms. Their flat-brimmed black hats and solemnity suggest menace and malice.

He dismounts.

Ella stands with the Colt. The visitor extends a small silver Liberty Dime. "I am Brother Jacob, and this is my wife, Sarah. I wish to buy water."

"The Unetlanvhi provides drink free." Ella advises. "Keep your coin."

"The water's not for thirst. She is sixteen and not baptized in the Mennonite faith. Your creek offers a holy opportunity."

Dideyohvsgi joins Ella. "Do Mennonites follow the White man's Christ?"

"Yes." The gentleman replies.

"Take his money." The shaman inspects the couple.

She accepts the dime. "Come, I'll walk you to the water."

"Thank you." The man nods and leads his mules with Sarah.

"Any news of the world?" Oldest sibling asks.

"Last month, Chief Bowles died at the battle of the Neches," the Mennonite begins.

"We've heard nothing." The woman listens.

"He fought with Sam Houston's sword." The visitor shakes his head in disbelief. "Mirabeau B. Lamar, Texas's new President, herded his Cherokee survivors together and sent them to the territory."

"Houston was a friend of our people." The Waters matriarch muses. "And Chief Bowles was an influential leader."

At the creek, the Mennonite's mules drink as he lifts his wife to the ground. "Sarah, today is the day. We renew life and confess faith as required by Christ to be a loyal follower of Him."

Ella glances upward. From a hackberry tree limb hangs Benjamin Waters' hand-carved water spider medallion, the same talisman Tesali ripped from Lisa's neck, recently suspended.

She grabs the strap and looks around, panicked. The woman abandons her pious visitors and runs to the house. In haste, she trips and drops the Colt. On hands and knees, she crawls to grab the firearm. Imagining the warrior is behind her, in fear, she grasps and points the pistol. A sound flips the point in a new direction.

The Waters eldest dashes for the cabin and flings open its door. Inside, Dideyohvsgi and Lisa stare. "Where's One Eye?" She trembles in dread and from exertion.

"Out back chopping wood." The medicine man stands with concern. "Those Mennonites make trouble?"

Ella spins and charges out, brandishing Ezra's Colt 45. She looks both ways and creeps to a stop at the house's corner. Panicked, she fights to control her breathing as she listens intently. The woman cocks the weapon with both thumbs. She cringes at the loud click, a fire-ready sound. The inept gunman steps around the building's edge with the Colt extended.

Nobody.

The oldest strains to un-cock the heavy gun as Dideyohvsgi joins her.

"One Eye's gone."

"Slave catcher?" The old fellow scans the area.

She shows the medallion to the shaman. "Yes. But not just any bounty hunter. Tesali's got him, and they're away by now."

"The warrior came silently in the night's wind."

"And left father's water spider as a thank you gift."

"More, I think, a victory totem." The medicine man shakes his shoulders and cautiously looks in different directions.

Nothing moves.

"They will whip a slave until he acts a victim." Ella walks and stares at the ground.

"Better than the whip that did our Bella." The old medicine man dawdles as his eyes search the hills.

"I failed them both, Dideyohvsgi."

"When you join our ancestors, ask them. I believe they won't agree." The wise Indian rubs his hands together with concern for Benjamin's daughter.

They round the corner of the sod house. The two Mennonites ride mules to the cabin door. Wife's dark clothes stain darker, wet from baptismal water.

"Thank you. We'll be returning to our place."

"Where's that, Brother Jacob?" Ella looks at her potential neighbor.

"Sarah and I have a homestead ten miles west. We're just hanging onto the land. The closest creek is here. We collect rainwater for the corn, but it's been a dry summer."

The leader of the Waters family digs in a pocket and hands the Mennonite's dime back to the man. "I don't want this silver. There's no cost to cleanse a soul in my creek."

CHAPTER THIRTY-TWO — Locusts

ᎠᏓᏔᏬᎣᎢᏍᎤᏝᏯᎠᎫᎬᎤᎢᏆᎯᎦᏚᎳᏫᏍᎥᏖᎻᎡᏍᎤᎣᏂᎲᎫᏯᎣᏖᎤᎡᏗᎭᏃᎦᎤᵛ

Six weeks after One Eye's abduction, Ella, Lisa, and Dideyohvsgi stand in their farm's corn patch and inspect ears. Elder Waters peals back the husks from a cob. Interior kernels display healthy yellow nobs. "What do you think?"

"Each stalk is a skin layer off my knee." Lisa examines a husk. "I'll never marry a farmer."

The medicine man chuckles. "Find you a young Cherokee shaman."

A grasshopper lands on Lisa's cheek, and she swats the insect. "Ugh! Nasty thing."

"We have a good crop." Ella surveys her production.

"Let's have a new corn ceremony." Her old friend claps his palms together.

"I wish we could, but there's no one to invite. But, better than that, we'll eat well this winter. How about an early supper tonight?"

With Ella between Dideyohvsgi and Lisa, the three link arms over shoulders and move to the house. "Think we have neighbors anywhere near other than the Mennonites?" The youngest wonders.

"I say we take the wagon and explore tomorrow," big sibling replies.

"Oh! Can we?"

"Bound to be somebody out there."

"A young man?" Lisa claps her hands. "And we could invite him to our new corn ceremony."

"Who knows, but we will go explore. Lulu and Hetty need the exercise." Ella's voice brims with anticipation. "Let's get out of this valley for a day or so."

"I'm so excited!" Younger jumps with enthusiasm.

"I think Paw wished us to have…" The Waters matriarch stalls in mid-sentence. "…look!"

The sky to the north looms with a great white cloud, blocking out the sun as vapor, as if a winter front threatens.

As they watch the ominous storm move into their valley, Rocky Mountain Locusts pop their faces.

Ella slaps an insect, and youngest rips her bonnet off and throws it to the ground. She attempts to dislodge insects from her hair.

Dideyohvsgi stomps another under his heel. "Get to the house!" oldest sister yells, and the three dash for sanctuary.

Inside, Ella slams the door as Lisa shutters the windows. The medicine man dances as he crushes grasshoppers. One window shutter sticks, and older sibling leaps to help force it closed. The barrier presses several insects into greasy smears on its interior sill.

The youngest chokes in disgust. "Dirty things!" Lisa shrinks from the stains.

Outside, the sod roof vibrates as gentle patter becomes a menacing roar, and moments later, continuous thunder.

"They're coming under the door!" young sibling screams. Big sister grabs a blanket and fills the space between the floor.

With the base blocked, grasshoppers pop their heads into the house from around the door's sides and top, and the youngest girl recoils in fear.

Outside, the patter on the roof crescendos to a snap-and-crackle clamor.

"More blankets!" Ella looks to her sister.

Lisa huddles in a corner of the cabin, shaking with repulsion.

Dideyohvsgi, with more rags and padding, dumps his load at the base of the front door. The old man works to stuff cloth into cracks in the door, window, and roof. A supper fire in the fireplace provides the only light in the house as the pounding outside crescendos.

Older Waters wraps her little sister in a blanket as the young girl trembles in her corner. She checks the shaman, who watches insects drop into the hot ash and coals at the chimney's floor.

Boiling water in a pot bubbles on the fire. Grasshoppers cook with a pop that sounds like raindrops.

The eldest woman leaps to help. "More firewood! They're coming in the chimney!"

Clamor through the cabin's walls grows as if a flock of giant turkey vultures pound the house for fresh meat.

The medicine man dumps more wood into the cooking space, and its flames roar. A blitz of falling cooked locusts adds to the staccato.

Sisters huddle together in their corner while the old fellow tends the chimney. Older hugs younger as both listen to the menace pounding their walls.

"Make it stop!" Lisa trembles in fear.

Oldest pulls her sister tighter, "They won't get in, I promise."

"They are in! Can't you see?" Younger blubbers her fear and frustration.

Big sibling holds sister's head against her chest and clamps her own hands over the woman's ears. "I lost our Bella. I refuse to let it happen to you."

Dideyohvsgi picks up a roasted grasshopper from the fireplace and eats it. "Crispy and sweet. Anybody want one?" The youngest sibling shudders as he reaches for another charred insect.

Like an absurd ambiguity, they cower in their corner, while across the space, the shaman sits and chomps grasshopper popcorn.

***

Next morning, with little sister in her arms, Ella wakens, cocks her head, and listens. Dideyohvsgi snores, the only sound in the cabin. She stands and tiptoes. One by one, she removes the rags and blankets that protect the front door.

Ella cracks an open space, and a stripe of soft light streams across the cabin's floor.

She peeks into the yard.

A gentle and peaceful landscape greets her, bathed by a sun that just tips the horizon. Grass and skeletal hackberry trees mimic Cherokee burial grounds.

The landowner looks to her cornfield, and it lays barren in rows of stubble.

Metal hoops of the Conestoga wagon's canopy supports remnants of its canvas top, and leather straps hang, chewed but not completely devoured by the locust swarm.

The Waters matriarch staggers outdoors, floored by the devastation.

She meanders in the crop.

The bonnet her sibling dropped lays at her feet, shredded and unrecognizable.

"Was that my hat?" Lisa points at the item as she and Dideyohvsgi join Ella in the field.

"Did you see the wagon's canopy?" The shaman hooks his thumb. "There's a spare in the wakis chest, but I didn't know grasshoppers ate canvas and leather."

A locust-devoured and broken corn crop, so promising the day before, now spreads around the three.

They walk together and survey what's left. The matriarch sits, drops her forehead into her hands, and cries.

Youngest touches her sister. "This may be tough, but we'll be fine."

"Why is life so hard for Cherokees, always?" The frustrated woman thumps her head in her hands. "And I've had enough! Without corn, we can't make it!"

The shaman surveys the property. "We have little choice. The soldiers won't allow us to leave." He salutes like a trooper.

"Then where's the good in Cherokee? This is the promised land. We have nowhere else to go." The landowner blubbers tears from swollen eyes.

"You forget too soon."

"What?"

Dideyohvsgi grasps his friend's shoulders. "You were the great mother who nursed Indian children and buried Cherokee dead."

"Because it was right. Where did it get me?" Ella looks at the medicine man and clenches her fists. "I quit! I resign from that pitiful race!"

"That's fine by me, Sister!" Lisa stomps a foot. "But remember, it's your mistake. You made us come here!"

"No, United States of America's soldiers did." Dideyohvsgi releases Ella.

"What will happen to us?" Lisa sobs into her hands.

The Waters matriarch struggles to stand in her ravaged field and looks at her devastated territorial homestead. "We do what our heritage tells us and what our tribe does."

The shaman peers at her. "And what is that, leader of our Cherokee clan?"

She glances back and forth between her sibling and her friend. "We're going to have a renewal ceremony, a New Corn Festival."

Lisa recoils from Ella as if she is crazy. Dideyohvsgi grins and nods his head with approval.

***

Days later, in the late summer of 1839, the hot, dry smell of territorial dust floats over Ella's allotment in the territory. A breeze ventilates the family's celebration of restoration. The farm bustles with an annual Cherokee ritual and thanksgiving.

Lisa Waters performs the purifying Ribbon Dance at her people's new corn ceremony. She circles a fire in the center of a four-crosswise log fire pit. Each timber aligns in a cardinal direction.

Two Mennonite guests, Jacob and Sarah, sit on stumps and watch.

Lisa waves colorful ribbons attached to the tips of sticks.

The banners float in the air in a primary color visual riot contrasted to the dry and colorless insect-eaten farm.

From the four corners of ceremonial fire, hickory branches extend above the women, the cloth strips, and the flames to join as a quad-pod tied by rope at the top. More bright ribbons hang grasshopper-devoured cobs and, in the breeze, they turn and sway much like the dancer.

Near the farm's log and sod cabin, in a buckskin shirt and skirt, the Mekko, Ella Waters, watches her sister dance. Her father's hand-carved stone water spider medallion hangs around her neck. The carving displays quality craftsmanship and detail far exceeding normal Cherokee crafts.

The daughter of Benjamin hosts from a hewn hickory log table. She points and beams a smile toward her sister.

Dideyohvsgi joins Lisa and surveys the cornpone and venison. "Nothing is coated in bear oil. Won't taste as good as a corn ceremony." The medicine man shakes his head.

"I have a small pot left. Sorry, I'm going to save it for Lisa's marriage." Older shrugs in apology.

"But your father's medallion looks good on you. And that buckskin. Worth the weight from Georgia?"

"It was." Eldest defends her sentimentality.

"Our guests aren't much fun." The shaman peers at the two Mennonites on their tree stumps.

"I am not being a suitable host." Ella lifts a plate of cornpone and venison. "Which I will remedy right now. Come with me and make conversation easier."

The woman and her assistant approach Jacob on his stump. "Welcome to our Corn Ceremony." She offers the crunchy bread.

"Thank you. This observance is different." The man stands and takes one sample.

"It is a renewal ceremony." The hostess waits for him to taste the food.

"Like when Sarah accepted Christ as an adult, and I baptized her?"

"Yes and no. More a triumph of the new year and home," the Mekko replies and then looks into her guest's eyes. "You appear not to be enjoying yourselves. Have we offended you or your religion?" She offers venison.

"You know our faith?" He accepts the meat.

"No. But we never intend to offend a guest."

"We believe in salvation through Jesus Christ, adult baptism, nonviolence, and oath avoidance." He munches venison. "And we want to express our appreciation to our hosts. Sarah?"

His wife stands and steps to the serving table where she lifts a pottery jar. She returns to her husband's side.

The husband takes his hostess's hands. "Please sit on my stump."

Ella sits, and the Mennonite drops to his knees before her. He reaches and slips off her moccasins. Husband looks to his helper, and she removes her gray apron and soaks it with water. She extends the cloth.

The man prays. With the damp washrag, the guest swabs and cleans Ella's dusty feet.

When finished, he nods and bows. "Thank you for the hospitality of your home. Sarah and I will walk back. You need not take us."

Ella slips her moccasins on her feet. "Praise you for sharing our renewal celebration."

"The plague of locusts destroyed your life. We were lucky and had no pests. So we share what we have with you if you hope to rebuild." The husband looks at his wife, and she smiles in agreement.

"That is most generous," the Waters matriarch responds. "The United States cares for us by treaty. They traded for our lands in Georgia. I expect their help. With respect, you have no obligation, and your sharing is too much to ask."

Jacob nods, crestfallen, and she notices. "If the government fails us and the need arises, we will accept your offer." The man smiles and takes his wife's hand. Together they walk away from Ella's farm.

The host family watches the couple go. "I wonder if they faced a genuine threat." Ella poses the question to herself. "Aren't they nonviolent?"

"I think so." Dideyohvsgi responds.

Lisa watches the guests leave. "Then they are hypocritical."

"You call a Mennonite a hypocrite?" big sister's eyebrows arch.

"That's not it. I meant ridiculous." Lisa pouts. "None of us are renewing. This territory offers little. How long can we stand this joke?"

CHAPTER THIRTY-THREE — Decisions

DRTₒᏫᏫᎥᏚᏫᎥᎩᎪᎫᎬⱷᎮᎪᎥᎱᏚᎳᏍᎱᏀᎷᎪᏍᏣᎥᎲᎫᎩᎾᏫᎾᏁᎻᏃᏂᎤᏫ

Weeks after the grasshoppers and their sparse Corn Ceremony, Ella sits against a hackberry tree trunk and chunks rocks into the creek.

Beside her, a charred stick lays next to a piece of stationery. The paper surface lays covered with charcoal-inscribed words. Elder sibling reads her composition.

She smiles, digs under her neckline, and removes a pouch of gold. She empties the contents into her hand. Two nuggets shine on her palm.

She writes a last sentence on her document, folds the sheet, and inserts it with the Dolomite.

The sun's highlights ripple from the creek across her eyes as her mind wanders to Georgia.

At her father's Corn Ceremony, over a year past, Ella's mother, Bella, and Lisa—along with the family's women guests—circle dance a bonfire in the center of four crosswise logs.

The eldest's memories focus on her Bella, on how she moves, smiles, laughs, and how her demeanor projects warmth and graciousness.

Her mind drifts from the corn celebration to the creek in the foothills of the Blue Ridge Mountains above her father's farm.

Ezra wades into the water with a sharpened stick poised. He searches the bubbles, spies a small fish, and hurls the spear. Her friend jumps to retrieve the cane without a prize on its point, and she laughs.

Laughter fades to somberness in the Dahlonega Court House as she probates her parents' will. She reaches out as Judge Steel takes her hand and escorts the young woman to chambers. The oldest Waters glances for the assurance that Ezra follows.

Lisa's call interrupts Ella's musings.

She twists around the base of a hackberry tree and looks at their sod farmhouse. Hetty and Lulu stand hitched to her loaded Conestoga beside the house.

Lisa motions to come and climbs into the rear of the wagon.

Dideyohvsgi waves as he clambers onto the wakis seat behind the team.

The Waters matriarch pats the pouch lump under her bodice, throws one more rock into the creek, and turns to join and lead her family.

She walks near the devastated corn field, and the rows that displayed such promise now appear as scars on a wilderness intent upon returning to the untamed. Weeds and natural grass spread among the dead stalk stubs but show dry and reddish tan color matching the rocky soil.

"Come! Let's go." Lisa calls from the wagon.

Older sister steps to the log and sod lean-to home and through its open front door. She gazes into the small, dark room. The fireplace lies abandoned, and a shaft of light from the single window spotlights a stripe on the empty floor.

A grasshopper jumps from the window's sill to the center of the spotlight and preens in victory.

With resignation, Ella steps out of the house and joins the departure.

She looks at their dream destination, paid for in sweat and blood and now in pathetic ruin, and her eyes cloud with another vision of home.

In her mind, Ella watches her father's farm burn, and she observes the smoke.

Eldest shakes her head clear, leaves the lean-to cabin, and returns to Lulu and Hetty. "Get up!" The wagon lurches into the trail up incline, away from Ella's promised land and her treaty with the White man.

As with so many agreements before, like leaves in the wind, words turn sour and become history.

***

Two days along the return route, around a substantial mud block and tree log home, farmland supports cotton fields lined with burlap-strapped bales. Six slaves load the product on a flatbed with wheels, but the laborers stop and stare as the Waters group passes. Four men work shirtless, and obvious whipping scars crisscross their backs. The women wear old dresses and carry a heavy roll of rough weave wrapping.

The pickers gaze at the unusual dusty clothes and defeated body language of the passersby.

In contrast to the slave women, the travelers' much newer and better conditioned dresses gleam.

The oxen's walker wears a ribbon in clean hair and a bonnet for sun protection. "Whoa!" Ella stops the team and steps to the side of the trail. "Does anyone know One Eye?"

The slaves stand silent and stare at the intruder.

"He was my friend." A man limps forward. The foot drag, from a severed Achilles tendon cut by his master because he ran, pains the old fellow, and he grimaces as he moves. "Slave catcher brought him back. Whipped him so bad that he died. We buried him under that Hickory up there."

The broken human points to a tree beside the trail at the crest of incline.

Oldest sibling locates the specific landmark, "Much obliged."

"The bounty hunter who captured One Eye was a Cherokee, one of your tribe." The crippled gentleman's attitude ripples disdain.

"Yes, sir. An Indian like your master and I." Ella accepts half-responsibility.

The remnants of a man stare and consider the woman's words. "And Amen."

The Waters matriarch commands the oxen and moves on up the incline atop the hill where they stop. Beside the trail, little evidence of a grave remains.

The soil shows minor disturbance other than a long rectangle of stubby recent growth surrounded by thicker grass.

At the top, a small slab of limestone lays. On its surface, a crude hand carving of an eye looks at the clouds.

Ella pats Hetty, walks to the memorial, and stands for a moment.

Dideyohvsgi joins his friend and pokes the quill end of an eagle feather under the rock. Lisa takes the old medicine man's arm and helps him regain his feet. They remember their friend.

A gentle breeze sweeps across the hilltop and stirs the grass of the gravesite as if One Eye sighs, finally relaxed from oppression.

Oldest sibling looks back at the slope to the slaves in the cotton field.

Six watch the group at the top of the ridge.

The old man with the crippled heel removes a battered hat and covers his shattered heart.

He bows a head, and the others follow.

***

Two days later, with her mind still on the old slave with the broken heart and body, Ella watches the Federal Depot at Woodhall Farm approach.

The oxen plod along and creep closer to the army-maintained debarkation point. The place bustles.

Several soldiers unload US Army supply wagons into one storehouse erected on the farm's property. They joke, jostle each other, and pay no attention to Ella's Conestoga.

A blacksmith works in the next shelter and watches Ella and Dideyohvsgi as the oxen stop before his shop. The muscular man meets the wagon.

"Need new cues." Ella points at Hetty's hooves.

"Both oxen's claws?"

"Yes."

"Taking a long trip?" The smith eyes his customer.

She pats Hetty's shoulder. "No. We wore these out getting here."

"Hear about the murders?" The fellow spreads current talk.

She shakes her head.

"Someone murdered Ridge Faction leaders at home."

"Which ones?" Dideyohvsgi, on the wakis chest, jerks his head to attention.

"John, Major, and Elias Boudinot."

Ella slaps trail dust off her bonnet. "Rich people. Bet the army caught the murderers."

"No." The blacksmith scratches his beard. "No suspects. Funny thing was the bodies had bear's claws hanging out of their mouths."

"Ugh!" Lisa, next to the medicine man, gags in disgust.

"Come on." Older takes little sister's elbow. "You're going to be fine."

The family leaves the oxen and the wagon and walks to check in at the official registration table near the storehouse. A sign on the building reads "Federal Rations."

Soldiers and Cherokee workers move items on its wide porch.

"I'm Ella Waters, allotment parcel 318."

One worker listens and responds. "We'll get your supplies but stack the stuff here. You got to load 'em, but where's your wagon?"

"We'll load up in the morning." Ella looks at the man.

A second Indian leans against a roof support and reads the *Phoenix* newspaper aloud, "A council of old settlers and latecomers to the territory met at Double Springs to compromise. John Brown, leader of the Nation West, argued with Ross and called him inflexible because he insisted he was Principal Leader. They blamed the Treaty Party, the Ridge, and Watie families."

The Waters matriarch listens, and then spits on the ground. "The tribe can't even live together."

The reader looks to see who pays attention. "Ross supporters hired a US Army Scout to enforce Cherokee law."

"No law's valid unless a White man says so." Dideyohvsgi steps near Ella.

The depot employee reading the paper looks at the pair. "We sure don't want to leave provisions on the deck tonight. Too many toughs in the territory. That's inviting theft."

"My Conestoga's at the blacksmith. Oxen are getting new clews."

"I know you, Miss Waters." The newspaper reader asserts, "Read a story about you in the paper. You're the famous Cherokee Rose. We'll deliver your supplies to the wagon at the blacksmith's."

Ella lies. "Something else, please. I have a ring from my mother that's gold. Know anyone here who buys?"

"Sure do, Miss Waters." The Indian responds. "Third tent past the blacksmith. White man named Willacy, but he'll try to take you. Don't let the crook beat you."

"Thanks for the warning." She looks toward the blacksmith's establishment. "What's gold selling for?"

"Read in the *Phoenix* twenty dollar an ounce, but that's two months old," the Cherokee on the porch replies.

"Much obliged. We've been out of touch at least that long."

The Waters three walk in the direction indicated, but Lisa spies a temporary space provisioned as a general store. "Ella, meet me in there." Older sister nods agreement, and younger investigates the temptations.

The matriarch and the shaman stroll on to the third canvas house. Tent flaps hang closed, and no signs or markers identify the place.

Ella slaps the flap. "Mr. Willacy? Anybody in there?"

The makeshift door opens from the inside and a cigar-smoking White speculator in flannel pants tucked into boots emerges without a shirt. Suspenders hold up britches, and a hairy tummy hangs over his beltline. "What do you want?"

"They say you buy gold. Is that right?" Ella steps back a pace.

"Got some?" The broker puffs smoke that floats in the air.

"A little that we will sell." She fans the drift.

"Come on in." Willacy holds an opening.

At one end, a cot with messy blankets serves as a bedroom, and near the flap door, a small table supports a scale. Behind, a stool sits where the stogie sucker plops. "What you got?"

Oldest Waters removes the pouch and empties the last gold nuggets from Georgia into her hand. Willacy's eyes expand double at the sight.

"These are from Dahlonega." Ella watches greed paint the man's face. "I want to sell them for fair value."

"They are. I worked those fields back in twenty-nine. Call me one of the first in that rush." Willacy pats his belly. "I'll pay ten dollars. Think I can move them for fifteen."

The Waters woman leans forward and plants her hands on the table, unimpressed. "I am not an ignorant seller and know the market price. Twenty an ounce is current."

"Maybe. But yours are a Dolomite mix."

"That's so. Starting point is weight," older sister suggests.

The broker nods and points to the scales on the table.

She places the nuggets in one hanging dish, and it drops to the table's surface.

"Well, let's see." The smoker puts a measure on the second measuring cup, and nothing moves. He tries a heavier and then another. The plate lifts, but the dealer adds smaller ones to balance. "A pound and a half?"

"May I see those?" The Waters matriarch requests.

Willacy hands Ella the weights, which she holds in one hand, estimating weight. Their values lay surface engraved. She calculates the sum.

"That's twenty-three ounces," the oldest sister states.

"I estimate 15 percent ore and the rest Dolomite." The smoker retrieves his property. "Figure about two and a half ounces. Buy them for fifty bucks."

Ella's tone and body language vibrates frustration. "We've sold this gold before. It's seventy-five, twenty-five. That's seventeen-and-a-quarter ounces, maybe more. Take three hundred forty-five dollars, not a penny less."

"Not in this tent! Three hundred. Best offer!" Willacy huffs. "And only because you're good with numbers!"

Ella picks up the goods and slips the two nuggets back in their pouch. She looks at Dideyohvsgi and jerks her head to the tent's flap door.

"You win! Three hundred forty-five, and never say I tried to take a dumb Injun. You don't qualify, lady!" The dealer puffs his stogie and removes a box from under a cot. He counts Ella's money.

The Waters matriarch removes the folded paper from the pouch and flips her gold bag to the man, and he catches it. She slips the stationary into her belt.

With cash, Ella and Dideyohvsgi join Lisa in the general store tent. The girl browses at a clothing table as her sibling steps close. "Look, the dresses are so different and lovely," the younger gushes.

A Cherokee woman clerk joins them. "The new silhouette is a nipped waist above the natural waistline." She holds a garment to her chest in demonstration. "Skirts end at the ankle, and these sleeves are wonderful." The salesperson spreads out the dress's sleeve. "This sample is a standard Gigot. See, full to the wrist." She picks up another dress. "And here, a Demi-Gigot, fitted from the elbow."

The younger sister sweeps up a third style. "And this one?" The arms on the fashion feature fullness, banded in intervals to a series of puffs.

"Those are the newest." The Cherokee clerk displays the garment as Dideyohvsgi eyes the older sibling and retreats to the outdoors. "This is 'a la giraffe' from France."

The Waters matriarch comments. "I need an inkwell and a quill pen. Do you sell parchment?"

"Always so practical." Younger sister observes.

"Yes I am, but today, pick you a dress." Ella smiles, and the other one jumps with excitement.

That night in the wagon by candlelight, the leader of the family transcribes the charcoal-written document composed under the Hickory tree by the creek in the territory into pen and ink. She copies the words on a fresh sheet of parchment.

Dideyohvsgi watches, and youngest sibling sleeps on a mat nearby. "Change frustrates. Do you believe what you write?" her old friend asks.

"Yes. Lisa is my responsibility, but you are not." The Waters matriarch frowns at her traveling companion. "You with me on this?"

"The soldiers will not tolerate your words," the medicine man muses. "Cherokee they dislike find quick graves."

"Ever since Georgia." Ella nods understanding.

"I talked to Unetlanvhi, and He/She is with us." The old fellow's tired eyes don't blink.

***

The next morning, Ella, Lisa, and Dideyohvsgi halt the wagon at the government's supply house. The Woodhall Farm's blacksmith stands on the porch. Older sister extends payment for the oxen's new clews. "May I use your hammer and one nail?"

The big blacksmith slips the tools from his vest and hands both to the woman.

She withdraws the parchment copied the night prior. With the manifesto, Benjamin Water's daughter climbs from the Conestoga. The half-Indian stalks to the door of the depot and nails the document at eye-level, direct center.

"That is what my Cherokee allotment was worth." Ella looks at the blacksmith and clambers up to the wakis seat.

Lisa scrambles out of the farm's general store tent with a new bonnet. She models for Dideyohvsgi, who stands with the oxen.

A rising sun in the east warms the leader's face as she points the shaman to lead the team forward.

The White man scratches his head as the wagon travels eastward. The stock clerk who quoted Ella the current price of gold emerges from the supply house, and the blacksmith glances at the fellow. "Ain't her allotment west of here?"

"Yep. They're heading in the wrong direction. You see she nailed something to the door?" The Indian newspaper reader steps to the manifesto and reads the document.

He turns and eyes the Conestoga as it pulls out of sight. "No. Cherokee Rose picked her direction. Unetlanvhi walks with her."

CHAPTER THIRTY-FOUR — Escape

ᎠᏡᏍᏬᎢᏍᏲᎭᏴᎠᎫᎬᏁᎯᏆᎭᎥᎶᏩᏚᎵᏥᎷᏇᎮᏠᎤᎯᎲᎶᎩᏣᏟᎿᎭᏁᏂᎭᏃᏊᎤ

Days from Woodhall's Farm, Ella leads her oxen southward with Dideyohvsgi. They struggle with Hetty and Lulu and search for a navigable path through thick woods. The bramble wildness east of Tahlequah demands attentive navigation. The team follows their wagon masters off trail, even when the leaders become disoriented.

"We should turn soon." Ella looks at the countryside ahead. "This rough country fights us. It's hard on the animals. This land's spirit devours the lost."

"We off course? Not a good thing out here. This territory hides bandits and ruffians," Dideyohvsgi scrutinizes the surrounding wilderness.

"And by now I'm afraid soldiers trail us." Ella looks behind the wagon.

"I doubt any follow. They won't miss deserters from that desolate corn farm."

"They could send a professional hunter." Her voice cracks with worry. "If Tesali tracks us, we have no chance."

"I'm sure we are the only ones aware we're missing." Dideyohvsgi chuckles and looks at his friend. "The Cherokee Rose and Stone Cloud's shaman are not important in this part of the territory."

"Unless the government knows we've jumped the allotment." Ella shrugs her speculation.

"If they learn, it counts as a revolution, not reservation jumping." The medicine man chops one hand on his palm. "They'll send General Winfield Scott himself with an army."

"Then let's keep this between you and me." Oldest sister touches a lip with a forefinger.

"Nobody will recognize we're gone until time to pick up our next ration at the depot." The shaman pats his friend's shoulder.

"That's a three-month head start." Ella clasps his hand. "We have enough money to buy steamboat passage on the Arkansas. Then on to the Mississippi. We can make Georgia before they check."

"If our luck holds." The shaman strokes the eagle feather in his hair. The oxen's leaders walk in silent thought for a moment. "Did you know Sequoyah lives a day or so from here?"

"Does he?" Ella's attitude perks at the great teacher's name.

"Spent time with him once, when he was teaching Cherokee children to write, in Dahlonega."

"The man's a legend. Father called him the source and soul of the seven clans. Mother worshipped him."

"He has a farm on Big Skin Bayou about five miles southeast of here," Dideyohvsgi spreads his hands wide and points. "We could rest at his place. He welcomes his tribe."

"I'm only half his, remember," Ella raises her eyebrows at the older man.

"Sequoya has vision," the shaman responds. "He sees tribes, clans, governments, and soldiers. The prophet in him believes they should live together in peace. I think he's delusional, but we'll be welcome, I'm sure."

"Good. I say look for a campsite for tonight." The Waters daughter reads the sun above the horizon.

The matron and her fellow travelers dry camp under the sky, and night descends. She lies awake on a mat beside the wagon and watches the stars. Lulu and Hetty, with front legs tethered, munch grass on a remuda.

"Kik, kik, kik!" breaks the night's silence. A prairie falcon hunts. Its high-pitched call resonates wild overhead. The bird's predatory flight sweeps the terrain. The aerial hunter scans for movement as it flies low and fast.

A surprised ground squirrel scrambles for a protecting den. Too slow for escape, its neck snaps in vicious talons.

Ella, on her back with her body under the wagon, watches the Big Dipper creep across the sky. Sleepy eyes hang heavy, and her thoughts drift into dreamland.

The night's spirit hunter, the prairie falcon, swoops from the moon and perches on Ella's shoulder. Pupils of the predatory hawk examine her heart. The bird finds it pure. "Why do you wander in my lands, Cherokee woman?"

"I am lost without direction." The oldest sister stares into the bird's gaze.

"For what do you search?" The falcon pecks a wing.

"A place to nest. Your earth is harsh. I cannot grow corn," the Indian grasps soil and filters the rocks through her fingers.

"Part of your clan wanders. She walks through the spirit land," the hawk observes. "I see her when I hunt."

"That is my sister Bella. You spoke to her?"

"Yes. We talk. She wonders if her old world exists. She speaks of you, of a third sister, of her mother and father. Your wanderer tells of how you left home to journey through this country."

"Does she hate me for causing her death?" Ella's dream fills with mists of dread.

"No. You did not take life. Another Indian did," the spirit bird stretches and flaps wide wings. The air movement fans the oldest sister's hair.

The falcon observes his audience's concern and attentiveness. "She loves and cares for you. Plus, you care for her little sister now that she cannot." The prairie falcon fluffs its feathers. "For the strength and courage that guides you, she thanks Unetlanvhi. She only wonders when it might end."

The Waters matriarch's voice softens, "On your next hunt, tell her I defy the president of the United States and flee his territory. More than anyone, she knows the punishment."

"I think I will not tell her." The falcon states, "She is happy and walks where travelers are white, red, or any color. If some are purple, no one cares."

"It pleases me to know she is peaceful."

"I do not wish to disturb your loved one." The bird stretches wings and springs upward for the tree's tops. From a high perch, the falcon looks at the Waters woman on the ground. "From here, you are no hue, and I do not care." The spirit soars from the lofty treetop and circles the moon.

Ella wakens, lifts a head from the mat, and peers around the dry camp. Nothing moves. Fireflies speckle the surrounding brush.

Reassured, the oldest sister lies back and watches a shooting star traverse the horizon. As the streak fades, she thinks, "There's Bella. She travels the sky where the falcon hunts prairie dogs."

***

The following day arrives.

Ella helps the others break camp, load, and push on through the wilderness. Mid-morning, as Dideyohvsgi leads the oxen, the wagon meets two Indians on foot. The pair surprises the travelers as they emerge from the surrounding brush.

Both men stand tall, over six feet, and wear buckskin breechcloths. Thigh-high deerskin boots protect their legs from the underbrush. With removed body hair, except on heads, they display total facial tattoos. With skulls that slope flat by tribal tradition adjusted in childhood, the Indians' physicality awe a half asleep, old medicine man.

The shaman reacts. "Whoa, Lulu! Ella! Visitors!"

"Chokma, chinchokma?" The visitor welcomes in his language.

Dideyohvsgi understands. "I am well. How are my Chickasaw brothers?"

The oldest sister sticks a head out of the Conestoga. She holds the Colt ready.

The Indian eyes the pistol.

The shaman turns and beckons for reduced threat. Weapon and its holder withdraw under the wagon's cover.

"Thank you. We hunt for meat. We caught rabbits. Seen any deer sign?"

"Nothing for several days." Dideyohvsgi shakes his head.

"Luck travels with you, then. Comanche, Kiowa, and Wichita war parties roam this land. Pawnee and Osage too. Texas Rangers from the south ride this far north to shoot and murder. Watch for them—all Indians are targets."

"You're not armed?" The old man eyes the visitors.

"Weeks ago, in the west, Kiowas stole our weapons and horses. We are the ones who escaped. Can you spare something to eat?"

"We have venison. I will trade jerky for information." Dideyohvsgi leads the hungry to the wagon's rear.

"Lisa, food for our guests, please," the medicine man calls.

"This is fine transport," the visitor observes. "The oxen follow your lead and pull well. They are prize animals."

The youngest sister leans out with a wrapped package, which she hands to the shaman.

The two Chickasaw men eye the young half-Cherokee.

Waters most adventuresome sibling glances at the pair, sees ages and flat foreheads, and ducks under the wagon's canvas concealment.

"I travel to the home of the great Sequoyah. I believe we are close?"

"Yes, turn south from this trail at a dead Bald Cypress on top of a hill. Then when you meet the bayou, go East. You will arrive by sunset." The Indian accepts the venison.

"Good hunting." The medicine man returns to the oxen and resumes travel.

When the Chickasaw pair walk west and the Conestoga distances, Dideyohvsgi, out of hearing range in the opposite direction, calls, "Ella. Sit on the wakis chest. Put the Colt in plain view."

A mile further along the trail, she sits with the revolver on her lap. As the wagon bumps, she watches the surroundings.

Off the path, concealed by trees, the Chickasaws wait, crouched among rocks.

Oldest grips her pistol.

The two do not move as she rolls past their concealment.

Well beyond the ambush, Dideyohvsgi turns to his armed escort and brandishes a clenched victory fist.

She waves thumbs up and returns to the wagon's interior comfort.

***

Midday, the shaman spots the dead cypress. He directs the team toward Big Skin Bayou.

That night, Ella's Conestoga wagon rests near Sequoyah's cabin. Hetty and Lulu, tied to a tree, graze.

The man's lodging of logs with a chimney on one end exhibits a front door and windows. Posts support a porch.

Sequoyah, the great Cherokee learned man who created the tribe's syllabary in 1820, sits beside his wife Sally at Ella's fire. He rocks in a chair brought from his house and smokes a long, thin-stemmed black pipe with a small bowl. He wears a frock coat with his head covered by a red turban trimmed in white lace.

"This morning, we met two Chickasaw in the brush." Dideyohvsgi mentions.

"They were far from their allotment," Sequoya observes. "But you were lucky. Comanche and Kiowa parties ride these brambles often."

"The hunters told me where to find you." The medicine man leans forward. "Are you not concerned with your safety out here?"

"No, my friend. I live on the bayou because of its isolation. We see few people, but guests are welcome, including Comanche."

"And you do not fear visitors?"

"No. Army soldiers patrol. Troops visit often. Because of my stature with the White man, others know to leave me alone." Sequoya winks at Ella. "Those most proficient in war guarantee my peace."

As the evening continues, the Waters party watches the campfire's flames and listens at the feet of a life hero. "It is tragic our people are so divided. Those who moved to the territory early fight those who, by force, came later. We divide over slave and free. I fear civil conflict, our clans against each other. A White man's dispute comes soon, I expect. They hold tremendous power to war and kill each other, and I predict they will."

"When we traveled through the state of Illinois . . ." the oldest Waters sister begins.

"Your journey lives in Cherokee lore." The wise man interrupts. "Ani-yun-wiya speak of 'Nunna daul Tsuny' forever."

"Hundreds died, thousands cried." Ella clasps her palms together. "And the government lied."

"My apologies for interrupting." Sequoya draws smoke from his pipe. "You were saying Illinois."

"Yes, people spoke of a lawyer named Lincoln who predicts a conflict. His speech at a social club denounced slavery." She enjoys that the learned Indian nods acknowledgment.

"I heard of this politician." The wise Cherokee muses. "In Washington they talk of him. I believe he may become a leader if a national battle comes." Sequoya exhales, and a cloud of tobacco smoke engulfs the camp's fire.

"War is sad. Today, I am here in safety. Tomorrow, we must continue to flee the territory. The White man's government promised land for our rich cotton fields in Georgia. That promise became rocks in the territory that will not grow corn." Ella looks at the wise man.

"A few give up. Many should. That I have no influence to stop." The wise one drags on his pipe. "I tried to unite our people in a peace conference only weeks ago. Tempers resulted. Good men died over issues not as important as yours."

"I believe the Treaty Party and the followers of John Ross are tools. Both have Indian hearts but dance to White music," Ella asserts.

"And I sense none of Unetlanvhi in the territory. Our Cherokee tribesmen lost course and are forced here, but we return to Georgia. Home is where the old ways can find us." Dideyohvsgi presses for endorsement. "You are the wisest in the clans, do you understand our plight?"

Sequoyah sucks a long draw from his pipe and exhales smoke that drifts toward the fire. "I do. The genuine people must grow corn."

Ella nods as she ducks his tobacco smoke.

Lisa sits politely but views the Indian father in the lace turban as a relic of history.

"I wish you well." The smoker blesses his visitor's actions and warns, "but the White man's soldiers will not approve. Stay invisible and blend with the dropouts from the deportation. Travel the water route out of Fort Smith. It is safer."

"Don't tell the troopers we came this way, please," Ella requests.

"They patrol but leave me alone, not because I created our writing but because I visited with their President." Sequoyah squints through tobacco smoke.

"Thank you." She nods respect for the great man.

"They believe their leader knows me." Sequoya chuckles with deep-seated pleasure. "In reality, their President sees me as I do, just another meddlesome Injun."

CHAPTER THIRTY-FIVE — Capture

ᎠᎡᏣᏫᎣᎢᏍᏯᎢᏴᏯᎫᎴᏫᏇᏗᏏᎦᏛᏝᎳᏍᎦᎻᎷᏇᎠᏦᎲᏝᏴᎠᏔᏪᏰᏏᎭᏃᏇᎧ

Weeks later, Ella walks her oxen into Phillips Landing on the Arkansas River near Fort Smith. A boat dock and large wood-yard feature two steamboats that load coal. Around their pier, goods stack high for shipment, and the place bustles with tradesmen, riverboat passengers, and crew. Muleskinners, slaves, gamblers, and others involved with passage and trade crowd the site.

Lisa sits in front on the wakis chest and relishes the exuberant spectacle. Several workers roll whiskey barrels up a ramp and stack the containers on top of an earlier layer.

A man in a wide-brimmed hat and ten-dollar suit parades alongside her wagon. With one hand, the gambler manipulates a deck of cards. His other tips his brim to the youngest Waters, and she beams pleasure with the attention.

Following the card shark, a drunk crumples against stacks of wooden barrels full of his favorite alcoholic drink. Unaware he is near his weakness, the sloppy stumbler collapses to his butt with his back against many years' supply of whiskey. He attempts to focus on the container's label, fails, and watches the Waters' oxen plod by.

A muleskinner in a deerskin jacket with arm fringes spies Ella's Conestoga wagon and her two powerful animals. The teamster eyes the group. The man falls in step with the eldest sister. "Hundred dollars cash for your rig!"

"Plus, fifty." Ella commands the oxen, "Whoa."

The potential buyer feels the team's muscles and examines the animals' teeth. "I'll offer that."

Ella looks from her oxen to Dideyohvsgi in the wagon.

He gestures palms up. "Lulu and Hetty can't swim to Georgia."

The Waters leader faces the muleskinner. "Federal cash?"

The fellow digs in his pocket. "You're a Cherokee, ain't you? You hear they arrested one of your tribe for the murder of those Ridge Party folks?"

"Hadn't heard. You got the money or not?"

"Sure, I do. Them's splendid animals. Here. Count it." The agreement seals. "The trial's going on right now in Fort Smith. Big to-do. They say an army scout named Tesali will hang for doing it."

Ella shivers at the name. "Politics! I am only part-Indian. I need passage for three to Georgia. Those steamboats at the dock take passengers?"

The new oxen owner turns and points at one steamboat on the landing. "That's the Arkansas Belle. She is bound for the upper Mississippi. You can get land transport from there to the Tennessee and further east."

"Much obliged, Mister, for the money and the information."

"See the Ticketmaster. His name is Bailey. He'll be near the boat."

Ella, Lisa, and Dideyohvsgi gather their meager belongings into burlap sacks from the wagon and abandon anything old and worn. Hauling luggage as if on the northern route trail, the three walk toward the passenger dock.

The group pauses and looks for a last time at their dependable wagon and trustworthy oxen. Their team stands, two massive pillars of strength and endurance. Enormous ox's eyes follow their trusted owners.

"George Sears left you for us, Lulu." Lisa's cheeks moisten with tears. "Blame him."

"We have little choice. Hetty, the family and those sick people you pulled say thank you." Ella waves as if the animals understand.

"Same for me. Downhill trails, Lulu. May your road be smooth." The medicine man turns toward the future as the Arkansas Belle whistles.

***

The steamboat's berth at Phillips Landing hums as the hub of the yard. Two loading ramps extend from the lower deck rail to its pier. Constant traffic flows on the incline. Freight, luggage, animals, and people percolate back and forth.

In a flat top straw hat with a band around its crown that reads "Arkansas Belle," ticket master Bailey hawks his product. "Tickets here! Six dollars each to the Mississippi."

Ella steps up to the sales table. "I need three."

The salesman tests the family. "Injuns got to stay in the Nigra section. Still same price."

The older sister nods okay and hands the man eighteen bills. With passage in hand, the group walks up the loading ramp of the Arkansas Belle. In awe of the boat's size and atmosphere, the youngest bubbles excitement. "Oh! This is wonderful!"

The riverboat features two stacks and a single rear paddle-wheel. A main deck supports cotton bales and whiskey barrels. Tucked among freight, a few small cabins give the non-White passenger classification a sleeping spot. A second level, more luxurious, accommodates Whites and social interaction.

Dideyohvsgi finds their space, an eight by eight-foot wooden-walled cubicle with a curtain door. Its entrance features cloth over an opening for privacy.

As the medicine man holds the drape open, young sister enters. "Look, fresh, white sheets!"

"How clean." Ella pats the sleeping surface. "Lisa, you take the bed."

The youngest stows her burlap bag under the sleep space. Dideyohvsgi settles against the wall and older sibling on the floor.

"With this excitement, I will not sit on this sheet the whole trip, no matter how clean it is," Adventuresome Waters announces, "This might be my only steamboat ride."

"Fine. Come on, let's explore." Ella stands.

"Think I'll take a nap." The medicine man lumps in his corner.

The sisters walk the lower deck as the steamboat's whistle screeches. Thick, coal-smelling puffs from the boat's stack and the clamor of chains and winches mark the loading ramp's removal. The paddle wheel churns, and the craft separates from the landing.

The boat lurches from reverse to forward as its engine forces entry into the Arkansas. Smoke billows over the sisters, then shifts with the wind. The Belle slices the water en route to its next stop while the oldest sister watches the wet, even roll of the current. Lisa eyes the same gambler in his wide-brimmed headgear and ten-dollar suit she noticed before the oxen sale.

The dandy tips his brim. "Good day, Miss. Fine weather on the river, don't you think?"

"Yes. It's so wonderful," the youngest sister gushes.

The man slips a deck of cards from his vest and fans them across the top of a whiskey barrel. "Pick a card."

Ella joins her sibling and eyes the trickster.

Lisa takes one card from the fan and holds it close.

Noticing Ella's suspicion, the gambler-turned-magician includes her in his performance. "Give it to your companion for safe keeping, please."

Lisa giggles and complies.

The magician collects the remaining cards.

"Now you're going to tell us what it is, right?" Young Waters claps her hands in delight.

"No, Miss, I can't do that. I'm not a miracle maker, just a riverboat gambler. You tell me what it is and then let me buy you a drink in the parlor."

The older sibling intrudes. "On the second deck?"

Youngest sputters, "Ella, you gave up drinking."

"This man knows they don't allow our kind up there." Ella glares.

"I know. I can bring the drinks here." The dandy smiles. "Your card is the Jack of Diamonds."

Lisa blushes and shows her sister the card.

"No, thank you." Ella stiffens, and her welcoming demeanor changes. "I believe your magic is as deceptive as your offer. Find a conquest with your own people."

Ella hands the lothario his playing card without further comment, but her eyes direct his exit. The two Waters women stand together as the ten-dollar suit walks away.

***

Onshore and far from Phillips Landing, Lulu and Hetty pull their first load of whiskey barrels from on the road to Fort Smith. Their new wagon master strolls, as their past ones did, to the left of Lulu's horns. The trained team follows as they should, and the muleskinner smiles with pleasure.

He watches horsemen approach. Three riders close, two soldiers and one civilian. As the groups meet, an Arkansas Deputy Marshal inspects Lulu and Hetty as he passes. Several yards beyond, the officer turns his mount and trots back to the oxen.

"Wagon master, where did you get these animals?" Hiram Colly inquires.

"Bought them in Phillips Landing," the muleskinner answers. "Why are you asking? Paid cash."

The lawman rides around the wagon and peers into its rear. The vehicle transports whiskey barrels. "I know this Conestoga and those oxen."

"I should have done a bill of sale!" The oxen's owner smashes his fist into his hand. "They're stolen, ain't they?"

"No. Don't worry. I believe you." The deputy waves his hand. "You bought them from three Cherokee, an old man with two women?"

"I did, but they said they were half. All Injuns look alike to me."

"They jumped their land in the territory, I suspect." Colly stands in his stirrups and gazes toward Phillips Landing.

"I can't tell the independent farmers from the wild ones." Lulu's owner chuckles. "Hauled buff hides on the 'Llano Estacado' years back. Comanches were the real Injuns."

"They say their destination?" The deputy settles onto his saddle.

"Yeah, said they were booking on the Arkansas Belle."

"Upriver?"

"To the Mississippi, but it's left the landing by now. The boat's next stop is Russellville." The muleskinner points.

"Thanks. I know those animals. You got good oxen." Colly turns his horse to rejoin his soldiers.

***

Two days later, Ella, Dideyohvsgi, and Lisa lean against the Arkansas Belle's rail as the river passes underneath into the next landing. The steamboat chugs into the first stop upriver from Phillips.

Its giant paddlewheel churns in reverse and kicks muddy water bubbles as it slows to dock at Russellville.

The steamship bumps as its loading ramp lowers, and the three travelers wave back to Indians, slaves, and roustabouts that greet their arrival. On the waiting dock, unseen by her party, Hiram Colly and two armed soldiers sit on horseback.

The oldest Waters hangs on the rail and rubs the water spider rock around her neck. She stares across the river.

"How come you never gave Papa's medallion back to me?" Lisa touches her lower lip.

"You outgrew it."

"Glad you're wearing it." The younger sibling straightens her spine. "I am grown up, and Paw protects you with it."

"So, I need protecting?" Ella looks at her sister. "When we left Georgia, I didn't think so. But when I tremble inside for whiskey these days, I believe I do."

"We've traveled a long way." Lisa puts her arm around her big sister. "We could not have done that without you."

Dideyohvsgi joins the family huddle and embraces both women. "Yes, you wear the water spider for your father. The little spirit belongs to the Mekko."

"Them's the ones, Marshal!" The Waters matriarch twists at the sound of a roustabout who points at her.

Hiram Colly brushes the crewman aside. "You are under arrest by the State of Arkansas for unlawful departure from Indian Territory."

"No!" Ella screams.

"Take them," the deputy orders.

Troopers tie rope around the family, under their armpits, and pull them, like leading dogs across the deck. Several bystanders do nothing as the soldiers drag the Indians. Nobody protests or cares except one.

The gambler in the ten-dollar suit stands at the base of the stairs and tips his hat to Lisa as she drags close to him.

He removes the playing cards from his vest and flips a face diamond toward the youngest sister. "Missy, yours was the Jack. Should have played when you had the chance."

Deputy Colly and his soldiers drag their prisoner cargo across the lower level of the Arkansas Belle.

They pass Ticketmaster Bailey, who descends the ramp to sell new passages. The steamboat ticket hawker shows lack of respect. "Sorry Injuns, no ticket refunds."

A roustabout with burlap bags reports to Hiram Colly and transfers the Waters' luggage. The deputy withdraws Ella's Colt 45 revolver from one bag and stuffs it into his own belt.

He dumps the rest of the contents onto the wharf, kicks the items overboard, and flips the sacks into the Arkansas river.

The prisoners watch their worldly possessions drift away on muddy water.

At the bottom of the loading ramp, Hiram Colly and the soldiers mount their horses and drag Ella, Lisa, and Dideyohvsgi—cattle roped and on foot—downriver.

The three struggle forward, and their minds and attitudes revert to their unaccustomed status as worthless deportees on the trail where women cried.

CHAPTER THIRTY-SIX — Habeas Corpus

DRTᏠᎣᎥꜱⱭᏏYAJEᏙᏔ₽ᎯᏆᏍᏔWᎦᏒGMᎯᏠᎣᏲᏅᏔZᏀᎣꮼ

A week after their arrest on the Arkansas Belle, Ella, Lisa, and Dideyohvsgi huddle together in a log building within the Fort Smith Internment Camp.

The group's cleanliness and mental acuity screams new arrival status.

Several older Cherokees pace around the room and sing ancient chants to spirits that no longer remember their names.

Lisa whispers, "What's the matter with these people?"

"They walk in the spirit world." Dideyohvsgi leans closer and slips a protective arm around the girl.

In one corner, a Cherokee woman with stringy hair and long nails prays to a cross made from two sticks.

Another middle-aged man lies against a wall and shakes.

"Excuse me, did Paul come visit?" Ella recognizes the prayer.

"Shh, Ella! What are you doing?" Lisa hisses.

The stringy-haired one halts her devotional. "Mary! You have returned! Last time, we prayed in the crazy wagon. I am so glad you are back. My Apostles came, but no Disciples."

"I'm sorry. I know you have been lonely." Oldest Waters pats the disturbed individual.

"Yes, but now you are here. You can tell me how you saw Christ's death and resurrection." The woman's face glows with anticipation and pleasure.

"Is wife-killer here?" the cautious elder sister inquires.

"What!" Lisa sputters. "Who?"

The stringy-haired woman points. "Over there."

Dideyohvsgi and Ella look in the woman's pointed direction.

Across the room, the drinker murderer from the crazy wagon keeps his seat but grins and waves acknowledgment.

"Who's that?" the medicine man whispers.

"He killed his wife and ate her gizzard." Ella scoots closer for comfort.

"People don't have gizzards." The shaman looks at his friend. "Just turkeys and other birds."

"Maybe he meant liver or something?" She shrugs her shoulders.

Lisa gags. "Stop! I'm going to vomit."

"Not in here!" Big sister objects.

"Smells as if these crazies already have." The younger wrinkles her nose.

The door to the log building opens, and Ezra stands for a moment as his eyes adjust to the dim interior light. In a wide-brimmed hat, he wears a store-bought butternut shirt and gray trousers that tuck into high-top black boots.

Lisa sucks in a breath and touches Ella's hand.

The lawyer scans the dimness and locates Ella. As he walks across the room, stringy hair has an epiphany. "Behold, the Son of God! Hallelujah!"

The Waters ex-slave shies away from the woman and drops to knees beside the family. "Are you all right? This place is awful."

"How did you know we were here?" Ella relaxes in relief.

"The judge's court roll listed your case." The young man takes his friend's hands.

"Jumping the reservation." The counselor's ex-owner tears. "They charged us, and we did!"

"And will do so again if they force us back!" Dideyohvsgi extends his hand to shake.

"I talked to Judge Steel." The young lawyer grips the medicine man's hand. "We are going to file a writ of habeas corpus."

"A what?" Lisa studies the attorney.

"Means to produce a body," Ezra responds.

"I would rather you smuggle in another Colt 45." The shaman shakes the attorney's hand.

"It's a legal order that demands a public official deliver jailed individuals to the court and show valid reasons for detention." The counselor notices the Waters younger sister as she stares at the young barrister with rapt attention.

Ella looks at her childhood friend in amazement. "Such a thing for a Cherokee?"

"This is the first filed in a federal jurisdiction for an Indian." He extends a forefinger. "Before a White jury."

"I thought I was a reformer." Oldest sibling chuckles. "At least I try the possible."

"Priority is to get you folks out of here. The paperwork will not be here until tomorrow. That means another night in this place." Ezra directs the last statement to Lisa.

The younger sister nods affirmative with stars sparkling in her eyes.

"Judge Steel reviewed the case and wants to push you earlier in the court's docket. Wants a trial soon. He believes principals are at stake here with national impact." The new attorney stares at his old friends and now clients.

"Do we have a choice?" Dideyohvsgi glances away. "White men usually offer no choices."

"Don't worry. The judge is on your side. He can't be too public with it and has to try the case." Ezra's demeanor assures his friends for a moment.

"A White court cannot be impartial." The older man shakes his head. "You were the boy who drank from Benjamin Waters' Passv pot . I remember. Now you support these rules!"

The young attorney bump fists the shaman's shoulder. "I was immature then, and boyhood died with my wife on that farm in Georgia. I have studied their principals with one of the greatest advocates for justice in our time. He advanced my knowledge, understanding, and standing in this world. The division between prejudice and principal, between inbred racism and outsourced injustice, I understand. That boy you knew is qualified to stand before any tribunal—White, Unetlanvhi, or the heavenly."

Ella and the medicine man sit and stare at their friend for a moment.

Lisa speaks first. "Ezra, we are proud to choose you as our representative."

The young attorney stands and towers over the three detainees, "Out of here tomorrow, I promise."

***

That night, few prisoners rest. Out of mind chatter, ailing groans, and illness reverberate and make the prisoner populace uncomfortable.

The stringy hair, long nail woman sees the Angel Gabriel descend through the fireplace. She prays to stay still until he invites her otherwise. With the handmade cross gripped until knuckles redden, she talks to the vision.

The Waters group curl together on the floor and try to sleep with confidence that freedom awaits the sunrise.

The sick old man murderer prowls the darkness. He mutters under his breath, "I'm hungry. Come, my delicate. I taste your vitality."

Ella hears the psychotic ramblings and wakens Dideyohvsgi. They both listen as the threat moves closer.

With a horrendous scream, stringy hair pounces and lands atop the old, ill murderer.

Screaming Bible verses of God's wrath, she stabs her cross into the man's eye.

The woman yells, "I am the apostle Paul!" With full weight, she drives the spike home. "Death to disbelievers!" Pacified, the woman collapses and settles into sleep.

Ella and Dideyohvsgi sit against the wall the remainder of the night and protect Lisa, who sleeps. They wait for dawn.

***

The following afternoon, after release from imprisonment, Ezra provides an opportunity to clean their bodies and minds in a Fort Smith boarding house.

Refreshed, the ex-prisoners wear fresh clothing and approach the courthouse.

"I'm apprehensive. Does Judge Steel remember us?" Ella walks with her attorney.

"He seldom forgets." Her friend opens the door into the building.

The older Waters sisters stops and surveys the wooden building. "Not as imposing as Dahlonega. Remember?"

Ezra smiles and waits. "School together, court together. Remember?"

She steps over the threshold.

The group moves to a stair to the second floor. Their legal representative knocks at an entrance.

He hears a voice and opens the door to Judge Bennett Steel's chambers. The room stands comfortable but not opulent like the office in Georgia.

The magistrate rises from the chair behind his desk. "Hello, Miss Waters. These must be your sister and traveling companion?"

"Yes, sir. Lisa and Dideyohvsgi." Ella nods a greeting.

"My pleasure." The older and wiser-appearing gentleman sweeps his black gown clad arm toward chairs in welcome. He inspects the medicine man. "My wife tells me of you. I am impressed with your qualifications and training as a respected shaman."

"Thank you, Judge Steel," the Indian responds.

"An accomplishment." The magistrate settles into an armchair as the others seat themselves.

Lisa moves a chair closer to and sits next to Ezra.

Dideyohvsgi leans forward for attention. "You remember we met in Georgia."

"Yes. At the time, I was not aware of your stature." The arbiter of law chuckles. "I was younger and not impressed with reputations beyond my own."

"Perceptions change with age." The medicine man settles into a chair. "Why did you come West? Life in Georgia was more comfortable, I expect."

"My wife's people were moved to the territory." The human in black robes changes his expression from greeting to introspection. "The real reason is I am no good with family. I isolate in work, focus, and concentrate on legal concepts. What better place for me? On this frontier, law is new. We examine its precepts in fresh ways."

The judge's audience stares, not empathizing with his eccentricity.

The magistrate reads the faces and changes the conversation. "And Miss Waters has changed the most. I remember a timid young woman brave enough to confront a bigoted clerk, and now I read of you in the newspapers."

"The trip from Georgia was challenging." Ella smiles.

"On the most devastating, racist separations in the history of this country, you not only survived but became your people's Cherokee Rose." The judge exudes admiration. His voice shifts from pride to suppression. "But now, oppression is why we meet again. So sad, in a way."

"And I lost a sister in addition to my parents." The oldest Waters sibling's eyes tear"We have a ruffian imprisoned that rumor says had something to do with your father's murder. No actual evidence. They convicted him in another matter."

"That's not why we are here, Judge Steel. I appreciate you removing us from that holding pen at the fort." Ella stiffens her back.

"A writ of habeas corpus, the first ever undertaken to free an Indian. This is an action I am most interested in pursuing. I should be the one to thank you." Bennett Steel clasps his hands together on his desk.

"Before I abandon those poor souls in your Fort Smith holding cell, there was a murder the night before we left. Their imprisonment is inhumane. Those prisoners act disturbed and dysfunctional. I protest those conditions!" The older Waters advocates for the downtrodden.

The judge leans back at the outburst. "You are the Cherokee Rose! I wish you were a prosecutor in my court. Ezra, she should have studied for the bar!"

"Don't sneer at those people's plight. Those poor souls suffer without legal protection!" The eldest's face flushes red, and Ella's body language confronts.

The magistrate changes tone. "I do not belittle. I promise we will investigate." The judge adjusts to business. "Your case is going to trial for escaping the territory without knowledge or permission from the government."

"That is an injustice, sir!" The oldest sibling grits her teeth.

"Please, I am on your side." Bennett Steel leans forward with hands clenched on his desk. "But abandonment of your allotment does not concern me beyond your personal inconvenience."

"Ella." Ezra uses a calm, comforting voice. "He is why you are not imprisoned."

"Then what is your interest here, Judge?" The oldest sister trembles.

The magistrate relaxes. "Your case allows the opportunity to explore questions of the law. What does intrigue me are several challenges. Is an Indian a 'person' who deserves justice of this country?"

"No. Neither is he a slave," she answers.

"May a Cherokee sue out a writ of habeas corpus in a federal court when confined for violation of the constitution or its laws?"

"You said no one has tried." The Waters daughter's voice becomes more indignant.

"Does the commander of the military department of the territory, General Winfield Scott, have custody under the laws of the United States if that detention violates the same?" The judge's eyebrows arch.

"I have been in his imprisonment!" Ella stands.

"Is there a rightful reason to remove by force individuals to allotments?"

"Only to watch more women cry!"

"Do you possess the right of expatriation and expectation to life, liberty, and pursuit of happiness as long as you obey the law?" The judge pounds a fist on the desk.

The entire room sits in silence.

Ella breaks the mood. "Do those questions release my sister, my friend, and I out from under the burden of the United States government?"

Steel leans forward. "I do not know, Miss Waters. That is why we go to trial."

CHAPTER THIRTY-SEVEN — Fort Smith

DRTᏠᎣⁱᏒᏉᏝYAJEᏁᏞᎯⱠᎬᏔᏛᏐᎬMᎯᏕᎣᏐHᎫYᎾᏎᎾᏗhZᎯᎣᵛ

Ella, Dideyohvsgi, Lisa, and Ezra stand in the court-house's entrance outside the door on its porch many brick steps from street level. "Aren't we prisoners?" the eldest sister asks. "Soldiers guard our boarding house."

"You are, but I instructed them to leave you in peace. Judge Steel placed you in my custody."

Lisa beams at the young attorney, "I enjoy your company better than the soldiers."

A commotion interrupts the conversation. Several dozen White tradesmen and laborers parade in the street before the courthouse. The workers shout and talk, but because of heavy northeastern accents, their speech is difficult to understand.

Dideyohvsgi yells to one tradesman. "What's the celebration?"

"Contract's expired!" A stumpy fellow with a huge beard and less accent pumps a fist in the air. "No more work on the fort. We're getting out of this steaming heat and going home!"

"Where's that?" The shaman calls back.

"Maine! Blessed Bangor, My Man!"

Ella looks to Ezra for more information.

"Tradesmen constructing a fortification at Bell's Point under a year's contract with the army. Their contract ended yesterday, and they just got paid, I expect. I heard most were going home."

"He called Dideyohvsgi 'My Man'." Ella turns her attention to the lawyer and points out the nomenclature. "Not Injun or something worse."

"I noticed. Not unusual. Nobody ever sees a slave that far north." Her escort watches the men parade.

"If we don't head for Georgia, the State of Maine would be fine." The shaman's voice ripples with pleasure.

***

Atop a bluff overlooking the Poteau and Arkansas rivers' conjunction, Fort Smith settlement stretches from the courthouse a few hundred yards as buildings on two sides of a main street that accommodate a thousand soldiers, civilians, Indians, and slaves.

An older stockade, constructed years earlier to control warfare between the Cherokee and the Osage, sits nearby. A new fortification rises adjacent to it. Protecting the territory from Indian uprisings and guarding against incursion from the east is its primary role. A secondary reason, which becomes more important, is to offer law and jurisprudence to the wild frontier. Along the street originating near the fort's half-constructed wall, most governmental activities center.

To Ella, Lisa, and their medicine man from a small farm in Georgia, the place thrives as an impressive urban center. Most structures work as saloons and rooming houses. A massive storage house stands at the opposite end, under construction, with several governmental and commercial buildings established between them.

Ella's group exits the courthouse steps and strolls on one side of the street. An imposing jail dominates the lane a block away. Beside it, an unusual, temporary gallows looms. The visitors walk a historic spot, fifty years before the town's more famous era under the tenure of the hanging judge, Isaac Charles Parker.

The local political power structure, comprised of slave-owners, display three whipping posts in the ground near the hangman's stand. A crowd mingles and churns around the hanging stand. Nearby, a medicine wagon hawks elixir, but no one pays attention.

As the four stroll, Dideyohvsgi stops another Indian. "What's going on there?"

The Choctaw looks at the shaman. "Where have you been? Great Tesali, Chief Army Scout and the murderer of John and Major Ridge plus Elias Boudinot, is right there in the lockup."

She looks at the jail and oldest Waters responds. "He is?"

"And he hangs day after tomorrow." The gossiper moves on along the lane.

Ella turns and stares. Several soldiers guard the building's entrance. A group of individuals sit or stand on the premises and wait. They watch the windows and the doors of the jail as if they expect imminent escape action.

"What are they watching?" Lisa questions.

"They convicted the scout for multiple murders. Treaty Party leaders. He jammed a bear claw into each victim's upper gum, some sort of a psychotic death marker." Ezra shudders. "When they found the victims, the newspaper said they looked bloated, like walruses with tusks."

"Oh, my!" Lisa fans her face.

"He didn't do that to our father." The oldest daughter watches the jail. "But I hope I can see him hang."

***

That evening, at supper in the boarding house, Dideyohvsgi and the two Waters sisters sit at their own table for four. "Ezra's not joining us?" Ella places a cloth napkin on her lap.

"Not tonight." Lisa smiles. "At dark, he's picking me up for a carriage ride."

"He is?" Older sister's voice expresses surprise.

"Yes. We are going to drive around the fort's construction, and then I thought moonlight air along the river sounded fun." The youngest speaks as if nothing is unusual.

"That is proper?" Ella stammers. "Dideyohvsgi?"

"Proper? Hmmm." The shaman responds. "Unetlanvhi tells me they may even take a swim."

"Hush! I am not the least bit hungry. Please excuse me. I must do my hair." Younger sashays away from the table.

Older watches her sibling ascend stairs to the boarding house's second floor. "Did you know of this, Dideyohvsgi?"

"Of what?" The medicine man pretends ignorance.

"Lisa and Ezra!"

"I knew. I am not blind. Neither are you, but you choose to ignore it." The shaman covers his eyes and peeks through his fingers for a reaction.

"He's married!"

"A widower. Over a year now."

"Lisa's too young!"

"She's sixteen."

"That's too inexperienced."

The two friends sit in silence and stare at each other as a slave of the boarding house's owner serves their supper. Ella watches the woman place bowls of stew with cornbread before them. The server returns to the kitchen. "We have to find other accommodations." The oldest Waters daughter leans over the table to her dinner companion.

"Why? This food tastes great." The shaman slurps the soup. "And my bed's fit for Stone Cloud. After our wagon, this place is wonderful."

"Don't be dense. I refuse slave service. That woman should eat with us." Ella points her fork at her friend.

"Judge Steel's court is paying for this." The old man glances at the utensil. "Be careful with that White man's hay pitcher! You might hurt somebody."

"I say we buy a wagon and a team." Older Waters lays her silverware beside her plate.

"They'll just bring us back again." The meal partner looks at his trail companion. "What's got you riled?"

She sputters, "I'm not upset!"

The eldest Waters sister sits and picks at her food. Her old friend watches. After a moment, the woman reaches across the table and grasps her friend's hand.

"I think I feel like a racist. I don't want Lisa and Ezra to be a pair." She squeezes his palm.

"You might be, Ella, but I know you well. If you are, you'll be heroic and reform yourself."

***

After dinner, in her boarding house room, the older sister stands beside her bedroom window on the second floor and watches pedestrian and wagon traffic.

Fort Smith, as the sun sets on the day, wakens from an afternoon snooze and steps into the evening. Men in the saloons stumble from drinking establishment to bordello. Workers lumber homeward or visit food servers, including the lower level of the Waters sibling's building.

As a carriage with large back wheels and smaller fronts stops below Ella's window, she moves away for concealment and releases her lace curtains. Concealed, she watches Ezra step from his ride, tie his team, and enter.

A few moments later, the dapper attorney in a suit and shiny black, knee-high boots guides Lisa and helps her into the passenger seat. As she shifts her weight and smooths her dress, her date unties the horses and climbs into the seat beside her.

The young man leans over and kisses the younger Waters sister on her lips, clicks the team's reins on their rumps, and pulls away. Ella switches sides of the window and watches the couple talk and smile as they move. She draws the window's heavier curtains together and erases her outside view.

Lisa's older sibling stands for a moment. She looks at her hands. The wrinkles of a forty-year-old and the callouses of a muleskinner show trail time and hundreds of oxen yoke changes.

The woman walks across her bedroom to a dresser with a mirror. She stares into the glass. A middle-age, half-Cherokee virgin with tired cheeks and thin lips stands before its reflective surface.

Tears fill Ella's eyes. "I'm not prejudiced, just jealous."

The oldest Waters daughter steps to the bedroom's closet and removes an Indian blanket from the sparse collection of her belongings. She swings the cover over her shoulders and leaves her room. In her wrap and obscured, the woman walks through the hall and descends the staircase into the eating establishment on the first floor.

Several customers, men, sit at the tables and have their evening meal. None notice an Indian as she walks along the wall, through the doors and onto the street of Fort Smith. Ella pulls her blanket close as she walks and defers to fellows, couples, and an occasional wagon.

Boisterous celebration shakes a building the older Waters ambles toward, and bright light from within spills upon the dirt lane. A sign with large red letters advertises the building's saloon identity. Staggering out its front entrance, a drunk reinforces the ad.

Ella the alcoholic steps to a window and peers through filthy glass.

Soldiers and Fort Smith citizens drink and carouse. A smaller, adjacent room with its own exterior door welcomes Indians and a few freedmen.

Ella watches a Cherokee woman stagger from one customer to another as she hustles drinks.

The Waters sister focuses on one bottle of whiskey abandoned at a table. The liquor beckons. Light twinkles off its lip, and its contents swirl an exotic, seductive dance that reflects the social intercourse within the room.

Ella shudders and steps away from the window. She continues, one foot before the other, past the gallows to the jail. Lit from inside, shafts of luminance fall outside, and Bella's sister finds a shadow to camouflage herself. She peers at the lockup.

Nothing moves around the building, and the daytime spectators no longer stand vigil. A sheriff or deputy strolls across one of the front lower floor's windows, but others stay dark.

The older Waters hides in the darkness and watches.

***

Hours later, the last non-saloon lights on the street blink out from within the jail, and the building sleeps.

Ella creeps through the shadows and avoids the light from saloons to her boarding house. She slips through the eating room where a slave mops the floor and up the stairs to her room. Inside, she drops her blanket into her closet and climbs into bed.

The clip-clop sound of hooves drift through her window. Big sister tiptoes to the curtains and watches Ezra offer his hand to Lisa as the younger sibling stands in the carriage. She steps to the ground and embraces the young attorney. They kiss.

After a moment, Ella pads across the floor to bed.

***

The next morning, after the sun floods Fort Smith with warmth, Ella, Dideyohvsgi, and a sleepy yawner sit at a downstairs table. They sip coffee with finished breakfast plates before them.

"How was your ride, Lisa?" The eldest smiles.

"Delightful," Younger covers the remnants of her momentary drowse. "We toured the old place, then drove along the river. The moonlight on the water reminded me of Georgia." Lisa beams as she describes her evening.

"I didn't hear you come in." Ella's instincts rise.

"We were quiet. No need to wake anyone." The younger taps her lips with a napkin and glances at her sister. "What did you do last night?"

"Nothing. Watched street life from my window until it got dark, then I went to bed." Older sibling, through the window, notices Ezra pull up in his carriage. "Slept well. I see your friend out there. Are you going for another ride?"

CHAPTER THIRTY-EIGHT — Court

DRTⱭO'ⁱSⱭⱣYAJEᏇꝚAⱧᎦⱭWⱭᎱGMꝚᏸⱰⱧꝚⱭYꝚⱰↄⱰⱧZꝚOᵘ

A week later, seats in a stuffed courtroom contain White men. Cherokees, along with slaves, freedmen, and soldiers of lower ranks crowd the windows.

A court clerk steps forward, looks at the bustling room, and announces the docket. "This sixteenth day of October 1839, Case No. 891, United States Circuit Court, Fort Smith, Arkansas - Ella Waters versus Hiram Colly and US Army General Winfield Scott is now in session."

The bailiff executes a militaristic about-face, strides to the bench, and hands his paper to Judge Bennett Steel.

Before the magistrate, to his left, Captain Jessup, the Fort Wool and detachment's military commanding officer for the debarkation, sits as prosecuting attorney.

To the judge's right. Ella, Lisa, and Dideyohvsgi sit with Ezra, their appointed public defender.

Her legal representative leans to the family leader's ear and whispers, "Remember in the territory with One Eye? You said if you ever needed a lawyer, he would be she?"

"I wish, but you'll do just fine." Ella pats her counsel's hand.

The presiding officer takes a moment. He surveys the packed courtroom. The magistrate clears his throat, sips water

383

from a glass before him, and begins. "During my twenty years on the bench, I have never heard or decided a case that appealed so strongly to my sympathy as the one now under consideration."

A murmur ripples through the audience and lands in a crowded press section. Reporters await the trial from far away newspapers, including the Richmond, Virginia Enquirer.

Steel waves one open hand showing Ella, Dideyohvsgi, and Lisa. "We have a few of the remnants of a once many and powerful race, now weak, insignificant, and despised."

He scans the Cherokee observers outside who peek through windows. "The representatives of this wasted people often come into our national tribunal and ask for justice and liberty to enable them to adopt our boasted civilization, and to pursue the arts of peace."

The man on the bench looks at Colly and Captain Jessup. "We have agents of one of the most powerful, enlightened, and Christianized nations of modern times."

Turning to the American flag near his shoulder, he continues, "This magnificent, if not magnanimous, govern-ment resists this application and is determined to send these people back to the territory, which to them is less desirable than imprisonment."

The magistrate looks at the crowd inside the room and the throng with noses to windows. "Law regulates liberty. Something more satisfactory and enduring than sympathy must base judicial action."

He turns at once to the twelve men of the jury. They are White, of differing ages, and of varying degrees of prosperity.

Steel addresses these individuals. "We examine this case and decide its outcome on the principles of law. Unless we discharge Ella Waters and her party under the constitution or laws of the United States, she must return to the custody of her arresting officer and Indian Territory, which she left without consent or permission."

The judge turns to Captain Jessup. "Call your first witness."

The prosecutor rises. "The government calls Hiram Colly."

Bathed and beard trimmed, with a new store-bought cotton shirt under a leather vest that never carried trail dust, the law enforcement officer stands and walks to the stand.

"State your name and occupation."

"Hiram Colly, Deputy Marshal."

"And the United States Army once employed you?"

"In Georgia, I was a militiaman and territorial guard. Following that, the government appointed me to serve as detachment manager during the Cherokee deportation. Upon completion of those duties, they hired me in Fort Smith as a peace officer."

"Then, as a civilian scout during the removal of Indians from Georgia to the territory, you were obeying orders from General Winfield Scott?"

"Yes. Then and now. These Cherokees fled a reservation without government permission. By standing order from him, my duty to Arkansas was to arrest these Injuns."

Captain Jessup glances at Judge Steel and returns to his table. He sits. "No further questions, your Honor."

"Your witness, Counselor." The magistrate addresses, Ezra who stands, and the crowd spies his skin color. A rumbling murmur passes outside and through the room. The newspaper section buzzes with excitement.

"Deputy Marshal Colly, the Cherokee woman next to me, have you ever seen her before you arrested the same for fleeing the territory's reservation?" Ezra looks to the witness.

"I have."

"Please tell the jury when and where that occurred?"

"As I stated, I served as manager of civilian and military guards, and this woman was a deportee. The detachment traveled last winter along the northern route from Georgia to the territory. I was aware of her several times."

"Did you control rations, blankets, camp sites, travel stipends, cemetery arrangements, tolls, and everything else about deportees during that trek?" Ella's lawyer approaches the stand.

"Yes."

"At the expense of the government?"

"They provided for the Injuns."

Ezra pauses and looks at the jury. "And you made no personal profit from these items?"

"I did not."

The attorney pivots and stares at the witness. "Were you not planning to buy a cotton plantation upon arrival in the territory?"

"No, I was not."

The lawyer changes his line of inquiry. "Are you aware the relators, upon arrest, had before withdrawn and severed their connection to the Cherokee tribe?"

"Once an Injun, always an Injun."

Ezra's voice steels. "Mr. Colly, this court does not care what your opinion is." The crowd in the courtroom ripples with anger and objection at the upstart attorney's tone. "We are only interested in what occurred. Did you profit from your responsibility?" Ezra presses.

"I did as the army ordered."

"Did you sell Indians rations, blankets, camp sites, travel stipends, cemetery arrangements, tolls, and everything else to deportees provided at no cost by the government?" the young defender thunders.

"Only when ordered to do so. Never for personal benefit!" The marshal slaps the box's rail.

"You were privy to costs?" Ezra follows.

"Yes, I mean, no. I knew some." Colly backtracks.

The defense spins to his table and picks up a sheet of paper. He scans the document as he rejoins the deputy. "A slab of salt pork lists at thirteen cents. What was your price?"

The marshal squirms. "Best I can recall, between three-bits and one dollar."

"To me, that's extraordinary profit." Ezra stares at the witness.

"I . . . I don't consider it large. There are transportation and distribution costs, and they wrapped each slab in burlap." Colly coughs into his hand. "I did not set the cost."

"Did that include sales of rations and supplies to citizens?" The defense moves closer to the stand.

Colly's tone fakes annoyance. "The army did not sell to civilians!"

"Not what I asked. Did you?"

"No!"

Ezra stands for a moment and eyes the law enforcement officer. The young attorney steps to his table and scans paperwork. From there, he poses his next question. "As a member of the Georgia militia, did you profit from supplies intended for detainee use sold to any of the civilian populace?"

Captain Jessup leaps to his feet. "Don't answer that, Deputy Colly! Judge, the courageous soldiers from that great state are not on trial in this matter."

"Sustained." Bennett Steel yawns. "Please proceed."

"No further questions, your honor. I ask the right to recall this witness." The defense addresses the bench.

"Objection!" Captain Jessup interjects a second time.

The judge hand signals both the attorneys to gather before him. He whispers, "Gentlemen, in this trial we can consider only the facts of our question that occurred under US Army or the federal government supervision. Fort Wool through imprisonment here is the span. Don't waste my energy with extraneous incidents. Do we understand?"

"Even if events show moral character and inclinations of the participants?" Ezra questions at a whisper.

"If we tried the quality and inclination of every person involved with this pitiful display of human depravity, we will die of old age. I am sure the prosecution would call Andrew Jackson and Martin Van Buren, and you would subpoena Sequoyah and Chief John Ross. Move this along," the federal magistrate directs.

The judge excuses the witness as the attorneys return to their tables.

Ella leans to her friend and legal representative. "How can he do that? Colly's a liar. He was the prime offender!"

"But he's not on trial. You are. Now please, keep silent and let me do my job." The young lawyer stares at Lisa.

The younger Waters daughter smiles and nods encouragement.

Captain Steel looks over the rail into the court audience. "The prosecution calls Emily Brooks."

A Cherokee woman enters from the rear of the courtroom with the court's bailiff and walks forward in the aisle.

At the defense table, Ezra leans to Ella and whispers, "Is that the woman? Remember, from the list I gave you?"

"I am not sure. It was dark. I barley heard her voice." The defendant covers her mouth as she eyes the new witness.

The summoned walks to the stand, and the bailiff issues the oath for truthfulness.

Captain Jessup begins. "Please state your name for the court."

"Emily Brooks."

"Speak louder. We want to hear." The prosecutor puts a hand to ear. "Last winter, were you one of the Cherokee tribal members deported by the US Army on the northern route?"

"I was."

"During that deportation, did you come in contact with Ella Waters?"

"Yes."

"Point to the individual in this room you knew, if she is present," the prosecution requests, and the witness points at Ella. "How did you meet this woman?"

"They incarcerated her with me. They confined us in the crazy wagon, and she escaped. I asked her to take me with her. She refused, and the man who was helping her locked me in."

Emily Brooks stares at the Waters elder with resentment in her eyes.

"Was this place for army prisoner transport? Why were you there?" Captain Jessup poses two questions.

"It was. They imprisoned me for stealing a blanket."

"And why was she, do you know?"

"No. I do not. She was drunk on arrival and had a bottle of whiskey with her and buddied up with a man who had murdered his wife. Also tried to get friendly with a crazy lady who talked to disciples and apostles at night."

"Did you witness her escape?" Captain Steel attempts to focus the woman's testimony.

"Yes, she spoke to someone. She promised gold if he helped her. The man returned and opened the rear of the wagon. He only let her out. I looked at him. He was a slave, but I did not know his name. Loaded her into a wheelbarrow under a pile of hay, and that was the last time I saw either of them." The woman relaxes in the witness chair and glances at Judge Steel.

Captain Jessup concludes, "Confined by the army and the government, Ella Waters escaped from detention without approval or knowledge of military authorities or release by any official act. Is that what you saw?"

"Yes, sir. It was."

The prosecutor nods and returns to his seat. Ezra rises and approaches the witness.

"What were the conditions of this 'crazy' or 'prisoner' wagon, Mrs. Brooks?" the defense begins.

The woman withdraws within herself away from her questioner. "Terrible. Most inside were out of their minds, delirious. We were starving. They fed prisoners scraps from the troops every couple of days. No regular water. We drank snow melt off the top of the wagon."

"And they confined you for stealing a blanket?" Ezra nods his head in sympathy.

"Yes."

"Is it possible they imprisoned Ella Waters for an offense as serious as yours?"

"Others in there did terrible things. I know she stunk of whiskey. You could smell it over the prisoners' stench," the woman answers.

"I am sorry you experienced these horrors, Mrs. Brooks, but I have one last question." Ezra looks at the jury.

"You wanted to go with her, you testified. That implies conditions were such that if they had not restrained you, you would have joined Ella Waters' escape from army detention that night?"

A mummer ripples through the courtroom.

The witness sits straight in her chair. "Anyone in their right mind would escape if they could."

CHAPTER THIRTY-NINE — Water Beetle

DRTᏐᎤᎢᏍᎠᎥᎩᎠᎫᎬᎤᏩᏆᎯᏋᎾᏔᎤᏞᎬᎷᎷᎠᏲᎣᏲᎰᎶᎩᎥᎾᎦᎡᏁᎰᎳᏃᏆᎣ

After midday break, Ella and her party watch the jury file into the room and settle into box seats. Several jurors appear winded and red-faced.

The bailiff stomps the floor. "All rise, the honorable Bennett Steel."

Judge Steel settles into his seat between the American and State of Arkansas flags. The magistrate breathes deeply. "It is unfortunate that society is so polarized on opposite sides of slavery, bigotry, race, and even social intercourse that impartial citizens in a trial face reaction and potential violence."

The magistrate clears his voice. "There was an incident during break, suppressed by authorities of this court, that forced me to sequester the jury for peace of mind and safety. I applaud these twelve individuals for courage and intent to continue. I am not declaring a mistrial, and we, as these men lead, continue our quest for justice and sanity. Proceed, gentlemen."

Jessup rises. "The prosecution calls the Cherokee shaman, Dideyohvsgi Waters."

The old fellow steps from the defense table to the witness stand and settles into a chair.

"Please state your name and occupation, sir,"

"Dideyohvsgi Waters, spiritual advisor."

"And your relationship to the defendant?" The captain looks at Ella.

"Friend, companion traveler, tribal clan, and dream translator." The shaman nods.

"Your last names are the same?" The prosecutor attempts clarification.

"Yes. When the army registered me into the territory, a form had blanks for two labels, so they borrowed my friend's second name." The old man claps his hands at the nonsense.

"You are not blood-related but only cooperative escapees?" Jessup's tone reverberates implication.

"Our entire tribe shares the life in our veins. The little water beetle made the world and the first brother and sister," the shaman preaches. "When you say escapee, don't you mean liberated?"

The prosecutor turns to Judge Steel. "This gentleman offers important testimony. He is aggressive and defensive. May I consider the witness hostile?"

"Yes," the magistrate replies.

Dideyohvsgi glances to Ella, Lisa, and Ezra at the defense table. "They hang hostiles, don't they?"

"Mr. Waters, please control the sarcasm. I won't convict over comments, but I might throw this case out of court." Steel's voice implies he enjoyed the humor. "Proceed, Captain."

"Were you deported by order of General Winfield Scott from Georgia to the territory?"

"I was."

"And assigned a land allotment according to treaty, purpose to farm?"

"Yes, along with my companions."

"Are they members of the Cherokee tribe?"

"Yes."

"Did you abandon those lands without notice or approval of the army or the government and flee that property?"

"We did."

"Your witness, Counselor."

Ezra walks from the defense table to the stand. "Are you full-blooded, Mr. Waters?"

"Yes."

"Are you aware that the others are only half?" The young attorney points at the defense table.

"Their mother was a genuine person, and their father was a freedman."

The defense nods understanding. "So not obligated to migrate to the territory?"

"When the militia did the round-up in Georgia, no one cared."

Ezra rubs his chin as if in thought. "Those were militia from the state. Was this "no care" also true after transfer into army custody?"

"It was. The reason for removal was not lineage but land appropriation." The medicine man's voice rises with indignation.

The room erupts with conversation and protest as Captain Jessup jumps to his feet. "Objection! The last part of that must strike!"

Judge Steel pounds a gavel for order. “Sustained.”

“They are as much Cherokee as I!” The old man slams his fist on the stand’s rail.

Ezra questions, “Did you, sir, sever your connection to the tribe?”

“No, they severed me.”

“You practice religion. How can you disconnect?”

“When the Captain was talking of escaping, I explained that the Earth is an island surrounded by seawater that hangs from the sky by chords. He created it, Doyunisi (ᏙᏯᎤᏂᏏ do-hyi-u-ni-si,) when the little water beetle descended from the cloud realm.”

“Water beetle?” Ezra steps away from the witness.

“It dove to the bottom and brought up soft mud. This expanded and became where we live.”

“Cherokee are Christian, correct?” The defense attorney attempts to bring the testimony into the present.

“Yes. They believe the Christ’s father created the heavens and the earth in seven days. White men battled each other for the best land, so the Son settled it by dying on a cross. They herd Indians off their property ever since he died.”

“When did you sever your connection?”

“When the people forgot the old ways. In times as warm as today, I always wear the loincloth.”

“So, let me understand.” Ezra steps closer to the jury. “You are Cherokee but denounce tribal concepts. You consider yourself different, independent of the group led by Chief John Ross. You are not Christian, and no matter how the army qualifies, the beliefs you hold are not those of your peers.”

"True. But I try to bring society back to the real." The old man beams proudly and strokes the eagle feather in his hair.

"You know your companions are half-Cherokee and not true candidates for government subsidized residence, is that right?" The defense attorney separates the defendants from the tribe.

"My companions may do as they please." Dideyohvsgi refuses to cooperate, and his representative shrugs frustration toward Ella and the family.

"That's enough." Judge Steel interrupts.

Captain Jessup stands, "The prosecution requests re-direct with this witness when the court reconvenes."

"Approved. May I see both of you attorneys in chambers?"

***

Later, Ezra and the prosecutor sit across a desk from the court's magistrate. The younger lawyer fidgets as the older calmly watches Bennett Steel read the court's record. After a few moments, the judge addresses the two. "I am not pleased with progress. In the morning, we focus on the issues at question."

"Please clarify, your honor." Captain Jessup leans forward.

"Yes, you try these poor Indians for jumping the reservation. I do not care if they are guilty or not. I only want justice served. More important, larger questions complicate simple guilt or innocence."

"I care, sir!" Ella's friend and Lisa's new love confronts his mentor.

"Then divert that old medicine man's ramble! We are not trying water bugs here! This case defines Indian rights, military, and government use of power and the Constitution of the United States! Do both of you understand?"

Captain Jessup sits for a moment and nods yes. The captain's younger colleague nurses his ego over the rebuke.

***

Later the same afternoon, the sun approaches the horizon, and shadows cast long over Fort Smith. Dressed in ceremonial buckskins from her Corn Ceremony in the territory, Ella steps into the front office of the town's jail. She carries a basket of venison, corn, beans, squash, and pumpkin slices.

The only person in the reception room, a middle-aged, White constable, leans back in a chair and stares at the oldest Waters. "Injuns ain't allowed in here unless they're prisoners."

"I wish to visit Tesali."

"Not today."

"He hangs tomorrow."

"You heard me, Injun."

She removes money from a skirt pocket and puts it on the constable's desk.

The guard stands and opens a window's curtain. After a quick survey of the outside of the jail, the officer takes a key ring from a peg nearby. As the official moves past the cash, he discreetly sweeps the bribe into a hand and steps to a locked door. The man turns the lock.

"Wait. What's in there."

The woman in buckskin finery extends the basket and lifts the cloth napkin that protects its content from flies.

"Uggg! Injun food. You bought yourself ten minutes." The jailer opens the entrance to the interior of the building, and daylight from the front office windows floods the room.

A sweaty prisoner in the first cell covers his eyes and curls away as if sunlight is a rare occurrence.

Ella smothers her mouth and nose with her bonnet against the stench.

A hallway leads ahead between the bars of cells. Each set of bars imprisons an occupant, most unidentifiable in the windowless dimness.

A small window illuminates the far enclosure, and Tesali sits cross-legged on the floor next to a wooden pail in a rectangle of light. He looks upward, and the beam sparkles off his bear claw neckwear. In a traditional loincloth and leggings with moccasins and a leather vest, the warrior confronts imprisonment as a Cherokee, not an army scout.

Ella stops, bends, withdraws its covering, and sets her basket on the floor.

The constable draws a pistol, unlocks the iron gate, and with a boot, pushes the food into the confined space. He closes and relocks the security. "Eight minutes, and keep a distance." The man slips the weapon into its holster, rechecks the prisoner, and saunters to the jail office. He pauses and stares into the dimness.

Tesali does not move. He only looks up at the window. Ella sits on her heels several feet from the cell's bars.

After the Constable disappears, the Indian turns a head to the items in the basket. Unimpressed, the man's eyes return to the light.

"In honor of a famous warrior, the meal is coated with bear oil." Ella whispers.

They stare at each other.

"You are Cherokee Rose, the owner of the spirit's medicine wagon."

"And you are the great Tesali, Chief Scout of General Winfield Scott."

"Who the army hangs tomorrow."

Ella nods affirmation.

She and the murderer sit quietly and study each other.

He reaches into the basket and selects a strip of bear-oiled venison. Under the meat, Benjamin Waters' water spider lies tied to a leather strap. The Cherokee looks at the medallion for a long moment. "That spirit brought fire to the people."

"It belonged to my father, a gift from my mother, which you returned when you captured my slave." The oldest sister's voice holds strong and true, but subdued.

"They paid me well for that. His owner took the slave's last eye for running." Tesali does not offer an apology, he clarifies.

"Was the pay worth the man's vision?" Ella's vocal tone questions.

The man-catcher jerks physically, but his aggression remains blocked by iron bars. "No. The next night, I cut the owner's throat and carved out his eyeballs."

"Did you leave a bear claw in his mouth?"

The murderer does not reply for a moment. "The mark tells true men the corpse is not human. It is an animal." The army scout lifts the water spider, glances at Ella, and drops it around his neck. He returns to the spot in dim light and chews venison. "The beetle brought fire in a basket to earth, but you bring proper food."

"Do you remember Benjamin Waters?"

"Yes."

"And my sister, the woman you bull-whipped to death at Fort Dahlonega?"

"You and she were his daughters."

The Great Scout and the Cherokee Rose study each other.

"How did you get that scar?" Ella leans forward.

"The mark is not on my face, it is on my heart." Tesali rubs the spider medallion around his neck. "When I was a boy, soldiers came and raped my mother. I hid in the cotton. For pleasure, they skinned my sister and slit my father's belly. They dragged him to death behind a horse by his intestines."

Tesali stares at Ella. She gazes back silently.

"I killed one soldier. Another slashed my face with a saber. They left me for dead."

A shaft of light sweeps through the dimness as the office's door opens, and the constable's silhouette breaks the luminance.

"Time's up."

CHAPTER FORTY — Identity

ᎠᎡᎢᎣᎤᎥᎦᎧᎨᎩᎪᎫᎬᎭᎮᎯᎰᎱᎲᎳᎴᎵᎶᎷᎸᎹᎺᎻᎼᎽᎾᎿᏀᏁᏂᏃᏄᏅ

As court reconvenes the following morning, more interested and concerned observers crowd the windows. Most of the Fort Smith populace gathers around the courthouse. Several appointed translators and reporters surround the building and pass the events to their audience.

Inside, the bailiff calls Dideyohvsgi, and he returns to the stand for redirect by the prosecution.

Captain Jessup begins. “I remind you, sir, that you are still under oath. They released you from imprisonment in Fort Smith by writ of habeas corpus. Who or what held you in custody?”

“The fort’s army guards. Deputy Marshal Colly arrested me,” the medicine man responds.

“Both are federal officers. If we can entitle an Indian to a writ, the law requires we must restrain them of liberty and violate a provision of their treaty.”

“They restrained us.” The shaman looks to Ella for support. She smiles and nods an affirmative.

“Signed by your tribal representatives on March the third, eighteen hundred and thirty-six at New Echota, your tribe agreed to move to the territory and live on those lands. Your arrest for violating that agreement was lawful.”

"My family and I did not agree to or sign that document." Dideyohvsgi's voice ripples protest.

"The habeas corpus act describes applicants eligible as persons, or parties, not as citizens." The prosecutor looks at the witness.

The shaman responds, "Was that a question?"

"No. Established custom in Arkansas does not recognize a Cherokee as a person with full rights under the law. You are subhuman, more than a slave, but below the humanity of a White. Do you understand that is the reason an Indian has never sued a writ of habeas corpus?"

Dideyohvsgi shifts in the witness chair. "I have been told that is true."

"Then we should return you to lawful confinement?"

"That is out of our control." The medicine man glares at his uniformed army opposition.

"Are water spiders and beetles?" Captain Jessup smiles. When the Indian nods his head in the affirmative, the government turns to the defense. "Your witness."

Ezra accepts. "Nathanial Webster, the authority on word meaning, describes a person as, I quote, 'a living soul; a self-conscious being, a moral agent, a man, woman, or child, an individual.' This includes even an Indian. Do you agree, Mr. Waters?"

"Webster must have been a Cherokee." Dideyohvsgi claps his hands and enjoys his humor. He squares his shoulders, reaches to his belt and withdraws an eagle feather. The rebellious Indian slides the symbol into his hair.

"In defining generic terms, the Revised Statutes declares that the word person includes partnerships and corporations."

The young attorney glances at Lisa before he focuses on the stand. "We intend the comprehensive language used to apply to humankind, as well the more favored race. Do you agree, sir?"

"Yes," the medicine man concludes.

The crowd within the room erupts with dissent. When the words ripple outside, human emotion rises.

Judge Steel bangs his gavel for order and pounds until the clamor subsides.

"Without harming our vocabulary, or the spirit or letter of the law, are Indians, and our defendants, persons?"

The medicine man's voice rings above rising noise. "Yes!"

The young lawyer takes a breath. "This first instance on record where we let an Indian sue out a writ of habeas corpus in a federal court must be without jurisdiction in the premises. This is a non sequitur. Don't you believe it is time?"

"No greater than decades ago." Dideyohvsgi disagrees, but nods understanding of the young man's point of view.

"Arkansas has experienced much bloodshed in Indian wars. Mr. Waters, maybe the Indians think it wiser and better to resort to the peaceful march of law than to undertake the hopeless task of redressing alleged wrongs by force of arms."

The old man nods yes. "Only young men bleed without thinking."

"The sad experience of others has taught Indians the folly and madness of the sword. They can see serious resistance is a signal for utter extermination. Mr. Waters, have you not chosen the wise approach by resorting to the very tribunal erected by those you claim have wronged and oppressed?"

"Still unlikely to redress our grievances." The medicine man leans back in his chair.

"We will wait for a verdict. This is not the Cherokee choice, but the only one into which they can go for deliverance." The young lawyer steps to the jury box. "We cannot say, Mr. Waters, that because no Indian ever before invoked the aid of this writ in a federal court, the rightful jurisdiction to issue it does not exist."

"Power and authority do not cease. Many generations passed who never sought its use!" the medicine man nods his head.

"Every person who comes within our purview, whether he be European, Asiatic, African, White, or 'Native,' must obey the laws of the United States. Don't you agree, Mr. Waters?"

"In theory, yes, but in actual life, that's not the rule." The shaman's tone questions his attorney's motivation.

"When an individual commits a crime, we do not inquire where the accused was born, nor to what sovereign or government his allegiance is due, nor to what race he belongs." Ezra looks at the jury. The defense attorney poses his question. "Guilt and innocence only form the subjects of inquiry. Don't you think a sad commentary on the justice and impartiality of our laws is to hold that Indians, though natives of our own country, cannot test the validity of an alleged illegal imprisonment?"

Dideyohvsgi considers the dispute for a moment. "I cannot doubt every person restrained of liberty has the right to the writ of habeas corpus."

Ezra turns to the bench. "No more questions of this witness, your honor."

Captain Jessup stands. "The prosecution calls Lisa Waters."

She and the shaman, as they cross paths to and from the stand, clench hands in unity.

The youngest sibling sits in the chair, and the prosecutor approaches. "Please state your name and your relationship to the other defendants."

"Lisa Waters, sister to Ella Waters and family friend to Dideyohvsgi Waters."

"And your age?" The army captain's voice softens.

"Sixteen, sir."

"I will question you concerning adult matters. You have sworn to speak truth. Do these proceedings intimidate you or fill you with fear?"

"Yes," she responds and glances at her older sister. The younger stiffens and her testimony continues strong. "I am young. We walked from Georgia to Arkansas. That is more than anyone my age you know has done." A ripple of approval sweeps across the courtroom.

"I'll question you on the rights of government to arrest and hold you for return to the territory." The prosecutor advances.

"I am not vain enough to explain the state's power," Lisa answers. "But I shall try from my standpoint."

"You lived upon your own land in Georgia. Are you aware your tribal leaders ceded claims to those lands to the Secretary of the Interior for $5 million?" The prosecutor begins.

"Yes. I read of it in the *Phoenix*."

"You and your family relocated to Indian Territory." Captain Jessup rubs his chin. "Out of three thousand eighty-one Indians with you, eight hundred fifty-nine died within a year, and a major proportion of the others were sick and disabled."

"You don't have to tell me, sir," she replies. "I was there."

"So was I, young lady." The captain regains control. "Death and illness caused by drought that fall and the harshest winter on record."

"It was freezing." Younger sibling shivers, recalling the ice and snow.

"You settled with your family on an allotment in the territory?" The prosecutor returns to and sits at his desk.

"We did. And grew corn, but the land was rocky, and grasshoppers ate our crop." Lisa looks at her sister for reinforcement. "We returned to our old home."

"Did any of your household, to your knowledge, inform a government agent of their ultimate purpose to leave, never to return?" The prosecutor leans back.

"My sister might have."

"Might have?" The captain thumps his chair to the floor for emphasis. "Your family planned to sever their connection with the Cherokee and resolved to cut loose from the public's care, to go to work, become self-sustaining, and adopt the habits and customs of a higher civilization. That required legal notice!"

"If Indian tribes are separate, dependent nations, any woman can pull out!" Lisa loses her temper, "Your country revolted! You withdrew from England. And I am only half-Cherokee."

"For a sixteen-year-old, you have strong opinions." Captain Jessup points at his witness.

"I think anyone possesses the God-given right to resign a group and forever live away from it, as though it no longer exists!" The youngest sister looks around the room for approval. The audience stares without empathy.

"The law protects the individual and the tribe while in the territory. For that reason, desertion is unlawful. Did you and your family disregard that code?"

"Yes! Because there was none!" She crosses her arms in contempt.

Captain Jessup turns to the defense's table. "Your witness."

Ezra approaches the stand, and Lisa's entire body language and voice changes to cooperation.

"Miss Waters, when someone violates a rule formed for the peace and welfare of the Cherokee, should the government use necessary force to enforce it?" The defense begins.

"Like having Deputy Colly arrest us?" The young woman looks up at the lawyer with her eyelids flickering.

"That's what I mean."

"I guess, but he was rude doing it," she pouts.

The trial continues, and later, Ella sits in the witness chair as Captain Jessup paces before her. Judge Steel commands the bench, and Ezra and Dideyohvsgi listen to the proceedings.

"The relators are individual persons of the Cherokee tribe who have fled from a reservation in Indian Territory." Jessup begins.

The defense stands. "Can we expect a question?"

"Sustained."

"Are you, Ella Waters, by birth and by deportation from the State of Georgia, a member of the Cherokee Nation?"

"I am, by the cruelest extended means, and born of a freedman and his full-blooded wife."

"And did you flee Indian Territory?"

"I was returning home."

"Without government permission? Or the Secretary of the Interior's, the army's?"

"By approval of Doyunisi, the water beetle who made this land."

"It gave you permission to leave the reservation?"

"Yes."

"Your witness, Counselor."

Ezra rises, looks at the seated Dideyohvsgi for a moment, then begins. "Are you, Ella Waters, well known among your tribe as Cherokee Rose, keeper of the Unetlanvhi medicine wagon?"

"They call me that."

"We define a person as a living soul; a self-conscious being and a moral agent; a functioning human man, woman, or child of humanity. This is comprehensive enough, Miss Waters, to even include you?"

"I am those things."

"The statutes of the United States declare that the word person includes partnerships and corporations. Do you believe this applies to humankind as well the more favored White race?"

"That is my opinion."

"Are you aware this case is the first instance in which they have permitted an Indian to sue out and support a writ of habeas corpus in a federal court?"

"Yes, and that does not surprise me."

"When we charge a person with a crime, we do not inquire in what country the accused was born, to what sovereign or government the person's allegiance is due, nor to what culture he belongs. Why do we question you? Because you are an Indian?"

"Yes, but more. Because you view me as a woman. A female of a distinct but different race."

"Have you repudiated your membership in your Cherokee clan?"

"Resembling the water beetle, the White man with his power and by force and intimidation has created a new tribe. I have no affiliation with either."

"Does the individual own the God-given right to withdraw from his clan and forever live away from it, as though it had no further existence?"

"Yes."

Ezra lifts a document from his table and presents one piece of paper to Ella.

"Do you recognize this?"

"I do."

"When did you last see it?"

"When I nailed it to the door at Woodhall's Farm, our detachment's relocation headquarters."

"Please read the item to the court."

Captain Jessup leaps to his feet. "I object. It is not original. We are not even sure that this woman wrote it."

"Your honor, Thomas Jefferson penned these thoughts." Ezra looks at his mentor on the bench.

"Jefferson's concepts are basic to the law that I swear us to enforce and protect. Please, Miss Waters, read," Judge Steel concludes.

The witness holds her manifesto and reads the words, "We, Ella Waters, Lisa Waters, and Dideyohvsgi Waters, declare our independence from the Cherokee nation. We hold this action to be self-evident, that it creates everyone equal, that our Creator endows us with rights, such as life, liberty and pursuing happiness. When governments, nations, or tribes become destructive of these ends, our right is to sever our ties and find our own future security."

Ezra turns to and looks at Judge Steel. "Your Honor, I rest our case."

Bennett clears his throat. "Thank you. The jury will retire for deliberations, stay sequestered, and we reconvene to hear your verdict Monday."

CHAPTER FORTY-ONE — Visitors

ᎠᏕᎢᏃᏅᎢᏍᏲᏈᏯᎠᏎᎥᎮᏛᎯᎦᏉᏪᏛᎵᏕᎹᎱᏼᎣᎯᎲᎫᏯᎾᏛᎾᏂᎻᏃᏅᵛ

The night following the evidence phase of the trial, the matriarch of the Waters clan lies in her boarding house bed and frets, unable to sleep. She tosses from her back to her other side. The woman's mind slips between dreams and reality.

A younger Ella walks in the hills of Georgia as early fog drifts. Grass and foliage drip dew. A frog croaks in the meadow. In the distance, a rooster crows to encourage morning. The girl's thoughts recall her mother as she hangs wet wash on a clothesline, and her ears enjoy the pop sound as one of her damp dresses catches the wind.

In her mind, she walks to Presbyterian school. She waves at Ezra, who trudges along behind her and motions for him to catch her. As her friend joins her, a carriage pulled by a matched team clatters to the front of the building before her.

A slave coachman jumps from the reins to open a door. At the sight of the servant, Ella grabs her friend's arm and halts his progress.

Emily Ross, a plantation owner's daughter in a frilly blue dress and with blond curls, does not thank or even notice the man. She steps to the ground, sees the Waters girl with Ezra, and waves.

"Wow! Look at that hair," Benjamin's young servant comments.

"Can you imagine riding in that?" His friend points.

Both approach the building as the Ross driver returns from opening the gate for his Emily. "You going to school or just walking your master's daughter?"

"Sixth grade," Ella's escort replies.

"They let you go?"

"Yes, Benjamin Waters requires it," he responds.

"My mama taught me. I can read parts of the Bible. She made me learn at night." The slave climbs upon the carriage's driver's seat. "Waters a White man?"

"No. A freedman."

The servant flicks a rope with a knot on its end across the flanks of his team, and they move. "That's why," he calls back.

The oldest daughter and her companion enter the school-house. Emily Ross waits in the foyer.

"What do you think of my new dress, Ella?" The girl spins in place, and her blue store-bought garment with puffy shoulders fans around her.

The Waters' eldest stands in a plain cotton homespun made by her mother, with her schoolbooks cradled in her arms. "It's fabulous."

"Thank you. You are so sweet. Have your boy take your notebooks and touch this cloth. Linen."

"I'm no boy, and she can hold her own things," Ezra's voice responds.

Ross slaps Ezra with the back of her hand. "Don't get uppity with me! Ella, tell your man to do as he's told."

The eldest Waters daughter squirms in her homespun dress. "Now wait, my family doesn't command people."

"Expect not! Since you are a half-slave!" The White girl spins away, opens the main door, and disappears.

"Rude little viper!" The older sibling spits her words between her teeth.

"I liked the way she walked, but she has no interest in a young fellow below her station. That's obvious." Ezra chuckles.

"But not fair. Our skin's dark. But her heart's blacker." The school-girl's mind drifts back to the fog in the hills of Georgia.

The eldest daughter of Benjamin Waters shivers in the dampness. She hurries her pace. Menacing dream shadows, derivative humans, follow. The girl flushes red with fear and runs from her dreams.

Dark and dreaded apparitions chase. She grasps her skirt with both hands and pulls her hem to her knees to run faster. The somber shapes close.

Ella slips and falls. She rolls into a ravine, picks herself to her feet, and scrambles into a grove of trees. Gasping for breath, she hides behind one immense trunk, and from that concealment, peeks and checks on her pursuers.

They leap from tree to tree ever closer.

In panic, the young half-Cherokee girl abandons her hideaway and dashes for low-hanging fog over a decline. Penetrating the cloud, her vision dims to a gray mist.

Tree trunks stand around her as fence posts. Not protective, the foliage presses, resembling an enclosure stockade. Ella stumbles, falls to her knees, and feels her way through the smog.

Behind her, the stalkers chase.

The young girl screams in fear, and panic flees.

Glow blossoms in the vapor before her, an opening flower.

Light calms the escapee, and she investigates her hunters. Hazards she fears stand frozen and cower from the illumination. The radiance blooms and becomes individual life forms as the older sister creeps forward. They drift in a comforting slide in step with music that soothes Ella's ears and soul.

"Are you the Nunne'hi?" The Cherokee half of the Waters child questions at low volume, not to disturb the song.

"Yes, we are the immortals." Their brilliance coalesces into individual men and women, even children. "We dance and sing to warm the fog. Why do your shadows chase you?"

"They are from my life. I am not permanent and only visit the mists." Ella drops to her knees in awe of the spirit people. "The sinister ones want to capture me."

A child steps forward. "If they catch you?"

"They arraign me before their peers." Waters shakes her head with doubt. "I am found wanting before I testify."

"Then they know you?" a woman apparition questions.

"Yes. They build gallows in their homeland where a noose waits. I run from its reach for my life." The older sister breathes in gasps.

"You dream as an Indian." A ghostly warrior floats forward. "But our tribe does not flee threats."

"I retreat from my inner self." The matriarch of the Waters family bows her head. "Because I journey into darkness with those that stalk."

One glowing grandmother Nunne'hi steps closer. "Child, they trouble you. This we know. As you walk the highlands of the Cherokee Nation, have no fear. We can help you."

Ella looks behind her, and the dark threats lurk. "You are the spirit people, the ones unseen. How can you defeat the darkness?"

The matron spreads her arms, and her white buckskin robe sparkles; its sleeves' fringes shimmer. "They will catch you, but be not afraid. I protect you. In return, soften the hatred in your heart. You must reach out to your bitter enemy and soothe your troubled conscience."

"Whom do you speak of, Grandmother?"

"You know, Child. Search within your dreams."

The Nunne'hi drifts from the world. Her light fades and fog returns.

***

Ella tosses to one side in her bed and sits up upon its edge.

The curtains at her open window flutter and drift with the night's air.

She shakes her head to halt her dream and focus on noise.

"You people leave my place in peace!" The owner of the boarding house joins people on the street.

The Waters oldest sister pads to her window's opening and holds its curtain for a view.

A crowd mills in a tense, frustrated churn.

Individuals carry torches for light, and many tote side arms or muskets. They scream hatred and shake fists in the air.

A hysterical woman carries two split-open feather pillows. Men suspend from their shoulders a steaming tar bucket on a rail.

"We want the uppity Injun!" the vicious attacker with feathers screams. "We support law and order!"

"Move her back to the territory!" One man shouldering the pot shakes his fist in the air. "Give them land and food, and they only demand more!"

Many in the crowd wave torches near business fronts and porch overhangs. "Burn Injuns or ship them to hell!" A mob mentality surges the participants to the boarding house.

Ella slips into a robe from her closet and shuffles across the room to peek out her bedroom door. The hall stands quiet and empty. The big sister leaps through the space and bangs on Lisa's door.

"What? Who's out there?" Little sister's voice trembles with fear, awakened by the clamor.

The rooming house's owner screams downstairs, "Stop! You can't come in here. I sent for a marshal!"

A crash reverberates through the building as its entrance collapses inward. The mob surges into the house. Several attackers throw torches against window curtains and behind the bar.

"Open, Lisa!" Ella yells into the locked wood.

Below the Waters women on the ground level, flames sweep the floor, and alcohol explodes. The mass attackers panic with the flash fire, and individuals fight each other to crowd through the opening and escape.

Younger sister opens her room, and older yanks her into the hall. Both run to the building's rear second-floor viewpoint.

Ella pulls the window's frame, but it stays frozen to its sill. At the opposite end of the hall, flames climb from below up the wall to second level.

Lisa panics and grabs her sibling. Her eyes sparkle fear. "We're trapped!"

"My room's window is open!" The two sisters rush to the room they just left. Younger flings wide the door and both recoil from heat, smoke, and fire.

Ella hugs her sister as if the closeness protects them together.

A peaceful glow engulfs both women.

Grandmother Nunne'hi from the older one's dream spreads her arms, and her white buckskin robe sparkles. Its sleeves' fringes shimmer as she pulls both girls into her embrace. "Come with me, my children."

They walk to the stairs and descend into the flames of the ground floor. Interior blazes and the heat ignite the restaurant's wood in an out-of-control bonfire. The Nunne'hi's buckskins protect the Waters pair through falling ceiling beams and intense sparks as they float to the boarding house's back door.

Outside in the cool night air, Lisa opens her eyes. "How did you do that?"

Ella turns to the Nunne'hi grandmother as she, with the smoke from the building fire, dissipates in the fresh breeze. Her words drift on the wind. "Remember, soften the hatred in your heart. Sooth your enemies' troubled conscience."

Ella hugs her younger sister. "We are safe, now. Did you see her?"

"Who?"

"The Nunne'hi."

"Be serious." The youngest one adores her older sibling. "I saw the woman they call the Cherokee Rose."

Both sisters hug each other.

"There's dark shadows out front with tar and feathers. We need another place to sleep." Ella takes charge.

CHAPTER FORTY-TWO — Liberation

ᎠᎡᏗᏐᎣᎢᏎᏍᎳᏫᎽᎠᎫᎬᏁᏇᏄᎲᏛᏫᏍᎡᎦᎹᎠᏕᎣᎲᎵᏴᎾᏜᎠᏁᎭᏃᎡᏍᏐᎤ

Saturday morning, without court in session, Ella and Lisa buy replenishment clothing. The women shop in a dry goods store near the courthouse.

Oldest admires ceremonial buckskins on display and for sale. The store's clerk hovers nearby.

"What's changed?" Lisa's voice flirts with laughter. "You've not spent an unnecessary penny since we left Georgia. We are paupers, and you shop for party clothes. You must have a beau?"

"No. Now that everybody calls me the Cherokee Rose, I'd better look good in court Monday." Ella laughs.

"Don't mean to hurry you folks, but I wasn't planning on opening today." The nervous owner frets. "My wife is in early labor. I opened to check the store, but I need to close."

"We only happened into your place. But I want this jacket." The elder Waters sister empathizes. "I'll pay, then we'll let you go home."

The storekeeper steps to a cash register near the establishment's front windows.

The eldest glances through the glass. From the storefront window view, the middle-age White constable in charge of the Fort Smith lockup picks his teeth and ambles from breakfast to work. He reaches the jail's door and grabs its latch. The heavy, wooden entry smashes his hand as it opens.

The jail guard stumbles backward and trips. He lands on his butt.

Tesali leaps from the boardwalk as the peace officer draws his pistol. The scout grasps the man's wrist, and they struggle on the ground for control of the weapon.

"Lisa! Go find Ezra or Dideyohvsgi!" Ella ushers her little sister out the front door and watches her from the general store as she hurries from the melee.

"What's going on?" The clerk's concern ripples in his voice.

The eldest sister's attention whips to the fighting men in the street as a pistol's blast echoes. Tesali and the constable lie intertwined. As the guard twitches, the escapee pushes the man's body aside and stands. His right hand carries the officer's pistol.

Several citizens of Fort Smith pop from their business establishments, curious about the commotion. Walking traffic stops and observes the calamity.

The warrior unbuckles the guard's gun belt and straps it around his waist. He rips a bear claw from his neck collection and hammers the marker into the deputy's mouth with the butt of the man's revolver. The victor stands over the peace officer and reloads.

On the street, people stand frozen and fearful. They watch the escapee.

Tesali holsters his weapon and glares at the Cherokee bystanders. The murderer hisses a striking water moccasin's warning, and several terrified onlookers cower away.

After a moment, the ex-army outrider steps to a nearby horseman who watches from horseback. The Indian jerks his head in command.

The rider dismounts and surrenders his mount. Tesali swings onto the horse's saddle and turns. He rides away on the Fort Smith street.

As if struck by lightning, with the boom of a buffalo gun, the scout's horse collapses. Its human rider sprawls on the dirt.

Ella twists and shifts her view toward the explosive shot.

A hundred yards from the window of the general store, Arkansas Deputy Marshal Hiram Colly emerges visible as black powder smoke dissipates. He lowers his high caliber, single-fire buffalo gun.

Unharmed but horseless, Colly's old colleague from the trail scrambles off the road and ducks behind a building.

The weapon's discharge attracts army conscripts from Fort Smith's contingent into the street along with a gathering crowd of gawkers.

The civilian peace officer assumes authority and directs the troopers. "Take both sides of the roadway. Shut the businesses," Colly orders. "He won't get far. Soldier, go tell the captain to send help!"

Ella turns to the general store's clerk, "Fort Smith's a dangerous place to shop."

The merchant frets, agitated. "We don't need gunfire. I am closing. Did you want that buckskin jacket or not?"

"I do, please." Oldest sibling moves to pay for her selections.

"Thank you." He counts his customer's money.

An army soldier bursts into the shop. "You people stay put! Army's got a murderer on the loose. Lock this place! Stay low."

"Wait! I have a baby coming! I must go!" The merchant protests.

"All right. I can escort you. But woman, you stick here. We'll lock you in and I'll come back for you." The trooper ushers the clerk out the front door, and the man locks his store.

Ella peeks out the window. Army troopers move along both sides of the street and check each building for occupants. A few civilians scurry for safety, and a column of mounted soldiers clatter into town from the stockade.

The elder Waters daughter carries her new buckskin jacket and slips through the store to its backroom. She checks the space. By a rear fireplace, several rocking chairs with comfortable cushions for warm winter breaks face an unlit fire pit. Wooden racks support retail back stock and stuff the rest of the area.

The hideaway customer settles into one seat before the furnace to wait and listen.

Horses' hooves pound along the street. Soldiers shout to each other as they search the road and its buildings. Ella identifies a voice as Hiram Colly. "He's armed. Shoot him on sight!"

A shuffle noise, resembling a mouse, attracts the Waters sister's attention. She peers through the dimness. Near a rear door, as her eyes adjust to the subdued place, Tesali crouches behind a box of dry goods.

"A warrior need not fear a woman." Her voice trembles as she speaks.

The army scout stands with his revolver cocked and ready. "Don't you hear the guards?"

"Yes," she whispers. "I do."

"And you do not scream for help?"

"I have hidden from guards many times. As you have, like when you were a boy in the cotton field. We both know how to not make noise."

The warrior stares at the Waters sister. With graceful movement and no fear, the Cherokee steps to and peeks out a heavily curtained window. He surveys the environment behind the store.

Several armed, mounted soldiers inspect water barrels and under wagons, any potential hiding place.

The warrior moves to the door that opens into the store's product display room and pauses. He considers the woman in the rocking chair for a moment, then slides into the principal sales space.

***

Ella sits and trembles with fear. She listens for any sounds. For minutes, nothing.

The outside rattles. Someone checks the lock.

The sound stimulates Ella's mind to memories from Georgia, and she visualizes Georgia Militia Sergeant Colly as he shakes the exterior entrance of the storeroom of the Fort Dahlonega stockade. He carries a leather satchel stuffed with cash.

Across the room through a door ajar to the yard, oldest sibling's watches.

Colly opens his bag and counts money.

Bella's older sister looks at the musket abandoned by the young guard that lays at her feet. With trembling hands, the woman picks up the weapon and cocks it. She freezes in fear at the sound. A quick glance assures her the militia manager inside did not hear the lever action.

The long gun's butt settles with purpose against her shoulder as she slips her finger onto the trigger.

Colly's head centers in the rifle's sight. Ella's index tremors upon the metal for brief seconds, then relaxes. Bella's potential avenger steps away.

***

Ella rubs her forehead for clarity and turns to another sound in a present-day Fort Smith storeroom. Someone rattles the lock at the front entrance to the general store.

A hefty kick from the outside slams the entry doorway inside to the floor. The Waters daughter listens as a body lunges into the room. Quiet follows.

"Tesali. I know you're in here." Sergeant Colly's voice sounds calm and controlled. "A soldier watched you break in."

No response, except Ella hears her own quick breaths.

"We trailed together, partner. That counts for something with me." The deputy lies.

In the silence, the oldest Waters sister slips out of her rocking chair and crawls across the floor to the backroom's entry. She cracks the door open for a slim view.

"Leave, then." Tesali's voice breaks the impasse.

"Can't do, compadre. I am a federal officer. I don't do things my own way anymore."

Stillness encompasses the standoff. A wall clock ticks, and Ella's pulse imitates its pace.

From a distinct part of the store, the scout intones. "You always have your will. In the Georgia militia, my tribe's trail money, you do what you want."

The lawman looks to the voice. "Pitch your pistol where I can see it. Make it easy on both of us."

"Eat donkey dung," the Cherokee hisses.

Both men wait in silence and from Ella's view; no one moves.

"Why no surrender? Is it because you hang tomorrow?" The deputy chuckles. "You ain't escaping, my friend. I got two hundred federal troops out there."

"I have you in here."

"Nobody wants to die." The peace officer's words drop low and mean.

***

As Colly speaks, from the Waters woman's crack at the door, the shadow of Tesali leaps at the sound of the lawman.

His opponent jumps from behind a counter and slaps the attacker's face with the butt of his buffalo gun. The impact flies and slides Tesali's pistol across the store's wooden floor, two inches from Ella's nose.

The deputy points the threatening rifle at his prey's chest. "Don't move a muscle, friend, or you won't hang."

Tesali grits his teeth. "You value our trail time so much. Remember the 'Twenty-Niner' with the 'Brown Bess' whose name was Whitley?"

Sergeant Colly relaxes but shows no recognition.

"He worked for your land scheme. You paid him to have us kill a freedman. That cotton farmer, remember?"

The marshal stares at the scout and shakes his head no.

Tesali nods toward the backroom. "Farmer's name was Benjamin Waters. That's his daughter."

The deputy looks at Ella as he hears a pistol cock.

With her back against the jamb, the oldest Waters aims Tesali's firearm. She jerks the trigger and blows a hole through Hiram Colly's forehead.

As the smoke clears, she trembles.

***

Tesali stands with his palm outreached to help her stand.

The older sibling places her handgun in the scout's hand. The warrior stares at the weapon and switches to Benjamin Waters' daughter. Piercing Cherokee eyes dive deep into Ella's soul and finds it without shadows.

The man grips the Colt and spins toward Colly's body. He whips a bear claw from the string on his neck and jams it into the corpse's upper gums. His pistol's butt pounds and functions as a hammer.

Over the deputy marshal for a long moment, the warrior stands and then turns to Ella. "They heard your shot and will be here soon."

The scout peers through the dim rear room at its exit. He looks at the oldest Waters daughter and smiles. "They'll think I killed him. Escape while you can, Cherokee Rose."

CHAPTER FORTY-THREE — The Gallows

DRTↀOⁱSⴹⳑYAJEⴔꝑAⱧⲦⱮWↈℾGMꝗⴙOⱵℨⳆⱯᎾ₵Ᏹ∿hZꝗO

Sunday afternoon, the day designated for the murderer Tesali's execution, in her new deerskin finery bought in the general store, Ella explores a raucous crowd around the Fort Smith gallows.

An Indian corn-on-the-cob vendor pedals product from a tent in the traffic pattern around the built-for-a-lethal-purpose construction. Near the rear of the canvas-covered food stand, a black, deep, belly pot sits over a fire and boils cobs. The delicious smell floats over the people and promotes sales.

Attracted by the scent, Ella stops and buys herself golden tastiness. She accepts the product, a cob with a horseshoe nail in both ends. Holding the nails, the Waters sister bites the treat and nods approval.

"Fresh corn's the trick." The woman vendor offers her secret, delighted by her customer's endorsement. "We raise the finest, but not tasty as back home in Georgia."

"Best of everything was there, don't you think?" Ella looks to the peddler.

"Hangings were better. More people, more sales." The lady claps in delight.

"This is a sizable crowd." The older Waters sister observes.

"That Tesali's as famous as those Treaty Party folks he murdered." The merchant acts as if she wishes to make a friend, and her customer shies away.

Several whiskey vendors work tents in the jail's yard with brisk business. Two canvas tarps suspend from poles at each establishment and give shade with hay bales for chairs. These impromptu saloons host animated customers who talk politics and the day's news. The crowd mills through the makeshift bars, unsteady from too much liquor.

Ella watches a Cherokee woman in one of the whiskey tents laugh and swig her booze. The woman plays with two guys that hang on her. With the elder Waters sister's lack of men in life plus her natural thirst for excessive alcohol, the sight holds appeal.

The matriarch of her clan firms her shoulders and looks for other pursuits. She watches several children giggle and play roll-a-hoop with the metal from a small wheel. They push the object between themselves and roar when one of their participants falters.

A fellow in a dark suit carries a Bible and pulls a low bed cart past the children's rolling rim. The man moves his conveyance as near to the center of the action as possible.

The preacher climbs upon his flat pulpit. He stands and surveys the crowd, who pays him little attention. The orator waits as if he expects a congregation.

Ella walks to the stage. "You act as if you have something to say."

The dark clad gentleman extends his Bible. "Not I. But this book has much to tell you."

"Be glad to listen. I have an open mind." The oldest Waters smiles. "Most of these people are drunk. Hard to get their attention."

The pastor slips a flask from his inside pocket and slugs a sip. "Attention's easy, Sister. Please join my congregation." From under his coat, the man of God pulls a Colt Forty-Five. The weapon explodes into the air in a deafening discharge.

The throng's chatter, clamor, and anticipation turn to the preacher.

"See what a noise can do?" The pastor winks at Ella, then turns to his found audience. "This great assembly knows that this poor prisoner dies for murdering innocent people."

"You mean them New Echota rich folks?" A Cherokee shakes his fist in the air.

"I'm speaking of Deuteronomy, Chapter Nineteen, Verse Thirteen. 'Thine eye shall not pity him, but thou shall put away the guilt of blood from Israel, that it may go well with thee'," the preacher slaps his black book.

"They weren't from the Bible, just greedy land grabbers!" The heckler laughs.

"This is a solemn and melancholy occasion." The speaker spreads his arm over the congregation in warning. The throng around the gallows pays attention. "This heinous crime meets justice so that we will detest and avoid repetition. In the days of Noah, we filled the earth with violence: violence! Cain bloodied his hands with his brother's innocence. Take notice of the true import of the first clause of the verse, thine eye shalt not pity him."

"He ain't responsible, preacher?" Someone's voice in the crowd rises above the clamor.

"It is plain from my text that shedding innocent blood contracts guilt. The will of the Holy Spirit dictates they should turn away this sin."

"God's not hanging Tesali!" A second heckler loses composure. "The White men are."

"We see the special reason God sets it aside, expressed in the latter part of the verse, that it may go well with thee." The wagon minister sweeps the audience but ends his hand sweep pointed at Ella.

The preacher stares at his reluctant rhetorical example, who freezes under the scrutiny.

A voice in the cluster rises above the others. "That's Cherokee Rose! She knew him. Did she follow God's word and put Tesali's guilt away?"

The Bible thumper inflates his chest and drops his point at Ella. He turns to the inquirer. "If they assault a man, he should stand upon his safety and kill his antagonist. That is Cherokee blood law! He is not chargeable with murder in the eye of God's law!"

"Ask her if the killings were self-defense!" The yeller screams louder.

The preacher confronts the aggressive loudmouth. "If war is lawful, even conflict between the Treaty Party and Chief John Ross, it cannot then be said that if enemies die in it, those who slay them are guilty of shedding innocent blood."

"Them people ain't the only ones Tesali murdered! Ask Cherokee Rose. They say he killed her father!" The man yells.

Ella stands alone in a crowd of haters, those for and those against the execution.

The preacher peers at the Waters family matriarch as she examines her own feelings.

"I am not a believer in the White man's black book. Nor do my veins bleed full, as do Tesali's. I walked the old Cherokee hills with the warrior. He is not a follower. We both face our destiny."

The White advocate of God straightens his back and attempts to summarize for the crowd. "I answer, by inflicting the penalty of the law upon the breakers of it, this price is nothing less than the destruction of his temporal body. Genesis Nine, Verses Five and Six, at the hand of every person's brother, I need the life of man. Who so sheddeth, by his be shed."

The preacher's last words echo in Ella's head with a gender change, "She who takes blood shall bleed her own."

Ella flashes back to the previous day. With her back against the doorjamb, the oldest Waters daughter aims Tesali's firearm. She jerks the trigger and blows a hole through Hiram Colly's forehead. Her thoughts return to the preacher.

He spreads his hands wide in benediction. "This awful spectacle now before us awakens our souls to a sense of the great evil of sin, that we escape from guilt and condemnation, brought to the fruition of eternal life in Heaven."

The man folds his arms and climbs to the ground. He steps to Ella's side. "May we keep from falling, sister. Do you wish cleansing by God's mighty power, through faith into salvation?"

"Will that save Tesali?" The oldest Waters peers at the preacher.

"No." He shakes his head. "God looks in tender compassion upon this poor prisoner, and will admit him when he departs, to be with Jesus in paradise."

The rear door of the jail opens, and two US Army troopers step outside and adopt guard positions on each side of the exit.

The spectators surge from the wagon pulpit to capture prime viewing spots from the lockup to a circle at the gallows.

They wait in silent anticipation.

***

From within the shadows, Tesali steps out into the morning light.

A blood-thirsty gurgle sweeps the witnesses, and they jostle for better views.

Clad in a traditional breechcloth and leggings suspended by waist belt, the prisoner wears his calico turban. Both of his hands meet at the wrists tied together.

Benjamin Waters' hand-carved water spider hangs from the warrior's neck. Bear claws click, strung on a leather strap.

Worn and dusty US Army-issued boots protect his feet.

From Tesali's upper lip, a fearsome bear's claw, a fang, suspends, forced between his teeth.

The facial scar runs from under his headgear, across his cheek, and onto his chest. The old wound disappears near the man's heart.

He looks around, and his eyes blink from unaccustomed light. As they adjust, a steely gaze examines the crowd gathered to watch him hang.

When the people spot the Indian's mouth and bear claw fang, a collective inhale and fear-filled gasp suck hatred and animosity from the air.

Ella watches two more army guards follow Tesali as he steps forward. By the power of his presence, the warrior clears a path through onlookers to the gallows.

On its second step, the scout recognizes the Waters' eldest in the crowd and stops.

***

From within her buckskin jacket, the oldest daughter withdraws one of Dideyohvsgi's feathers. She holds the item in front of her face for the murderer to see. When sure the prisoner has identified the symbol, she lays the plume on her palm, purses her lips, and blows its lightness into the air.

It floats and catches a breeze to circle like an eagle above the crowd.

Tesali watches the feather's flight.

The object catches an updraft and climbs. Swooping, it sweeps from the dirty and oppressed land of men upward to disappear on the path of the spirit.

From then forward, the prisoner never takes his eyes off Ella.

***

A soldier nudges the prisoner's ribs, and he moves up each step. The ex-army scout gains the gallows deck, where he stops. Tesali grasps the carved water spider from his neck in a bound palm and grips.

An executioner steps to Tesali's side. The grim White man carries a gray hood. "Does the prisoner have any last words?" The black clad man faces his prisoner. "You may speak them now."

A collective breath of anticipation sweeps through the crowd, and several onlookers murmur excited expectations.

435

The Cherokee sneers at the audience and shakes his chin negatively.

The court's executioner guides the army scout to a noose. He covers Tesali's face with the hood and fastens the rope around his victim's neck.

The official steps back and pulls a lever. The murderer drops, kicks several times, and hangs still.

Ella stares in stunned silence, as does the crowd.

***

One woman in her language sings the Cherokee song, "Amazing Grace." "u ne la nv i u we tsi i ga go yv he i - hna quo tso sv wi yu lo se i ga gu yv ho nv - a se no i u ne tse i - i yu no du le nv - ta li ne dv tsi lu tsi li - u dv ne u ne tsv"

An Indian man in English joins. "God's Son paid for us. Now to heaven He went after paying for us. Then He spoke when He rose. I will come the second time He said when He spoke. The world ends when He returns..."

Crowd voices swell and overwhelm the lyric with an older death lament. "The sun sets in night and the stars shun the day. but glory remains when their lights fade away. Begin ye tormentors. your threats are in vain, for the spirit of Tesali will never complain."

Ella joins in with the ancient lyrics. "Remember the arrows he shot from his bow. Remember your chiefs by his hatchet laid low. He goes to the land where his father has gone, whose ghost shall rejoice in the fame of his son."

The oldest Waters bows her head for a moment, turns, and trudges toward the Fort Smith Courthouse.

CHAPTER FORTY-FOUR — The Verdict

ᎠᎡᎢᎣᎤᎥᎦᎧᎨᎩᎪᎫᎬᎭᎮᎯᎰᎱᎲᎳᎴᎵᎶᎷᎸᎹᎺᎻᎼᎽᎾᎿᏀᏁᏂᏃᏄᏅ

Monday morning in Steel's chambers, the participants in Ella Waters versus Hiram Colly and US Army General Winfield Scott await a verdict.

"I go on record, Judge, that this trial has been a travesty." Captain Jessup stands before the presiding officer's desk. "If the decision is dis-favorable, the government intends to appeal."

"On what grounds, sir?" The man in black robes leans back in his chair.

"You are the reason." The prosecutor asserts. "Never have I seen in my many years of court-martial action a magistrate more inclined to one argument."

The judge relaxes and smiles.

Jessup points in accusation. "Your rulings appear designed to promote liberal, anti-American philosophies not yet explored by law."

"I plead guilty, Captain." Bennett Steel laughs.

The accuser's jaw drops at the admission.

The magistrate spreads his hands apart and clasps them together in a containing gesture. "I have spent my entire judicial career exploring issues of jurisprudence selected to expand our interpretation of the Constitution. But your concern won't float in the appellate process."

Jessup sputters. "I differ, sir!"

"Because of your experience with court-martial, I respect your years of duty." Steel salutes with one finger. "But a civilian tribunal is a Cherokee town meeting compared to your military courts."

"Then we have the matter of the unfortunate death of the prosecution's witness, Deputy Marshal Hiram Colly." The captain leans forward across the desk and confronts the judge.

Ella, who sits with Lisa, freezes at the mention of the marshal's name. She looks at Ezra and Dideyohvsgi, who sit nearby. Both watch the magistrate and the trial's prosecutor.

Older sister grasps little sister's hand for reassurance that her loved one is still there.

"The deputy's death was unfortunate. I understand that his murderer paid for another crime on the gallows yesterday." Steel touches his fingertips together.

"Our principal witness is no longer available for appellate action. Convenient. And that serves you." The captain slams a fist into his palm.

"Colly's killer hung for a political offense." The Judge's voice reflects his surname. "Your commanding officer, not to mention the President, have no interest in reopening that case."

Both men stare into defiant eyes.

Judge Steel breaks the standoff. "The reason I summoned you to my chambers is to thank you, including the prosecution, for your diligent efforts."

The Waters group nods recognition.

"This trial may set new legal positions unseen in these United States before this action. As you know, I have presented the jury with questions to answer. Their responses will decide guilt or innocence." The presiding officer looks at the prosecutor. "And set up precedents for decades."

The court's clerk opens the chamber's door and interrupts. "Judge. You asked me to tell you when they are ready. The foreman says its time."

Bennett Steel rises. "Thank you. Ladies and gentlemen, we entertain a verdict."

Ella sits with Dideyohvsgi, Lisa, and Ezra in the Fort Smith federal courthouse.

The magistrate enters the courtroom. Captain Jessup waits at the table for the prosecution.

"Please rise. This court is now in session," the clerk intones. Older Waters scans the stuffed occupants and the mass of people who strain to see inside the building. She recognizes many of the outsiders as tar-and-feather advocates.

"Be seated, please. Bailiff, bring in our heroes." The judge turns and watches the twelve file in and take their seats. "Has the jury reached its verdict?"

The jury's foreman stands. "We have, your honor." He hands a document to the court clerk, who walks it to the bench.

Steel sits in silence for a moment as he reads a sheet of paper. "The jurors returned their decree in five points. Before we read that decision, I, on behalf of the State of Arkansas and the United States government, thank each of you for your service. This was not a popular proceeding, and each of you did your duty under perilous circumstances. We congratulate and applaud you." The magistrate nods at his assistant.

"The defendants will rise," the clerk directs as Ella, Ezra, Dideyohvsgi, and Lisa stand.

Bennett Steel clicks the papers before him on the bench. "The jury concludes: One, an Indian is a 'person' within the meaning of the laws of the United States and may sue out a writ of habeas corpus in a federal court where he is in custody in violation of the constitution or those precepts."

The crowd rumbles disagreement.

"Two, General Winfield Scott, commander of the military department of Indian Territory, has imprisoned the relators under the authority of this country but against its legal principals."

Army personnel in the room shout protests.

"Three, no rightful reason exists for removing by force any of the defendants in the manner they endured."

Captain Jessup leaps to his feet. "Orders were orders!"

"Four, Indians have the inherent ideal of expatriation, as the more fortunate White race, and have the inalienable right to life, liberty, and pursuing happiness, so long as they obey the law."

The Cherokee outside the courtroom cheer.

"And last, being restrained of freedom under color of authority of the United States, and in violation of its laws, the relators Ella, Lisa, and Dideyohvsgi Waters are free from custody! Be it so ordered!"

Judge Steel slams his gavel onto its pedestal, and the sound reverberates throughout the nation.

***

The court explodes with joy, freedom, exaltation, and simultaneously spite, vicious catcalls, and bigotry.

Ezra stands and shakes hands with Ella. Lisa hugs her big sister. She turns and holds her attorney longer. Over the lawyer's shoulder, she winks at her sibling.

Jessup, in frustration and anger, shoves his way to the bench. "The government will appeal, sir. This is a joke!"

Judge Steel leans forward so the prosecutor can hear. "Without you as the representative."

"My training prepares me to do my duty and serve my country," the officer pontificates.

"I intend to send the transcript of these proceedings to General Scott. After his staff reviews this trial, I am sure your command during the Cherokee transfer may be in question. You might prepare a defense for your own court martial."

Moments later, Ella and Ezra, with Lisa attached to his arm, step from the Fort Smith Courthouse's main entrance.

A clamorous crowd erupts in excitement and noise.

Three army soldiers jostle the attorney and spit at the oldest Waters. "Go back to Georgia, ya' filthy Injun!"

Several Cherokee wave placards written in their language. They translate, "Abolitionist traitor! You disgrace our people!"

Dideyohvsgi steps to Ella's side. "Ezra! Get us out of here."

The crowd presses around the half-Indian matriarch and her family.

"Move aside!" the attorney directs.

A White cotton farmer and his wife push forward. "Negras are slaves! Find you a slave pen!"

"And take your fancy Nigra lawyer with you!" The woman screams.

Lisa grasps Ezra's arm and slips behind him. "I'm scared."

A studious appearing fellow pushes next to Ella. "Hello, Finial Jackson with the *Arkansas Gazette* in Little Rock."

"The newspaper?"

"Yes. Do you realize history will record you as a hero and the person inspiring this court's decision?"

"Listen to these people. Think that ruling changes any of this?" She questions as the crowd jostles the two together.

"Over time, I believe so."

"The law, the White man's God, Unetlanvhi, the Water Beetle," Benjamin Waters' oldest stammers with nerves. "They change nothing. Human beings just struggle through life."

"May I use that in my newspaper?"

A rabid pastor waves a cross. "Hang the heathen!"

"Tell your paper I said only ethical humans can be heroic."

Ezra pulls Ella away from the reporter and the crowd into the courthouse. He nudges his friends into the building.

Lisa takes her sister's shoulders. "Paw is proud of you."

"I'm not sure. His daughter tried but wasn't ethical or heroic." Older sibling shudders, and her eyes fill with tears. "But Mama would be proud."

"This is a mad man's scorn. Haters of all kinds." Dideyohvsgi trembles. "I am too old. What choice do we have? What does this mean?"

The Waters matriarch looks at the medicine man for a moment, and then bends and hugs his frail figure. "Freedman, White, or Cherokee, their hate can't keep us from travel to the Unetlanvhi proper home in Georgia."

Dideyohvsgi calms and stares into the eyes of his old friend's daughter. "All this hatred makes my blood fear, even as a White court stands with us. Your father's blood flows in your veins with more reason to be afraid. But I think the Cherokee Rose can make the trip without Lulu and Hetty."

– END –

ACKNOWLEDGEMENTS

ᎠᎡᎢᎣᎤᎥᎦᎧᎨᎩᎪᎫᎬᎭᎮᎯᎰᎱᎲᎳᎴᎵᎶᎷᎸᎹᎺᎻᎼᎽᎾᎿᏀᏁᏂᏃᏄᏅ

The author acknowledges the following contributors to this book:

My wife, who enabled endless hours of research and writing time.

Ella Waters, my paternal grandmother and Dawes Roll signee, who inspired my interest in all things Cherokee - even though we never met.

Ed Fields and Mary Rae, who teach the Cherokee online language classes from the Cherokee Nation. And their language department for expanding my interest in our culture, syllabary and speech. The author reccommends their book, *Journeying Into Cherokee*, for help and encouragement learning the Cherokee Language.

The author, Grace Steel Woodward, who introduced me to Cherokee history through her book, *The Cherokees* published by University of Oklahoma Press, Norman.

ABOUT THE AUTHOR

ᎠᏰᎵᏍᎣᎢᏍᏚᎢᏯᎠᏎᎤᏓᎢᎦᎭᏥᏣᎳᏩᏐᎠᏫᎦᎷᎦᎹᏝᎤᎢᎲᏚᏯᏗᎦᏁᏍᏁᏁᎵᎵᏃᏆᎣ

ᎤᏆᎲ ᎲᏐᏓ

Thank you for reading *Cherokee Rose*. I hope you enjoyed the book and ask you to recommend it to your friends.

That recommendation is important to spread Cherokee culture, history, and language awareness.

I am a citizen of the Cherokee Nation and work daily to learn our Class IV language and our history's nuances.

Married for over fifty years with two children and four grandchildren, I live in Grapevine, Texas. Other than writing, my interests include painting in oils and watercolors, making short films, plus anything that makes my grandchildren happy.

ᎦᏬ (Wa-do Thank you.)

James A. Humphrey

ALSO BY JAMES A. HUMPHREY

ᎴᏒᏣᎣᎢᏚᏗᏴᎠᏲᎬᏆᏚᎯᎦᏬᏪᏛᏥᎬᎷᎠᏝᎣᏅᏅᏛᏯᎾᏖᏋᎾᏂᏃᎠᎣᵛ

    This historical novel, *Cherokee Rose,* is book two of the Cherokee Trilogy, the story of the extended Waters family from 1779 through Civil War Reconstruction.

The other two are:

Cherokee Rock, the first book, tells an epic story as exploitation sweeps westward over the Appalachians in 1779 and engulfs a Tsalagi boy who loses his mother to smallpox, allies with a mentor squirrel, and trains as a shaman. A tribal fountain-head, Cherokee Rock, shelters his growth to manhood. Through decades of pestilence and war, with a Freedman blood brother, he battles a malignant medicine man for their peoples' hearts. The life-long enemies collide in an epic revelation.

Cherokee Reel, the trilogy's concluding book, follows Lisa, the frivolous daughter of freedman Benjamin Waters and his wife Walela, who strives to imitate her white socialite philanthropist friend. Cultural conflict, the civil war, her sister's murder, and the death of a beloved husband compels a basic "Who am I?" confrontation with a Confederate demigod's racist immorality that avenges her loved one's deaths and molds her individual and indigenous identity.

All three historical novels are available for purchase at www.cherokeetrilogy.com or from Tsalagi Books, tsalagibooks.com

ᎦᎥ (Wa-do) Thank you.